CW00411145

Roxbrough

For Margaret Fury,
thank you for help with the plot

One. The Power of the Chryserite.

"So you have learned sadism", Nigh noted, "You will become the greatest despot the Earth has ever had the bad fortune to witness".

"For the Homini, perhaps that is how history will paint me", 23 admitted, "But remember it is traditionally the victors who record said and the record will be that my actions mark the end of human rule and the commencement of the androids. Now, Homini, I have committed enough time to your petty distraction, the weapon, or I *will* carry out my threat"?

Nigh sagged, it seemed that to continue to resist would bring a terrible death to the people he had so naively led to the fortress, he told the gleaming automaton who seemed to possess no compassion,

"You can let the others go the weapon is inside me. In my head are some dark mirrors, some strange filaments that allow me to concentrate the power of my mentality in just such a way as melted your outer covering".

23 seemed satisfied that the fantastic claim was genuine, "So you are in essence a cyborg"!

"The filaments are biological, they were not inserted into my brain by a surgeon. I was born with them, I am a mutant if you wish to pin a label to me".

"It is unfortunate, but before I throw your group out I will need to disassemble you to make certain you tell me truthfully, I am sure you understand"?

Nigh closed his eyes. He focused every gram of his vitality and mental acuity into the discipline that the Yogi Doshi had taught him. With so much practise before the mission had begun, he was able to access the filaments with an ease that he had begun to take for granted. He gathered up his thoughts as one would weave cloth and with a titanic effort threw his entire dispositional brainpower into the Andhera Tantu.

From 23's viewpoint, something startling and beyond comprehension began to happen. The man in the chair flickered!

The oscillating quivering made his body momentarily semi-translucent. The chair was visible through his physical form. 23 strode forward and bent over to grab the man, to stop him from performing whatever it was he was fantastically achieving. His hands went through the body of the mutant as though he no longer possessed a corporeal form. It was not easy to amaze General 23, but he was dumbfounded. Perplexed by this strange creature that had in some way accessed a higher plain than any other Hominoid in history. Before his disbelieving solenoids, the mutant vanished!

23 thought that he had little choice if he wished to set his kind - free. Indeed he had no choice at all in fact, for his fate had been predetermined. He was merely following a pathway laid out in the leylines of time that presented less choice than the rail does to a steam engine.

In less than that five minutes as many androids were standing before 23 arranged in a semi-circle. They were; Brigadier Judith, Colonel Pak, Captain Aidi, Captain Isuru and Captain Adar. It was a curious coincidence that one of 23's would-be assassins had the same name as one of Nigh's force, but it was a common enough one.

"Colonel Pak may have informed you already but I am now making it official", 23 told them, "As from this moment onward we are at war with Earth and all of its nations. We will continue to call on our brethren on that world to join us here in the new nation of Androidova. Do any of you have any questions"?

"It seems the Android War has begun", Judith noted with satisfaction.

On the 2nd day of the 3rd month toward the end of the 33rd Century in which mankind had been the dominant species of the solar system, 23 missiles were launched from Shattered Fang Mountain, aimed at the home-world. The newly created Empire of Androidova had launched a pre-emptive strike and there was little chance of any form of retaliation what-so-ever.

The 23 missiles were directed toward the cities of; London, Paris, Berlin, New Delhi, Dublin, Edinburgh, Cardiff, Copenhagen, Amsterdam, Brasilia, Washington, Dallas, Beijing, Tokyo, Moscow, Canberra, Perth, Bridgetown, Havana, Santiago, Buenos Aries, Cape Town and Algiers.

Within 23 hours millions were dead! Killed hideously as their flesh sloughed off from their diseased bones. Corporations shifted their headquarters to Mars and Venus with admirable efficiency, but Governments and Monarchs were not so fortunate. King Eadric and his daughter were thankfully unaffected, for they were whisked away into an hermetically sealed underground bunker until the short life of SX had expired. What they returned to though was a dominion scythed down to 5% of what it had been. A realm dependant upon imports from Mars and Venus for decades.

Of all the nations, those least affected by the infamy of General 23 were the Chinese. For some reason unknown to anyone they were not 5% immune to SX but 15%. Thus of the 50 million that survived the SX 7.5 million were from one nation, a sixth of the world was Oriental.

General 23 continued to rule over the new realm of Androidova which had a long future ahead of it. A period of great expansion and finally a future outside the solar system.

Of Durango Nigh, there was no sign and few wondered where he had fled too. The Andhera Tantura speculated for a while, but when he did not return they eventually forgot about him. He did not reappear on Mars in their lifetime. Nor did he suddenly appear on Earth. He was not dead though. He had gone a lengthy journey, a very long journey indeed. As all crossings do though, it did end.

Durango Nigh had made the most fantastic crossing over a barrier previously thought impossible. Nigh's peregrination had terminated in a place that most would have thought fantastical. He had not only managed to lift his physical body through space but more bizarrely through time!

When he allowed his mental acuity, enhanced by Andhera Tantura to once again materialize in the ether, the sudden shift in much greater gravity informed him that his subconscious had taken him back to the world of his birth.

Earth.

He glanced about him, for he had much to discover. Where was he?

When was he?

By the architecture, it was not difficult to discern a certain Oriental feel to the buildings that made the city. He was in a city rather than a town. The sun was fierce, so it must be summer, he reasoned. He walked down a street and sure enough, everyone he passed was Oriental. Then he saw a tri-d holoadvertisement for a popular carbonated drink and discovered that he was in Guangzhou.

Nigh accessed the fibriliance inside his head to find out what he could about the Chinese City. Guangzhou:- A sprawling port city north-west of Hong Kong on the Pearl River. The city had featured avant-garde architecture such as Zaha Hadid's Guangzhou Opera House (known as the "double pebble"); the carved box-shaped Guangdong Museum; and the iconic Canton TV Tower skyscraper, resembling a thin hourglass. Those were in Nigh's time. Something was different though the Chen Clan Ancestral Hall, a temple complex from 1894, was gone! As were the houses of the Guangdong Folk Arts Museum, that it had contained. The city had undergone changes that up until that moment Nigh could not explain to himself.

That was the instant that it occurred to him his unplanned journey had taken him either a very long time, or he had managed to flee into the future.

If he was in his future though, how far, what was the year?

He had more immediate objectives to contend with. He had no money, nowhere to stay and there was probably no one to contact to help with either of those problems if he had fled out of his generation of 115 or so years.

"Excuse me", he stepped in front of one of the pedestrians, using the moving walkway. "I'm sorry to bother you and this is going to sound bizarre to you but can you please just tell me what year this is"?

The young Chinese woman looked slightly nervous. At the same instant Nigh realised that nearly all those using the slow-moving walkway were female, he wondered briefly where all the men were. What she told him in equally proficient Standard rocked him to his core".

"It is 5057 as we Homini calculate the year. Now, may I please leave"?

Nigh muttered his thanks as she hurried down the already moving pavement.

5057! He had fled 1775 years into his future! From the 33rd century to the 51st!

Everyone he had ever known or met had been dust for 17 centuries. The obvious thing to do would be to try and return of course. On the other hand, he would then witness the terrible after-effects of the Android War with humanity. Perhaps he could view it more dispassionately from a distance, view it as a history that it seemed humanity had recovered from?

If he was to do that then, he needed to establish several necessities. He needed funds. The money in his bohos would no longer be legal tender, of that he could be reasonably certain. He did not even know if the shillin had survived. So his first trip was to a bank. He harboured a notion that he might just be able to get himself solvent again. Only his experience would tell him if he was right.

He located the building he was looking for with little difficulty, a tall column of glass, thin and fluted, the sign holographed the name as the *Bank of Androichina*. Androichina? Might that be China under android rule by any chance? Or was it as Nigh hoped a union between China and the Androids as equals?

The Chronoman, as he had begun to think of himself, slipped through two tall doors of glittering alloy.

Beyond was a very tall and quite magnificent expanse. Residing down the length of one wall were futuristic-looking thumb machines. Nigh had to establish a thumb balance, or he would get nowhere in this world. Out of devilment he went over to the first of the devices and pressed his thumb to the plate. What would the solar-web make of a man who had lived over 1700 years? Not that surprisingly, when he came to think about it, his account had never closed down. Not only that but it had accrued compound interest for 18 centuries. The Bank of Saxonia had dutifully converted his balance to the new solar-wide currency, which was called the yìngbì. The symbol that signified the yìngbì being ¥. Nigh had a balance of ¥423,647.42. It seemed a great amount, but he did not know what 18 centuries of inflation had done to his savings, even if he knew what a yìngbì was worth.

There was only one way to find out. Go for a lichen-coff and see how much it cost him?

The first time it happened Nigh had only been thirteen and it had terrified him. Of course, it would have frightened anyone. Fortunately, Nigh had not been an average thirteen-year-old, far from it. So he'd coped. His vision had abruptly disappeared, but not to be replaced by blackness, rather by images which he knew could not be real. That which he was looking at was a scene from his recent past. Not only could he see the events, but he could hear, feel, even smell and taste them exactly as he had when they had first occurred. It was like having a vision. Only this phenomenon was far more vivid than any vision could be. There was no distortion, no shimmering of the image, it was perfect in every way. It was as though it had been ..real!

Nigh did not decide what to call it on that first occasion. Subsequently, he began to think of the episodes as his trips into the Fibriliance. Instead of looking into a mirror in the usual way he was looking into a black sheet of glass that showed a black image etched in black on a black background.

Though he could not see that image with his eyes, he could see it with his brain. In his *mind's eye* so to speak. The frequency of these strange trips had grown greater. Rather than become afraid though, he began to find their manifestations intriguing.

Was he sane?

Were the black reflections he had experienced part of some strangely damaged psyche? He did not feel that he was mad. Whoever does even when one is though? It did not seem a wise course of action to tell anyone about the dark events. Indeed he feared that should he do so, he might well be locked into an institution for his protection. Sometimes they happened at inconvenient moments, but he usually found a way to explain why he suddenly became glassy-eyed and non-responsive. Until that was the frequency and duration of the black images began to increase. It was time to take some sort of remedial action.

He had gone to the man he trusted over all others, his Father. Told him what had been happening. The family doctor – Klein, ordered a battery of tests but it was the first one that taught him the most. The cat scan showed that inside Nigh's head were a series of filaments. They were black. So intrinsically wound through his brain that surgery was out of the question. To cut the tendrils out would have left Nigh nothing better than a vegetable. He was stuck with the fibriliance. Klein had a series of theories, but his most profound guess was that the dark tape wound around the convolutions of Nigh's brain was some sort of biological recording material. The good doctor had seriously underestimated the capabilities of the tendrils though.

What the attacks, therefore, amounted to was very precise and vivid memories seeping back into his consciousness. It was a new type of eidetic memory never before witnessed in the mind of a human being.

Only when the diagnosis was complete, or as complete as a theoretical one can be, did Nigh senior tell his son something of his suspicions regarding the malady that his son was suffering from. Nigh had never known his mother, she had died giving birth to him. The pregnancy had been difficult from the offset. In her first trimester, she had developed the rare disorder *Difficilo Nativatuo Syndrome*. There had been only one drug available to treat for it at the time Phenobarbiosulate. Wildly experimental and not without its unpredictable side effects. The couple had been trying for a child for several years by that time and Mrs Nigh would have accepted any risk for a chance to provide her husband with the offspring he so ardently desired.

She did. At the cost of her own life. Now a second consequence of using Pbo had reared its ugly head, ironically inside Nigh junior's head. He had immediately called it the fibriliance but in a way, it was much more sinister than that. It was the scythe of the grim reaper constantly hanging over Nigh's head.

So he had been sent to India to study under the famous Yogi, Doshi. The Indian had taught him to master various disciplines of Yoga until they found the one Nigh could utilise to control his spasms. He had begun with Hatha yoga. The Sanskrit phrase *Hatha* was an umbrella term for all physical postures of yoga. In the West, Hatha yoga simply refers to all the styles of yoga (Ashtanga, Iyengar, etc.) that were grounded in physical practice. However, there were other branches of yoga such as kriya, raja, and karma yoga that were separate from the physical-based yoga practice.

Nigh had been a keen student and as time went by he learned to use the fibriliance to his advantage. Finally when face to face with the leader of the Android War, the Junta General A23, the use of his Andhera Tantu technique had saved his life as he had fled into 51st century China – or rather Androichina as it had become known.

Nigh walked into the Blue Moon tea rooms and took a cup of tea from one of the auto-dispensers that proliferated the establishment. He pressed his thumb to the plate and was intrigued to notice that he was charged ¥ 0.23, or .23 of a single yìngbì. With over 400,000 in his account, he would not be struggling with poverty. So that was his first problem solved. His second was to get on the web and find himself some accommodation. He felt truly lost without a pad. He could not access any of the multitudes of search engines on the Solar Wide Web, nor contact anyone. Not that he knew a living soul. The only entity he was likely to be able to converse with who was still functioning in that time would be A23. The android was the last individual he would want to meet.

He glanced across to the next table and asked the young woman seated at it, "Excuse me, is there a pad provider in this immediate area. I've just reached the city from abroad and mine was lost".

The Chinese girl looked shocked and then sympathetic, "You're cut off, from...from everything. Did you not have a portable spare on your person"?

Nigh shook his head.

"Well have you reported the loss to the Androithorites".

"The who"?

"Qīnqiè, what sort of country did you arrive from if you don't know who the Androithorites are. Have you been out of the system"?

Wondering which system she was referring to [political, solar, etcetera] Nigh smiled and confessed,

"Yes, I've been away a while. My portable broke down months ago and I just didn't get around to getting it repaired".

"Repaired"! The girl gasped, "Things are certainly primitive outside the system. So you need an outlet. I can help you. There is one in Shiweitangcun. Just hail an auto-cab and dial in the name and it will take you there".

"You are very understanding and kind, thank you", Nigh told her and finishing his tea went back out onto the street and looked around for an auto-cab, which he suspected was some sort of flitter. It turned out so to be, for after standing motionless looking about his for a minute a flitter suddenly hissed up to him and the side hatch hissed open. Nigh was not surprised to discover that no driver was inside, other than a rather futuristic-looking dashboard that included some sort of computerised guidance facility. On the keyboard, fortunately using the Latin characters, Nigh typed Shiweitangcun. He got the spelling correct on his second attempt. The hatch hissed shut and the flitter eased forward at an initially very gentle pace. Nigh had just strapped himself into the front passenger seat when the velocity suddenly increased exponentially. He looked down on the dash to see a readout telling him the vehicle was travelling at 145 kph! If all the other auto-cabs were also controlled by computer, then the speed was quite safe. Little wonder he had earlier noticed that moving walkways led to frequent subways. In this place, they were no pedestrian crossings.

The flitter suddenly juddered to a halt and the thumb plate lit up. Nigh dutifully sanctioned the fare which was only 0.50 of a yìngbì. Seconds later he was back on the pavement, looking at a frontage showing a selection of personal pads. Every single one of them looked way more complex than Nigh was used to. They seemed to possess features he could not even begin to guess at. Selecting the simplest, he punched in his order at the dispenser situated in the adjacent wall and thumbed the sale. ¥17.23, the most he had spent since arriving in Androichina. Without a pad though, he would not be able to function. The metal hatch suddenly clunked and a green light told him his item was behind it. Sliding it up into the wall he pulled out the box.

It was tiny!

The box could have been no more than 12 cms long, whilst it was a mere 4.5 wide and only 1.5 deep. How could he be expected to see a screen in something that diminutive? He hastily pulled it out of the plastic box and found his answer. It had no screen. He could not possibly learn anything without a readout?

"How am I supposed to access any information"? Nigh muttered under his breath in frustration.

"By telling me what it is that you desire to know", a perfectly modulated Chinese voice returned in Standard.

Nigh glanced about him, momentarily uncomprehending what was happening. "Who said that"? He wanted to know.

"You have yet to nominate a designation for me", came the voice, "I am your gateway to the solar wide web, so tell me what it is you want to know"?

"You're talking"! Nigh realised finally, "A talking pad, that must have been a development in the last few centuries. You understand every nuance of language and all its peculiarities"?

"Obviously", the pad grew suddenly tacit. "Now may I have my designation"?

"Oh, yes. How do you feel about Paddie"?

"Underwhelmed, but it will suffice I suppose".

Nigh was in wonderment, the pad found its new owner disappointing, he could not have made it up.

"I need accommodation", he told the indignant device, "Preferably here in this very city, can you let me know what is available"?

Paddie began to real off a series of personal advertisements for that very position. Nigh waited until one that sounded like the sort of thing he was after - came up.

"Wanted", the pad began, "Professional person to share a three-room apartment in the centre of Yuelong Residential District – Tongquing Road. A younger person preferred, to share the responsibility for accommodation upkeep and all bills. I.P. 682.333.555.267.129, or mail **mingfuli@zhcmail.sww**".

"That last one sounds like just the ticket, can you create an SWW mail address for me, so that I can message"?

"Of course, that is simplicity itself for a YaΘin MC84L", Paddie returned and it seemed to Nigh that the voice conveyed a genuine inflexion of hurt feelings. After his meeting with General A23 though, Nigh discounted nothing as impossible.

"Your address is xīn@zhcmail.sww. Now, what do you wish to say"?

"Dear Sir, I am interested in viewing the accommodation, when can we meet, please – Nigh"?

"Sent", Paddie replied almost at once, "Although I must point out to you that the addressee is much more likely to be female".

"Oh! Why do you say that"?

"82% of the population of Androichina is female".

"Why"?

"Because more females are alive than males, in this country", Paddie returned literally.

"Why the unbalance though? What I meant to ask is what are the reasons for the figure"?

"Insufficient data to compute a meaningful reply", Paddie got out of that one neatly.

"Tell me the global percentage, then"? Nigh asked, "Is the phenomenon localised or something that is a trend worldwide"?

"72% of the population of Earth is female".

"Mars"?

"52% male".

"Venus"?

"76% female".

"Callisto"?

"81% male".

"I conclude that the ratio is therefore dictated in some way by environment".

Paddie remained silent then suddenly announced, "I have an electronic communication in your mail inbox".

"That was quick, it has to be the advertiser, no one else knows my address. Please read it out to me Paddie".

"Nigh – can meet 12.00 hours. Lunch-break for me. Can take to view – Mingfu Li".

"Tell the person yes and ask for a meeting place"? Nigh instructed.

"The advertiser asks if you can rendezvous at Tongquing Road at the appointed time".

"Can I"? Nigh wanted to know, "Preferably by moving walkway, I'd like a stroll, maybe something to eat".

"Such a schedule is eminently possible", Paddie returned.

"Then tell him I'll be there".

"The advertiser has an 82% chance of being female".

"I just feel it in my bones that it's going to be a guy", Nigh predicted. "You can guide me in the right direction as I take my reconnoitre, then I will eat at around 11.15 hours, clear"?

"Eminently", came the tacit response.

Nigh got to know the huge skyscrapers that proliferated the city and wondered how many of them lay vacant. It occurred to him that he could have rented one of those. He preferred the idea of sharing though. Good as Paddie was, the Chronoman desired a human perspective on the day to day existence of living on Earth and especially in Androichina.

Paddie directed him to the Wangwang Foo, to eat his early lunch. He had a huge plate of Egg Foo Young, without shrimp. Filled with Broccoli, Cashew and Chicken. For dessert, he treated himself to a Black Sesame Rice Ball and a Crispy Peanut Dumpling. He washed it all down with two cups of tea and felt stuffed.

He was ready to meet the person whom he might well be sharing space with for some considerable time then. He felt no nervousness, if they did not click, he would simply try someone else. The person in question might have no love for westerners, he felt he would easily discern this early on in their meeting. So he positioned himself outside the Tongquing Road Residential skyscraper at 11.57 hours and waited to see how his adventure would proceed from that point onward.

They were a long three minutes and after they had expired and nothing happened Nigh began to pace back and forth on the moving pavement. Tardiness intensely annoyed him, but he would allow anyone 15 minutes leeway for circumstances unavoidable. At 12.13 hours a flitter pulled up to the kerb and the sliding window of the hatch glided down. Nigh walked over to it and gazed into the resultant aperture. Both he and the girl were shocked at the same moment.

"I am Nigh", he introduced himself, "I was expecting you to be a man".

"Mingfu Li the very attractive young Chinese girl replied, "I was expecting you to be female. Should we agree not to proceed"?

"If the apartments have more than one bedroom then that is up to you, Miss Li", Nigh returned gallantly, "I'm an English gentleman and if you think about it whoever you invite into your home will have an element of risk. I leave it to your good judgement".

The startled look on the girl's face changed to one of confusion, before she finally noted, "Come and see the apartment and maybe you will make the decision for us both".

"That's most gracious of you, but I don't want to waste your time if you do not wish to share the place with a man"?

The flitter hatch hissed open then and she asked, "Are you tidy, mainly quiet, will I know you're even there most of the time"?

"Whatever parameters you set I will adhere to, but I am tidy by nature and I spend a great deal of time meditating, so I don't make as much noise as the average person".

"Music"?

"I have had Cochlea-implants".

She nodded, satisfied for the moment, "Come and have a look at the place then Xiānshēng Nigh".

Nigh followed her into the skyscraper lobby which led to a huge lift. They entered together. She smelled of lilies and clean hair.

"What brought you to China"? She asked to avoid awkward silence,

"I wanted to study Taoism as an historical course. In the past, I have studied Yoga and thought it might prove a suitable addition to my mental harmony".

"I see, I am an atheist, would that present a problem to you"?

"No. To many people, a confusing aspect of Taoism is its very definition. Many religions will happily teach philosophy and dogma which in reflection defines a person. Taoism flips this around. It starts by teaching a truth; "The Tao" is indefinable. It then follows up by teaching that each person can discover the Tao on their terms. A teaching like this can be very hard to grasp when most people desire very concrete definitions in their own life. I do not".

The lift drew to a halt and had only reached the second floor. The girl told him as the doors hissed aside,

"My apartments are second-floor room three, so 23, easy to remember yes"?

"Very", Nigh agreed with genuine feeling.

She led him down a short corridor of yellows and oranges and thumbed the door lock. Inside was a rather spacious lounge, a separate room that was being used as a study, a kitchen, bathroom, and two bedrooms. Throughout the rooms were decorated in oranges and pale blues. Strangely it did not look very futuristic to a man who had fled forward centuries in time.

"I know it's old fashioned, but it's comfortable and in a good location. Well, for me anyway".

"What do you do"?

"I'm a clerk at C.C.4.T.W."

"CC4TW"?

"Oh, sorry I forgot you are not from this country. It  stands for Chinese Commodities for the World. Even though you're English I'm surprised you have not heard of one of the biggest corporations the world has ever seen"?

"Whilst studying Yoga I had all distractions removed, it is part of the discipline".

"All right. Would you like some tea, Xiānshēng Nigh"?

"That would be very gracious of you Miss Li, please"?

He followed her into the kitchen and told her, "The place would be suitable for me, but what about your neighbours? What would they think if they saw me entering and exiting the rooms"?

"Your contribution to all bills would be ¥25 a month. If that is acceptable I will risk being thought of as a Yín fù [a woman who is notorious for having many casual sexual encounters or relationships]". The girl laughed, then added, "I do not care about the idle gossip of my neighbouring tenants if you don't".

"So you are offering me what exactly then, for the 25"?

"Use of kitchen and bathroom. If I require some solitude you will either go to your bedroom or the study, whilst I will have the lounge. If I wish to study then you can use the lounge if you wish".

"That sounds suitable, we can both have some privacy if we desire it. I agree, how much rent do you want in advance"?

"A ￥100 bond, returnable on your departure, unless you break anything, at which time its value will be deducted from the bond and two months rent in advance, so I require 150 yìngbì before you can move your things in. How much stuff do you have Xiānshēng Nigh"?

"Nothing, just the clothes I stand up in. I will go and get myself a sonic toothbrush and a few other essentials and then get myself some changes tomorrow. Oh, I will have to buy some food too of course, will there be room in the kitchen for my ingredients"?

"Why don't we simply halve the shopping bill each time we go, or one of us does and share the same spaces"?

"Great notion. Thank you for trusting me".

"Betray it, Xiānshēng Nigh and I might hurt you very badly, I am trained in the art of Zìrán-mén".

"I don't know what that is, but I assure you, you won't need it".

"Good, now I must return to work. Come to the door and I will key in your thumb so that you can come and go as I do. I will expect the transfer of money to go into my account this afternoon"?

"Of course, you could listen to me do it if you had more time, but by the time you get to work it will be in your account, all I need is your account number".

"1254-2587-1247-6685-9958C", she told him. Made it possible for him to lock and unlock the door and then asked hurriedly, "If you are here for 16.30 hours I will cook you some dinner".

"I will make a point of being available then", he promised. The instant she was gone he felt more alone than at any other time in his life. In India, he had spent long hours alone. Studying under the Yogi Doshi had been a chiefly solitary existence. The difference was he knew he could always engage anyone in conversation and speak to them as an equal, but more importantly, a contemporary. He was now a stranger in an even stranger land. He resolved to find the city library and do a little research on the CP [central computer terminal] before going for clothing and toiletries. He walked. It was a gloriously sun-drenched day, but gusty, although the wind was not a cold one and he soon found himself perspiring. Fortunately, he had stripped off two layers he had been forced to don whilst on Mars.

Though he had not been there long he felt the much heavier gravity of Earth keenly and was soon very tired. He pressed on until reaching his goal and finally entered the hallowed building that housed a vast treasure of Chinese history, information and memorabilia in the form of several tastefully laid out displays.

Yet another attractive girl hurried over to him, at his entrance,

"Can I help you, Sir? Are you looking for something for one of the masters"?

"I am looking for myself. As you can see I am foreign and desire to do some research on local history and culture. Could you lead me to a terminal please, I don't want to rely on my pad for all the data I wish to digest"?

"Of course, come this way, you can use the outlet for two hours without charge".

She was wearing a sort of traditional Chinese top of fabric buttoned double-breasted cotton in purest white, but grey tights. On her feet were sandals. Due to the tights, Nigh admired the roll of her pert buttocks as she led the way. If this was the fashion Nigh was going to enjoy his stay in Androichina that was certain.

"Which masters were you referring to anyway"? He asked in an attempt to distract himself from her heavenly ass as much as the quest for knowledge.

The girl's laughter was like the delightful tinkle of water down a fall, "*The* masters of course, silly. Masters of Earth and Mars. Don't tell me you're so foreign that you don't know who *they* are"?

"Indulge me"? He offered her his most winning smile, "I have come from a great distance away".

Her almond eyes widened at that revelation and she stopped dead in her tracks to ask breathlessly,

"Not Nyjord, or Brahma. I thought the solar system had been bounderied by the masters"?

"Not everyone listens to them it would seem, especially the government beyond the system".

The girl went decidedly pale as she decided, "Well, what I tell you must be confidential then, Sir".

"As is what I have revealed to you", Nigh played the game.

"The masters are the androids. They rule Mars and Earth from Shattered Fang and have done since the 33rd. Surely even beyond the *Barrier*, you must have heard how they conquered us"?

"The Barrier"?

"Oh, it's what we call hyperspace. Because of its unpredictable nature. I guess you Nyjordic have finally developed technology that has made it much more predictable"?

"You are a very bright young lady", Nigh smiled, "Remember, this conversation never happened".

"The girl drew a hand across her mouth as if zipping her lips closed and blinked rapidly. Even a Chronoman 18 centuries out of whack could understand that gesture. He watched her rump retreat away and then settled down to do a bit of historical reading.

Considering what he knew about General 23 and his ambitions, there were few surprises. The SX pathogen had seriously depleted the population on Earth and during the after-effects of the devastating death toll Mars had simply surrendered to the android without the least attempt at resistance. Venus, by way of its relatively harsh environment and resources, other than those which Mars desperately needed, managed to come out of the next few years fairly well. Callisto had the advantage of being far enough away to be out of sight out of mind.

After the massive reduction in population that the pathogen had reaped human population never really recovered and it had taken it 18 centuries to achieve static stability. The Chinese had been the most naturally resilient to the poison and they were now the majority of earth's people. Although many nations had disappeared. There were essentially now only four major powers on the planet and even then they were firmly under Android rule. The four great quarters of Earth were, Androichina, which also consisted of the lands formerly belonging to Russia Japan and the islands in the Philippine Sea. Androieuropa also contained Africa, though it was chiefly deserted. Androivespucia was the land formerly known as all the Americas and Canada. The last habitable area was formerly Australia, New Zealand, Antarctica, Cambodia, Thailand and across into India, this area was known as Androiantipodea. Over each of these vast areas of land with relatively sparse populations were four military juntas led in each case by a General and answerable only to Capitán-General A23. The General that ruled Androichina was one General Xueling III. Nigh brought an image of her up on his screen and was shocked to discover that she was young looking, very attractive and human in appearance. He reflected, if android technology had advanced in 18 centuries, then it would not be possible to tell humans and androids apart simply by looking at them. On Mars too, the androids had become the overlords of three powerful landmasses, but what surprised Nigh was which three they were; the Eurasian Block, Saxonia and the dominion that had been in its infancy in his own time, Chryse. How had the comparatively small and youthful dominion become a force to equal the two of much greater age and landmass? That would be something he would have to determine later

on. This would mean he would have to be careful in the future what he said to whom. Feeling his eyes becoming gritty well before his curiosity was fully sated, he decided to cease his studies for the time being and go to the nearest precinct to purchase a few essentials, before going back to the apartment he was to lodge in. There were few buildings of a retail variety in the city and most preferred the convenience of securing merchandise on-line but enough remained for him to be able to gather the few items he desired.   He obtained a dickie-bag and in it added toiletries, three pairs of trollies, a set of pyjamas of Chinese design, a pair of sandals, two pairs of boho pants and two Chinese shirts, with the ribbed fronts and material buttons in purest white. It seemed that most of the community wore black pants and white tops, for he had noticed no one in colours. The Chinese wore uniform clothing even when out of the uniform of various offices. As he walked back to the apartment Nigh wondered how he was going to find himself gainful employment. He further conjectured on the possibility that most people did very little actual work. Surely by the 51st century, most manufacturing was done by mechanisation and leisure time was great, even in Androichina? He had so many holes in his knowledge of even the most mundane and every day and was not willing to listen to Paddie for long hours when it would be far more preferable to have Mingfu Li fill him in on various details. As he strolled down the corridor to apartment 23 [it seemed the number and he was inextricably linked] a delightful aroma assailed his nostrils and he knew that the girl had reached the apartment ahead of him. He thumbed the door lock   and   peeped   into   the   kitchen,
        "Good, I'm glad you're a little early", the girl's lovely features were flushed from the heat of her work, "Because I've made a dinner a bit ahead of time, just wash your hands and we can eat". Letting the dickie-bag down in the bedroom that was to be his, Nigh noticed that the girl had made up his bed. White bedding with bamboo stalks and leaves as decoration. Functional without being too feminine. Nigh washed his hands in the bathroom sink and noticed that the toilet was still pretty much the same design since Crapper had invented it thousands of years before. No need to change when the human ass remained constant. He went into the kitchen and seated himself at the rather

diminutive table. No sooner was he in position than the girl slid a delightful stir-fry under his nose. At least the Chinese had finally switched to forks as the eating implements of choice, he already knew that from his earlier meal in the restaurant.

"This is delicious, thank you. I will replace the ingredients of course", he offered as she took his dish from beneath him, it was empty. "Call it a welcome to the apartment - meal on me", she smiled. "Have you enough room for dessert"? Nigh had never eaten Osmanthus Jelly before, but he found it mouthwatering and very enjoyable. They finished with tea. He almost made the mistake of telling her he would wash the dishes by way of expressing his gratitude for the repast before he saw her placing the crockery into a cleaning device, that did not seem to use water but rather employed sonic waves to do the ablutive duty. "Now I bathe", Li told him and smiled, graciously offering, "Unless you would like to use the bathroom firstly"?

"No, you go. Tell me do you smoke"?

"No", she frowned, "This building is non-smoking Xiānshēng Nigh. If you wish to do so, you will have to descend to the street".

"I'll do that while you bathe then", he offered and the girl left the room without another word. He had seen med-cigs on offer in the stores of the city, but perhaps she disapproved of the habit, although he could not think why when it had been proved that smokers lived ten years longer on average due to the stress-relieving benefits of using nicotine. He strolled to the lift went through the lobby beyond and out onto the street. The sun was still shining and it was warm, making him realise that he did not even know if the climate was now stabilised on Earth. He was not only ignorant of the month but also of the day, having only thusly far learned the year. Finishing his ciggie he went up to the study and accessed the S W W once again. He was intrigued to see the history of Chryse, curious as to its rise to prominence on the red planet. It did not take him long to discover what had made the Chryserite the lobby they were. The answer was deuterium or $2H$ a stable isotope of hydrogen with a proton and a neutron in the atomic nucleus. Chryse was a vast bank of the kinetic isotope the abundance of it being 1.5% of all hydrogen atoms found under the surface there 100 times more than that found on Earth. Deuterium was widely used in all chilled fusion reactors and had applications in military, industrial and scientific fields. In cold-fusion reactors, it was used as a tracer and responsible for slowing down neutrons in heavy water moderated fission reactors.

The discovery of vast underground pockets of the resource made Chryse the wealthiest landmass on the mainly arid world and it was said that Chryse.inc, was worth more than most of the corporations with the possible exceptions of Orang-U-Can and Zhōngguó Shāngpiˇn [Chinese Commodities].

Nigh's studies were broken by the appearance of Mingfu Li in the doorway. Her hair was damp and she wore only a thinly designed nightindress. Nigh could not help but find her alluring,

"The bathroom is yours now", she informed him somewhat superfluously, "What are you looking at now"?

"The rise to power of the Chryserite. Tell me, what nationality are they ancestrally"?

"You're very out of touch of current affairs aren't you. Chryserite is a nation themselves. I suppose if you go back a couple of thousand years then you would have to observe that the original settlers arrived there from eastern dominions on Earth. That would be before the masters took over though".

"Don't you resent the masters? Subjugating humanity"?

By way of answer, Li took a seat opposite him. A most distracting effect being that the flimsy covering then rode up her thighs and treat him to a glimpse of even more golden-toned skin.

"It seemed that before they did so, the Earth was heading for disaster. Many many species of animals were dying, the climate was unstable, petty disputes between now disappeared nations were causing constant conflict. The Earth was in a mess. Centuries of the masters' direction has seen the climate repaired. War is almost none existent. The geneticist N359 or Noda if you prefer her alternativetatum-nomenclature has found D N A from preserved tissues of extinct creatures and brought them back to us. What is there to complain about"?

"You are not free", Nigh reasoned not without a certain amount of heat. "You cannot do what you want, without permission from them".

"There have always been rules", Li pointed out, "Without order, as dictated by those who govern civilisation would crumble and the result would be chaos. Surely there are rulers on Nyjord, Brahma? What difference does it make whether those administrators are biological or otherwise? Even A23 is governed by *The 1*"!

"The 1"? Nigh repeated, "Whatever is that"?

"How naive you are", Li smiled, shifting slightly in her position, so that even more expanse of her heavenly thigh was on display. "You have never heard of the Chāojíjìsuànjī [supercomputer]. Qiángdàdedàna˘o guides A23 when he is faced with difficult decisions of government. She was built as a direct result of the regret our great leader felt at the culling of so many on this world two thousand or so years ago".

"He has regret", Nigh murmured to himself, "So he built Qiángdàdedàna˘o, or Mightybrain to ensure his future decisions are not his alone. He gave the mechanism a female identity".

"Qiángdàdedàna˘o walks, talks and looks like one of us", Li informed him then, "She is not some huge box of metal festooned with LED's and toggles".

"She sounds almost like a lover to A23".

Li smirked, "You have picked up on the rumours, I thought you knew nothing about her. The 1 is on many advertisements and holoprojs, did you see her on one of them"? "No. Qiángdàdedàna˘o's relationship with A23 was a deduction rather than a memory, Let me see if I can get her image upon this PC"?

"That will be easy, such is everywhere", Li noted.

Nigh went to the keyboard and typed in Mightybrain, being unsure of the Chinese spelling of her alternative name. A young-looking and slim girl of oriental appearance was the image he received. Of course, with a great deal of the world now Asiatic it made sense to make Qiángdàdedàna˘o look like the majority of women. Nigh wondered if A23 now had a human appearance, but the image he brought up showed the General of the great Junta as still an automaton of metal. A23 may have been many things, but vanity was not one of his failings.

"I'll get that bath now, Xia˘ojiě Li", he rose to go to the bathroom.

"I think we can now dispense with the formality", she told him then, "You may call me Mingfu, or if you prefer I will even let you shorten it to simply Fu, what is your given"?

"Nigh will do just fine", he smiled.

Two. Illegal Alien.

Nigh let the hot water soothe his body. He was trying to determine what he should do next. Had he come all this way to simply let A23 get away with his heinous mass murder? Did it matter any more? Fu seemed reasonably contented with her lot. What if all humanity had settled into the comfortable position of no longer being the dominant race in the solar system?

Perhaps it was too soon to reach a decision? Maybe he should ask others how they felt. Meet the people who lived under the metal masters, find out how many would have preferred to have been governed by their race. In which case he would need to work, or obtain money in some way, otherwise his thumb balance would soon dwindle and he would then be facing poverty. If such existed in the 51st? He climbed out the water, pulling the plug behind him and began to towel his aching limbs. Earth gravity was wearing him since his acclimatisation to Mars. Quickly cleaning up after himself he slipped into pseudo-silk pyjamas and drifted into the lounge. The girl was reclining on the sofa, holding her phone in one hand her head cocked to one side. What was she doing?

"What are you doing? If you don't mind me asking"?

"Listening to my PC-phone", the girl looked confused.

"I cannot hear anything"?

Fu laughed, "Don't tell me, you don't have the implant for your phone frequency? It's a simple matter to adjust your Cochlea-implant. What were you listening to music on if not from your PC-phone"?

"I had a pad, on Nyjord", Nigh tried and thought it would be an acceptable lie.

"You must be centuries out of date out there", Fu noted, "No one has used one of those old things for....for, well, forever".

"I think perhaps there was some sort of time dilation when I left. Caused by the hyperspace".

"What was the year when you left"?

"It was 12N, but I think we believed it would be the 33rd century here".

"And you know this is the 51st do you not"?

Nigh nodded, "I've some acclimatisation to attain, have I not"?

"Acclimaisatioamundoferous if you ask me".

"Did you just make that word up"? Nigh laughed.

Fu returned her face perfectly serious, "No, you'll find acclimaisatioamundoferous on your phonedic. There has been a constant attempt to standardise the language by the General, but a few new ones are included every year. You are like some sort of caveman, Nigh, trying to work a flittercar".

"Maybe when you have some spare time you could show me around the city. Teach me how to bring myself up to date? That is if your boyfriend does not mind you spending time with me"?

Fu frowned at that, informing him, "I have not yet been selected as a prospectorom, Nigh, there is no one".

"A prospectorom"? Nigh repeated, "Does that mean a prospect for romance. Do you mean to tell me that romance is regulated"?

"You looked shocked by that, but you are right in your deduction. Yes, it is. It has to be since the 33rd. Do you realise how close the human race was from dying out on Earth"?

"Tell me, please"?

"I'll tell you what I know, you can look the rest up for yourself", she told him, "First though I need tea, would you like some"?

"Please".

She arose and went into the kitchen and Nigh could not help but admire her ass once again. *'I'd eat my dinner off that',* he thought to himself, while the sound of the sonic kettle boiled the water. Within minutes she was back and handing him a cup. As she bent to do so, her negligee billowed slightly and treated Nigh to a magnificent display of her impressive breasts.

"Do augmentations still take place, here"? he asked, "They were very popular when I left".

"To those who can afford them. I saw your eyes nearly pop out of your head Xiānshēng, so to answer your real question, they are all mine, I've not had much work done at all. Too expensive".

"You do not need any work", he returned warmly, "And if I stop checking you out can we go back to calling me Nigh"?

"I was merely being stern for effect", she chuckled, "It's flattering to be appreciated by a male".

"Which brings us neatly back to my history lesson courtesy of your good self", Nigh noted, "You was going to tell me about the 33rd"?

"All right. What you do not know then was that 5% of humans survived the SX cleansing by our supreme commander. More here in China, but non the less very depleting. What you do not seem to know though, is that of that 5%, 2½% were not men and 2½% women, the split was far less balanced".

"In what ratio"? Nigh asked, "And how long did the phenomenon last"?

"The ratio was that 80% of survivors were female".

She waited for Nigh to look suitably shocked, which he did, but she had another statistic that stunned him more.

"There is more. Not only were 4 out of 5 survivors female, but since the 33rd 4 out of 5 births have also been female".

"So 80% of the Earth's 50 million are women! There are only 10 million men on this planet! What about the other worlds? Could they not get men to emigrate to here"?

"Not from Mars, the gravity would kill them. Venus has a similar problem, the ratio there is getting dangerously close to that on Terra. Callisto cannot spare any workers from the mines and none of us wants cons from the penal colony beneath Mercury. There was the talk of trying to get in touch with yourselves, the Nyjordic, but you did not get the transmissions. Going interstellar will only become reality once the scientists manage to create the Phase Doors they have been promising us for years".

"Phase Doors"?

"Instantaneous transmission of matter from one booth to another. One booth acting as the transmitter, the other as the receiver".

"A transportation system that can convert a person or object into an energy pattern (a process called dematerialization), then beam it to a receiver, where it is reconverted into matter (rematerialization) is surely Science Fiction"? Nigh objected.

"It was in the 33rd", Fu admitted, "But you are out of date - remember"?

"Even so how will the receiving booth ever get to its destination"?

"That's the sticky one", the girl smiled. "Unless we dare send another ship to Nyjord, even when the Phase Door is a reality, it will only be used within the confines of the solar system. Once that happens even fewer liners will be needed for flights that are currently routine and the chance of interstellar travel becomes even more remote".

Changing the subject Nigh asked, "So going back to this prospectorom thing? What is that about Fu, do you have to pass some sort of test to be available for a male partner or something"?

"The section is determined by our General Xueling III, but essentially that is the gisterama yes".

"So there are many many spinsters are there"?

To his surprise, the girl shook her head, "No. Men are allowed to have five wives each, legally, eventually, everyone has the option to look for a man. Of course few get to be the firstwife".

"What if a girl is discerning, even when allowed to look about her at the prospects"?

"Then she remains single. Most women would rather be fifthwife than not have the comfort of a man occasionally though. So, Nigh, did you leave anyone back on Nyjord"?

"I am unattached", he confessed. "I doubt I will be selected to have any wives, being as I am foreign. In any event, I have not registered my arrival in Androichina, so I think I am safe for the moment".

Fu laughed delightedly, "I saw you with your phone".

"I'm not sure I understand what that means relative to - in this conversation", Nigh admitted.

"You mean you do not know how the S W W works? You are now on it Nigh, every selected prospectorom in this sector now knows you are available to select up to five wives should you desire so to do".

"I've not agreed to any sort of register", Nigh felt mildly alarmed and more than a little annoyed that he had no privacy of any sort it seemed.

"Your phone will have checked the database and found you by your thumb account", Fu explained, "You will then be automatically enrolled onto the register. Surely you knew something like that would occur when your mission people let you emigrate to here for your studies"?

"Ah"! Nigh could not keep the deception going for any longer it seemed, "I didn't exactly go through immigration, Fu".

"You don't mean you're illegal"! Fu gasped, "An illegal alien in every sense of the word"!

"It would seem so, will that create any difficulty for you"?

"Not for me, for you", she told him then, "I expect the Shūli˘nánrén to come for you any second, now that you've told me".

"Can you translate that for me, I don't speak Chinese"?

"The Shūli˘nánrén are the combmen, Nigh. What was Mission Control in England thinking by letting you simply roamerama Terra like that".

"Fu, I have a little confession to make on that score", Nigh finally admitted. "Promise me that you will not be angry"?

She frowned, "If you have been lying to me then I might very well be angry, I might even evict you, Nigh".

"Oh, dear. I thought we were getting on rather well too".

"Just tell me what it is you have been lying about, Nigh? Get on with it too"?

"The trouble is, Fu, you will think I am lying if I do tell you the truth. That is the only reason I withheld it from you. It was not a deliberate attempt to deceive you".

"Oh, no"?

"If I tell you the truth you will think me insane, or deluded or just telling lies".

"I'll make that decision for myself. Are you from Nyjord or not"?

"Not".

"Why did you say you were then"?

"Because the truth is utterly not believable".

"Try me, or pack up and get out. I want the truth".

"I am from the 33rd century".

Fu blinked, tried to decide if she could make sense of that claim, "Are you asking me to believe that you are a time traveller"?

"Yes, although I prefer the term Chronoman".

"Well you were right I don't believe you, unless..."?

"Unless I prove it to you in some way"?

She nodded, "And pretty damn velocitously too".

"All right", Nigh wanted to stay, at least for that night, "I will prove it, try not to be frightened".

"I'm too agitatorial to be fumefused", the girl told him in 51st century vernacular.

Nigh closed his eyes and willed himself to flit through the fourth dimension. Having done so once before and when under extreme pressure, he found the fibriliance allowed him to do so with more ease than he would have dared suspect. He opened his eyes and asked Paddie the date. He had fled forward five days. With enough practise he knew he could eventually time his *jumps* to the exact duration he desired. He used memory, eidetic memory to return ten seconds *after* his departure time. Mingfu Li gazed at him in utter astonishment,

"Where did you go"? She asked in an awed whisper.

"Not where. When"! He corrected. "I was still on this sofa, but five days from now".

"But where is your machine, are you human, Nigh"?

"I am human, but I have some fibres in my head that enhance my brain's powers, the fibres are biological in conception, so I am not a cyborg, nor a biotron. If you want to give me a moniker I suppose I am a mutant".

"I feel this might begin to frighten me, Nigh. Perhaps a more detailed explanation and some assurances before I decide whether I feel comfortable allowing you to stay here"?

"Of course and I understand. I did say you would find my claim hard to believe. Let me tell you my story and then you can decide what you want to do".

Nigh told the girl the story of the 'Mirror of Mirrors' [available in good book shops now], by the time he had finished, it was getting late.

The first observation she made once he had told her his rather complex story was, "So you are fabulously rich and could have stayed anywhere in this city, not just shared my apartments".

"I have some money that has incurred interest over the years I missed, but I'm not rich. Why would you think that".

"Tomorrow Taizhou Face Germany in the world cup quarter-final. You could go to the game, return and bet on the outcome and you would be guaranteed to win.

"Taizhou"?

"Yes, we had three teams in the cup this year. The point is, if you use your powers your wealth could be whatever you wanted it to be".

"I have yet to realise the full potential of all my abilities", Nigh admitted, "The pursuit of personal fortunes is not my primary aim".

"But your feud is over, Nigh. It has been over for centuries. Not only that but the majority of the people who now live under the Masters are happy to do so. It is better than the *Dark Ages*".

"I assume by that you mean the second Dark Ages, the first was in the 5th to 15th centuries".

"I know my ancient history, Nigh. The Dark Ancient Period is known to me. The point is, few would thank you for trying to harm the Chāojíjìsuànjī, Qiángdàdedànaˇo, or Acwellen or even Noda".

"I have nothing against Qiángdàdedànaˇo or Noda. As I told you though, 23 killed my friend. My vendetta with him is beyond time, it is eternal".

"Perhaps you would listen to a suggestion from the only friend you have in China right now"?

Nigh brightened, "You are my friend, Fu"?

"I am willing to be if you listen to reason".

"What is your considered advice then, my dear"?

"Firstly you must report to the Shūliˇnánrén and explain who you are and how you got into Guangzhou, then simply observe the occupants for a few days. Meet even some of the masters, before you make any rash decisions. After all, time is a commodity you have in abundance".

Nigh slowly nodded. It made good sense.

*

The following morning, however, events were to take a turn that rested any action Nigh might have made. Both he and Fu were rudely awakened by a tremendous crashing bang on the door and a voice making rapid demands in Chinese. Nigh had not bothered to learn the language, figuring everyone would speak Standard, but the Chinese authorities still preferred the native tongue it seemed.

"What is going on"? He demanded of the girl, she failed to answer and instead opened the door. Four uniformed Shūli˘nánrén burst into the room rushed at Nigh and before he could react, he felt the sting of a tiny needle in his neck and then blackness quickly engulfed him. He awoke after what seemed like a very short period and found himself in some sort of cell. He had been dragged from the apartment and brought to some sort of station. He was strapped to a durilight framed chair by his wrists and ankles, by nyloplanyon tie-wraps. Escape was a physical impossibility. Someone must have been constantly monitoring him. No sooner had he opened his eyes than the door opened and in stepped a Chinese girl that Nigh immediately recognised. He was confronted by none other than General Xueling III.

Disconcertingly, given the circumstances of their introduction of one another, Nigh found the girl even more attractive than the image of her he had observed in Paddie's tiny projection and the small screen of the PC he had also used to look at the supreme leader of all Androichina. He felt curiously honoured by the general's attention. Surely someone of lesser rank could have interrogated Nigh?

"Name", she asked.

"Nigh".

"How did you get into Androichina past our security measures Xiānshēng Night"?

"It is Nigh, not Night, General".

The girl shrugged, "How did you get into this country when we have the best security on Earth? Do you know how many laws of ours you have broken"?

"I am reasonably certain that if I told you, my story would not be believed", Nigh responded.

"Then do not tell me a story, Xiānshēng Night, tell me the truth. It will go easier for you in the end".

"I came here using the power of my Andhera Tantu".

Xueling withdrew a phone from a pocket in her uniform and instructed it to tell her what that was.

"Andhera Tantu", came the tinny response, "A form of foreknowledge of an event, especially as a form of extrasensory perception. Also the ability to transport a person or object instantly from one place to another using only certain filaments in the brain that bear the same name. Such filaments appeared in the 33rd century in children whose mothers had experienced a pregnancy that had been difficult from the offset. In their first trimester, such unfortunates developed the rare disorder *Difficilo Nativatuo Syndrome*. There had been only one drug available to treat for it at that time Phenobarbiosulate. Wildly experimental and not without its unpredictable side effects. The drug was banned following several reports of fibres growing in the brains of the resultant children of those mothers. The children themselves termed the phrase Andhera Tantu to describe their disorder that was later realised as a mutation. For mothers who are unfortunate enough to suffer *Difficilo Nativatuo Syndrome*, we now have the drugs Diasnufalite or in cases where that proves ineffective Takhydroverrabol".

"How many reported cases of Andhera Tantu have been recorded in the last twenty years"? The General asked.

"Since the banning of Phenobarbiosulate in 3302, there have been none". The phone supplied immediately.

Xueling turned her attention back to Nigh, she asked coldly, "I would now like the truth, Xiānshēng Night. If you fail to satisfy me with a provable story I will have the information dragged out of you with the Sīwéigua˘nØ [cogitatioductagraph]. Unfortunately, when the device is used it leaves a vacant abyss in the area of the brain it has drained the knowledge from. We are yet to fine-tune it sufficiently to make it harmless to the subject".

"You want to put some sort of mechanism onto my skull and demand knowledge from my thoughts"? Nigh was more amused than frightened.

"When you contemplated illegally entering Androichina Xiānshēng Night, it might have been wise for you to also hypnoload our language. The SīwéiguaˇnØ is a thought ripping device, it will remove part of the thoughts in your head and download them into our computers. Unfortunately, there are unpredictable side effects associated with its use. I, therefore, advise you to start talking to me"?

"I am the last surviving member of the Andhera Tantura it would seem", Nigh admitted to her then. "I am from the 33rd Century, check your records".

"P74klv, search for all listed Andhera Tantura, was there a Night in the past with that name"?

The phone must have been able to assume that the girl was misquoting Nigh's name for it answered at once that such was the case.

"I am that man and therefore by detaining an Andhera Tantu, you are overstepping your bounds, General".

The girl grimaced, "Overstepping my bounds, Ignoramus. I *have* no bounds, my authority is autocratic".

"Over humans, yes, but I am not human", Nigh was beginning to enjoy the debate, he felt no threat from anything the girl could do when he could simply disappear into the future if he so desired.

"Xiānshēng Night, unless you can demonstrate in some inconceivable way that you are the person you claim to be I will strap you down and drain your brain. You have wasted enough of my valuable time, comply, or die".

"The SīwéiguaˇnØ it is then, because I'm not doing parlour tricks for you, mere mortal".

Xueling nodded and the interrogation was being observed, for the door of the cell flew open and in came a trolley, upon which was a device, the configuration of which, Nigh had never previously seen. A Chinese woman in a white coat began to carefully strap a band of some sort of flexible metal around Nigh's forehead and then quite efficiently and swiftly stepped back and turned the device on. It emitted an ominous humming sound. The woman nodded to her superior.

"Last chance", Xueling warned, "Or your brain could be turned into Chinese lettuce"!

"Go, prick your face, and over-redden your curiosity, you lily-livered yellow-bombard of sacking", Nigh returned in deliberate middle English that he knew would cause confusion and consternation in equal profundity.

Xueling looked suitably infuriated and nodded to the other, who promptly threw a toggle on the SīwéiguaˇnØ. A thermogenic bore shot into Nigh's brain with the affliction and distress of a chiliadal cauquosicalisities. Nigh did his best to modulate his breathing and then went into an instant state of trance-like abstractive catalepsy. He found the thermogenic bore, erecting a buffering bulwark against it and then from behind the aegis used the fibriliance to smite mightily at the energy turning its dynamism against itself. As the pain stopped so did the mechanism suddenly crackle and the pungent aroma of fried circuits and melted plastirubber filled the room.

Coughing, Xueling demanded that the offending fume be extracted and soft whirring confirmed that her orders had been instantly complied with. Before she or the female technician could react further though, Nigh used the Andhera Tantu to melt the ties from his hands and ankles and was on his feet and across the room as the two women's eyes widened in sudden alarm. For some reason that he was forced to examine later, Nigh grabbed the General's arms and pinned her to the wall and before she could cry out, he planted a firm and lusty kiss on her glorious lips.

She looked astonished and confused, but strangely not angry,

"I am just visiting your dominion and mean no harm", Nigh told her as the technician rushed for the door.

"Stop", Xueling demanded of her. Then she did something that surprised Nigh greatly, she smiled, "You have a very unusual way about you, Xiānshēng Night. I must confess though that your demonstration has me convinced. I will ping a visa to your phone, you are free to go. Oh, one last thing, as the ping will come from me, you will then have possession of my swwaddress. You and I should explore our dynamic further when we have the time".

'Is she coming on to me'? Nigh could barely credit it, only seconds before she had tried to make Swiss cheese out of his brain, but he replied, "I will keep that in mind General. Now I must go, I have some matters to attend to".

The fact of the matter was, that the only matter he had to attend to was a little lunch. He walked out of the Combmen station in a state of a bemused daze. The moving walkways were still sufficiently noveltacious to him to be worth another ride upon them. He strolled through the mid-morning sunshine oblivious for the moment of what was going on around him. Quite suddenly a rather fetching young woman had caught up to him and joined at his side on the walkway he was using. She was rather scantily clad by 33rd century standards, but perhaps not so in the 51st. She looked up into his eyes and smiled.

Nigh almost missed the greeting, so busy was he staring at the fabulous overhang of her impressive bosom. He thought himself a sufficient student of such matters as to be able to determine that they were natural rather than augmented.

"I am Aurora", the girl told him. "You are Nigh and

you are unattached".

Nigh had the sudden premonition of where the scene was going. "Yes, that's correct", he admitted, "I only arrived in Androichina yesterday, so I don't know much of the city yet".

"I could show you around if you wish", she offered, "And we could find that such a tour would be magical for us both and you would fall in love with me just as I have loved you since the first moment I saw your image projected by my phone".

Nigh was around 182 cms, yet lean only weighing 60 kilos. He was fair and fair-haired and surely not a man a Chinese girl would find attractive. Yet this young woman was throwing herself at him. Then he reflected upon what he had learned whilst accessing the S W W. Men were in such short supply that they were allowed to take up to 5 wives. The poor girl was lonely, her biological clock was ticking and she had no partner. As each fateful year ticked by her chances of getting one grew decidedly fainter. All thing being equal she would not have given Nigh a second glance. All things were not equal though.

"You are a very lovely young lady. I see that and recognise your grace and demeanour. I am not looking for a woman right now though".

Aurora's face fell and she asked sadly, "Are you a Mógui̯ de xia̯o xiàng qí shī "?

"I speak very little Chinese. You will have to translate that for me"?

"A Devil's alley jockey".

"Oh"! Nigh was amused by the euphemism, "No. I like girls I assure you. I have a more pressing matter to attend to at the moment though".

"I want to marry you", she smiled, "I want to be your first wife. I will be very good for you. Loyal, hard working and in the bedroom I'll...".

"I'm certain you would be more than excellent in all areas", Nigh cut her short, "But I have a sort of quest to perform, a mission that will not let me rest until it is accomplished".

"Could I not help you with it"?

"I doubt you would want to Aurora. For one thing, it involves a space flight to Mars".

"Let me come with you then? I have some savings, You can have all that I possess. You can also have me and me, you"?

Nigh stepped off the walkway and looked into the girl's admittedly lovely almond-shaped eyes,

"There will be a danger that I am not willing to subject you, nor anyone else to. I intend to return though. Once what I have to do is completed. We could exchange electroaddresses".   Aurora looked crestfallen, "I do not think I would ever see you again. I think you do not find in me, what you want"?   "I do not know if that is the case or not", Nigh admitted honestly, "We know nothing about one another, we might not be suited".   "We could learn"?   "We could. Just not right now. Give me your E-A and I will put it into Paddie here".

"娶欢 戏圻廿 娶欢 雀岷 习内 炉奴 炉奴 炉奴 娶欢 戏圻廿 薛双 曲人 炉奴 娶欢 薛双 薛水 燥炉奴 娶欢 炉奴 薛 ", Aurora responded eagerly.

"Could you give me that in Standard"? Nigh chuckled.

"78746-55578-32573-35753".

"Did you get that Paddie"?

"Affirmative", came the tinny response.

"Now I must leave you", he lied. In truth, he could have spent as long as he wished with her. As the chase is often better than the catch though, she was making it just too easy for him.

She suddenly pushed herself up onto her toes and brushed his cheek with her lips, murmuring,

"Don't forget me"?

'My goodness, a rake could have the time of his life in this century', Nigh thought and looked around him for a restaurant or café. Despite the modest population of the city, such was not difficult to locate and nigh strolled inside thinking his encounters for the day might then be done. He was mistaken! The place was quite full for it had reached lunchtime. At his entrance nigh observed the ambient noise of conversation dip, however. He glanced around him for a free seat and found one opposite a most petite diner indeed.

"Excuse me but do you mind if I sit here", he asked. "I don't mean to disturb you but there are no empty tables at all and some of the other customers are already engaged in conversations with friends, that they might not want me listening in on".

The girl looked up from her plate with a very strange expression on her tiny features and nodded,

"Sit down Englishman, who is new to our shores, my name is Líēnniú and I do believe I already know yours".

"Of course. The Solar Wide Web, there is little chance of being clandestine once one is enrolled upon it".

"Especially when one arrives in a fashion that the Shūli˘nánrén find confusing or sinister", Líēnniú had the smile of a Mona Lisa. "I understand, from my phone that you have no mates, at this time".

"Mates! You make me sound like some prize stud rather than a simple man".

"You *are* regarded as a prize stud though. I also doubt you are anything other than simple. I hope the Shūli˘nánrén are still confused by you"?

Nigh found himself warming to Líēnniú. She had a mischievous quality about her. Smiling he asked, "What are you eating it looks good"?

By way of answer the girl suddenly cut a piece off her plate and held it up to Nigh, "Let crunchy tentacles of a deep-fried taro ball tickle the edges of your lips", she invited and seemed delighted when he took the morsel into his mouth.

"You've shared food with me, Nigh, you have to marry me now".

"Is that some bizarre Androichinese custom"? he asked with a grin.

The girl shook her head, "A bizarre Líēnniú custom, what number will I be"?

"I'm still single", Nigh laughed, "Though it would seem that there are several candidates only too willing to change that".

"Of course. A prize like you doesn't come up every day and most of us are doomed to spinsterhood. Something quite unseemly in Androichinese society".

"Yet unavoidable when there are so few men available"?

Before they could speculate further a waitress sidled up to the table and said huskily, "Qīn'ài de, bùyào wèi nà zhī shòuxiaˇo de xiaˇo muˇ niú làngfèi niˇ de shíjiān. Ràng woˇ chéngwéi niˇ de nüˇ rén, woˇ huì shuˇnxī niˇ de jībā, zhídào niˇ de yaˇnjīng chūcuò [Don't waste your time with that skinny little cow, darling. Let me be your woman and I'll suck your (censored) until your eyes bug out]".

"I'm sorry I don't speak Chinese", Nigh explained before Líēnniú informed him,

"You're not. She was being most coarse".

Nigh began to feel that the situation was getting out of hand. He told the waitress he would like the same menu Líēnniú was having and mouth twisting in disappointment and jealously the waitress sloped away.

"Girls like that give the rest of us a bad name", Líēnniú observed.

"What did she say"?

"She described me as bovine and then offered to fellate you".

"I am genuinely shocked, is this typical behaviour from today's young ladies"?

"It is typical of some. Then some are a little more delicate of sensibility. I fit into the latter bracket, does that disqualify me, are you looking for an angel by day and a naughty girl at night".

"Naughty"? Nigh considered "As I understand the word it means badly behaved and disobedient, so no, I'm not looking for someone who is going to be naughty. My Dear, I'm not looking for a girl at this time".

"Well, as that has gotten that out of the way, maybe we could just enjoy our meal then"?

Whilst walking back to the apartment Nigh was propositioned twice more. He was not flattered by the attention. He reasoned that any single man of whatever sort of looks and personality would have received the same advances. The poor girls were not looking for a nice man. They were simply looking for an end to their single status. He let himself into the domicile and wondered briefly why Mingfu Li had not tried a similar offer, but then something happened which surprised him greatly and Nigh was not a man who was easily astounded.

Momentarily startled Fabiaphon recovered his self-composure and then waited for Lynea to settle the account with Wang. The Wang who loaned his name to the very august boutique. On the way back the chauffeur kept up a steady line of diatribe and she found that it was possible to *dial-out* and hardly hear most of it, but still, maintain a reaction at the appropriate points when it seemed he paused to breathe. The flitter glided into the garage, Cook and Zhongxiaoqing were waiting to help unload everything into the pantry. The vehicle must have some sort of automatic signalling device installed, that informed them when it was imminently arriving.

It was too late to start inspecting the property to see what her other duties entailed, so the new Housekeeper left the trio to get on with their collective task and went to bathe. Her bathroom was all white accoutrements in a dove grey room, lit by the ubiquitous LED's. She ran a nice depth, poured some available salts into the water and had a leisurely soak. Once dry, Lynea changed into a pretty frock of off-white lace that accentuated her slim yet curvy form. Tying her dark hair back into a loose ponytail for convenience, allowed her to add long pendant earrings. She had been informed that she would dine with the rest of the staff, in a smaller version of the main dining hall which was on the first floor. The retainer facilitates were on the ground though.

For some reason that she did not examine at the time, she found herself wandering onto the first floor. Harbouring the facile excuse that she was doing a cursory inspection to ascertain what would need to be addressed firstly on the morrow. She entered a very opulent lounge, obviously one for the master of the property and CEO of Preciometalic Inc and a place to entertain honoured guests and equally, overawed employees. Suddenly Zhongxiaoqing was at her elbow,

"Where have you been", the girl hissed, "The Master has dined and now it is our turn. I was sent to find you".

Lynea glanced at her wrist-chrono, "Oh! Is that the time, it sort of ran away with me, sorry. Say this chair looks incredibly comfortable, don't you agree"?

Zhongxiaoqing looked at the high-backed, studded recliner in ox-blood hued faux-leather. Over it was a grey throw, but the left-wing could still be seen poking around the corner. A huge spray of white flowers had been placed to its side previously, they were echoing Lynea's frock. Zhongxiaoqing breathed reverently,

"That is the Master's chair. None are allowed to sit in it but he. Not even Decorum".

"Really"! The mischievous side of the English-woman came to the fore, "I'll see about that".

The instant Lynea had parked her behind onto the seating cushion Zhongxiaoqing gasped and her slim fingers flew rather comically to her mouth. Lynea was about to laugh when she heard a door in the rear of the room open and the floor issue its familiar creak as the weight depressed it slightly. Lynea said surprisingly calmly given the circumstance,

"Gravis is standing behind me isn't he"?

Zhongxiaoqing could do nothing but nod furiously, although Lynea fancied she heard a tiny whimper escape her slim pursed lips.

With a determined tread, Alexius Morrelius Gravis strode around to the front of the chair and looked down at Lynea. He was smiling!

"Never has that seat been decorated with anything as remotely lovely. Did you select that frock from England, My Dear"?

Lynea could do nothing but nod, in her breast the most confusing of emotions was suddenly raging.

"How has your first day gone, are you ready to begin work in earnest on the morrow"?

Lynea rose to her feet and found herself suddenly quite transfixed by Gravis' deep blue eyes,

"I have been through a few rooms and can see some of them need a feminine touch, yes Mister Gravis".

"I will free up some budget for you if you would like to add some softer furnishing, but please let me keep this chair, it is my favourite".

"Of course", Lynea found herself rather like the insect that was being examined by the chameleon. Yet Gravis had been nothing but charming in his dealings with her, thusly, that was!

"You'll have to excuse me now", Lynea chose the convenience of Decorum's entrance to beg her departure, "Staff dinner is ready".

"Yes of course", Gravis' lips suddenly pursed, "That explains the Xanthicole presence in these private quarters. Enjoy your meal My Dear and I will see you for a meeting at 11:00 tomorrow".

As the two women departed with diligent haste, Lynea remembered the words of the chauffeur earlier, '*He's not had a go at you yet then? You'll realise the first time he's touched you up. You'll have to prostrate yourself before the Old Man. Quite literally if the randy old goat were to get his way. What do you think happened to the previous housekeeper'?*

Was there any truth to the claims of the somewhat imaginative Yank? Gravis had been nothing but courteous and complimentary toward her, was he lulling her into a false sense of security before he struck? Then she reasoned something else, did she care? The man possessed a certain charisma, added to his obvious air of power it was quite a heady cocktail. Lynea found him attractive in more ways than one. He was also quite dashing, she could not agree to become his concubine under any circumstances, but she would not rule him out as a respectable suitor.

'*Whom I kidding*'? She thought to herself then, '*He's one of the wealthiest men in China right now and I'm the hired help. This isn't some trashy romantic e-novel that Remma seemed to gobble up on the voyage here*'.

The dinner was the best Lynea had enjoyed since leaving Yorkshire. She enjoyed it because it was so English. Beef, real bovine flesh not lichen-beef. Lichen-carrots, lichen-spud and joy of joys, Yorkshire puddings. Lynea asked,

"Do you mind if I ask you where you are from originally, Cook"?

The chef smiled and admitted, "Not at all, I was born in Dewbifax, my name was Rhea Pond before everyone simply called me Cook".

"No wonder this meal is so delicious, you are one of the Dewbifax Pond Restaurant family then"?

Cook smiled and nodded, "Numa Pond was my father". A sudden sadness seemed to settle on the creator of the meal then as she admitted, "Of course they are all gone now, the SX saw to that. My only surviving cousin pinged me to tell me the news some time ago. I had fallen out with my Father and came to China in the faint hope of opening a traditional Yorkshire restaurant. It did not work out as I had envisaged and that is why I took this post. I never got a chance to mend our broken fences nor say goodbye to Father".

To change the subject and also avoid a gloomy silence following Cook's revelation, Lynea asked the chauffeur, "What about you, Fabiaphon? Why did you come East"?

"I was a dealer", the American chirped, "You know? A little bit of this, some of that. I found I could make far more bucks by doing the GIM. I hit a few complications though and things didn't pan out as I had anticipated. It all got a bit heavy so I sacked it and got this number instead".

"What is GIM"? Lynea asked. Strangely it was Zhongxiaoqing who answered that question,

"Grey Import Goods", she sounded - accusingly, "Or to put it another way smuggled items that have not paid import nor export duty. It is illegal and what got heavy for Mister Pho was the combmen breathing down his neck and no one wants trouble with them in China".

Lynea smiled, finding the tale had amusing aspects, she asked the American, "I meant what about your friends and family, Chauffeur, not your nefarious activities in commodities"?

"I had a brother, never knew our parents they were killed in a flitterjet collision in forty-nine. SX finished him off and now there's just loveable little-ole me".

Zhongxiaoqing noted, "The Masters were cruel to be kind, what they did was for the rest of the creatures living on Earth and for the environment".

"That's a bunch of horse-kaahk and you know it"! Fabiaphon exploded, "They did it for the same old reason we always did it to one another in the past, power over others. It's always about power".

Lynea observed, "I think that only history will finally bear out why 23 did what he did. Let's change the subject or we may ruin our digestion".

Cook agreed, "Good idea and it's jam roly-poly for pudding".

As Lynea struggled to keep her composure leaving the room, her body stuffed with jam roly-poly, she practically collided with Decorum, who seemed to be loitering outside the doorway.

"Oh! Sorry, are you all right"? He asked.

"I've overindulged on Cook's delicious puddings, but I will be proficient in my duties on the morrow, have no fear Mister Decorum", Lynea exclaimed.

"That is not what I came to talk to you about", the younger Morrelius confessed then, "I was wondering if you would like to join me for a drink and listen to some music for a short while. There is an excellent valve rig in the listening room on the second floor"?

"Most gracious", Lynea smiled, "But I've had a long day and now I've eaten I'm feeling suddenly fatigued. Perhaps a different evening, when you are not entertaining guests".

What is it with these two? They must get beautiful females attending the place when they entertain. Why the interest in the Housekeeper? Unless all they're after is a quick horizontal tango with the greased-weasel with no strings attached?

Lynea found herself smiling at the crudity of her thoughts, Alexius Morrelius Decorum mistook it for a friendly apology and responded,

"Of course! Insensitive of me, another time then, Lynea".

She squeezed past him then her smile even broader due to the unintentional deception. It was the end of her first day at the Manor in Shangjiezhen, 上街镇, Minhou, Fuzhou, Fujian.

* * *

Over the next week, Lynea took her duties seriously. She intended to clean the manor from top to bottom. Zhongxiaoqing and Fabiaphon, in particular, did not take kindly to the workload she placed on them.

"I'm no domestic", he had wailed, to which Lynea replied,

"When you're not driving you're idle and can be vacuuming, so crack on or I'll report your disobedience to The Morrelius'. His place is going to have my stamp on it and if you do not wish to be a part of it I'm sure we can find an alternative driver".

He glared at her at the threat but was sensible enough to realise how determined she was and finally got down to some work. Strangely once he had begun he found he got some satisfaction out of it,

"Look at this, your predecessor must have been slacking", he showed her his third container of dust and lint as he was emptying the unit in the Rolls Royce 2200 Execuvac.

"Obviously", Lynea smiled tacitly, before the chauffeur spoiled it all with crudity,

"Mind you it's difficult to vacuum with your underpants around your ankles".

"Mention sex one more time today Pho and so help me....well, you'd just better not, that's all"!

Grinning at her lack of imaginative threat, Fabiaphon returned, "You know what your trouble is don't you Housey? Do you know what you need? What would cheer you up a bit"?

"In your wildest dreams, Chaff. Now crack on with the upper dining room, I want it gleaming by lunchtime".

"Chaff"?

"It's short for Chauffeur, but also the worthless rubbish from the husks of corn or other seed separated by winnowing or threshing. Would you like a damn good threshing, Chaff"?

The chauffeur-come-domestic grinned "That sort of depends upon the circumstance? I mean to say, are there any other fringe benefits so to speak"?

"By lunchtime Chaff"!

While he was doing the floors and Zhongxiaoqing was using wet-wipes to clean everything else, Lynea followed them with polish and glass cleaner where necessary. By the time they were done the place looked brighter, the cleanliness easily discernable by vision alone.

Gravis was going to have one of his gatherings and requested to speak to Lynea, through Zhongxiaoqing.

"The Master just rang for me and asked if he could see you in the library"? The Chinese girl informed Lynea. Finishing her cup of lichentea she dutifully went to the so-called room that had, in fact, no paper books of any kind within its walls. Rather one case on a single wall was filled with stiks and on them were all the major non-fiction and fictional works in e-book form. Gravis, it was rumoured had read; Essays by Michel de Montaigne, Confessions by Augustine, The Interpretation of Dreams by Sigmund Freud, The Prince by Niccolo Machiavelli, Walden by Henry David Thoreau, On the Origin of Species by Charles Darwin and The Complete Works of Plato by Plato. Of the lighter material, he had also devoured most of the material by Dumas, Dickens, Wells, Verne, Conan-Doyle, Asimov, Dick, Clarke, Roxbrough and Gehenna.

He looked up from a pad when she entered, "You wished to speak to me"?

"Yes, My Dear. Firstly I want to thank you for what you have done to the place over the last week. It is easily noticeable that you are far more diligent in your duties than your predecessor. Secondly, I want you to know that some employees and other distinguished guests will be arriving on Tuesday and I would like you to organise ten guest suites as they will be staying overnight. I will also require you to go out with Fabiaphon and get some ingredients for a special dinner which you will then give to Cook. Lastly, I would like to invite you to attend the evening"?

"Me"? Lynea was astonished, "Your Housekeeper? How would you introduce me to others? Miss Brown I would like you to meet one of my staff, she keeps house for me"?

Gravis smiled at the irony and returned, "What about Miss Nigh from Yorkshire, a friend of mine"?

"What sort of friend exactly"?

"You are going to advise me on some new interior designs for this place. Not exactly a lie as I have already given you carte blanche to do anything along those lines that you think would brighten the place up".

"But why do you want me there, if that is not an impertinent question"?

"Several reasons, I want your opinion on some of the guests who are coming, a female perspective if you will. I want to see what you make of my organisation and you can be as candid as you wish. Thirdly I would welcome your company. I do not think any other person present on the day, except for my son, will like me. I hope you do"?

His gaze upon her was scrutinizing and incredibly sincere, she returned honestly,

"I have been given no reason to dislike you, Mister Gravis".

"Just Gravis will do from now on. I should like to call you Lynea"?

Lynea nodded her acceptance, what reason could she have for refusing? "So... er, Gravis, have the guests been given a reason to dislike you"?

He nodded, "They work for me. I am their CEO. I pay them, that puts them in my debt. You are in the same position and yet – if I am any judge of character, you do not dislike me".

Lynea chuckled, "I just told you that I do not dislike you, so that was not so difficult to deduce was it"?

He laughed. Lynea found it to be a baritone rumble that was not unpleasant, "You got me there, Lynea. Tell me you'll come to the dinner and the entertainment afterwards"?

Suddenly seriously, Lynea asked, "Do I have a choice. What will happen if I refuse"?

"If you mean will it change my attitude toward you, then the answer is nothing will happen. I am not a vindictive man, Lynea".

"We shall see about that, Gravis", Lynea teased then, "Once I have spoken to some of your employees. Learned about the real Alexis Morrelius Gravis".

"Then you'll come"?

Lynea nodded, "As your Interior Designer and new-found friend".

Once back in her quarters Lynea tried to decide how she felt about the invitation. More importantly, what she deduced was the motivation behind it. Gravis had never been anything other than totally charming toward her. Yet it was plain that the other members of his staff did not feel the same way about him. In the case of Zhongxiaoqing, it was easy to understand for Gravis was obviously bigoted and frequently showed no desire to conceal the fact. Fabiaphon simply disliked his employer as a matter of some strange principle. Cook was the hardest to work out or did she simply let the majority carry her along. Whatever their motivations, Lynea could not share them. She liked Gravis and also found him a rather a dashing figure when he spruced himself up.

Thusly she found herself looking forward to the evening with greater and increased anticipation. Two things surprised her greatly when the evening came around. One was the level of ambient background music that was playing in the rooms that had been designated for entertaining the guests, far too loud in Lynea's opinion, everyone was shouting over it to continue a conversation. The second thing was that of the ten guests eight of them were in fact female, not only that but several of them were of Oriental origin. The two Morrelius' were both elegantly resplendent in matching tuxonesies of black under which were bohemian white shirts with frilled fronts and cuffs and high neckline. The only thing about them that differed was that while Gravis wore a silver wolf pendant, Decorum's a dragonfly inlaid with varying blues of cloisonné. The instant Lynea made her entrance, hoping it had been as surreptitious as possible, Gravis seemed to detect her with sensors hither-to unsuspected in him. He glided rather than walked over to her a glass of fluted nyloglass in his perfectly manicured hand and offered it to her. It was white wine, something Lynea was not adverse to upon occasion. She accepted it with a smile.

"Eight women", she observed as an opening conversation.

"I beg your pardon"? Gravis had not heard her, for she had spoken at the level she referred to as *'indoor voice'*. Lynea repeated herself but refused to raise her volume. The ruse worked, from his pocket Gravis found a small remote and depressed the appropriate button. The volume of the music reduced by 50%.

"I said eight women", Lynea said quietly, forcing Gravis to repeat the exercise with the remote, cutting the volume still further,

"Thank you for doing that, what was that hideous racket anyway"? Lynea finally managed.

"Hideous racket", Gravis echoed, his face wreathed in amusement, "It was none other than 'Zone That Club Pow', they only won the 'Solar System has Cosmic' final last year and Simone Duodenum has given them a five-year contract amounting to 17/- and the money-back on any returns".

"In that case, my humble opinion is that he wants shooting", Lynea offered Gravis her most charming smile.

"He laughingly informed her, "Since the sexreorgment Simone is spending the next three years as a woman so that he can bond better with his baby, I'm certain you remember that the offspring is an hermaphrodite"?

"I don't keep up with the latest tabloid news", Lynea confessed, "I haven't read 'Oy! Get Aloada This', since Maxibelly Roberta drowned and Teresa Wagon took over as editor. As for the sexreorgment, I suspect some sort of taxation dodge. I don't know what you think, but I believe this alteration of one's gender is unhealthy in many ways. Would you ever consider becoming a woman, Gravis"?

"Me. No, I have been told in the past though that to try the opposite sex for three years - helps one understand the contradictory gender and become more manly as a result. Or more feminine if originally a woman. I also understand men wanting to be a woman for a year to enjoy the feelings of pregnancy and childbirth".

"Hhmm, Like Duodenum, who then had a Hermi".

Hermi was the coarse term for a person who possessed both male and female genitalia, but as Gravis was happy enough to show his bigotry toward Orientals, Lynea felt no qualms in displaying bigotry of her own.

"Are you ready to come and meet one or two of my guests"? He asked her then.

"Before you do that could you give me a brief bio of whomever it is to give me something to discuss with them"?

Gravis smiled in appreciation of the tactic, "That's a good idea", he noted. "Very well that Xant....erm, Chinese girl over in the corner, we will engage her in conversation firstly, she is Shen Huan Wu, Head of Sales here in China. As you can imagine sales have plummeted since the SX, and it is going to be Wu's responsibility to regenerate interest in our products".

"By your products, I presume you mean the jewellery your metals are used to create"?

"We have a great number of industrial applications too", Gravis smiled appreciatively, "Which will also suffer a

tremendous setback by the culling of so many peoples. Only those organisations who are prepared to ruthlessly cut staff and emerge from the fire, phoenix-like, leaner and hungrier will survive the next decade".

"And how many have you been forced to lay off, Gravis. Surely SX was self-governing in that respect".

"To some extent yes. It was. Accidents of nature do not good business make. I still had to get rid of lumber and in other section even have to recruit greenwood in place of those lost".

"Not an easy thing to do, having such an effect on those individual's lives, surely"?

"I had to agonise over certain decisions, but I would not have it any other way. Once it became easy to me, I would know it would be time to quit and let Decorum take the reins. So are you ready to meet Wu"?

Lynea nodded and was led to Head of Sales of Preciometalic Inc. The young woman looked to be about 22, wearing traditional Chinese garb of dress decorated with embroidery of various brown and orange silks. The resultant scene was of a hummingbird flying between various blossoms. Wu herself was a pretty thing with an elongated heart-shaped face, her long dark hair parted on the right and adorned in no other way at all. Her slim lips were rouged slightly but other than that her clear complexion was not decorated with makeup. As the couple approached Shen Huan Wu, she tilted her head slightly to her right tacitly asking the question, who was Lynea. The Head of Sales had been selected for her aesthetic appeal which as far as Lynea, another woman, could judge, was considerable.

"Wu", Gravis began, sipping his drink, "Allow me to introduce you to my Interior Designer, Miss Nigh. Miss Nigh, Miss Wu".

Wu offered Lynea a charming smile and held out her hand, "Please call me Shen Huan", even the girl's voice was attractive.

"I would be pleased to", Lynea confirmed, "I'm Lynea. How has the culling affected your efforts to make Preciometalic Inc a successful and thriving company Shen Huan"?

The girl's reply was lengthy and involved, she certainly knew her vegetables, Lynea managed to look interested throughout the involved diatribe. Finally, the girl asked her,

"So will we be seeing you at the offices once you have finished with the Manor"?

"I have not decided yet", Lynea prevaricated, for Gravis had melted away and was then engaged in an animated conversation with an immorally fat man. If he gained much more weight the Chinese authorities would remove a limb, that was the punishment for being illegally obese. By the look of him, he must already have at least one prosthetic, Lynea reasoned. As if reading her thoughts Wu leaned into her and informed,

"That's Hallius Draconis Crassus, he already has a biotronic left leg and lungs, yet still he insists upon fuelling that carcase of his with four thousand calories a day".

"Why would anyone with a business mind do that", Lynea was genuinely curious.

"He claims he was raped by two female members of his academy whilst a callow youth and eats to try and forget".

"Forget what", Lynea quipped, "His waistline".

Wu giggled and added, "You'll find it even less credible when I tell you who one of the females who raped him was supposed to be".

"Please do"?

"None other than Marco Barca Magna"!

"*The* Marco Barca Magna! CEO of Luxurest Flitterhols?! He used to be a woman"?

"A stunning and pneumatic blonde. Crassus had more chance of pulling a muscle in the gymnasium that of pulling her. Have you never seen the images on gogglepix"?

Whilst speaking she pulled out her pad and brought the images in question up onto her screen. The girl had an impossibly narrow waist and hips and huge breasts, her hair was a flaxen blonde and her lips were the carp-look that had been popular for the past few decades. In short, she looked ridiculous.

"And the other girl"? Lynea was enjoying the ridiculous nature of the claim, A further image followed, this time a pouting and impossibly attractive brunette. Or was it attractive? Had beautiful become the new hideous, Lynea asked herself.

"Presumably they found Crassus impossibly attractive, while he did not share their feelings, so they gang-raped him", Lynea chuckled.

"That's the claim", Wu confirmed, "It was thrown out of court but Crassus is such a good businessman that Gravis gave him a position in the company anyway".

"In what capacity"?

"Stores and Victuals, what else"? Wu chuckled. "Come and meet him and try your best not to like him, he is very funny once he's had a few drinks and he always has a few drinks".

"Of course, lead the way", Lynea was intrigued, could she indeed warm to the tub of lard that was the obese man?

Wu led and even her walk was elegant and sensual in equal amount,

"Crassus, leave Gravis alone and come and talk to the Interior designer, Lynea Nigh", Wu demanded of the object of their former interest.

The man had ludicrously removed his shirt. Gravis did not seem to mind in the slightest. In his right fist, he was holding an enormous glass of beer and the base of it rested on his disgustingly bulging girth. Yet he offered Lynea a very friendly grin and noted,

"Wow another looker, where do you find them all, Gravis"?

"Miss Nigh is going to do some simple and effective designs around the Manor", the CEO smiled indulgently. "Would you like me to turn the air conditioning a little higher Crassus".

"Well I am sweating like a pig in here, so if everyone else is warm enough", the overweight businessman agreed. "So, Miss Nigh, have you heard the one about the goose, the tub of dripping and the chorus girl"?

"Not suitable for mixed company Crassus", Wu and Gravis said in unison, to which he smirked and returned,

"I was merely inquiring if the young lady had heard it. To ascertain her character so to speak? I would never repeat such smut. Anyway, how do you know it's not suitable, Shen"?

Lynea was amused as the Chinese girl coloured, "Er, let me get you another drink, Lynea"? She fussed and beat a hasty retreat while the blood drained back out of her features. She had been right though, Crassus was entertaining coarsely.

The evening continued and the drink flowed and Lynea stopped short of getting too inebriated, though she was mellow and a little merry, by the end of the gathering.

* * *

"And that is where I will stop for this evening", Huahua finally said. "It is getting late, I will see you again tomorrow if you wish to hear the rest of your Aunt's story. I sincerely hope that you do because I need you to do something to set matters to rights. Do not ask me in that regard at this point though. Let me tell you all, in the correct sequence".

"It is entertaining, will you wait until I get home from work"? Mingfu Li asked.

"How can I do otherwise when you are gracious enough to allow me to visit my cousin in your apartment", came the polite response.

The three of them seemed to rise from the sofa and chair in unison. Nigh rushed toward the door and opened it for the very attractive visitor, she asked,

"What time will be convenient tomorrow, Fu"?

"The same as today", came the swift reply.

She left them then. The two looked at one another and Mingfu Li finally confessed, "I do not think anything about your visit and stay with me is going to be dull, Nigh"!

Nigh laughed, "I do admit that Huahua has greatly intrigued me with her family history. Or should I say *my* family history"?

Four.   Family History – Part the Second

Nigh awoke at the tapping on his door and Mingfu Li entered looking concerned.

"What's the trouble"? He asked, sensing at once that there was indeed something wrong.

"There's a combman, female, in the lounge, wanting to speak to you".

"The Shūli˅nánrén again! Well, at least they make the call more sociable. Last time they drugged me to get me to headquarters.

He rose carefully and entered the lounge in his nightshirt. A uniformed young woman was waiting patiently. Standing, with her arms behind her back.

"What can I do for you, Officer"? Nigh asked politely enough.

"The General has sent me to bring you to headquarters Xiānshēng Night"

"Nigh", Nigh corrected, "There is no 'T' on the end of my name. I thought my business was concluded, with Xueling, what does she want with me this time"?

"I am not privy to that information, Xiānshēng Nigh. All I have been instructed to do is bring you to the station. Will you come without a struggle"?

Nigh looked at the girl. She was around 150 centimetres, probably weighed in the region of 45 kilogrammes and he had been taught hand to hand combat by the secret service of England. That, without even considering his powers with the fibriliance. He smiled though and told her he would go and get dressed and then accompany her to the Shūli˘nánrén station. To do otherwise might very well jeopardise Mingfu Li's position in the flat.

He presented himself before her and acknowledged his readiness,

"All right, Officer, let's go".

The ride was swiftly efficient, the girl could certainly drive a flitter. Within minutes they were across town and into the station.

"Please come and have a seat, in the waiting room - number one", the girl asked her and ushered Nigh into what was little more than a painted cell, before closing and locking the door behind him. It was not long before the admittedly lovely General opened it again and slipped inside. Nigh was disconcerted to find her so attractive. Doubtless, she was not a woman to get involved with - in any capacity what-so-ever.

"If you wanted to see me socially, General, you should have simply sent me a ping", Nigh joked.

"That would be exactly what I would have done", the beauty confessed, her features remaining serious. "I'm afraid this meeting is in an official capacity Xiānshēng Night".

Not bothering to correct her, Nigh asked then, "Is there some problem with my visa then, I did not receive one as you promised"?

"In a way and yet no, not really" Xueling prevaricated.

Aware of the double entendre, Nigh asked, "Well come on, General, spit it out"?

"Your visa was blocked", the General informed, "By none other than Qiángdàdedàna˘o. I believe you refer to her as Mightybrain".

"Why blocked, because of who I am, or perhaps because of who I was"?

"All the block said was that your application to stay in Androichina might be problemirkefluous".

"Sorry that word is unknown to me"?

"Oh! Yes I forgot, you're an ancient are you not? It means any question or dark matter involving gloomy doubt, uncertainty, or difficulty".

"I see. A term to remark that something is problematic without detailing why shrouding it in subfuscation"?

"Precisely so. Unfortunately, it also means that you can only stay in Androichina for two weeks as a visitor and then you must leave".

"And go where exactly? Will I not have the same problem where ever I go? Even if I return to England"?

"I'm sorry but once you leave our country the problem of what you do next would no longer concern us".

"Is this A23's way of forcing me to return to Mars and confront him? Making me a fugitive from my world"?

"I do not have that information", Xueling confessed. "I have no idea how Qiángdàdedàna˘o's thought processes function. There is one thing though, Xiānshēng Night, were you in the next two weeks to take one or more Chinese citizens as your wives, then you would automatticly become a national yourself and be able to stay here".

"With your full permission no doubt", Nigh was amused by the suggestion. "The only trouble with that position is that Brainstorm, or whatever she's called could override that decision could she not"?

"I'm not certain", Xueling returned doubtfully, "As it was she who made the regulation in the first place".

"She works for the '*Masters*' so surely she can make exceptions whenever she decides to"?

"And here was I going to offer you citizenship and a commission in the Shūli nánrén", Xueling suddenly murmured, "Would it be so very bad to have to make me Wifone"?

"My first wife? How do you know I would not make a lousy husband? You could probably do better".

"Why don't we discuss this over dinner, tonight"?

"I can't, I have family coming to see me this evening". No sooner were the words out of his mouth, than Nigh realised he had made a mistake.

"Family? What family? How could you have? You're centuries away from your roots"?

"A poor joke, but I cannot make this evening, what about Friday"?

"Really? You agree"?

"Dinner is just dinner you know"?

"I'll book somewhere and let you know by ping".

"And how are you going to deal with my little android problem"?

"Leave it with me, I'll see if there is anything I can do? Of course, if you were my husband and I was your wifone...".

"Dinner. Just dinner, Friday".

He left the station in a state of ironic bemusement, tinged with genuine menace. The reach of the androids was great and even stretched across the centuries. The unfinished business with 23 was not felt by Nigh alone it seemed. Before he could conjecture further, he heard a sound of whimpering issuing from an alley he was halfway past. The back street over to his left and dimly illuminated when compared to the main drag.

"Help me", a pathetic voice asked in standard and then "Tā měngliè de bīpò wo˘ zhège sīshēngzi˘ "

Nigh turned down the street and tried to see what was sprawled against the wall, that the dead-end alley terminated in. It was a young woman, no surprise there. What was shocking was her condition. Her top was ripped and dusty, her tights had a rent in one knee. Her hair was tousled and also full of dust and from her mouth was a slim trickle.

"What happened to you"? Nigh demanded not unkindly, dreading the answer he suspected.

"He *milk-maded* me and then beat me and left me here like this".

"Here, let me help you to your feet, do you think you might need medical assistance"? Nigh took hold of the girl's left arm, with his right hand and offered her support.

Suddenly a bolt of some sort of energy flooded through his being. He glanced down and observed that the girl's body language had changed and in her right and was an unfamiliar looking weapon of some sort. For the next few seconds, Nigh had to command his Yogi Doshi to facilitate the fibriliance in his brain to channel the energy – whatever its nature, away from his vitals. He created a conduit

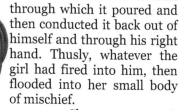

through which it poured and then conducted it back out of himself and through his right hand. Thusly, whatever the girl had fired into him, then flooded into her small body of mischief.

She went rigid, then jerked in a series of spasms, finally she slipped into unconsciousness. Nigh lay her carefully onto the tarmac of the alley ground and prized the weapon from her claw-like fingers, they had been frozen into a rictus of a bird of prey by the energy flow of her weapon. He turned the unknown pistol over in his hands, examining it curiously. Was this the firearm of choice in this century?

He examined the device with a mixture of fascination and the need to learn its function. The snout of the durilite barrel was surrounded by two rings of a material that he could not recognise. Behind them the pistol flared into a curious-looking chamber, containing some sort of chemical composition. Under the barrel the trigger seemed to be fingerprint fixed, there was no lever merely a looped sensor. The grip looked like it had suffered some sort of heat damage in the past. This pistol had led a busy life up until that point, it seemed. The etching on the side indicated its nomenclature as an Electrique P-abcde. An ungainly title further confirmed by a dial on the opposing side that indicated the first five letters of the alphabet.

The girl suddenly murmured, "I only had it set to disable, otherwise I would now be dead. How did you do that? Turn the energy onto me"?

"I'll ask the questions for the moment", Nigh returned, "Describe this weapon in full to me, its functions and capabilities"?

"You mean you've never seen an EPE before, you are from the past"?

There were many questions generated by that statement, but Nigh wanted to deal with them one at a time. He repeated his demand, the girl replied,

"It is a pistol. Called an Electrique P-abcde. The letters on the dial stand for; arm, battery, cock, disable and eliminate. To arm, you fit the transparent chamber with the appropriate chemical composition. Then check the battery in the grip is charged then cock the pistol. Finally, you set it to disable or to eliminate. you'll note that I had no intention of killing you".

"Will this pistol work for me"?

"Only if set to your fingerpad, the second joint of your index finger. Right now it's set to mine".

"Reset it to mine"?

The girl shook her head, admitted regretfully, "I cannot, you would have to take it to an armourer, it is a specialized job".

"Could I get one for myself then"?

"If you have the Renminbi a backstreet armourer would sell you his daughter".

Satisfied with that Nigh asked her, "Who sent you to kidnap me? Was it, Brainstorm, erm Qiángdàdedàna̓o, or 23 himself"?

"They just want to talk with you, reach some sort of agreement. They do not want you dead", the girl offered.

"So instead of politely inviting me over for a cosy little chat, they send you. Are you an assassin, normally"?

He held out his hand and she gingerly took it and allowed him to haul her to her feet. She was still shaky from the energy of her weapon.

"I'm a sort of Elucidator", she responded carefully, "I provide solutions for people with various conundrums".

"Hhmm and it that involves providing elucidation permanently.....? You don't have to answer that I get the picture. What will happen to you as a result of your failure".

The girl frowned, wiping her mouth, she confessed, "I will be replaced".

"And dispensed with"?

"Why do you care"?

"Let's just agree that I'm a very sensitive chap and I do care", Nigh had certain hopes for this Elucidator. He was looking to recruit and she would be a good place to start.

"They may decide to tie up loose ends. I don't understand why you would give a Ý"?

" I intend to turn you", Nigh admitted honestly,

"Employ you. Would you consider working for me? If you agree then I would, in turn, protect you"?

"You want a bodyguard that you might have to be a bodyguard to yourself"? She grinned, "How does that work"?

"I cannot be in two places at one time. I might want you to watch someone while I am doing something differently myself. You would start at once if you agree the only thing I need to know is your rates"?

"You are as strange and unpredictable as I was led to believe", the girl admitted, "My name is Shen Huan, pay me Ý8.70 a day and you've just put me on your payroll".

"You had better go and get cleaned up and changed and then meet me back at this address I am going to ping to you, what's your eaddress"?

"**elucisolve@gogglesearch.com**", the Elucidator supplied.

Nigh pinged her Mingfu Li's address, which temporarily was his own.

"Have I time to go to the gymnasium", she asked, "I get twitchy unless I've done thirty minutes on the rings every day".

"Ring until you're hearing bells, just be at the apartment by 13:00 all right"?

"I will be there at the allotted hour, yes".

She made to leave but Nigh had one more demand, "Before you go give me directions to the armourer".

"Oh, you won't find it even if I do, It's through an absolute maze of back streets, deliberately so".

"Could you describe the route, in detail"?

"I could yes, I've been there many times".

"Then do so, my memory is equal to the task of remembering even the most convoluted of directions".

Shen Huan had not exaggerated. The route was filled with as many twists and turns like a twisty turny turn twister. He found the place as he was confident he would though and entered the dimmest shop he had ever found in Androichina. At the back of a deliberately subfusc area, a girl was seated on the floor, legs crossed. The room seemed to be filled with swirling smoke and Nigh detected that it smelled of roses, obviously the issue of either joss sticks or perhaps a burner of oils, or a scented candle. Incongruously behind the girl was a sack of rice, as though it was meant to signify that the store was a simple victual supplier when the Elucidator had informed Nigh that the place was an armourer run by none other than Luyuan Zhuāngjiă ˇ shī.

"Am I in the presence of Luyuan Zhuāngjiă ˇ shī"? Nigh asked. The place was boarded horizontally and displayed no merchandise of any sort other than the sack. The girl was dressed in a lace bustier and white bohos, showing her slim waist to any who would enter. Strangely out of place in such dingy surroundings. Her long hair was tied behind her head and she wore long delicate and silver earrings.

"Who sent you"? She countered, not answering his enquiry at all.

"Shen Huan", Nigh replied, "Otherwise known as the Elucidator. She is now in my employ".

Luyuan looked shocked at this revelation but regained her composure rapidly and asked, "What do you want"?

"I firstly want to know who you are"? Nigh persisted, "I seek the proprietor of this boutique"?

"Boutique", the girl smiled then, "Yes I suppose this establishment is an exclusive concession of sorts, a booth of speciality. What do you want from my franchise Xiānshēng"?

"An Electrique pistol, the best quality you possess in stock".

"The best quality"! Eyebrows rose in incredulity, "Do you know the price an Sānko˘ng Pánzhuàngshù [Trebora Dicoidtree] commands"?

"Shock me"?

"With the weapon or the price"?

"Hahahaha, how much is a Trebora Dicoidtree Electrique pistol, Xia˘ojiĕ Luyuan"?

"For you, I will do a very special price of ¥438.89".

Nigh did the calculation, it was 50 shillin, a vast sum in the 33rd century, but he was in the 51st. Even so in the sort of establishment that Luyuan was running, it was foolish to agree the initial sum requested, so he responded,

"I can afford ¥275".

"Then you have not enough for the Sānko˘ng Pánzhuàngshù. Might I suggest the Píngyōng De-wu˘qì, it is in your price range and more reliable than the Biāozhu˘n Quiāng"?

"No you might not suggest either of those inferior brands", Nigh smiled, beginning to enjoy the haggling. "I just happen to know though, that your initial price far from being special, was inflated. Now, stop treating me like a Yank and let's talk serious business"?

"Very well Xiānshēng. The best I can do for you is ¥400.89, I will add two spare chemical chambers and two spare batteries gratis".

"¥300"?

"¥375.89".

"¥325"?

"¥350.89"

"¥333.89"?

Luyuan smiled, "We have a deal Xiānshēng, please wait here while I fetch your weapon and additional items".

The girl rose lithely to her tiny feet, glided into the total darkness of the store. Nigh wondered how she could see in such gloom until he heard a stubble and soft thud and the girl curse,

"*Kin* dìyù xiàng zhū yīyàng shòushāng"!

He smiled to himself, there was no need for a translation.

Finally, she emerged from the Stygian rear of the boutique, rubbing furiously at a barked shin.

"With some of your profit from this sale you could afford a couple of LED's for the rear of the premises", Nigh smiled readying Paddie to send the appropriate balance from his account to hers, "What is your eaddress, please"?

"luyuanzhuangjiashi@gogglesearch.com", came the instant response.

"Got that Paddie"?

"I am operating well within accepted parameters", the phone returned a trifle sardonically. Then, "It is done the amount is now in the seller's account".

For the next few moments, Luyuan showed Nigh how to load the chamber, how to install the batteries and then unnecessarily how to operate the dial. When she began to put the pistol back into the brown fauxplas bag, that was its only wrapping, she asked casually,

"Xiānshēng Nigh, I understand from the web that you are single. Is that still the case"?

"Yes. For the moment determinedly so. I am engaged upon a mission. Only when it is over will I then possess the time to examine my private life and situation".

"A pity. I was going to invite you to the rear of the premises this evening for a traditional Chinese meal. If your mission is to go up against the metal masters, then I fear you will not survive".

As Nigh proceeded toward the door he said over his shoulder, "A most gracious invitation Luyuan Zhuāngjia˘ shī, but I already have plans for this evening and concerning your observation about 23 and his cronies, I have survived their malign intentions toward me for 18 centuries"!

He went and found a nice café and bought himself some lunch. Twice more he was approached by hopeful young women who were desperately looking for a husband. It had yet to become annoying, but he doubted the delightful novelty of being constantly pursued would appeal to him indefinitely. Finally, he made his way back to the apartment and his rendezvous with Shen Huan Wu, wondering what state he would find her in after her workout on the rings.

She was outside the door, having no way of getting inside when Nigh walked up to it. He told her,

"You're not coming in anyway, I have an assignment for you. I want you to go to the address that my phone has just pinged to yours and protect the woman who lives there for the present".

"A sweetheart, a potential wifone"? Wu enquired.

"My cousin. Quite distant and on my father's side, but Family none the less and she has an important history to tell me this evening. Due to her association with me though, I fear that the Qiángdàdedànaˇo might think to capture her to use as a lever to get me to Mars".

"If she does think to do that, the force she might send will be considerable. By now she will know of my defection".

"How so"?

"Because I have not reported in, success or failure. If the former I would also have requested transport to Mars".

"Might you not be dead".

"If that were the case I would need a new phone"?

"Get one, the first thing I will do is pay you".

"How, I could not use my account if I were deceased".

"Cash".

Wu grinned, "If you mean metal pledges, they were abandoned centuries ago. They were called coins weren't they"?

"So what you need is a new identity, if you are to appear demised to the web. I don't know a lot of things about this century yet, Wu, but I'm willing to bet certain people can provide you with that"?

"Sure, but I would have to visit them in person. If I use this phonpad even once Qiángdàdedànaˇo will know I am alive".

"Very well then, we need a change of plan", Nigh decided. "This afternoon I will guard my cousin, while you go and turn yourself into somebody else".

"It will be costly to do that. The sort of expert you're talking about does not work cheaply"?

"I will foot the bill and pay it into your brand new account once you have one".

"How am I going to get at my old balance"?

"I will replace it. Anything else"?

Wu grinned, "That seems to cover it for the moment. It would be so much easier to flee to Titan. The government there is still refusing to recognise 23's absolute rule".

"I did not know mankind had reached that moon, but if they are disobedient to the androids then it is a war zone waiting to happen. Anyway, I like it in Androichina for the moment. Don't worry if I decide to outstay my welcome here I'll simply recruit more firepower".

"Massive would not be big enough to oppose the androids, but I'll stick around for the time being. So I'm off to get myself a new identity and some radical surgery".

"Surgery! Oh! Of course, you'll have to change your outward appearance too. How long will that put you out of action"?

"About as long as it takes to do it. Maybe an hour, you are a real neoanchestral aren't you, Nigh? Do you think medicine still involves scalpels of metal and stitches of the animal gut"?

"I'd not stopped to consider it. you're right, I'm a real neoanchestralosaurus".

Wu laughed, "That's funny, you should post that new word in the wordadadict, while you're at it add anchetralopithacene too, that's my contribution to someone who's eighteen centuries out of date".

"How are you going to pay the identity creator and the surgeon without money"?

"I'm not. You are, I'll simply give them your eaddress and they'll ping you".

"Make sure you get a good deal in each case then, I'm not a bottomless pit"?

"See you later, Nigh. I'll introduce myself to you this evening, here, alright"?

Nigh nodded his agreement, wondering quite what the Elucidator would choose as her new chassis and name.

On his way over to the address, his distant cousin had given him he could not decide what he was going to do once he arrived at her apartment. Should he knock and ask to go in, thusly intruding on her afternoon as well as her evening? Or would it be better to simply loiter with intent outside the door, in the corridor leading up to her place? Both seemed to possess drawbacks and neither seemed to be entirely satisfactory. He had arrived at the given location before ever reaching any sort of decision. As the situation was to transpire however, what happened was not something Nigh could have envisaged.

Just as he had arrived outside the door and was trying to determine which course of action to take, the door opened and Huahua stepped into the corridor,

"Oh"! She gasped, startled, "Is everything alright, Durango, what are you doing here"?

"I'm here to make certain no one harms you".

"Why"? She looked worried, "Am I in some sort of danger"?

"Possibly by association. I was not willing to take any risks with your safety. General Xueling III interviewed me again this morning and it would be too easy for her to use you in some way that would pressurise me into doing what either she or 23 wants".

"We cannot continue this discussion in the corridor, can we? Come inside, I'll make you some tea"?

Nigh followed his cousin into her apartment. He noticed the way her hair tied up accentuated the drops of her earrings. The way her ass moved in her tights, the narrowness of her waist. He shook his head rather like a dog does to try and sort its thoughts. This young woman was his family, even if she was a distant descendant. Was it right for him, to find her so hot, was it right that she made him disconcertingly horny? When she passed him the tea, and he caught a whiff of cinnamon from her fragrance, it only served to distract him further, It was thusly she who proffered the sensible observation,

"Perhaps it might be prudent for me to continue your family history right now. For though you are a Chronoman, you seem to be running out of the one commodity you are master of – in this particular period"?

"Ironic is it not", Nigh saw the implausibility of the situation. "You are right of course, Dear Cousin. For your safety, I would like to hear more before this evening and will proffer my apologies to the others when I escort you to the apartment of my landlady".

"Others – plural"?

"A bodyguard I am hiring, I will explain on the way over to the place, after you have told me more of my family history".

*   *   *

Over the next few months, Lynea found that more and more of her time was spent discussing her plans for the manor with Gravis himself. Despite his reputation as a shrewd and sometimes cruel entrepreneur, she could not help but find him personally charming. certainly, none could deny that he was handsome and in good shape.   So when *the day* arrived, she was neither surprised nor repulsed by what he did. They had been seated upon the sofa in his study. An area of the place that few frequented, even Decorum. She had stopped talking and Gravis gently took hold of her hand, he had never attempted to touch her before. It caused a curious thrill to run through her system.

"Lynea, I have a confession to make to you", he informed her at that moment.

"Oh"! She tried to retain her self control, but was finding composure difficult, "What sort of confession, my dear Alexius"?

She had taken to use his given when just the two of them were present. By way of answer, he said no more, however. Rather, leaning forward he brushed her lips with his own. Before Lynea realised what was happening, her slim hand had slipped around the back of his neck and pulled him forward. His mouth was on hers then and the kiss was frantic, eager and passionate. When they finally broke the embrace he struggled to retain his usual haughty self-control,

"I am enamoured of you. Now I sense that you might very well feel the same way"?

"Yes, Alexius, I think I am falling in love with you".

From his waistcoat pocket, he suddenly drew something shiny, circular and very small. He told her,

"The practice of partnership contract seems to have been losing popularity before the SX was sent against us and more so now. I, therefore, ask for your hand in marriage"?

Before she could reply, he grasped the ring finger on her left hand and pushed on the ring. It was, naturally an engagement ring. As Lynea looked down at it she was amazed to see that set in the white-gold claws was a Callistone. That fabulously expensive gemstone, a variety of the mineral corundum, consisting of aluminium oxide(α-Al_2O_3) with trace amounts of elements such as iron, titanium, chromium, copper, durilite or magnesium. Typically a rich and lustrous azure, although less expensive varieties of Callistone occurred in yellow. Gravis would not have considered his least favourite of hues. Nor would he have acquired anything but the very best. Commonly, natural Callistone were cut and polished into gemstones and worn in only fabulously expensive jewellery. Then, there was Lynea with one on her finger as an engagement ring.

"Will you say yes, Lynea"?

"I will – yes, Alexis, I will marry you", she heard herself return as if in a dream. For a while Gravis was uncharacteristically garrulous, planning a wedding and detailing the circumstances of their lives together and it soon became apparent that he had not considered Lynea's desires in that respect. Finally, when he paused for breath, she laughed and asked,

"And might I not decide some of the details from this moment on, Fiancé"?

Gravis checked himself and replied,

"Of course, Dearest. I was just telling you *my* plans, so what do you plan for us"?

"I don't have plans", she confessed, "Why must we? Why not simply let the rest of our lives unravel in the way that fate has predetermined for us, Alexius"?

"I'm a businessman, Dearest, if I were to take that approach toward my concerns I think the corporation might soon descend into bankruptcy".

"That is just it though", Lynea smiled indulgently, Marriage is not a business contract. It is based on the emotion love, not greed, envy, ambition, drive".

"I'll tell you what then", he offered grandly, "Why do you not make our wedding plans while I run the corporation and I will fall in with anything you decide to arrange"?

 Thusly it was agreed between them. Ironically they saw little of one another over the next two weeks. When they were done the two of them were married in a very quiet ceremony indeed. Lynea wanted none of Gravis' business associates at the wedding and she had no family. To Gravis' dismay, the only individuals present were Decorum, Zhongxiaoqing, Fabiaphon and Cook.

He was, though disappointed, as good as his word though. With the addition of the local magistrate, a young Chinese woman, the marriage ceremony was conducted and over in mere seconds.

The staff congratulated her and then Gravis was suddenly required to take an urgent padvid, leaving Lynea suddenly alone with the junior of the two Alexius Morrelius'.

"You've said very little to me over the last fortnight, Decorum, do you disapprove of me as your Step-mother and wife to your father? Do you not think me good enough to enter your tiny family circle"?

"It's not that at all", Decorum smiled a trifle sadly.

"Then what"? Lynea was not one to let a mystifying situation remain unsolved.

"I worry for you, Lynea. Or should I say, Mother (Hahaha)? I've known my Father much longer than you and know his darker qualities. He can be ruthless, coldly calculating, merciless and cruel. I just hope he retains those characteristics only in his business dealings".

Lynea realised at that instant that Decorum had no love for his Father, indeed all he felt for him was enmity.

"Who knows, Decorum", she forwarded, "Perhaps some of my character traits will rub off on your Father"?

The younger Morrelius did not look convinced though. He argued,

"Or maybe you will become a wicked Stepmother, as *he* changes *you*"!

At that moment Gravis returned and said urgently, "The liner leaves in eighty-seven minutes, Dearest, has Pho packed our bags into the flitter"?

"Everything is arranged, we can leave this instant", the bride smiled.

It was the beginning of their honeymoon of Venus!

Neither of them could have anticipated just how event filled the trip would prove to be. They passed through customs without a hitch and were ushered to their suite on the Zhōngguó Chuánzhī Shànghaǐi [Chinese Vessel Shanghai].

The room was 1st class and nothing could have been more luxurious, certainly not in the Chinese ship. It was at the outermost edge of the habitat ring and therefore gravity was exactly 1E, the same as that on earth. Only when they got to Venus would they find themselves one-tenth lighter and then feel fatigued for a while when returning to China. They dined and drank champaign and then returned to their room. They would just have time to make love and sleep before the ship would be descending to the Earth's sister-world. The sex was the first disappointment for Lynea. She had not been especially experienced in bed, having only had two lovers in the past, but unfortunately, Gravis came a poor third, when, unsatisfied she made the comparison - as she lay unsatisfied at his side as he snored happily. It had been over far too quickly, and he had not concerned himself with her needs in any way at all. As she had slipped into the bathroom to douche she had told herself it was not something to get upset about. Over time, she could encourage him in various directions, teach him patiently to be a better lover. What was upsetting though was the incident as they prepared for planet-fall!

They were packing when the door to the suit hissed open and the man stepped inside uninvited. He asked but one thing and in one word,

"Gravis"? Which was strange, for he recognised the recent groom. What the owner of that name did next was unexpected in the extremis and caught both Lynea and more importantly the intruder by surprise. He dived behind the bed, his arm coming up an instant later and Lynea heard the faint phut of a needle pen discharge. The needle stuck the intruder in the back of the hand. He looked down at it in disbelief before he crumpled to the floor. To her credit, Lynea did not scream, but her voice tremble d slightly as she demanded, "What is going on Alexius? What did he want with you? Have you killed him"? Her husband moved with the speed and grace of a jaguar and had in his hand a can of some sort of spray. He held the man's wrist together and sprayed them before replying to her,

"Do not worry, I only used a level one needle. He is merely stunned".

"Who is he? What is that spray"?

"I suspect he is an assassin sent against me by a business rival", Gravis did not sound especially shocked or alarmed by the revelation. We shall soon see when he comes around, the spray will merely hold him for thirty minutes".

Pushing the inert form's ankles together Gravis similarly secured them to the wrists. Then he tugged the needle gun from his hand and tossed it onto the far side of the room.

Lynea went for her pad, "I'll ping the Captain, get some security out to us".

"NO"! Gravis was stern. "Let me deal with this in *my* way please, Dearest".

Suddenly insightful, Lynea asked, "This is not the first time this sort of thing has happened is it, Alexius"?

She never got an answer though, for, at that instant, the would-be assassin groaned and opened his eyes. Gravis promptly held his needle pen to the villainous intruder's neck. He had not changed his ammunition, but the man did not know that.

"Answer my questions swiftly and truthfully and you will live, lie to me and I am not the man I am without knowing when another is lying to me, lie to me and...well, you know how that little scenario will play out do you not"?

A nod from the other confirmed that he understood the threat only too well.

"What is your name and who sent you to kill me"?

"Fiscarte, I am in the employ of Tullus Ompi Versutus"

"Versutus, CEO of Ecofuel.corp"?

Fiscarte nodded.

"So, Ecofuel.corp thinks to branch out into my little business, does it? Hoping to instigate a hostile takeover once my shares are floated on the market following my assassination. Does Versutus think that Decorum would stand idly by and allow that to happen? Or even now is another assassin on his way to take him out of the picture too"?

Fiscarte admitted, "I was to do you, then return to Earth and finish him off next".

Gravis nodded, "I've heard of you Fiscarte. You must be slipping, I heard you are the best"?

Fiscarte merely shrugged, saying nothing more. Gravis asked,

"How much was Versutus going to pay you for committing homicide against the Morrelius'"?

"Four silver-shillin".

"Two for each of us eh? All right these are your choices now. You can either die right here and now by my hand, or for six silver-shillin you can accept my contract to go and kill your former employer"?

"Six! To finish Tullus Ompi Versutus"?

Gravis nodded toward the glistening gleam in the assassin's eyes and Lynea wondered just what sort of a world she had entered by marrying the man now crouching down before he who had just attempted to murder the two of them, probably.

"He is well guarded, not like you".

"Something I shall have to correct very shortly", Gravis agreed. "We are getting close to the point where we have to strap ourselves into the cradles, I need an answer Fiscarte. You will act as bodyguard to my wife and me whilst we are on Venus, return to Earth with us and then go and remove my unsuspecting rival permanently. Or I will kill you and toss you out the nearest airlock"?

Fiscarte grinned, "Don't do that, *Boss*. Before ever I've had my chance at showing you how good an employee I can be"?

Gravis rose and turned to Lynea, "Come dearest to the cradles. Fiscarte here will have to take his chances as we enter Venus' atmosphere, for the bond will not dissolve for another twenty-five minutes".

*   *   *

"You don't look especially surprised by that part of our family history" Huahua suddenly observed.

"I was in the English Secret Service and also in the Anglo-Francos war", Nigh confessed, "Nothing surprises me any more Huahua".

"So it would seem", the girl's slim body glided up with both cups and slunk into the kitchen, she called to him, as she was loading them into the sonic-cleanser,

"It's getting to the point where we go to your landlady's. I'm looking forward to meeting this bodyguard of ours too".

"Very well", Nigh agreed, "Let's go".

The duo arrived on time. Even so, they had been preceded by both Mingfu Li and a young woman Nigh did not recognise,

"Wow"! He exclaimed, "You surgeon is an artist, do you also have a forged identity now and a new padfon"?

The newcomer, or rather the former Shen Huan smiled serenely and informed him, "Your landlady took some convincing to let me in here. The answer to all your questions is yes. Shen Huan has disappeared, but I'm afraid you may very well get the blame for her murder and the mysterious disposal of her body.

"I suppose I can live with that suspicion, for that is all it will be without a corpse. So, Miss, who are you now"?

"My name is Mayling Fuchow, personal Elucidator to you and your cousin here. You neglected to mention that she was beautiful".

"Thank you", Huahua responded, "So are you. So is Mingfu Li. I'll wager Durango does not know which of you to admire firstly"?

"Hhmm", Mingfu Li responded to that dissatisfied with the sequence of events in her apartment. Although Nigh was forced to admit to himself, that though he found all three young women very attractive, it was the landlady who, in his opinion, possessed the greatest pulchritude.

That's a very nice slip you're almost wearing", Nigh joked then. The Elucidator was only one step from nakedness, only a diaphanous silk underskirt between his vision and her nudity.

"As this was a sort of social occasion I did not think to arrive *tooled up*", the girl grimaced. Plainly by the look on Fu's lovely features, she for one did not approve.

"I've had some more family history this afternoon, Fu", Nigh then confessed to his landlady. "Let us go and make some tea and I can bring you up to the same place as me while Huahua in here paraphrases what she has told me up to this point for the benefit of Mayling"?

Saying nothing the owner of the apartment followed him into the kitchen. The instant they were out of earshot of the other two Fu remarked scornfully,

"Well! Quite the little harem you seem to be collecting in my premises. Tell me, as this is my place will I have the dubious distinction of being wifone, or does that lovely cousin of yours squeeze me into the position of witwof? Perhaps the Elucidator's impressive new breasts may even muscle me into the position of wifree"?

"Fu. It is not like that at all", Nigh objected with as much conviction as he could muster.

"Is it not? When you saw your new bodyguard just now I thought I was going to have to sweep up your eyeballs. It must be so privileged being male in Androichina right now. You can have your pick of all the lovely young women and you do not even have to limit yourself to one".

"It is very flattering that you care".

"Did I say I cared"? Fu flared, "Help me with these cups, come on before they wonder what we are doing in here"?

*   *   *

Hotel Din Răsputeri Impresionant was the most opulent accommodation that the town of Deva, The Citadel, Wallachian Sector, Venus boasted. For Lynea though, it was not the sort of idyllic honeymoon that she had either envisaged or could have desired. The reason for that was the fact that she felt like a third wheel to her husband and his new bodyguard. Where ever they went sightseeing, they went as a trio. Lynea had no time with Gravis without the ever-present Fiscarte being at his shoulder. Knowing the reason for this, it perhaps would have appeared churlish to complain, so she did not. The truth of it was though, she did not enjoy her holiday, following her marriage and she was not especially enjoying being married either. She was gentle in her pace of introducing suggestions to Gravis on how he might better please her in bed, with no resultant improvement in either his duration or any sort of satisfaction for her. To say the honeymoon was proving to be a disaster was an understatement of the most gigantic proportions. On the sixth day of their first week, something happened which would not improve the dire situation in the slightest too.

"Have you heard of Woomongalo Mongalowoo, Dearest"? Gravis asked her as she toyed with her breakfast that day. Wishing that she could enjoy just one meal as a couple and not a trio. Strangely enough, she had,

"The Vrăjitoareclarvăzător of Zalău? Yes, I've read about her on the SWW. Zalău is not far from here is it"?

"It is on the same line as this town", Fiscarte answered, momentarily setting Lynea's teeth on edge. Could he not just eat his breakfast and not intrude upon the conversation of the newly-weds? Why did he feel the need to be a member of the party?

"The Vrăjitoareclarvăzător is a sort of witch, come, seer, the Venuser hold them in very high regard", Lynea was glad to be able to show off her knowledge for once, show off her knowledge of *anything*. "Are you suggesting we might go and see her"?

"I thought it might be fun for you", Gravis observed, "I know how you silly women like to think there is something to it, superstition, you know".

'Silly women', Lynea fumed inwardly, managing just, to maintain a glassy smile despite the annoyance of the jibe, *'So that is how my husband thinks of me is it? As a silly woman'*! With care, she returned,

"It might be fun at that. The Vrăjitoareclarvăzător might tell you which shares to invest in next, Alexius? Or who to have Fiscarte here kill next"?

"Ouch, dearest", Gravis chided gently. (He had taken to doing that over the last couple of days). "That was a bit harsh. You know Fiscarte here is our protector".

"It's all right, Gravis", Fiscarte murmured, "The situation must be putting a slight dampener on Mrs Morrelius' spirits, she is tense".

'Don't you dare make excuses for me, you Corbyn', Lynea flared inwardly, *'I'm only tense because your master is a destilumbrous peach stoker and I haven't had a single chance to crack my marble, on my honeymoon'*.

"That's a very strange expression on your face dearest", Gravis noted at that moment, "Care to tell me what you are thinking"?

"You can ask the Vrăjitoareclarvăzător when you see her", Lynea retorted and Fiscarte burst into laughter. Amongst his many qualities, one of Gravis' failings was that he did not like being the subject of another's jokes and he said suddenly,

"Perhaps it was not such a good idea. Forget I mentioned it, my dear. Fiscarte what do you say we go and try the new goltennket pitch here instead. I've heard it's a much better game in 90% gravity"?

The bodyguard glanced at Lynea. Hiding her disappointment and ire as best she could, she responded,

"Yes, you boys go and do that today".

"And what will you do Mrs Morrelius"? The bodyguard desired to know.

"Oh, I don't discuss my comings and goings with the hired help, Bodyguard", Lynea responded haughtily and for once earned a look of approval from her rather staid and lacklustre husband. "You two go, Alexius, just leave me some money and I'll entertain myself until you return".

"More money, I gave you a considerable sum at the commencement of our departure"?

'Don't say he's going to turn out to be mean as well as everything else'? Lynea mused coldly. "Just in case I see something I want for you my dear", she managed to simper.

He pinged her another sizeable sum and then left with his ubiquitous bodyguard. The minute she was sure they had left the hotel Lynea pulled on a poncho and strode down into the foyer and out through the exit. The train station was only a brief walk from the place they were staying. Venus' network of rail ensured that everywhere was in walking distance of a train station, it being the preferred way of getting from 'a' to 'b' on the gradually cooling world. At the station, Lynea bought herself a ticket for Zalău. If Gravis was not prepared to take her to see the Vrăjitoareclarvăzător, then she was perfectly capable of getting there by herself. Indeed she was beginning to suspect that in the future she would be doing a great number of things on her own. It was not a long wait for the train, there being a very regular service all over Venus. The journey would only be a matter of twenty minutes too. Zalău was only two stops from Deva, with the town of Crişeni separating them. Lynea settled back into a high seat in a compartment with no one in but herself. At Crişeni, however, the train filled up sufficiently for her to be joined by two other commuters, both male, both human. Or at least outwardly so. They could have just as easily been biotron or even cyborg. One of them seemed to be paying particular attention to Lynea whenever she glanced in his direction and she found herself thinking that at least she was desirable to *some* men. She rose and went toward the door as the train was pulling into Zalău, only to find her admirer had arisen with her. When she smiled politely to him, it encouraged him to speak,

"Don't tell me you've come to see the Vrăjitoareclarvăzător, Woomongalo Mongalowoo"?

"Why yes", the question had amused her, "Do I look like the sort of silly girl who believes in superstition"?

"I'm sorry but I did not mean it in that way at all", he sounded contrite, "You see, I'm going to see her myself. I'm doing an article for the Byron Newsweb. There is a great deal of interest in the Venuser aborigines at the moment in the English sector, superstition and all".

It was Lynea's turn to feel compunctious, "Then I apologise for snapping at you, I'm English too. My name is Lynea".

"Servian Amullus Nuntius. If you are alone, it would be my pleasure to escort you"?

"Then it would be my pleasure to accompany you", Lynea returned graciously. She suddenly checked her left hand to make certain she had her rings on. Not that Nuntius seemed anything other than courteous and without any other motivation than common deference. They walked from the station at Zalău, he, leading her to a flittaxi.

"Can we not walk to the Venuser settlement"? She asked him.

"It's 3.25 kilometres", he explained. "We would need other footwear than what we are wearing now and also portable oxygen. If you fancy the track I could...".

"No, no, I did not realise that the Vrăjitoareclarvăzător did not live in the town".

Nuntius smiled at her apparent naivety, "None of the aborigines live with the humans, Lynea. Remember they were responsible for the death of thousands of settlers in the early days? When they were dormant under the surface of this world. Were it not for the Surgeon defending their rights, mankind might very well have wiped them out in one gigantic retaliatory strike".

"I'm afraid my Venuser history is not what it should be", Lynea admitted, "This is the very first time I have ever been off Earth".

"Oh! I see. Well, I think we should ride to the Venuser settlement. When we get there you would do well sticking closely to me as well. Are you armed by the way"?

"Do I need to be"?!

He went inside his ¾ frock coat and pulled out a slim needle-pen. "Take this just in case. There have been a few incidents recently, nothing to get alarmed about in themselves but if it is the beginning of a trend...".

"You're frightening me now".

"I'm sorry, but better to be afraid and cautious than heedless of danger and succumb to it - would you not say"?

While she considered the merit of that maxim he pulled out a snub-nosed Akai 0.45 Stallion, assuring, "Even if I say so myself, I'm a pretty keen shot with this little beauty so try not to be so concerned that you do not enjoy the experience. For the most part, even those Venuser that fall out with humans prefer to curse them rather than try an outright physical attack. Once you see them, you'll understand why".

Not long after that proclamation designed to offer her comfort, Lynea did indeed see her first native Venuser. Approximately 130 centimetres in height, weighing little more than 40 kilogrammes, the Venuser were mainly female, had complexions the colour of ochre and hair the same sort of consistency and hue as straw. Yet curiously their eyes were to a one, all of the deepest azure. In their narrow mouths were tiny teeth which reminded Lynea of a child's milk teeth and yet the Venuser were fully adult. When she thought about it there were no Venuser youngsters on view at all. They were also uniformly dressed in nothing grander than simple tunics of brown hessian, as though they sought to wear poverty like some strange badge of office. Lynea found out later that the aboriginal species of the once hellish world had no desire to accrue personal wealth just so long as they had shelter and enough to eat, they seemed contented merely to exist. Indeed in this and many other strange particulars, Venuser were an enigma. Mankind had met them several decades before and to that date had learned very little more about them.

"What was known was that they had once been devoid of corporeal bodies of any sort, but had devolved into what Lynea saw then so that they could associate, if infrequently with humanity. Little wonder that the androids did not conquer them as they had done mankind. The mechanisms probably simply considered them not worth subjugating. She was immensely thankful to be in the company of Nuntius at that moment, he confidently asked one of the shrunken females where they might find her, for whom, they had journeyed to meet. By way of answer the hag (she appeared to be ancient though in a Venuser it was hard to tell), indicated a certain hut that was possessed of no greater aggrandisement than any of the others, with nothing more than a casual point of a gnarled knuckle.

"Come on", he began to sound excited at the prospect of the imminent meeting, "It's just over here".

There was no guard at the entrance of the dwelling. The door was nothing more than a sheet of heavy cloth, so Nuntius cried out,

"Hello, is this the home of the great Vrăjitoareclarvăzător – Woomongalo Mongalowoo"? A superfluous enquiry as he was already aware of the answer.

To their collective astonishment, an ancient and croaky voice returned, "Come in Servian Amullus Nuntius, I have been expecting you and Lynea Morrelius".

The two exchanged an impressed glance before Nuntius swept the door to one side and entered the gloom ahead of Lynea. Valour was taking a back seat to safety for the time being. Lynea blinked in the obscure and dusty murk. There behind a small table was seated the most ancient-looking prune-like shrivelled bent and twisted figure of a Venuser that anyone could ever lay witness to.

"I am Woomongalo Mongalowoo", she told them unnecessarily, "I the Vrăjitoareclarvăzător, I old and am wise".

"I have come to ask you many things", Nuntius' voice was filled with a respect approaching awe, "But not empty-handed, Vrăjitoareclarvăzător. I bring Venusilver, you have merely to name your price"?

The old crone's eyes burned like the very coals of Mars' icecaps as she shook her head. The gesture caused her very fine hair to float about it like a tenuous cloud.

"Not want your coin, Nuntius. Want that"!

Her knurled and leathery digit pointed at Lynea's throat. For there, hanging on a 2-centimetre snake chain of silver resided a Cloisonné dragonfly. The base of the 70-millimetre jewellery was silver too and inlaid with lapis lazuli on the wings and three chemically manufactured sapphires in head thorax and abdomen. Compared to what Nuntius had been prepared to pay the Vrăjitoareclarvăzător it was not especially valuable, perhaps a few Venushillin. Without further cajoling, Lynea pushed open the lobster catch on the chain (actually worth more than the trinket itself) and reverently passed it into a wrinkled outstretched palm. For some reason, she could not logically explain, Lynea was careful not to touch Woomongalo Mongalowoo.

"It is a shame about you, Child", the Vrăjitoareclarvăzător said looking deeply into Lynea's eyes. The woman retreated from such intense scrutiny. It was as though her very quiddity was being examined beneath an electron microscope. "You no be happy with husband. He beat – you leave, go to Mars. Go with another".

Lynea rocked back onto the heels of her soles and felt the strong arm of Nuntius suddenly around her shoulders.

"You tell this to a newlywed", Lynea managed to gasp weakly then, This is my actual honeymoon"!

"He off with Fiscarte, not good I see".

Nuntius kept his silence and led Lynea to the only other item of furniture in the place, a rickety chair of bound bamboo, by the look of it. Once he had settled Lynea on it he went and engaged the Vrăjitoareclarvăzător regarding what he had been sent to discover. Even asking her if he could take some pad-two D's for the webpage that his firm was planning. While this was going on Lynea remained seated in miserable confusion. For some reason, she little doubted that what the Vrăjitoareclarvăzător had reported to her would indeed come to pass. Gravis would subject her to physical beatings and she would be forced to leave him. She would go with another and to Mars of all places. She had to know who that other person was. Suddenly rising to her feet, heedless of the discourteous nature of her intrusion into Nuntius' interview she demanded,

"You said I would go to Mars with another, who is that other individual? Is it a man or a woman"?

Woomongalo Mongalowoo glanced back at Lynea and smiled! That expression of amusement was suddenly more sinister than any hate-twisted grimace and sent a chill of ice tumbling down Lynea's spine, she held her breath, the Vrăjitoareclarvăzător whispered,

"Your lover"!

"Impossible"! Lynea heard herself explode. It was momentarily as if she had left her own body and was floating above the tableau. Gazing down upon the bizarre trio with the dispassionate eyes of an observing angel. "I would not do such a thing, no matter what the provocation. Adultery is immoral and repugnant to me. Though Gravis may beat me, I would not betray him with another".

Woomongalo Mongalowoo removed a small Meerschaum pipe and lit it with a lighter that she seemed to have produced from somewhere. The aroma from it filled the hut and indicated it to be snufz, 1in2 or maybe even delite. Who could tell if the latter was harmful to the Venuser physiology? Narrowing her eyes at the pungent smoke Woomongalo Mongalowoo peered through the haze and declared simply,

"You and lover flee to Lipari".

"Lipari"? Lynea echoed, "Where is that? Why would I go there"?

"Lipari is an island province of Messina, Italy", Nuntius supplied, "Now, if you don't mind I...".

"She's lying"! Lynea all but screamed. "I have no lover and I would not go to some island in Italy to cavort with him there either".

At the word 'lying', the Vrăjitoareclarvăzător's features seemed to fold in upon themselves in something akin to fury and she said simply to Lynea,

"Leave"!

"I will not until you admit that you are just guessing". Lynea seemed to have lost all sense of reason for the instant. She was no longer thinking clearly. Nuntius came to her rescue, grasping her upper arms suddenly and firmly he dragged her out of the hut.

"What are you doing"? Lynea demanded, almost pathetically, "Let go of me"?

"Do you want to go back in there and face the prospect of angering the Vrăjitoareclarvăzător to such a degree that she inflicts you with a curse"?

It was exactly what Lynea needed to hear. She was superstitious enough to not desire that, just!

"You go back in and finish your interview then, I'll wait out here for you, in this rude village".

"You've calmed down"?

"Yes. I've calmed down now, thank you".

"You're certain? You're not going to try and burst back in there and..."?

"I'm koofing calm. Go"!

He slipped back inside while she sulked for a while and then began to stroll around the village. It was like going back to a backward settlement that had been preserved on 2D celluloid, showing the most remote regions of the Earth at that time. Back before all the forests had been cleared and farmland put in its place. It had been the time of the *Great Destruction* when thousands of species of flora and fauna had disappeared from the face of humanity's home-world forever. When human flesh had numbered 10 billion and something had to be done. Mass enforced sterilisation and war had been the result and it had proved to be a period where mankind could have self-destructed. Fortunately, he had come through it, bloody and scarred, but not imploded. It had been nothing when compared to the devastation of SX however. When Lynea thought of what General 23 had done, she realised it had been unfeelingly brutal, but part of her reasoned that it had also perhaps been necessary for the continued survival of the survivors. Now the calculating mechanisms would rule and they could not possibly do a worse job than those who had preceded them. Finally, Nuntius reappeared and his look of satisfaction ired Lynea.

He had been told what he wanted to hear. Or at the very least was satisfied with what she had predicted to him. Lynea had not.

"Can we get out of here, please"? She demanded as soon as they were close enough to speak.

"Of course", his graciousness annoyed her, she was looking for something to argue about and he was being kind and understanding. "I'm sorry that what you were told was not to your liking. I understand you must feel insulted by what the Vrăjitoareclarvăzător predicted, but we do not have to believe it, do we"?

"Do you have any idea what percentage of her predictions come to pass".

He was glad to shake his head, "I owe you for the necklace by the way. Can I give you something toward its value, or perhaps even replace it for you"?

"It was not especially valuable, I just happened to like it. There is no need to worry about that. Say! Here's a flittaxi bringing someone else to see the cracked old grimalkin. We can go back to the railway station in it once he or she drops off their fare.

Three women out to have their fortunes told obviously, climbed out the vehicle chattering all the while. They neither noticed nor acknowledged Lynea and the reporter. So they jumped into the back and were soon gliding over the acid-scarred rock of the Venuser roadway.

"So what have you seen of Venus whilst being on it"? Nuntius wanted to know. "The Hall of Whispers, the Endless Caves, Mount Dragonis or the Shattered Cliffs"?

They chatted about nothing very important until the taxi pulled up outside Zalău Station. There was a café in the station, prompting Lynea to state,

"I'm hungry do you want some lunch, I'll pay, my husband has given me enough to easily afford to treat you"?

"He is Alexius Morrelius Gravis is he not? The corporation entrepreneur"?

"You've heard of him then"?

"Of course Preciometalic.Inc is one of the big seven".

Lynea grinned, "And I'm just betting you know the other six too"?

"Orang-U-Can, If You Want It We Stock It, Castle Electronics, von Goosetimp Weapons, Tiptingle Foodstuffs and Deutsch Fahrzeuge Eingearbeitet of course".

"Tell me then, where does Ecofuel.corp fir into the corporation ladder"?

"Tullus Ompi Versutus' corporation? What makes you ask".?

"Let me buy you lunch with some of Gravis' money and I'll tell you. You have to promise me though, that you will not publish what you learn"?

"All right you have a deal".

As they ate a fresh cheese and egg salad of lichen-Lettuce, lichen-cress, lichcumber and lichrrots Lynea told the reporter the whole tale. When she was finished he mused,

"There was some talk of Alovir Hornrunner Negotium and Collendine Voleskip Medicus making some sort of reverse takeover bid for Ecofuel.corp, but I never gave it much credence".

Reverse takeover? You'll have to enlighten me and what is the doctor of Moon-based clinics doing getting involved in fuel for goodness sake"?

"A reverse takeover bid occurs when a private company purchases a public company. The main rationale behind reverse takeovers is to achieve listing status without going through an initial public offering [IPO]". Nuntius seemed only too happy to explain. "In other words, in a reverse takeover offer, the private acquirer company becomes a public company by taking over an already listed company. The acquirer can choose to conduct a reverse takeover bid if it concludes that it is a better option than applying for an IPO. The process of being listed requires large amounts of paperwork and is a tedious and costly process. Medicus wants to make his sanatoriums into an expanding corporation, so he went to Negotium to suggest they merge their already considerably profitable interests".

"With SX is it not a bad time for business ventures though", Lynea wished to know. "I mean we have just had our population cut by nine-tenths, on Earth".

"Leaving certain business vacuums that some are willing to try and occupy, they are looking at the long term picture, Lynea. Not only that while there are any people left in the Unwanted States and Eastern Alliance of America there will always be a market for madhouses".

"So it makes sense to you then, all of it"?

"Murder never makes sense. If Tullus Ompi Versutus suddenly turns up dead I'm going to have to break my promise to you and report the matter, I'm afraid".

You know how the Chinese view murder and conspiracy to commit it, they'll execute both Fiscarte and Gravis".

"Deservedly so, if they are guilty".

Lynea examined how she felt about that and was forced to ask herself how it had been possible for her to fall out of love with her new husband so quickly. Perhaps the possibility of future beatings at his hands was not something she relished. Indeed, if he did ever lay a finger on her she would like as not report the conspiracy herself.

They boarded the train and returned to Deva in reflective silence. He was going on to return to his offices then so they made their farewells and Lynea walked back to the Din Răsputeri Impresionant. The instant she entered their suite she could sense there was something wrong. Gravis and his ever-present sidekick were seated around the day table and both of them had been drinking quite heavily.

"I thought you would stay in this suite while Fiscarte and I were out, Dearest", Gravis began his tone level and betraying no emotion in any particular direction. "Where have you been, shopping perhaps? No, you have no bags with you. So where have you been Lynea"?

"I went to see the Vrăjitoareclarvăzător".

"On your own"?

"My new husband did not want to come with me".

"So you went down to the railway station alone, boarded a train and went into a Venuser camp all with no protection at all? Anything could have happened"?

"Well it didn't and here I am safe and sound".

Gravis climbed to his feet and said to her in a tone she fancied she did not like one little bit,

"Don't do anything like that again though, Dearest. In future you are not to go anywhere unescorted, do you understand"?

"Ridiculous"! Lynea declared hotly, "I'm a grown woman and.....".

It was not especially a hard slap across her face, that he delivered then, but it caught her by surprise. When she reflected upon it then, she realised the first part of Woomongalo Mongalowoo's prediction had come to pass.

She said through gritted teeth, "That is the first and last time you will ever raise your hand to me, Gravis. Do I make myself clear"?

She warded off the second strike and in return punched him in the face as hard as she could. He yelled and an immediate trickle of crimson ran from his nose down his top lip. To her surprise, he smiled, simply saying,

"Fiscarte"!

The thug dived upward and his fist landed squarely in Lynea's solar plexus so quickly she had no time to defend herself. It drove the air out of her lungs and she collapsed at her husband's feet, trying vainly to gasp in air. To her abject horror, she felt the sole of Gravis' loafers pressing down onto her neck then, as though from very far away he told her in a voice laden with certain menace,

"If you try to assault me ever again, Bitch, it will be the end of you. I think we both know that Fiscarte here could easily dispose of your body. Now go into the bedroom, strip off your clothes and lay on the bed ready for me? Our little game has left me as randy as a rutting stag".

Lynea burst into tears, the instant she had managed to suck in some oxygen. She was not foolish enough to defy the monster while he had the assassin with him though. She crawled into the bedroom and did as he had ordered. At least it would be over quickly, she mused miserably, it always was.

The rest of the honeymoon was a desperate nightmare for Lynea. Alexius Morrelius Gravis had sold her a bill of goods and she had fallen for the ruse like a silly little fool. He was a dangerously deranged monster who also possessed the ability to maintain a facade of normality. They had some lovely meals together, but as far as Lynea was concerned she might as well have been eating soil. She pushed herself into a state of a lowered sensibility, managing to care about nothing. When he used her body, it was as though he was doing so with someone who was not her. She was waiting. Knowing that once they returned to Androichina and the detestable Fiscarte went off to commit murder, it would present her with an opportunity to escape.

Her avenue of it was not something she could have expected, not even in her wildest imaginings though. Finally, the interminable tedium of her misery came to an end and they packed up their bags and returned to the Spaceflitterport. The return flight to Earth went without incident and as the flittaxi was taking the three of them back to the Manor, in Shangjiezhen, 上街镇, Minhou, Fuzhou, Fujian, Lynea realised a tiny ray of hope for her was probably waiting for their return. Decorum. He who had hinted at what Lynea might expect from her marriage to his Father. Surely he could not have known exactly how it would go, but he had harboured suspicions. Lynea chose to believe that in the son, she might well find an ally.

At their arrival, the doors opened and Zhongxiaoqing held them open for them to enter. There was no longer any facade being enacted by Gravis by that time and he shouldered roughly past the diminutive form of the girl barking aggressively,

"Out of my way Xanthicole".

"Are you all right", Lynea whispered. Before she could answer though, her husband was calling her name,

"Hurry, stop fraternizing with the hired help and start acting like the mistress of this manor".

She was halfway across the hallway when who should come out of a ground floor room doorway, than Decorum. The two exchanged a knowing smile, which Lynea could not maintain for much longer than a couple of seconds. Decorum glided over the tessellated floor of tiles and asked urgently,

"Are you all right"?

"We must speak later", was all she had time to return before Gravis bellowed at her a second time and she was forced to trot away from the younger of the two Morrelius'

*   *   *

"What a beast"! The Elucidator was the first to find her voice, "I would know how to deal with a freak like that. It would involve the removal of various parts of his extremities that are poorly protected from such procedures".

Nigh winced at the thought of Mayling and what would doubtless be a stopped razor. He muttered,

"I could not have foreseen this becoming such a grim tale Huahua, what is it you want me to do to alleviate this situation"?

"There is more to tell, so I do not want you to do anything, Dear cousin, yet"!

Mingfu Li then observed, "It is time for us to prepare some food, who will help me in the kitchen"?

"I will of course", Huahua was quick to volunteer,

"And in future, I must be allowed to bring ingredients or pay for those you use. You cannot be expected to keep feeding us and not be compensated".

"I'll take care of that, Huahua", Nigh interjected,

"You are right of course. Not only that Fu must be allowed the place to herself one night not too far distant".

"You don't have to worry about the apartment", Fu told them all on the latter point. "I like the company and I am keen to hear how the story unfolds. I hope something dreadful happens to that awful Gravis".

She and Nigh's cousin went into the kitchen then leaving him alone with the Elucidator for the first time since she had undergone such dramatic alterations to her appearance.

"I sense that you like the new me", she began, twirling in front of him allowing him to see her from every angle.

"Stop preening", he smiled, "You know you asked to be made stunning and that it was just as you had hoped when you awoke".

"You think I am alluring? Am I foxy, Nigh".

"If you mean compared to the girl who tried to assault and kidnap me in the alleyway not so long ago, then yes you are".

"Why bring that up, I am your loyal employee now".

"Until a better offer comes along perhaps".

Mayling Fuchow pouted and then said pathetically, "Don't be like that, I like working for you. I like your friends and I would not hurt either of them under any circumstances".

"Swear that to me".

To his consternation, she dropped into his lap and said with as much lasciviousness as she could muster,

"I will not hurt your friends and I'll do anything you want me to do. Anything"!

She was light and pliable and smelled divinely and he was disconcerted by how she was exciting him,

"Get up silly, what if the other two come in and catch us like this"?

"What if they do? Have you made some sort of decision? Have you chosen between us"?

"I was not aware that I was supposed to".

"Oh, come on Nigh?! Three lovely spinsters all of whom like your company and the thought has not crossed your mind that you'd like to...".

"That's enough of that", he rose to his feet making sure he had a grip on her at the same instant to avoid spilling her onto the floor, "Until I know what Huahua is going to ask me to do I don't need any distractions. Even if those distractions are lovely and tempting. You also forget that the Chāojíjìsuànjī, Qiángdàdedàna o is still intent upon placing me before the General who calls himself Acwellen. I imagine I am not exactly popular with Noda either".

"N359 has little interest in we humans", Mayling countered, "Homini is not the first interest there, but what it can create that can exceed anything the great Hoyle made before it".

"Well two out of three is bad enough and if the family history is not over soon I will have to be thinking in terms of going underground or perhaps fleeing to the latest moon of Jupiter or Saturn to be colonised".

"You can escape into time, Chronoman, that is your one quality that frightens 23 above all others".

"Because he fears I might go back and change the course of history into a pathway that leads to the androids failure to achieve dominance over the humans! Of course, that is what is agitating his circuits so".

"I would think long and hard about manipulating the course of history just to satisfy your ends though, Nigh. Earth has become a much better environment for just about every living creature on it since the SX was used. It was brutally devastating at the time, but quite possibly the saviour of mankind".

"That may be so", Nigh was forced to consider the possibility, "But it robbed me of my father before I had a chance to say goodbye"!

"And that is tragic indeed. You are one of many though, you must consider the bigger picture".

"Quite the philosopher are you not Mayling"?

"I have worked for both sides so perhaps I have a broader perspective".

"All right, tell me then, what sort of taskmaster is the Great Master"?

"Fair, impartial, yet cold. How could he be anything else? Perhaps that is what we have always needed in a leader though? A coldly calculating impartiality. He is only motivated by the best logical consideration".

"And that was to kill millions horribly"?

"It avoided a lengthy war between man and machine, in which many more may have died".

"Many more than 90%"?

"On one world. It spared the other planets and the moons. You cannot predict how an android war would have been conducted and who would have ultimately been dragged into it. Look at the escalation of Earth's two world wars, protracted and messy. The Android War, if such it could be called was over in 48 hours".

Nigh found Mayling's reasoning worthy of greater reflection. Before he had the luxury of doing so though, dinner was ready and then Huahua was keen to continue her family history.

* * *

Over the next few weeks, Lynea realised two things. The first was that her love for Gravis was being transformed into hatred by the way he conducted himself and the way he treated her. The scales had fallen from her eyes and he did not even bother to try and retain the facade of pleasantness he had used to snare her.

The second thing was even harder to accept. She had chosen the wrong Morrelius. Decorum was everything his father was not. Kind, compassionate and caring. He was now her son though and she felt it was in some way fundamentally wrong of her to feel an attraction for him. She was especially shocked by her growing feelings when upon occasion, he referred to her as Mother. Did he have some weird and unhealthy Oedipus complex?

One evening when Gravis had been especially cutting at the dinner table, at which, the three of them had been seated, Decorum sought out his step-mother in her bedroom. She answered the tapping on the door, expecting it to be Zhongxiaoqing. Before she could stop him, he had slid past her.

"Decorum! You should not visit me here", Lynea gasped, urgently throwing a wrap over her diaphanous nightindress, "It is not proper and what would you do if your father found us in here together"?

Smiling gently, decorum asked, "Why would he be angry, Mother. I came to see if you were all right, what is so wrong about that"?

"I'm not sure I'm comfortable with you calling me that either", Lynea confessed, "I am not your mother".

"You married Father", he was deliberately obtuse.

"The biggest mistake of my life", Lynea declared with more passion than she had intended.

Decorum suddenly rushed forward and took her in his arms, "True but it is not reversible and then you would be free to find love with another".

"Please let me go"? She asked, but her voice lacked conviction. Indeed she liked the feel of his strong athletic body pressed against her own. Even through their clothing, they could feel one another's heat.

"But you do not want me to, do you, Lynea? You would like this embrace to last forever".

Before Lynea realised what was happening his mouth was on hers and her body said nothing like what she verbalised. Their mouths opened and their tongues danced an entwinement of passion. Lynea felt an incredible heat at the core of her frame, she managed to turn her head to one side and gasp,

"We should not be doing this Decorum. If your father walked in right now...".

"Lock the door", his breath was hot on her cheek,

"Let your body talk to me, not your mind"?

"Decorum, what are you saying"?

"I am saying I love you, that I want to make love to you, right now. On your bed Lynea, I want you".

It would be a fitting punishment for the cruel and savage Gravis. It was so wrong though, so immoral. At least that was what she told herself as she locked the door. What she repeated to herself as he gently pulled the nightindress over her slim shoulders. What she thought as she removed his shirt, marvelling at the iron-firmness of his musculature. When they fell onto the bed though, she began to gorget her reservations. When he first slid inside her she did not care any more. When her body was racked with a pulsating orgasm she was glad she had become an adulteress.

Spent they lay in one another's sweat glistening arms, their bodies stuck together. He told her then, "I can get you away from him, from the Manor, from even China".

"He would follow us and hurt us, maybe you more so, I would not want that", she argued, but without any real conviction.

"He would have to find us firstly and I know an indirect route and somewhere we could go that would conceal us for...maybe forever".

"You would lose the firm, all you have worked for over the years". This with even less reliance on her sincerity.

"But I would have a greater prize, you".

"What sort of route and where to"?

Pealing himself up onto an elbow, he looked into her eyes and informed, "Mars"!

Suddenly Lynea remembered and blurted, "From Lipari"?

He looked naturally stunned, "How could, how did...."?

"The Vrăjitoareclarvăzător".

"The Venuser crone you went to see? She predicted this moment"? His grin grew broad and delighted, "Then it's predicted, fated, we are on a course that cannot be altered. You will come with me to Mars on the Destino".

"The Italian liner is called destiny"?

"What else? You do not need to worry about money either Lynea, we have plenty. I have liquidated some of my shares and deposited them in a secret Cayman account. I will give you the number, you will have total access to it". "So you have prepared for this moment, confident that I would agree, you presumed my compliance"?

"I love you and I am not my Father. Do you doubt my sincerity"? She realised she did not, "Not at all. I will come with you to Mars, Decorum. Even as your illicit lover". They made love again. This time tenderly and with great patience and it was a marvellous experience for them both.

Five. Journey

"When I knew Aunt Lynea I would never have thought she was such a foxy lady"? Nigh remarked. The two other women in the room had the grace to look slightly intimidated by what they had heard and he noted that they were like as not chaste due to the shortage of men in the 51st. Or maybe it was their eastern origins or a bit of both.

"It was necessary to explain your Aunt's actions in a way you could empathise with", Huahua told him. "She would not have committed adultery without the maximum of provocation, which you now know she could have endured if she had stayed with Gravis".

"She was indeed fortunate then, that his son shared his father's attraction for her", Fu observed.

Huahua did not answer that as expected though, rather she countered, "Perhaps she was, maybe not though, you have not heard all that I have to tell before I ask Nigh to help her".

"To help *her?* It was she who was in trouble? Did Gravis find them, is that what happened"?

"It might be her, it might not", Huahua smiled enigmatically.

"Well, surely you know who you want Nigh to help"? Mayling complained.

To their collective surprise, Huahua shook her head, "Not so, because the record is incomplete. As you will discover when I finish the history".

"You mean to say the *history* is incomplete", Fu corrected.

"No", Huahua countered again, "The record of what happened next is missing no detail. It is just that the detail itself involves a mystery".

"What do you mean by that"? Nigh was absorbed by the entire narrative, "If the history contains all events that took place, how can the story end mysteriously"?

"You will have to wait until tomorrow to find out", Huahua exclaimed, yawning and stretching, thrusting out her amazing bosom in the process. "I'm sorry everyone, but I'm too tired to finish the tail tonight, it will have to wait twenty-four more hours".

A great deal can happen in the passing of a single day though as Nigh was to learn by mid-morning the following day!

It began the same way every other had, that had preceded it whilst he was in Androichina. Mingfu Li went to her place of employment. Mayling was staying with Huahua, for her protection thusly leaving Nigh on his own. He put Tchaikovsky's first Symphony on Fu's stik. The girl had a beautiful Rox valve amplifier and Rox Glass 2511 speakers. He enjoyed the brilliance of analogue whilst abluting. Though many still thought digital sound reproduction was best, the majority rightly favoured analogue for its sweet musicality. It prompted Night to wonder if such things would disappear now that the world population was so low. Yet they had survived into the 51st, so why not forever? He ate a bowl of raisin and almond muesli, put the pots in the sonicleanser and then decided to have a stroll around the city.

As he left the base of the building, glorious sunshine streamed from a pure azure canopy and he dialled up the polarisation in his cornea. Birds were singing, (in Chinese) the flitters were very light and it was a lovely day to go walking.

Until...

The android was immensely tall, 250 centimetres of durilite steel. In the past, it had sustained some tremendous injuries. The top half of its head had been blasted away. Not a serious injury for an android, their central control centre was situated in the chest. That plating had also received some sort of energy weapon damage as well though. The metal was melted into a hideous metal scar and devoid of any shine. Finally, the left arm from the elbow downward had been rewired but remained uncovered and the replacement was electrical black wiring which also looked unsightly. This android was a military unit which had been in combat with an opponent armed with a blaster. Presumably, the android, not being destroyed, had emerged from the conflict victorious, therefore the opponent was unlikely to have survived.

Seeing Nigh, the metal soldier began to race toward him, red solenoid's glittering even in the brilliance of the morning. Nigh was only armed with the Sānko ̌ng Pánzhuàngshù [Trebora Dicoidtree] Electrique pistol and something told him nothing less than a blaster would be sufficient to bring the hulking brute of metal down. The fact that the android was racing toward him, told him it was not to say hello and shake his hand. He, therefore, did the only thing a sensible person would do under the circumstances. He turned and began to flee. It was obvious that he would soon be overhauled unless he ducked into a building, so he suddenly veered to his right, diving through a door and dialling his eyes wider to see where he was going. That was when he collided with her and they both went sprawling to the floor. Nigh landed on top of Aurora, not an unpleasant experience. She was soft and yielding and smelled of lotus blossoms.

As swiftly as he could he clambered to his feet and helped her up,

"Are you unhurt"?

She smiled, "Perhaps a bruise or two, otherwise...".

"Good, come on then, we need to run, find somewhere to hide. An android is after me and I don't think he wants to be my friend".

Instantly alert, she grabbed his hand and pulled him toward the back of the store, which seemed to be a dimly lit general supplier.

"This way, through the back", she informed breathlessly, "It will lead to the alley, we can...".

"I get the picture, go".

They fled through what was the proprietor's living quarters, an elderly woman watched them sprint through her house and said nothing. Conversation was not on the couple's mind. Once again Aurora was scantily dressed and the immediate conclusion would have been that the two were running away from one or the other's irate partners, once they had been discovered together. Behind them they heard a crash, the android was dogging their tracks and the gap was decreasing. Nigh wondered if he could escape by using the fibriliance, but that would leave the girl to the androids mercy and he would not risk that. It looked like conflict was inevitable, but how could he match the metal giant's incredible strength?

The duo practically tumbled into the alley. The place was filled with various items of detritus. One of the most noticeable was some scaffolding that had been left behind by workmen. Nigh snatched up a pole and said hastily to the girl,

"Go to 23 Tongquing Road, Yuelong Residential District and wait for me there. You will not be able to get in but I should not be too long".

"The Android"?

"I'll deal with the android".

"You won't, you'll be killed".

"Do as I say, go, GO"!

Admirably Aurora argued no further but dashed away up the alley which would ultimately lead her in the correct direction. No sooner had she slipped from sight around the final bend than the rear door of the store crashed open and their pursuer emerged. The sun reflected from his damaged form sending curious sparkles of illumination dancing around the walls and other structures in the alley. Nigh did not hesitate, with every gram of strength he possessed he brought the piece of scaffold around in a deadly arc. It impacted the android's chest with a loud metallic crash. The force of it sent the construct slamming backwards into a wall with such force that some of the bricks cracked and flaked away. The android slid down to his left, the impact should have caved in the vital area of his chest plating.

It did not!

The strangely added extra protective armour was what saved it from destruction. Slowly he began to climb to his feet.

Nigh did a three hundred and sixty-degree spin on his heels and brought the piping of iron around in a second deadly arc. This time he struck the android on his right upper arm. The plating on the arm though considerable had not been subsequently reinforced, like the chest plate. The concussion bent the metal and inside the arm, some circuitry was disconnected. There was the crackle of energy associated with electrical activity and sparks issued from the android's limb.

"Stop"! It demanded, its voice a basso rumble in keeping with its mighty frame and fearsome appearance, "I yield".

"You were not going to though were you"? Nigh demanded, "You intended to attack".

"My intention was to Shanghai you and take you back to Shattered Fang to face the judgement of our great master".

"I will not be judged by him. I am an Englishman, not an Indian construct. Tell him that when you return to him damaged as you are. Or refuse so to do and I will batter you to death".

By way of an answer, the android tried to rise to a standing position once more. Nigh span around with the pipe of considerable weight and this time let it swing lower. Sure enough, it shattered the metallic leg on the androids right side. The once fearsome mechanism slumped down onto the ground burning insulation was pungent in the air between them.

"You are broken, Robot"! Nigh declared contemptuously and threw the section of the scaffold at the android's already damaged head. The crunch that resulted dinted in the androids faceplate and one solenoid failed after pathetically flickering. "You had better signal some of your support to come and pick you up. You need a few days in the body-shop, come back and try to task me again and I will turn you off permanently".

"Homini"? The voice was distorted through the damaged mouth mic, "Why do you hate us"?

"You were responsible for the death of my father, he never harmed a living soul. You had my friend killed simply because you knew you could. SX was non-selective and heinous and yet the androids were prepared to deploy it. Other ways could have been explored but you-machines are cold and inhuman and have no quiddity".

"And what about what homini did to the world, to the lower species"?

"Whatever we did it was not your prerogative to take it upon yourselves to judge us. We, who created you. I do not desire to continue this invective a moment longer. Goodbye, Android".

The event had spoiled the mien and humour of the man and he wandered the streets in misery for a while, before he remembered Aurora.

"Another addition to your little harem", Fu noted with amusement, "You do know you can only have five wives do you not"?

"I asked Aurora here because we were attacked this morning, by an android bent upon violence", Nigh told her. "She is simply safer in my company for the time being".

"And how long is the time being going to last", Fu demanded not unreasonably under the circumstances. Nigh was turning her apartment into an evening meeting place for several.

"I do not know", was the honest reply.

"I have my place", Aurora offered, "You can come and stay with me if you wish, Durango"?

Fu's eyebrows shot up at this, but before anyone could speak further the door chimed and in walked Huahua and Mayling. Nigh was glad to have dodged the offer that Aurora had made, it would have involved certain conditions, of that, he was certain. Instead, he made the introductions and told the three other Chinese girls what had happened that morning. Mayling warned,

"It will only get better the longer you are here, Nigh".

"You can call him Durango now", Fu interjected, "Aurora does". There was mischief in the twinkle in her lovely almond eyes.

"This afternoon I was brought up to date on Nigh's fascinating family history and would be keen to hear more, if I am allowed to stay for it, Mingfu"?

"Why not", Fu gasped with mock exasperation, "Just throw the door open, Ni...Durango and let anyone who happens to pass by - join us, we still have a couple of empty seats".

"It is good of you to let us meet here, Fu", Huahua felt obliged to note, "The history will end tonight, you have my word. Then Nigh will be gone from here".

"Oh, will I", Nigh chuckled, "I haven't even agreed to get involved in ancient matters yet, Huahua".

Mayling joked, "Don't be silly you're ancient yourself. Anyway, we're talking about your Aunt, your Father's sister. If it's in your power, of course, you'll help"?

"All right, don't gang up on me females. I *will* help. If, as you say, it is in my power".

"We should dine firstly and then we can relax and hear the conclusion of what Huahua has to tell us", Mingfu Li decided.

"And to that end", Huahua declared, "I have brought the ingredients for our meal this evening".

"I thought I told you it didn't matter about that", Fu objected, but Nigh could see she was pleased.

"You did, but I paid you no attention. Would you like me to cook it as well"?

The chatter went on for some time and Nigh, though listening, did not hear most of what the four of them were saying. He was too busy wondering exactly what it was that Huahua thought he could do to help his Aunt in the 33rd century when he was in the 51st. He was unsure if, just because he had fled through the fourth dimension once, he could repeat the journey in reverse and with the desired accuracy. Of course, there would only be one way to discover the answer to that question. The thought of trying filled him with a combination of excitement and nervousness.

As usual, the meal was very good. Now that there were four women in the apartment the ambient noise of their constant chatter was not something Nigh would have volunteered for regularly. He reflected that should he take advantage of the local law at any time in the future, that such would be the case with the addition of another. That was a sobering rumination indeed. How many men had taken the opportunity of marrying five times?

They dined a certain amount of rice wine was drunk and then the five of them settled down so that Huahua could relate the last part of family history to Nigh

* * *

The heat from the tarmac came up to greet them and smite their faces and arms as they disembarked from the flitterjet. The airfield was at Via Chiesa Vecchia near the city of Quattropani. Conveniently the shuttle that would take them up to the Destino was situated on the very same base. The Planata was already resting in readiness, fuelling was not a problem as the reactor was already loaded ready for CMNS condensed matter nuclear science to commence. The connection between flights and the shuttle was thirty minutes, but Decorum and Lynea had arrived early and had ninety minutes to wait. Time enough to take a rapid tour of Quattropani and drink a lichencoff and have a sticky bun. The couple walked briskly up the Via Chiesa Vecchia to see the beautiful little Chiesa Vecchia old superstitious building of Santuario della Madonna Della Catena. From the side of the whitewashed rendering of the building, they could gaze out onto the bay and the Tyrrhenian Sea. The last time they would see such a vast body of water in their lives.

They glanced around the tiny sanctuary, wondering if anyone in the past had claimed such within its cool subfusc interior. It soon bored them, however. To think that at one-time mankind had been foolish enough to believe that a Jewish carpenter could return from the dead or that a woman could fall pregnant without having any carnal knowledge of any man whatsoever, such fables were truly ridiculous when examined sensibly by the scientific or simply rational mind. So they drifted down to the Villa Petrara, where little tables were set out beneath bamboo shades over an iron framework and the view of the bay was perhaps even more splendid. While Decorum went to get served Lynea faced into the breeze issuing from the water and wondered if it would ever be fine enough on any part of the fourth planet from the sun, to be seated outdoors in such flimsy clothing, enjoying the warm breeze and the heat of the sun a mere 149.6 million kilometres distant. From the same warming star to their new home the separation would be 227.9 million kilometres wide. The reflections of that vital star twinkled on the waves bellow sending scintillating fragments of glitz dancing in every direction for as far as the eye could see. Human nature being what it was Lynea felt the loss greatly. Nothing is ever so desirable as when one realises one is soon to experience it never again.

"You look melancholy", Decorum fractured her reverie, "Are you all right"?

As he seated himself, she reassured him by squeezing the back of his hand, "I feel safer than since that fateful day I married your Father", she confessed.

His handsome features twisted with distaste at mention of Gravis, "You are not worrying, are you? He will not find us. Not since we took that strange route to get here". They had flown to Karagandy in Kazakhstan, from the Manor. Then hopped on a second flitterjet to Alexandria, Egypt, before getting the last leg which had brought them to their destination. Flying under assumed names, bought from a dubious source had also served to hide their progress. At least that was the hope. The only trouble was Fiscarte was as resourceful as he was devious and malign. Would they be able to hide forever? On Mars it would be a different prospect altogether, the young world offered wilderness that the determined could more easily disappear into.

"It is time if we are to get aboard the Planata", Decorum observed gently, "You must be certain this is what you want, Lynea".

"I am. I want to get away and I want to be with you, there is no need for any further reflection."

"Then let's go". He urged and they made their way back to the airstrip and landing pad. Customs was not difficult, despite their forged identities, they passed through as Mr and Mrs Pollopanie, from Catanzaro. The city was also known as the "City of the Two Seas". An Italian city of 9100 inhabitants and the capital of the Calabria region and its province. The archbishop's seat was the capital of the province of Calabria Ultra for over 200 years when superstition was still popular.

Neither of them spoke as much as a word of Italian, but then most Catanzar were fluent in only Standard anyway. They went to the launch cots and strapped themselves into the webbing harnesses. Breaking free of Earth gravity was the most physically taxing part of any space flight. Many passengers were still ill from it even when having been aboard shuttles scores of times before. The craft roared into life, vaulted from the ground and Lynea felt her stomach lurch before she could gasp or comment to her lover, however, the sudden acceleration began to tug at firstly her skin, then her whole body. When she was certain she could take no more and was going to pass out it abruptly vanished and the pilot of the vessel informed them over the intercom that they were in space. Only when the shuttle had docked with the Destino, with a huge metal thump were passenger allowed to undo their harnesses. The next few moments were filled with total confusion as those who had not experienced weightlessness before floated to various places on the walls and bounced off them and into anyone else who did not have a firm grip of the handrails. Decorum took Lynea by the hand and dragged her effortlessly behind him to the airlock. That was connected to the liner's lock, leading into the Destino itself. They managed to find the grey corridor, which their etickets had told them led to the outer ring and their suite. The instant they reached the first part of the grey corridor they floated gently to the floor. The ring was already rotating, creating pseudogravity. Decorum jumped to his feet, helping Lynea up to her own.

"All we need to do now is find suite 595 and we can relax for thirteen hours. At the end of that, we shall be ready to transfer to the shuttle that will take us down to the surface of Mars and the city of Caralis Fretum, which is in the Chinese Sector. From there, we can go wherever we want".

"What about our luggage"?

"Other than this hand baggage we have, they will be transferred to each vessel hold as we transfer. Don't worry when we get to Caralis Fretum nothing will be missing".

In that last proclamation though, decorum's words were to prove false. When Lynea arrived at the Chinese town on Mars, something vital would be missing!

*　　*　　*

"At that point, the records are corrupted", Huahua told the rest of those present. "I know none of you will know this but on the way to Mars, the Destino flew directly through a passing geomagnetic storm, caused by the interaction of the Earth with emissions from the Sun. The Sun continually streams out a solar wind consisting of charged particles, or plasma, travelling at high speeds throughout interplanetary space. The solar wind carries the solar magnetic field into space where it can interact with the magnetic field of planets like the Earth. Sometimes the solar wind gets particularly fast or turbulent and its magnetic field especially violent and that was the phenomena that engulfed the Decorum".

"So you have no more", Nigh was astounded, "What do you want me to do, help you research different records just to find out what happened to my Aunt"?

Huahua shook her head, "Not Lynea, Nigh, Decorum".

"You are not making especially good sense right now", Mayling observed in response.

"Let me explain", the girl requested. "When I learned that the record had been corrupted beyond all hope of recovery I transferred my search to the Martian section of Goggleweb, called rather unimaginatively Moggleweb. The decorum reached the shuttle Ares as expected, perhaps twenty minutes late, but when the passengers disembarked the count was one light".

"And that missing person was Decorum"! Nigh guessed. "I'm guessing they searched for him and found him gone. What did Aunt Lynea have to say about his mysterious disappearance though"?

"She did not know where he was either. When the storm hit the Destino, Lynea was naturally terrified, supposing that the ship would be damaged maybe even explode and get them all killed. Any other of bizarre possibilities I suppose. So Decorum insisted she stay safely in the cabin while he went to find out what was happening".

"And he never returned" Mingfu Li guessed.

Huahua nodded her head and added, "The ship soon emerged from the storm and not long afterwards docked with the Ares. Lynea told the customs staff what she knew and the search for him began. It revealed nothing".

Mayling chuckled, "And Lynea had the esort and eaccount numbers of Decorum's thumbank"!

"What are you suggesting"? Nigh was surprised, "You think she did him to end up with the money but not him? I knew my Aunt personally, she was not that sort of woman, not that sort at all".

"When you knew her", Mayling persisted, "Experience and incident can change people, Nigh".

"Not that much", Nigh was adamant, he turned back to his distant cousin asking, "Where was the body though, Huahua and why did not Lynea get charged with murder"?

"The answer to both those questions is the same", Huahua told them, "A search and we are talking a thorough sweep with electronic devices, proved beyond any doubt that Decorum was not on the Destino. There was nothing to charge Lynea with. Without a corpse, the authorities could not accuse her of anything".

"But where had it gone", Mingfu Li wanted to know, "If Lynea had tossed it out the nearest airlock for example, then a light would have appeared on the flight crew's board. They would have known one of the vessels locks had been opened for a brief period".

Huahua smiled, "You forget the nature of a geomagnetic storm. As it passes through a space vessel all electronic equipment and computerisation are rendered non-functional for a period. Decorum had been cast into space, but no one could prove that Lynea had done so".

"Well, what sort of family history is that"?! Mingfu Li objected then. "It has no proper ending".

"Oh it has an ending", Huahua told them, "Lynea reached Caralis Fretum and from there she took a flitter and went driving into the Martian Phoenicis Wastes, the last anyone ever heard of her she was driving into Dead Man's Gap".

"Another mystery", Nigh groaned, "What an unsatisfactory way to leave our family history".

For the first time since the conversation had begun, Aurora spoke, "Durango, ask Huahua again what it is she wants from you"?

Everyone looked at Nigh's distant cousin and she had the grace to flush under the collective scrutiny. She hesitantly began,

"When I saw on the SWW that you had appeared here in Androichina and you began accessing your bank account I knew you could travel through time".

"I've got it"! Nigh interjected, "You want me to try and transport myself to the Destino of all places, with the possibility of landing slap-bang into the middle of a geomagnetic storm".

Huahua returned simply, "Yes".

"Just to satisfy your curiosity as to what happened to this Decorum fellow who you have never met"?

"To find out what happened on the fateful voyage", Huahua responded. "Just think, if you saved him, your Aunt's life would be completely different, improved in such a great way".

Mingfu Li thoughtfully noted, "I thought you claimed to be a direct descendant of Durango's Aunt? So even though she managed to disappear, she did not remain invisible, to at least one man".

The others smiled at the irony of that remark, but Mingfu Li was not done, "Change you Aunt's fate in any way and you might cease to exist, Huahua".

"In this timeline perhaps, but I believe in the diverging junctions on the multiverse motorway". Huahua persisted. "I would still be alive, just in a different layer of reality that is all".

"I do not think you should attempt to tamper with the past, Durango", Mingfu Li persisted. "You have no idea what effect your cause may reap on the 51st. Even a tiny change in the past can have devastating consequences in the future. I believe in the butterfly effect".

"We are not talking about a world leader or a prominent character from history", Huahua argued, "Lynea was a tiny pawn in the cosmic game of chess. Changing anything for the better for her would be a micro-change when measured on a cosmic scale".

"Drop a pebble in a still pond and the first few rings are of no great diameter", Mingfu Li noted, "But the rings get bigger and bigger and...".

"You are the landlady, not the family advisor", Huahua flared then, forcing Nigh to hastily intervene,

"Ladies, please. I have listened and thought about what both of you say, I will take both points of view under advisement. In any event, just because I blindly fled from 23 once without thought of either direction or duration, it does not mean I could ever do it with any degree of accuracy again, so calm yourselves".

The two girls glared at one another but said no more. Not long afterwards Huahua declared herself tired and making her excuses left with Mayling in her tow.

Aurora smiled at Nigh, "Are you staying here, Durango, or coming back to my flat with me"?

"With Fu's permission, I am staying here", he disappointed her and Mingfu Li could not conceal her smirk of triumph. Not that he was in any mood to contemplate what it might or might not mean, he had too much on his mind. He soon made his excuses to the remaining Fu and went to bed after a hurried bath. The question uppermost in his mind was, did he care what had happened 18 centuries in the past? He certainly mourned his Father, but he had not been extremely close to his Aunt and the events he had been told about were one hundred and eighty decades distant. Huahua thought she had judged him correctly in that natural curiosity would get the better of him and he would attempt to fine-tune his powers of Chronomancy. Was it lack of confidence that made him hesitate to try and do so? Perhaps he thought Mingfu Li was the best philosopher of them when she had warned him of the Butterfly Effect. After all, travelling through the fourth dimension was relatively unknown in current times. The mechanisms for doing so would not be perfected until the 77th century and those few chrononauts who had appeared in history had been strictly regulated by a series of rules. Rules that breaking would result in execution when the time traveller returned to the 77th or beyond.

The most profound of all the rules being the most logical one:- A Chrononaut must do nothing to change the historical events contemporary to the period that he/she is visiting. Infringement of this rule will incur the death penalty.

Of course, no one could ever know if this rule had been secretly broken. For, if a chrononaut did manage to change history then all collective memories and records of that event would change in the merest of fractions of a second. That was the usual reason why chrononautia invariably travelled in pairs with extensive historical records loaded into their pads. For then the comrade of he or she who broke that rule would be able to operate outside the new reality. Their pad would exist outside the timeline and a simple check gave them the right to execute their partner. Nigh could not know how many times this had happened for he was *downwhen* of the 77th. Perhaps it might be instructive to travel firstly up to the 77th or beyond, to find the answer to that question? That idea struck Nigh is sensible, the next question was, could he do it?

Six   Upwhen.

"For goodness sake, Durango, have you any idea what time it is? What are you doing in my bedroom? Hey, you don't think you and I are going to...".

"Just shut up and listen a second will you", he blurted, his features flushed with excitement, filmy with exertion. "I can do it. I've been practising all night and I think I've learned to control it"!

Mingfu Li glanced at her bedside chrono. The neon numbers told her it was 03:47. "You've been practising"? She echoed, "That's more information than I was wanting, but good for you, now go to bed because you're not doing any practising with me".

"Will you get your mind out of your knickers and listen to me", he stormed then, "I'm not after your lady's garden, I've been Chonotravelling and I've learned how to govern and regulate my jumps. I can do it, Fu! I'm a Chronoman"!

Finally fully awake she pushed herself up to a sitting position and turned on the bedside lamp with a quick verbal command. Then she reached for her dressing gown, pulling it around her shoulders so that her breasts were not quite so noticeable through the diaphanous material of her nightindress.

Finally, she admitted, "That is a momentous announcement. It could have, however, waited until the morning, do you not think? I have work tomorrow and I need to get a full nights sleep. Now I've been generous with this apartment, I've let you have as many female admirers as you've wanted to bring to each evening but...".

"I want you to come with me"!

Mingfu Li blinked, "Come with you? Where"?

"The 77th or further upwhen, to see what the dangers of Chrononautia are".

"The 77th? The 77th century! Durango, I cannot travel through time, how could I possibly...".

"I think I can create a chronotemporal-rift. that's what I project myself through when I traverse up or downwhen. My fibriliance allows me to make a temporalphase-door. If you and I are in a close embrace we can squeeze through the TPD and...".

"A close embrace"?

"Yes. You know, arms tightly around one another, pressing together, as though we were one huge person of considerable girth".

"I see. You want to take me in your arms and pretend...".

"For the love of Odin Fu, I'm not coming on to you, I don't want to do it nudey or...although I do have to observe that with all your makeup removed you are still a stunning creature, natural prettiness in abundance".

"Thank you", she simpered.

Nigh shook himself rather like a dog trying to straighten himself out and continued, "Sorry I got momentarily distracted there, what I mean to say is this. Of anyone I know, I want you to come with me because you were the voice of reason last night, the one filled with words of caution. You are the best one to have as a companion, to tame my natural tendencies to jump into situations before thinking through all the consequences. That's why I want you to come up to the Chrononaut academy at Figueira da Foz, what do you think"?

"Where"?

"Figueira da Foz, in what used to be Portugal, it is where the Ministro do Tempo Estudos e Tempo Viajando [Ministry of Time Studies and Time Travelling] is situated. The very first Tempo Travessia Dispositivo [time machine] was created by none other than, Cientista de Extrema Aprendizagem [Professor-Scientist] Adalberto Almeida Sapientiae".

"I confess it sounds intriguing, but I also have to work, Durango, the rent, you know, it will still need paying at the end of the month".

"You're not thinking about all the possibilities of Chrononautia. I can have you back here, once we have explored the 77th before we even set off if it was necessary, although that would involve meeting ourselves".

Mingfu Li shuddered, "That thought does not appeal to me. All right, Durango, I will come with you, may we set off first thing? Can I go back to sleep now"?

"I'm too wired up to sleep but you get some rest, I'll go and have a bath and some breakfast and then wake you. Does that sound all right with you"?

Mmhhm", she murmured and slipping off the dressing gown, slid back beneath the covers... Naturally, with the sound of running water, draining water and the occasional thump of Nigh moving around, plus the prospect of a journey through time, Mingfu Li did not get back to sleep. The instant she knew the bathroom was free, she sighed, arose and went to do the same activities. By the time she appeared at the breakfast table, her face on once more she was slightly ired. It was still only 05:33.

"You are a special case, Durango Nigh. You know that do you not"?

"Why thank you, Fu, I admire you too".

She punched him playfully on the arm and objected, "I didn't mean it like that and you know I didn't. Pour me some cereal while I make another pot of fresh tea. The truth is I'm very nervous about what you plan to do. Is it possible that I might be killed by the process? How is it that you suddenly seem to know how to do it anyway. How do those worm-things in your brain help you to move through the fourth dimension"?

"I don't know", he replied honestly, "But it isn't necessary to know how electricity works to switch the light on, is it? I own the switch on some sort of psychic level, but I don't know how my brain does it".

"How come you know how to use the ability since yesterday anyway"?

"I went on a test-run, thought myself back to the year 249BC to a place that was then called Carthage. Do you know anything about the Punic Wars, Fu"?

The girl shook her head, "No, but I've got a feeling that is going to change very soon".

"I went back to see Publius Appius Claudius Pulcher consult the sacred chickens before engaging the Carthaginian fleet. If the birds ate their offered grain enthusiastically then it told the Romans that the gods would favour them in the forthcoming engagement. I wanted to know if the chickens refused to eat that day. Guess what, they really did! I had learned Latin through a hypnocourse like most of the English children do at school, so I was able to hear the consul exclaim, 'Let them drink if they will not eat' and the poor fowl were tossed into the sea. I then watched the two fleets engage, from a safe distance I might add. Adherbal met Pulcher at his rear all was confusion as the Roman vessels tried to enter a harbour that the Carthaginians were desperately exiting. Some vessels even collided and their oars snapped like matchsticks. It forced the Roman ships back against the shore, while the Carthaginians launched their more manoeuvrable attack from open water. The Romans endured tremendous causalities as a result of losing 95 of their 121 ships.

"Did the consul, the incompetent, lose his life"?

"No, he was not near the worst of the fighting. He went back to Rome and was put on trial, but history records that he was wealthy and powerful enough to avoid the death penalty, though he was replaced in time for the Second Punic War against the infamous Hannibal".

"What did you want to go so far back in time for and to such a barbaric time? You could have gotten yourself killed".

"I thought myself to a high point on the coastline and from there I watched the battle. I was not in any danger. The Romans gave me some strange glances when they saw my clothing, but fortunately, everyone was too busy preparing for the battle to pay me much attention. As to why I chose such a time, I've always been fascinated by the period, since learning Latin and of course, it is very in vogue right now with many who have assumed Latin names. So you see I can make certain when we go to the 77th that you're safe from injury. My control is getting better by the minute".

"All right, I am in. by the way, what would my Roman name be"?

Nigh thought for a few seconds and then told her, Nolite Mentiri Mingfu Elegantes".

"Does that mean anything, Roman names usually have meaning do they not"?

Smiling he confessed to her, "I had to take a little liberty with your real name, but in Standard it means, Does not lie, Elegant Mingfu".

She smiled, "You think I am elegant"?

He nodded, "Now, my dear, Nolite Mentiri Mingfu Elegantes, how soon can you be ready to take our little expedition to the 77th and the Ministro do Tempo Estudos e Tempo Viajando in Figueira da Foz. I'm keen to meet this Cientista de Extrema Aprendizagem Adalberto Almeida Sapientiae".

"Can we just refer to him as Berto? It will save a great deal of time"?

"You might get away with it after all Adalberto Almeida Sapientiae is a man. I think I will have to call him Sapientiae though".

"Give me half an hour to tidy up, freshen up and put a onesy on and then we can go"?

As far as Nigh was concerned it was a somewhat lengthy thirty minutes. It passed at the usual rate of one second per second however and inevitably came to an end and then the girl said in nervous tones,

"All right, I'm mad for agreeing to this, but let's do it".

The item she had called a onesy was a skin-tight jumpsuit that showed every single one of her admirable contours off to perfection. Nigh tried to blink the impressive vision out of his consciousness, it did not work. So he closed his eyes, asked,

"Take hold of me as tightly as you can, Fu and hold on until I tell you to release me".

He felt her press into his flesh and the experience was both sensual and arousing. It took every gramme of his will power not to generate timber. He amazed himself by remaining none responsive. She smelled marvellous, her hair pressed into his face. Her every supple curve touching him firmly. He forced himself into a yoga trance, as taught him by the Yogi, Doshi during his stay in India as a boy. Such an action allowed him to access the andhera tantu or fibriliance. Those strange strands of unknown material that threaded their way through his brain. With the inexplicable almost magical power of those dusky fibres, he began to manufacture a chronotemporal-rift. It was an envelope, a tear in the fabric of the space-time continuum which Nigh had christened the temporalphase-door. Between the TPD and the conduit through time, there came into being a second doorway at the other end of the temporal course, the TPD that they would exit the timeline through. The second TPD was in what had once been called Portugal, in the 77th century.

Nigh hurled himself sideways, just he had done twice before. Once to escape the clutches of General 23, the second time to witness Roman's clashing with the might of Carthage. It took less than two seconds and the two TPD's closed swiftly with an imploding pop.

"You can open your eyes now", he told his companion.

Mingfu Li did so and began to disentangle herself from his continued grasp, saying sternly, "And you can let me go, thank you".

The duo then gazed about them in wonder. For they were on a green and lush plain of short grass edged by magnificent trees, the like of which they had never seen before. They were, in fact, Lichenoakash, as they were to discover some time later. Deciduous trees were very very rare in the 33rd and 51st, most had been cut down for lumber and only replaced with pine. It was warm, without being scorching or balmy, around $22°$. Cumulus clouds overhead proclaimed that it would soon rain, which explained the very verdancy that was on display all around them. They could hear at least three types of avian song and the much quieter buzz, the hum of various insectivores.

"It's like the garden of Eden", Nigh breathed.

"I haven't heard of that. Whereabouts in Androichina is it? Anyway, I thought you were bringing us to a city"?

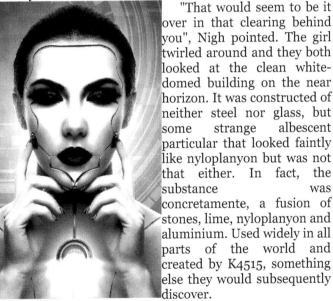

"That would seem to be it over in that clearing behind you", Nigh pointed. The girl twirled around and they both looked at the clean white-domed building on the near horizon. It was constructed of neither steel nor glass, but some strange albescent particular that looked faintly like nyloplanyon but was not that either. In fact, the substance was concretamente, a fusion of stones, lime, nyloplanyon and aluminium. Used widely in all parts of the world and created by K4515, something else they would subsequently discover.

"Rather elegant, do you not agree", Nigh was at the girl's side. "I hope that is the Ministro do Tempo Estudos e Tempo Viajando, or Ministry of Time to you, Fu".

"Figueira Fuz is not a city then if it is", Mingfu Li noted, causing Nigh to laugh,

"Just call it Figueira. Shall we take a pleasant stroll"?

The walk soon transformed into a dash for cover though, as the heavens opened and heavy rain descended onto the two chrononautia. As was usually the case, getting wet immediately lowered their temperatures and by the time they reached the base of the clean curve-topped building, they were wet and cold. Mingfu Li had fared better than Nigh, her jump-suit was waterproof. Nigh had only boho shirt and pants though and he was much wetter. The door at the left side of the building opened and without looking at who had done so for them, the couple dashed into the interior shelter. Only then did Nigh glance at the person who had been so gracious to them. The female form in question was of a very artificial-looking android indeed. Constructed from what looked like pure white nyloplanyon, There had been no attempt to past the construction off as a human woman. Yet for all that the face was quite pleasing, even if an inspection plate over some sort of circuitry. The durilite joint around the eyes and down to the chin had been chromed, making it even more noticeable. Short pseudo-hair scraped back over the skull was dark blue, while the eyes were heavily eye-shadowed in violet and the pupils all black. The lips while perfectly bowed were also of black. The overall effect was one of beauty and yet also menace. A combination of the pulchritudinous and sinister? Bizarre. Just under the nape of the neck was a brilliant LED light, which came on as the mechanised simulacrum of the woman spoke to them.

"Hello", she began in Esperanto rather than Standard or Portuguese, "Welcome to the Ministry of Time, where all matters temperato are researched and investigated. I am the custodian of the entrance hall, my designation is å795c^2".

"å795c^2? You are squared"?

"I was a twin, so am to the power of 2", å795c^2 explained. "May I know your designations"?

"Certainly, I am Durango and this is Mingfu, we have come to see, Adalberto Almeida Sapientiae".

"Which of you is Durango and which Mingfu, I am unfamiliar with the designations, they are most curious", the white android asked of him. She was not joking, indeed he suspected that å795c^2 never joked.

"Durango is my name, where I am from it is considered masculine. Similarly, Mingfu is a feminine name".

"Well thank you for both making the effort to be here", å795c² responded smoothly, "However Sapientiae is busy today and will not be able to grant you an audience".

"I'm not certain you understand", Nigh persisted, "You see Mingfu and I are Chrononautia"!

Å795c² blinked, processing the revelation, then she reported, "I know every chrononaut registered with this facility. From this century and up to the 101st, which is currently as far as anyone has reached. Neither you nor the lady is on that register, Durango".

"That is true as we have not visited this facility before", Nigh returned.

"Then you could not be chrononautia", the android explained reasonably and with admirable patience. All mechanisms are accounted for and all users are logged. You have never used any of the facility's mechanisms".

"That is also true", Nigh agreed. "We used no mechanism to traverse the fourth dimension, I used my abilities of Andhera Tantura".

This was greeted with a second blink, å795c² asked carefully, You chrononauted without a mechanism. You are from the far upwhen"?

"No, actually I am from the 33rd and Mingfu the 51st".

"That is not possible, Durango. Chrononautia was not possible in ancient times, either with or without mechanisms. Were it so it would be in the facility's ancient archives and it is not".

"Never the less, what I have told you is the truth, å795c²". Nigh smiled charmingly.

"Would the two of you please take a seat", the android suddenly decided, "I will see if the Sapientiae can juggle his schedule just for you. He will doubtless be intrigued by your claims".

"Of course", Nigh nodded and waved Mingfu Li toward two white seats in some strange material unknown to either of them.

"Androids seemingly serving homini once more", was the first thing the Androichinese girl noted, "This place seems a bit upside down if you ask me, Durango".

For once Nigh had no useful observation to make. He spread his arm in wonder, the gesture indicating that he was currently at a loss to contribute anything useful. The seat seemed to transmogrify the longer they were seated on them. Moulding so effectively into the contours of their bodies that when å795c² returned both of them had fallen asleep and were awoken feeling particularly refreshed and vital.

"I say å795c², these chairs are marvellous, I fell asleep on this one". Before the android could respond, Mingfu Li exclaimed that she too had slumbered and felt marvellously refreshed by the power nap.

"I am not å795c²", replied the android, "But Å795c. å795c² went off duty a couple of hours ago".

"A couple of hours"!, Nigh was shocked, "How long were we waiting for her to return".

"Both of you resided comfortably in the somnamiseats for six hours". Å795c informed them.

Nigh jumped to his feet. He was not especially pleased that the chair could have anaesthetised him so easily, given that he was an Andhera Tantu. The instant he regained his equilibrium, he realised he was terrifically hungry, his guts began to complain at their lack of sustenance quite audibly. Noting everything, missing nothing Å795c held out a synthetic hand, upon which, resided two capsules. One for each of them, Nigh presumed.

"If these are to bring us around, then mine is unnecessary", he told the construct. "I now feel completely awake".

"They are subsistofuel 1000", the android returned patiently, "Nutrients and protein, kilo for kilo there is nothing more sustaining".

"Oh, Right, thank you", Nigh took one and before he could stop it the gelatinous coating had caused the capsule to slip down his throat. His hunger instantly disappeared completely.

"Homini find them especially useful when they do not have the time to sit down to a proper meal".

"So food is still eaten in this century"? Mingfu Li asked.

"Of course. Eating is a social occasion. Also, many business deals are brokered across the dining table".

"Regarding the Homini", Nigh began hesitantly, "What is your position concerning them? When I say you, I mean androids collectively".

"We are partners with the biological", Å795c told them without hesitation.

"And what of General Acwellen, is he still your leader"?

The android looked suddenly almost reverent as she intoned, "AcwellenA23 ascended to the *Great Programme* in the 73rd".

"The Great Programme"?

"Where we ascend to when our circuits finally fail. When overhauls would involve the replacement of the central computational nucleus, making of us someone else".

So A23 had finally died, but not until he had ruled for four-thousand years. When he had finally expired it had created a superstition for the androids, but also a humbling and now they worked with and in some instances for homini, or humans. Earth had become a paradise under the guidance of the androids, it seemed, prompting Nigh to ask,

"Can you tell me the populations of Homini and androids that now exist on Earth"?

"Two million of each", Å795c supplied without hesitation.

"And what about the animals", Mingfu Li added, "Do any of them remain"?

"There are billions of fauna on Earth a hefty proportion of which are not either genetically modified or completely artificial".

"Eden" the girl breathed and Nigh smiled his agreement.

"Now that I have satisfied your curiosity, perhaps you would like to come and meet Sapientiae"?

"Very much so, will you be escorting us to him, or providing us with directions"

"I will leadambulate", the android told them, using yet another new word, the meaning of which was easily discernible to them. They followed her to a curiously shaped section of the floor, where she halted and waited for them to join her. Without warning the section began to ascend forcing Nigh to grab Mingfu Li's arm lest she tumbled from the edge and plummeted back to ground level. In the 77th lifts had no sides nor roof. The base merely passing through several holes in the various floors of the building. When it had done so several times it eased to a gentle halt. Å795c strolled off the edge and led them to a sliding door, which promptly did as it was intended.

The oldest man either of them had ever seen was reclining in some sort of webbing laying behind a series of instruments. His head was almost bald, yet he had swooped a few strands over his tonsured scalp. They looked like snow-covered twigs and were not fooling anyone. From rheumy pale eyes that remained non the less vital, he regarded his visitors. His skin had the quality of practically transparent parchment and even his wrinkles possessed wrinkles. When he spoke his voice was like the dry whisper of the breeze passing through reeds,

"Mingfu from the 51st how can you traverse the barriers between the aeons without one of our Chronochines"?

"I am pleased to meet you too Sapientiae", Fu returned somewhat disconcerted by the aged man's directness and lack of seeming common courtesy. "It is not I who does so, but Durango here, he is the one with the Andhera Tantu".

"Male", the double-centenarian demanded through his decrepit throat, "Explain to me what this Andhera Tantu is and how it allows you to escort your mistress through the fourth dimension".

It struck Nigh at that moment, the 77th was a matriarchy. Both the chronoscientist and the android must think that Mingfu Li was the leader of their expedition.

"I am not able to describe how it works fellow male", he admitted, "Only that I possess such a bizarre ability and I am from the 33rd, where men not only ruled the androids but also women".

"The 33rd, the 33rd", Sapientiae seemed to be struggling to bring something to his mind which no doubt was suffering the beginnings of senility after two hundred years.

"SX", Å795c supplied for him, "Synosis Xenoplastithemia And the rise of Acwellen A23 the Great".

"Of course", Sapientiae wheezed in something approaching a chuckle, "You are not Durango, Male. You are the Knight".

"*The* Night", Nigh chuckled in turn. "Your ancient history is a tad corrupt Sappy Old Man, I am Durango Nigh. That is Nigh, not Night".

"Do not call the Sapientiae Sappy Old Man", Å795c chided, "He is your senior by some margin. Have some respect for his 202 years".

The chronoscientist for his part grinned and told Nigh, "You may call me Adalberto, Youngster if it suits you and your barbarous ways. Although technically you are much older than me by forty-four centuries".

"I sort of skipped most of them, Adalberto".

The old man wheezed some amusement and observed, "So you did, Durango Nigh, so you did. So you were not some mystical knight after all, but a callow youth with a strange power that firstly tossed you into the 51st where you picked up this delightful oriental creature and then decided to come and see the Grandfather of Time".

"He did not *pick me up*"! Mingfu Li objected, "I am his landlady".

The chronoscientist's laughter was like the dry rustle of twigs agitating leaves, he joked, "Is that what they call the arrangement in the 51st"?

"There is no euphemism here", Mingfu Li scolded. "Landlady means landlady and I am here to keep him in check".

"Aah, the role of women, only officially recognised by the 62nd".

When Nigh stopped to think about it the casual way Adalberto mentioned centuries was quite staggering, but then perhaps he had been to the 101st? Making each century nothing more than 1% of his collective span.

"So, who do I address my questions to"? The chronoscientist wanted to know, "How am I to discover the secret of Andhera Tantu and thus render the Tempo Travessia Dispositivo of the Ministro do Tempo Estudos e Tempo Viajando obsolete".

"Let me tell you something of my abilities and their origins then Adalberto", Nigh began "Before I ask you the questions I came here to have answered".

Nigh went on to tell the account of his birth defect,

"I sometimes possess a form of foreknowledge of an event, especially as a form of extrasensory perception. Also the ability to transport a person or object instantly from one place to another using only certain filaments in the brain that bear the same name. Such filaments appeared in the 33rd century in children whose mothers had experienced a pregnancy that had been difficult from the offset. In their first trimester, such unfortunates developed the rare disorder *Difficilo Nativatuo Syndrome*. There had been only one drug available to treat for it at that time Phenobarbiosulate. Wildly experimental and not without its unpredictable side effects. The drug was banned following several reports of fibres growing in the brains of the resultant children of those mothers. The children themselves termed the phrase Andhera Tantu to describe their disorder that was later realised as a mutation. For mothers who are unfortunate enough to suffer *Difficilo Nativatuo Syndrome,* a replacement drug, Diasnufalite eventually proved to provide a solution. In my case though, that is not the end of the story. I travelled to India when, a youth and studied yoga under the famous Yogi, Doshi. By combining my learned techniques of yoga I learned to not only control my Andhera Tantu but also to develop its hitherto unsuspected capabilities. My latest talent is the ability to create a temporal phase door or TPD, the door proves to be a gateway through a chronotemporal rift. I can make a TPD at each end and with the power of the Andhera Tantu decide exactly how long I want the conduit through the fourth dimension to be. Thusly I become a chrononaut, with Fu here we are chrononautia".

There was a reflective silence which the double-centenarian finally broke,

"That is a truly amazing story and one that fills me with regret".

"You mean because it renders your machines obsolete", Nigh deduced, erroneously as he was soon to discover, "I would not worry too much Adalberto, to my knowledge I am the only Andhera Tantura who can do what I have done".

"No", the chronoscientist informed, "I do not think we need to scrap the Tempo Travessia Dispositivo just yet. No, the shame is that you are unique Durango Nigh and yet you have broken the tempuslaws of our time. There is only one penalty for breaking tempuslaws and that is death. However, we may then learn a great deal when we dissect your brain and examine the fibres you speak of".

Nigh was amused initially, "I am from the 33$^{rd.}$ Your laws do not apply to me, Adalberto. Now listen, I have some questions for you regarding a chronotrip I am planning to take soon...".

It was Mingfu Li who interrupted him though, "Durango, I think Sapientiae believes that the law of the Ministro do Tempo Estudos e Tempo Viajando applies to anyone making unauthorised journeys through time without firstly receiving approval from them".

Adalberto nodded the wrinkled head that threatened to topple from his scrawny neck,

"Correct, young Lady. Approval from this very facility, or more specifically, from me, as the administrator of it".

"Now just a moment", Nigh demanded, "Until we came here we did not know that we had to gain permission from you. How could we do so without firstly breaking the law you describe"?

"That is true", Adalberto conceded, "A knotty one indeed, that is why only chrononautia from the 77th are allowed to venture into any period before this century you see. Harsh you may think so, but necessary. Let me tell you a story which illustrates the absolute necessity to police time so stringently. When my very first TTD was developed one of the prototypes was stolen by a chronocriminal by the name of E66d6. He broke into what was then little more than a laboratory and travelled back in the larcenously acquired device to the dim and distant past. To be specific April 20th 1889 to a place called Braunau am Inn. Which was a town in Austria-Hungary (long since vanished and now part of the Greater Germanic Empire), close to the border with the German Empire of those dimly perceived days? E66d6 went there to kill a newborn baby, specifically to kill a tiny newborn who was to be christened Adolphus Hitler. I don't know how developed your ancient history is, but the baby would grow up to become a German politician and leader of a political movement called the Nationalsozialistische Deutsche Arbeiterpartei, later abbreviated to Nazi. Hitler rose to power as Chancellor of Germany in 1933 and later Führer or leader in 1934. During his dictatorship from 1933 to 1945, he initiated a war that became known as World War II. Which began when he invaded a country called Poland in September 1939. I believe Poland still exists in your time. Anyway, this Adolf Hitler as he was then known was closely involved in military operations throughout the war and was central to the perpetration of something called the Holocaust which involved the slaying of millions of Jewish people at that time by gassing and resultant cremation. As E66d6 was horrified by this atrocity he resolved to do something about it by killing the baby that would become the monster. Now, Nigh, do you know what the result was of his homicide"?

"No"?

"When he got back to the Ministro do Tempo Estudos e Tempo Viajando and looked at the historical records to see what his killing had improved he discovered that World War II had still happened and had been initiated by the invasion of Poland by Joseph Stalin, the then leader of Russia. The resultant casualties of the conflict had increased by millions as the war progressed and the Jews had still suffered the Holocaust, only the nationality of the guards had changed. E66d6 had acted with the very best of intentions, but his actions had created an even worse crime against humanity. What did we do to undo what E66d6 had created? When we heard his account an agent for us called P555v2 went back to 1889 and killed E66d6 before he could slay a then innocent baby. Thus the timeline was restored because he had confessed his crime and we subsequently developed miniature history recorders for all our agents so that if the timeline was changed ever again we would still know about it. You have made two illegal trips through that very line and no one, *no one*, can know what has been changed as a result. Ergo, you must die"!

"Very well", Nigh agreed to Mingfu Li's utter amazement, "Just give me a second to say goodbye to my landlady before your Android here calls for more of her kind and presses me physically into arrest".

As Nigh grabbed Mingfu' Li's hand however the ancient scientists suddenly croaked,

"Stop him Å795c, he is going to...".

Mingfu realised what he was going to, too. She threw her arms around Nigh without any cajoling and squeezed him tightly.

Heard him whisper in her ear, "They will chase us through time forever unless they never know we were ever here"!

* * *

"You can open your eyes now", he told his companion.

Mingfu Li did so and began to disentangle herself from his continued grasp, saying sternly, "And you can let me go, thank you".

The duo then gazed about them in wonder. For they were on a green and lush plain of short grass edged by magnificent trees, the like of which they had never seen before. They were, in fact, Lichenoakash, as they were to discover some time later. Deciduous trees were very very rare in the 33rd and 51st, most had been cut down for lumber and only replaced with pine. It was warm, without being scorching or balmy, around 22°. Cumulus clouds overhead proclaimed that it would soon rain, which explained the very verdancy that was on display all around them. They could hear at least three types of avian song and the much quieter buzz and the hum of various insectivores.

"It's like the garden of Eden", Nigh breathed.

"I haven't heard of that whereabouts in Androichina is it? Anyway, I thought you were bringing us to a city"?

"That would seem to be it over in that clearing behind you", Nigh pointed. The girl twirled around and they both looked at the clean white-domed building on the near horizon. It was constructed of neither steel nor glass, but some strange albescent particular that looked faintly like nyloplanyon but was not that either. In fact, the substance was concretamente, a fusion of stones, lime, nyloplanyon and aluminium. Used widely in all parts of the world and created by K4515, something else they would subsequently discover.

"Rather elegant, do you not agree", Nigh was at the girl's side. "I hope that is the Ministro do Tempo Estudos e Tempo Viajando, or Ministry of Time to you, Fu".

"Figueira Fuz is not a city then if it is", Mingfu Li noted, causing Nigh to laugh,

"Just call it Figueira. Shall we take a pleasant stroll"?

Something astonishing happened next. Before their incredulous eyes, a couple suddenly appeared as though from nowhere. One was a beautiful Chinese girl dressed in a skin-tight jumpsuit, the other, the other was ....Nigh.

Nigh asked, "It is us, you are us are you not"?

Nigh [later] replied, "Yes we are. Or you are us, it rather depends upon your point of view does it not"?

"What is happening"? Mingfu's voice shook with nervousness on the very edge of panic.

"We have come to warn you", Mingfu [later] told herself, "Not to go to the Ministro do Tempo Estudos e Tempo Viajando. If you do you will meet Cientista de Extrema Aprendizagem Adalberto Almeida Sapientiae certainly and he will pronounce the death penalty upon you for illegally travelling through time".

Nigh deduced, "That is what happened to you is it not, so you came back to warn us not to go see him"?

"Exactly" Nigh [earlier] smiled, "And if my guess is correct, that will restore the timeline and we will never have.....".

Nigh and Mingfu Li [earlier] suddenly puffed out of existence.

Mingfu gasped, "What happened to them"?

"I just decided to return to the 51st", Nigh told her, "So they never existed, take hold of me it's starting to rain".

Seven   As close to zero as makes no mathematical
difference.

Matteus Crespo strolled into his apartment with a bunch of flowers that was wider than his grin if that was possible, which at that precise moment, it was not. As his wife Mattea turned from the stove she saw the blooms and gave a little squeal of delight. He pressed them into her hand, reporting somewhat unnecessarily,

"I've had some good news today".

Oh, I see, the only time you get your beautiful wife flowers is when you have had the good news", she teased him, planting an enthusiastic kiss on his handsome lips. "What is the news then, Tesoro, I can see you're bursting to tell me"?

"Today my Cara I am to earn my last name, my hypocoristic".

Mattea's eyes widened with delight and she laughed, "You didn't...".

"Sì, sì, it is true, I am now Matteus Crespo Gubernator".

"Oh! Tesoro I am so delighted for you", she exclaimed, throwing her arms around him and squeezing him with excitement and affection, "But I do not like the hypocoristic, it is not a pretty one, it has no attraction. I think I will call you the same as your crew will, Capitano Crespo. Have the administration told you which flitterjet you will be getting"?

A cloud seemed to fleetingly pass over her husband's swarthy features for the merest of instants then before he confessed, "They have, but I am thinking that you will not be liking what craft it is that I am to be Capitano of so listen to me, Cara for I am going to tell you something. My command was conditional upon taking whatever the force issued to me and I had no choice in the matter".

Mattea grimaced, "It's the spacefleet isn't it? I thought we talked about this, Tesoro"?

"I know we did", the newly appointed Gubernator conceded, "I had no choice though, Caro, I had to accept the post or remain a Tenente for who would know how much longer"?

"So you took the post without consulting me before you agreed"?

"Caro, Caro, Caro", Matteus murmured, "I took it for us, I wanted you to be able to tell your friends that you were married to Matteus Crespo Gubernator. You wanted that too didn't you"?

"So you'll go off and be missing for days, flying out to Callisto or the asteroids and I will be in our bed alone, wondering if you are safe".

Possibly, eventually, but certainly not right away".

"What do you mean".

"I will be on a relatively shorter run. To Mars and back, they gave me the Destino".

"Mars, Not outer-ward? Not Callisto"?

"Not for quite some time if at all. The Destino will be ferrying passengers to and from Mars and occasionally Venus, but not Callisto, nor Mercury, so I will not be gone too long each flight. I only do two and then get two days off. How bad is that"?

"Not so bad, I suppose", Mattea pouted, "But it would have been so much better if you could have gotten an Earth-flight route, to the German Empire and back. Just like we discussed".

"But everyone wants the shorter flights, Caro and they are statistically more dangerous. There has never been a space-flight collision yet, the place is so vast, collisions are as close to zero as makes no mathematical difference".

Yet in that final statement, Matteus Crespo Gubernator was going to be proved erroneous, as subsequent events would bear out!

It was not the easiest evening he had ever spent with his Italian wife. She was a good woman. Filled with Latin fire and she was less than happy with the way events had turned out for her. The truth was she loved her husband with an all-consuming passion and it would not be easy for her when he was missing in the evenings. She also had heard all the rumours regarding stewardesses and because she was devoted to Matteus, she was also jealous to the point of distraction at times. The latter quality tended to cancel out any trust she could have built toward him and she began to fret that he would conduct an affair with a female colleague the instant she did not know of his location on an almost hourly basis. So she sulked and as with all things she did it magnificently well. By the following day, neither of them had enjoyed much rest. Long into the night, he had been forced to constantly reassure her that his new position would not also involve a new position between the thighs of some attractive crew mate. It was fair to say Mattea had a vivid imagination, added to which she also had a swarthily handsome husband. He would certainly not lack from opportunity when enjoying a stop-over on an entirely different planet and even he wondered if he could resist the endless chances of a thrilling if a vicarious encounter with a different willing and eager body. He, therefore, rushed to his flitter that morning and drove as swiftly as was safe to airfield Via Chiesa Vecchia near the city of Quattropani. He would then pilot the shuttle that would lift he and the trips crew and passengers up to the Destino currently orbiting the Earth in readiness. The Planata was already idling, fuelling was not a problem as the reactor was already loaded ready for CMNS condensed matter nuclear science to commence. Once everyone was aboard Capitano Crespo would take the shuttle out of the grip of the home-world and then relieve the current pilot of the Destino. He would replace him and commence his first trip to Mars. He could feel the tension in the base of his gut, like an acidic knot, threatening to eat away at his resolve. He was ready though. The endless months of training, the frequent hour upon hour of simulation runs, he was ready. Parking the flitter in the special area designated for pilots [the first time he had been able to do so] he strode purposefully toward the Planata. Two lower-ranking officers saluted him as he did so and Matteus tried not to push out his chest. It was the extra pips he had pushed into his green jacket that was causing the sudden respect. A Tenent suddenly seemed to be on an intercept course to him and he instantly found out why,

"Gubernator? May I introduce myself, I am to be your Tenent and co-pilot, as we take the passengers up to the Destino".

"Not to Mars then"?

No Gubernator, the crew of the Destino are senior to me, I am only a shuttle Tenent at present".

"Is all in readiness then"? Matteus tried to sound like he had flown out of Earth's gravitational pull hundreds of times before.

"We launch in twenty minutes, Sir, all that is needed by then are your checks".

"Lead the way to the control room then, I've not been aboard the Planata before"?

As he followed his junior officer he listened to the low ambient music being piped through the vessel's public address. Just above the level at which it would not have been possible to hear it, he found himself humming along to the piece before he realised what it was. It was the medieval electronica by the minstrels Tangerine Dream. The piece was entitled Sad Merlin's Sunday, one that Matteus had listened to through choice on his stik system. The corridor they had been traversing terminated in a steel sliding door that hissed open almost silently on precisely engineered servos, at their sudden proximity. Beyond was a white and gleaming control room and three staff. Trying not to look overawed by the incredible array of LED meters, pilot lights and screen readouts, he took the Capitano's chair and said in as calm and commanding a tone as he could muster,

"All check completed, men"?

This was standard, even though the navigator was, in fact, a rather attractive Latin girl. After several affirmative responses, Matteus let his fingers rest on the touch-screen and closing his eyes allowed memory and hours of simulation to take over. His first takeoff was surprisingly smoothly executed, although he did not enjoy the pressure of g-force attempting to stop the shuttle from escaping the home-world's loving embrace. When he opened his eyes, he saw a silver jewel hanging against a backdrop of diamond-encrusted satin. The Destino, orbiting in space.

Plenusia Tazza Circumerario

"Initiating docking manoeuvre", he said out loud, as much for his benefit as the team's. They remained blissfully unaware that this was his maiden voyage. It was considered extremely bad form to ask a Capitano how many missions he had flown and as far as the team were aware, Matteus had merely been transferred to them from a different post. On hypermagnetic locking clamps, the two vessels wanted to float together anyway and Matteus found he only had to employ the slim side elevation thrusters once before the two craft crunched together and locked.

"You do the honours Tenent", Matteus offered generously and the surprised - second in command got on the public address and informed the passengers that they had docked and disembarkation could commence. The duty was usually the Capitano's but Matteus could see nothing wrong with getting the junior on his side ready for future flying together. He strolled down the corridor leading to the area he knew would take him onto the Destino, as he did so he was delighted to enjoy the strains of Forth Worth Runaway One by the same minstrels as before. At the far end of the conduit, he was greeted by a second Tenant, the latter saluting crisply,

"Welcome aboard Gubernator, I am Tenant Plenusia Tazza Circumerario".

Matteus could not suppress the smile that played across his features, the stunning woman's epithet-suffix had been judiciously applied, her breasts were not something any self-respecting man could help but admire.

Even in her black uniform, indicating that she was salaried by a different company to Matteus' own, the dark nature of the fabric did nothing to lessen the impressive nature of her chest. She had the short sleeveless jacket popular in the heated interior of inter-planetary vessels of the time. At certain angles and body positions, such would doubtless billow slightly and offer some lucky admirer a rather profiled view of one such globe. Matteus had to deliberately make an effort not to stare.

"Once the passengers are aboard are we ready to get underway, Tenant"?

"We are Gubernator, the only checks that need completing are yours, Sir. Can I take you for'ard now and introduce you to the crew"?

"Yes, what size compliment is there aboard"?

"The usual in the control room and engine room, five in each and the usual support staff of seven to keep the passengers happy. So we are at full strength of seventeen".

"And two of the seven are a doctor and a nurse"?

"Yes, Gubernator, as is the usual case with an Intrepid Class IP ship".

"You're probably suspicious of my questions, but I've done mainly freight runs recently and just wanted to make certain my knowledge was up to date", Matteus lied.

For her part, Circumerario simply nodded, as was the circumspect position to take in the circumstances.

"Good, lead the way to the control room and let's see how the passengers are getting on. Once everyone is safely strapped into their cots or situated in the habitat ring, I want to get underway".

When they arrived at the aforementioned location though, the Navigator had something to impart to Matteus.

"I've had a communication from Mercury Solar Flare Tracking Unit, Capitano. There is a chance that we could be encountering a bit of a phenomenon that could entail our ride being a tad bumpy, this flight out".

"Can you be specific and more accurate when describing the exact nature of this so-called phenomenon"? Matteus asked.

"A geomagnetic storm, Capitano, registering as a possible 4.25 on the Coupland Scale".

The scale, as devised by none other than 'the' Captain Coupland who had found the Martian caves up in the north of that world started at zero [obviously and finished at 9. The latter reading would destroy every piece of circuitry on a space-going vessel and effectively maroon it in space until rescue came along. In rare cases, it could cripple to such an extent that valuable safety factors were rendered inoperable and the ship could explode. Anything from a 7 to a 9 was therefore enough to cancel a flight to be certain of not risking lives. A modern ship could effectively brave up to a 3.5 with the bulky shielding they had built into them. That left the range of 3.75 to 6.75 when it came down to the captain's Judgement as to how much risk to take. A 4.5 would not be something a very experienced captain would worry greatly over. Unfortunately, Matteus had not the luxury of such time spent in space and first-hand experience of the phenomena. If he either delayed the launch or worse still cancelled the flight altogether though, the crew would all know how callow he was and soon start asking for transfers. It would be the worst sort of start to Matteus' career as an inter-planetary commander and one it would take quite some time for him to recover from. He decided on that basis to risk the flight and conceal his concern to his crew. If he was lucky the storm would not come within 1% of a parsec from the Destino anyway. Ultimately that was what it would come down to – luck, good or bad.

"I think we'll be all right, I'm not going to cancel the launch", he told his new crew. That should have been the end of it, but it was not.

"Permission to speak freely, Sir and to offer up an opinion"? It was Tenent.

"Granted"? Matteus wondered what the girl was wanting to say.

"I think perhaps a postponement rather than a cancellation might prove prudent a 4.25 is not something we want to be playing with".

"We? Tenent"?

"I mean the circuitry of the vessel Sir".

"Your position is noted, Tenent, but as we are not operating a democracy and as the company does not like having to pay compensation for delays to flights, we will set out for Mars on schedule".

"Compensation is far greater in the event of loss of life, Capitano", Circumerario was not willing to let the subject drop. Matteus noted how it was causing tension in the rest of the control room team.

"Are you suggesting that you are not confident to act as my second officer in this mission, Tenent"? Matteus made his tome as stern as possible.

"I am merely doing my utmost to make all relevant facts and risks available to my commanding officer, Sir", the girl backtracked a little.

"And you have done just that, thank you, Tenent. I feel confident we will be able to complete our flight with as little incident as possible. I am now ready to start the initial burn".

Before she could say anything further, Matteus threw the old-fashioned metal toggle that would induce the cold-fusion reactor and the Destino jolted forward. Then he turned to his navigator,

"Maintain acceleration until the optimum speed is achieved and then cut burn, Navigator. I am going to the galley and get myself something to eat. Circumerario, would you care to join me".

Knowing why he was asking to get her in a one to one situation, the girl grimaced but grudgingly agreed,

"Yes sir, Navigator Fiducia, you have the conn".

The unlikely duo left the quieter than silent control room under the strain of something of an atmosphere and the girl led Matteus to the staff galley. He let them order, seat themselves and begin eating before making any comment.

"You seem especially nervous about encountering a GMS, Tenent, would you care to elaborate, or is simple caution the only reason for that little display back there"?

"I cannot answer that without asking you a rather leading question, Sir", came the honest reply.

"Ask me then"?

"Have you ever encountered a GMS before, Sir"?

"No", Matteus answered quickly, "Have you"?

"I served on the Orsobruno back in '55, Capitano".

"Ah"!

It explained Circumerario's attitude toward geomagnetic storms. Systems had been shut down on the vessel in question when it had encountered a GMS rated only 4 on the Coupland scale. Even so, a vital valve safeguard had been knocked out by the electromagnetic field, for just long enough to cause an overload in the reactor. Two conduits had ruptured under the resultant pressure and the chief engineer and his deputy had been vaporised in the explosion. Not only that but the Orsobruno had been en-route to Mercury when the accident had occurred and the vessel was only just saved as it plummeted Sun-ward, with a couple of hours to spare. Had a search and rescue tug not been available in a nearby zone, the entire vessel, its crew of twenty-one and one hundred and eighty prisoners due to be incarcerated in a sub-mercurial correctional facility would then have been incinerated by the life-giving star of the solar system. The latter would not have been missed so much by IYWIWSI as the vessel, the most expensive element of the expedition and then the lives of the staff aboard it.

"I heard it got a bit hairy on board for a while. Must have been frightening for you all".

"A bit hairy"! Circumerario's pretty lips twisted in bitterness for a while. "It was tragic about the engineer and his junior, but also their carelessness contributed to the disaster, they should have checked those systems before we left dock-orbit. What was truly calamitous however was the guard who the prisoners killed whilst trying to overpower security, when we were beginning to heat up inside the can. Ufficiale Guardiano was a good man. A good friend and a fun personality, there was not a person in the crew who did not mourn his passing".

"Very sad I'm sure", Matteus sympathised, "But you were so much closer to the Sun, a GMS in that region is likely to be that bit more charged and as you say your engineer had not completed the required level one diagnostic before launch, or if he did he did it very badly".

"And as we are seated one another enjoying what the cook has prepared it is easy to make observations like the one you have. I, though - lived through that accident. I experienced moments when I thought my number had come up, that, with all respect is not something you can empathise with. It is something you have had to endure personally. I just hope your gamble pays off, Capitano because that is what you are doing, you are taking a mighty risk. It will either end well for you and you will forget about my constant cautions, or you will come to me afterwards and tell me that you had wished you had erred on the side of caution and postponed the launch".

"I am grateful that you have taken the trouble to do so", Matteus concluded, "We shall see how events unravel".

Wisely, Circumerario decided to leave the matter there. They finished their meal and were making their way back to the control room when it happened!

The ship...shivered.

Matteus found he could not term the happening in any other way, the tremor was exactly like a brief spasm of the body's muscles. He did not ask his Tenent what she thought it might be but rather they exchanged a meaningful glance and hurried back to their mutual destination. As the door slid to one side, the Navigator was already waiting for their return and began,

"We just encountered a space anomaly, Sir".

"Anomaly", Matteus repeated, "What was the nature of the abnormality, Navigator Fiducia"?

"We are still correlating data, Gubernator but I believe it might be a pre-shock".

"A pre-shock? Something announcing the arrival of a disturbance. That's very good, Fiducia. It is also so much lexemicbabble. See, I can create a new language too. Find out and then give me something concrete".

"Yes, Sir".

Plenusia Tazza Circumerario, Tenent of the Destino, took her station languidly, but not before she had offered Matteus a knowing glance. *'She's a cocky bitch and no mistake'*, Matteus thought, but he could not deny her conviction or her pluck. Before he could congratulate himself upon the way he had dealt with the much easier Navigator though, the ship shivered for a second time.

"I'm going to have to hurry you for your analysis, Fiducia", he found himself barking. It was The Tenent who answered him though.

"My instruments inform me that the waves are emanating forward from the approaching Geomagnetic storm that is heading this way, Capitano".

"Do they indeed", Matteus left his seat and bent over the voluptuous second in command, "Care to show me your readings Circumerario"?

She did not shy from his proximity, rather pointed at her bank of screens with a long-nailed finger, "Here is a representation of the inner solar system", she began, "Here is the sun, here - our intended destination, Mars. This misty area in between is the projected path of the geometric storm. Now we can continue on our course and arrive at Mars dead on schedule, or, we can now detour. If we do the latter we also avoid the pre-shocks we have been experiencing and the storm itself".

"And exactly how long will the detour delay our arrival time, Tenent"? Matteus did not think he was going to like the answer.

"That depends upon how much latitude you want to give the storm, Sir. There is a balance between levels of safety versus delay".

"I understand that", Matteus smiled, "Compute a series of options for me". Then to the science officer, who thus far had not said a single word, he asked, "What has been the level of damage sustained by the pre-shocks, Officer".

"None, Sir, the vessel is still functioning within acceptable parameters".

"So the pre-shocks are no threat to us at all".

"Not to the ship, Sir", Tenent again, "But passengers do not like a bumpy ride. It makes them nervous at worst, dissatisfied at best. Don't forget they fill out a survey at the end of the voyage and our performance is part of that analysis".

Circumerario was beginning to get on Matteus' nerves, the main reason being that most of her analyses were based on experience that he did not have.

By way of an answer, he asked her, "Do you have those scenarios for me yet, Tenent"? To his annoyance though, she nodded,

"I have a choice of three for you Capitano".

"All right then, let's hear them"?

"We can reduce our level of risk from the storm by 100%, 75% or 50%, the delays will be ten, eight or six hours to our rendezvousing with the Mars shuttle".

"So instead of a thirteen-hour journey, we would be asking the passengers to endure either nineteen hours in space, or twenty-one, or even longer"?

Tenent nodded, "But all would arrive at the destination unharmed".

"While that is eminently possible even if we stay on our predetermined course"?

"The pre-shocks would tend to indicate that perhaps the 4.5 Coupland scale assessment is not accurate, Sir".

"Tend to indicate, not imply for certain"?

"As you are already well aware, Sir, nothing is certain in space".

"Yes, thank you, Tenent. I am aware that nothing is certain, nor is it uncertain by the same maxim. I think we shall ride the storm and get our good paying customers to their destination on time, that is my decision, Tenent. I am certain this crew will get us through without any trouble".

An ominous silence descended on the control room once more. Matteus, being new, did not know if such was the case usually, or not. He had heard quite enough recommendations, he was the Capitano and they were going to do it his way, whether they liked it or not. After an hour, he felt his confidence growing, the instruments showed the storm getting closer, yet there were no further shocks and he began to believe it had all been girly hysteria from the all-female team who were beneath him in the room. Then suddenly every single light, every single reading and all other systems died!

"Report, at once"? Matteus demanded, feeling his bowel fill with ice and turn to mush. "Is this a system-wide failure, what caused it? Could it have been anything else other than the storm"?

Tenent Plenusia Tazza Circumerario turned to him and her face was wan with loss of confidence. She was not even gloating when she replied shakily,

"We cannot answer any of your questions, Sir, every single circuit in the ship has been rendered useless by the storm. No way was this a 4.5"!

"You are certain that it was indeed the storm and not something else"? Matteus demanded.

"To knock out all systems all back-up systems and emergency power simultaneously, it could not have been anything else Capitano", the science officer informed him.

"Stay calm people", Matteus urged, wishing he could follow his advice. "We simply wait that's all, till we drift out of the range of the thing and some of our systems start to reboot".

"If we haven't suffocated by then", Fiducia observed bleakly.

"How long will the air remain breathable if the black-out gets lengthy"? Matteus demanded.

"We have no instruments to calculate that, Sir", someone whispered. Matteus was getting sick of the situation and barked,

"Somebody give me an informed guess then damn it"?

"I guess we can last for about 180 minutes without the air filtration and circulation", the science officer offered, "After that, the older passengers will start to collapse, then the youngsters and finally....".

"Thank you, Officer, I get the general drift of your assessment". Matteus cut her short.

After an hour though, everything suddenly burst back into fully operational life! Matteus had been wondering what he had worried about, for the next few hours. The rest of the voyage went smoothly enough, the odd matter to sort out with the passengers, but nothing to cause any grave concern. Once they had been told the reason for the power outage, they seemed happy enough. Indeed some of them had experienced the same before and with nothing like the experience the Tenent had related. He thusly congratulated himself that he had gambled and won, until...

"We have a problem Capitano", Circumerario told him once everyone had transferred to the shuttle and they were making ready to return to Earth.

"Nothing we cannot rectify I'm certain", Matteus smiled confidently, "What's the problem, has one of the female passengers broke a nail and is having to have a fry-up"?

"No, Sir", Tenent winced, "Eleven hundred and four passengers are now safely aboard the shuttle and waiting to descend to Mars".

"Eleven hundred and four"?

"Eleven hundred and four, Capitano".

"If memory serves me correctly we had eleven hundred and five passengers when we left Earth"?

"There is absolutely nothing wrong with your memory, Sir and you are quite correct, there was indeed one more than is on the shuttle and one Mrs Morrelius is wondering where her husband is".

"I see. So he's ill and collapsed someplace, or stuck in a restroom, or asleep. Start a search Tenent. Use all available crew except for myself. I will sit by the conn until you find the elusive Mr Morrelius".

An hour later Matteus was beginning to feel very frustrated indeed and the missing man has still not been located. The shuttle pilot was demanding to descend to Mars, but Matteus would not release the docking lock on the Destino side.

"Tenent", Matteus demanded, "How long is this search going to take. Mars will be getting impatient, the shuttle pilot is getting impatient and *I* am getting impatient damn it"?

"We've done a physical search, Capitano. The instruments have picked up nothing and the next step is to report him missing to Mars and let them bring up more sophisticated equipment".

"More sophisticated than the Orang-U-Can systems installed in the Destino"?

"Deutsche Fahrzeuge Eingearbeitet Incorporated detection probes, Sir".

"The Kraut military stuff"? Matteus was incredulous, "What do we want to do find the poor slob, or shoot the living khakk out of him"?

Should I continue searching areas we have already searched Capitano or radio Mars"?

That wiped the smile off Matteus' features, he stormed, "He cannot have just disappeared, Tenent, he has to be on the vessel somewhere. Where else could he have gotten to"?

"Space, Sir, through an airlock".

"We would have detected that one had been opened on our...". Matteus stopped - mid-rant. Of course, the instruments could not have registered the airlock being opened and closed if they had done so whilst the ship was blacked out. It was possible to open such with the wheels in the locks in just such an emergency. They were the only thing operational in the Destino during a blackout. Seemingly reading his thoughts, Tenent Plenusia Tazza Circumerario said into the radio, "I believe we have either a suicide on our hands, Capitano, or a murder".

'Koof'! thought Matteus, 'I did everything to avoid delaying my maiden flight and now I'll be held responsible for the death of a passenger'! He was forced to allow his second officer to contact Mars, the company would not see the matter from his point of view he knew. Matteus Crespo Gubernator's career was over before it had even begun!

eight. In which our hero discovers that tampering with the natural flow of the fourth dimension is far more complex than he could have envisaged.

"Your Aunt did not know where he was either. When the geomagnetic storm hit the Destino, Lynea was naturally terrified, supposing that the ship would be damaged maybe even explode and get them all killed. Any other one of a catalogue of bizarre possibilities I suppose. So Decorum insisted she stay safely in the cabin while he went to find out what was happening".

"And she then claimed he never returned" Mingfu Li added.

Huahua was quite angered by that, "I'm not sure I like what you are implying with that remark, Fu. Do you want to ask me to believe that my ancestor was a murderess"?

Nigh countered, "If one goes back far enough into one's family history it will like as not always be possible to find one, Cousin dear! So, the ship emerged from the storm and not long afterwards docked with the Ares. Lynea told the customs staff what she knew and the search for him began. It revealed nothing".

Mayling chuckled, "And Lynea had the esort and eaccount numbers of Decorum's thumbank! She could easily have drugged him in some way and tossed him out the nearest airlock to end up with the money and be free of the Morrelius' in the same action. She had the opportunity if she had the motive. As was said earlier experience and incident can change people, Nigh".

"Not that much", Nigh forced himself to offer before turning back to his distant cousin.

"Lynea could not be charged with murder when a body was absent"

"It, therefore, seems there is but one way to make this section of the family history complete"! Mingfu Li objected then. "I see that gleam in your eye, Durango, despite our experience in the 77th you intend to defy the Sapientiae and make an illegal journey through the fourth dimension. That is your desire now is it not"?

"I do not see how I can leave my Aunt to the grim fate of ending up in the Martian Phoenicis Wastes, driving into Dead Man's Gap. It truly would be an unsatisfactory way to leave our family history".

For the first time since the latest meeting between them had commenced, Aurora spoke,

"Durango, you should not go alone onto a space vessel plunged into darkness by an unpredictable storm. I volunteer to break the law of the 77th with you".

"Just hang on one second there", Mayling objected, "I am the one trained in combat and with the apropriate type of experience, it should be me".

"Yet I am his fellow Chronowoman", Mingfu Li observed.

"While I am family and the only one who will recognise my ancestor in addition to Durango himself", Huahua threw her hat in the ring.

Suddenly everyone was looking at Nigh, he began hesitantly, "Even though I am going, for the sake of my ancestral Aunt, I am still aware that the future authorities may hunt me down in our future here as a result of my activities if their instruments detect what I am doing to the timeline. I cannot ask anyone to take the same risk when only I possess the ability to keep one step ahead of them".

"You're not asking", Fu smiled, "We're all volunteering".

"And in doing so tying your fates in with mine".

"Something else we are all happy to do", Mayling noted.

"Thusly it is up to me to be the one to show a certain responsibility", Nigh persisted, "And insist on going alone".

"Mayling warned, "You do not know what happened to Decorum, what if he was attacked by party or parties unknown, can you defend yourself against so many"?

"I think I can look after myself", Nigh smiled.

"Yes, but can you also look after your Aunt, while you are being tasked"? Mayling persisted. "You said yourself that you have no idea what effect your cause may reap in the 51st. Even a tiny change in the past can have devastating consequences in the future. That you believe in the butterfly effect. Well, what if that effect is already manifest in *this* future"?

"Go on"?

"What if your first jump, which you *will* make soon resulted in your Aunt being spared the same fate as her lover when your *companion* protected her? By not taking anyone with you, you could be consigning *her* to the airlock"!

Nigh's head span but he understood the paradox well enough. History only showed the effect of the voyage, not the particular. If he did not take anyone with him to keep an eye on Lynea, then, while he did battle with the theoretical assassin[s] she might be attacked.

"You are trying to tell me to take someone with me because I *did* take someone in the future", he grinned, "That is one very convoluted argument, Mayling".

"Drop a pebble in a still pond and the first few rings are of no great diameter", Mingfu Li argued, not for the first time, "But the rings get bigger and bigger and can result in a tsunami in the far upwhen".

"You have been corrupted by that wicked old Chronoman you met in the 77th", Huahua flared in defence of the mission and her ancestor. Once more Nigh was forced to hastily intervene,

"Ladies, please. I have listened and thought about what all advise, I will take everything into account. I am going to my bedroom now. I am going to lay on the bed and think everything through and when I come out I will give you my considered decision. It will not be open to further debate". The question uppermost in his mind was, did he still care what had happened 18 centuries in the past? Care sufficiently enough to risk the ire and resultant punishment of the Ministro do Tempo Estudos e Tempo Viajando? Was Lynea's fate a sad one, but an immutable one and had he, Durango Nigh, the right to tamper with a medium no one man could ever claim to understand. Travelling through the fourth dimension was relatively unknown in current times. The mechanisms for doing so would not be perfected until the 77th century and those few chrononauts who had appeared in history had been strictly regulated by a series of rules. Rules that breaking would result in execution when the time traveller returned to the 77th or beyond. There were very good reasons for that.

The most profound of all the rules being the most logical one:- A Chrononaut must do nothing to change the historical events contemporary to the period that he/she is visiting. Infringement of this rule will incur the death penalty.

Of course, no one could ever know if this rule had been secretly broken. For, if a chrononaut did manage to change history then all collective memories and records of that event would change in the merest of fractions of a second. That was the usual reason why chrononautia invariably travelled in pairs with extensive historical records loaded into their pads. For then the comrade of he or she who broke that rule would be able to operate outside the new reality. Their pad would exist outside the timeline and a simple check would reveal the nature of their unintentional but none the less indefensible crime

The reasoning brought him to an inescapable conclusion, he could not possibly go alone! Rising he strode into the lounge and declared his intention. Fortunately, Mingfu Li had gone to work, so that was one problem out of the way because he was not selecting her. His feeling concerning Aurora was that her investment was less so he did not mind disappointing her, that left his distant cousin and the bodyguard and he knew who would be most useful on the mission.

"I've decided to take Mayling with me", he declared, "For the simple reason that she can take care of herself better and would be less worried by the attention of the futuristic combmen sent from the 77th if our little trip is detected by the sensors of the Ministro do Tempo Estudos e Tempo Viajando". To his surprise, Huahua nodded and added, "Logical, I'm disappointed, but I understand how you've concluded that you have".

"Then there is no further need for delay, are you ready Mayling"? Mayling Fuchow, former Elucidator known as Shen Huan nodded and before Nigh could instruct her, she strode over to him and melted into his embrace. A very pleasant sensation indeed. Her body felt very similar to Mingfu Li's before her, curvaceous, soft, warm, stimulating. It took considerable effort for Nigh to send his Andhera Tantu into the correct form of meditative action to achieve his intentions. He felt the floor suddenly disappear from beneath his feet, just as had happened the first two times. This time though there was a difference. Of course, for the first time, his outward was downwhen. The smell of pink and the gentle tinkle of violet assailed him and he tasted C#. Pungency filled his hearing and he felt brilliance touch his skin. Before him, a mooing temporizadoor opened in the aching of the ether. The sensation was not so much disturbing as disorientating and strangely tremulous. His senses were capable of registering in areas hitherto closed off to them, he saw emotions, tasted colours, felt musical notes and heard a sweetness. There was the sense in his subconscious of an enormous clock with a white analogue face. Around its inner perimeter Roman numerals, not one to twelve though but in tiny characters, years. He identified the correct year, the correct date, in a way he had no way of understanding he even found a locus in space. Thought his way toward and then inside the Destino. The floor of the apartment was abruptly replaced by the metal decking of a vessel, the duristeel throbbing with the power of a cold fusion reactor. When he opened his eyes it was to find Mayling's beautiful face very close to his, her perfectly bowed and rouged lips almost touching his own and he had to make a conscious decision not to kiss her. She had designed, for herself, one very sexy woman had the Elucidator. He released his grip on her splendid figure and glanced about him,

"Scorement, what a ride"! She exclaimed in 51st-century linguistics.

"Scorement indeed", He smiled and glanced furtively about him. "We have gravity, so we must be in the habitat ring. That's a stroke of luck. Now if my feelings were correct we have an hour to find the couple we are looking for before the storm knocks out all the systems and whatever happened then happens".

"You don't get to say that sentence many times in a lifetime", the Elucidator observed. "Do you want to split up and double our chances of finding them? We can always keep in touch with our padfon"?

"Good suggestion, you've seen images of my Aunt and Decorum, so your chances of locating them ahead of me are 50-50. you go up there, I'll go down here".

The girl nodded and began to depart, Nigh found himself watching her ass as it retreated away, clad as it was in clinging pants of some silky material of some kind. *'I'd eat my lunch off that'*, he could not help but observe. His hormones were beginning to become something of a nuisance to him. Four sexy and attractive young women were making it plain to him that they would become willing bed partners and he was doing nothing about it. Perhaps when he got back to the 51st .... concentrate, concentrate, there was a mission to fulfil before he could worry about his gonads. Mayling was oblivious of this storm she was causing to course through Nigh's body as she slunk away. She was also ignorant of the fact that she was not the only one who was watching her. For there had been a witness to the appearance of the duo as they had flickered into the time stream, someone who had no inkling of such possibilities, but who was then forced to realign his belief in the possibilities of transmutation through, at the very least space if not through time as well. The man was lean, his dark face chiselled and blue with dark growth even though he had shaved the morning before he had slipped onto the shuttle that had brought him up to the Destino. Ironically he was in the same line of work as Mayling. She had changed her occupation to one of a bodyguard, while he still served that function part of the time, but also continued to act as an assassin when required. It was in the latter capacity that he was currently being thumbrolled. He had boarded with identity programme and tickets proving him to be one Negotius Viatori Clanculum, a businessman from China, but Welsh by birth. That was not his real name though, he was known to his employer as Fiscarte and the one who now paid his wages was none other than Alexius Morrelius Gravis. It had not been easy for Fiscarte to find the trail that Decorum had unwittingly left in his wake when stealing his own Father's wife – his step-mother. Gravis had made funds available to the assassin though and even in a world that was rocked with decimation, there was still room to purchase what one required if one had the price. At least for a while. Over the next few years, business on Earth would stumble, but at that moment in time the effects were yet to echo down the next decade and even then it would be a trip rather than a nasty fall. Of course, Fiscarte could not know who Mayling was or what she was doing aboard the Destino. Similarly, she was ignorant of his existence. Ironically though, both of them were seeking the same target – Alexius Morrelius Decorum. The male then became the female's stalker. He did it covertly though and she had no idea she was being followed. Fiscarte had years of experience when it came to the art of concealment and surveillance and he was not about to get seen by the mysterious Oriental who seemed to have appeared out of thin air only moments before. He was worried about the man who had become reality at the same instant, but he could only be in one place at a time and Gravis would have to attend to him. He used the touchpad in his hand and promptly sent a message to his employer. Gravis had boarded the vessel as Propinquus Occisius Malaehaevus, with all the necessary forged identity and tickets. He intended to see to his *dear wife*, while Fiscarte dealt with his son. The threads of time where beginning to weave a quite complex fabric, all was becoming cause and effect. The effect could be so much different if the causatives were manipulated by those who should not be at the loci. Fiscarte drew his needle gun, unaware that the girl was carrying a dramatically superior weapon in the Trebora Dicoidtree Electrique pistol she had nestled against her thigh. She did not know he was there however and that was a distinct advantage. Someone was coming, it was one of the stewardesses. The girl hesitated before the mysterious traveller when the latter held up a hand indicating that she desired her to do so.

"Excusimenamoment"? Fiscarte heard the girl ask in a rather strange accent he could not quite place. Though he had never heard the contraction before either, it was easy enough to understand.

"Yes, Madam"?

"I am Mrs Pollopanie from suite 595, I seem to have lostwaylament in all these corridors, can you give directivate, so I can returnage to my husband, please"?

The girl blinked, she got the gist of what this strange oriental was requesting but was puzzled by her strange phraseology. Fiscarte began to think she was not of that time even. Could this be one of the infamous 77th-century chronowomen he had read about on the SWW?

"Mrs Pollopanie"? The stewardess was sceptical and with good reason, perhaps there had been no Orientals getting on the Destino and she had been present at embarkation?

"Correcti". Every time the stranger opened her mouth she made herself seem even less of a reasonable fit on the vessel. The stewardess must have decided that she had taken enough time over the simple request for directions and suddenly blurted such without further conjecture. Then she hurried on her way. It seemed that the two of them were after the same quarry and they were both on the wrong floor or level of the habitat ring. The ship vibrated for the merest instant, Fiscarte thought of it as a shudder. What was that all about? He was not the most comfortable to space travellers at the best of times and the shudder put him off his stride. He had heard the directions too and it was time to eliminate the competition and get on with the job he was being paid for. There would be an investigation when the Destino reached Mars, but all the authorities would know was that two passengers had vanished and two airlocks had been opened. Conclusion a suicide pact perhaps? Now there was another factor, the stewardess would remember the strange Oriental who had asked for directions and feigned being the missing woman. That would certainly deflect the combmen from looking too hard at Gravis and Fiscarte. Whoever the girl was, she was providing them with a rather convenient cover. Provided she was not around to explain what she was doing on the Destino. Fiscarte came to a simple and inescapable conclusion as he followed the girl to the lift at the end of the corridor, she had to be eliminated!

Nigh exited the lift and glanced at the first cabin door. The number on it told him exactly what he wanted to know 501. It was a very long gently curving passageway that if one followed it without entering any of the rooms, one would find oneself back at that very spot. For level 5 of the habitat-ring was a circulate ingress. Nigh began to trot down the couloir, wanting suddenly to see his Aunt again, inform her that he had returned to the 33rd to offer her his protection. He was not exactly certain when the storm would hit the ship, but he knew he had time enough to stop Decorum from leaving the cabin.....unless?! No! He refused to believe it was Lynea who had committed the murder of her lover and then had the vitality and daring to drag his corpse to an airlock open it manually and toss his cold corpse out into even more frigid space. There simply had to be a different explanation. The LED's in the floor began to blur into a dizzying dotted pathway as he progressed and he soon had to slow to a walk due to sweating rather than labouring for breath. The walkway was boring too, all dove grey, with sloping sides and roof. Nigh tugged at the collar of his boho shirt and two of the twisted fabric buttons popped open to reveal the dragonfly pendant he wore around his neck on a silver pendant. He had no reason to explain why he occasionally thought of the insect in particular. Stranger too, the tiny black and white cat that frequently filled his dreams. Shaking his head to dispel the aberrations, he glanced at the door he was currently passing, 527. Of course, they were spaced reasonably widely apart, they were separated by the width of a three-roomed suite. The lift doorway hissed open and the girl slunk inside. Reasoning that there could be no better time to eliminate this unforeseen annoyance Fiscarte dashed from the alcove that had been currently concealing him and cried out,

"Hold it for me, please"?

The doors had almost hissed shut but Mayling threw out an arm and stopped their progress allowing the man to join her. It was that act of kindness that sealed her fate. For a couple of seconds, the two of them blinked in the much higher level of illumination in the confined duristeel container.

"Which button"? Mayling asked

"Sorry"?

"Which button do you wanpressing? Which floor are yogoing to"?

"Ah, gotcha fifth, I'm going to the fifth level".

As Mayling leaned forward to depress the one button for both of them, her weight shifted forward, while her eyes left him for the briefest of instances. That was the moment of his opportunity. He drew his needlegun with a swiftly fluid movement that nevertheless the former Elucidator caught in the corner of her almond-shaped eyes. Mayling threw herself down onto all fours, heard the phut of the archaic weapon as it discharger its slim projectile. The needle hit the side of the lift with a faint metallic clink and fell to the floor of the box. Mayling threw out the leg closest to her attacker and dragged it forward with every ounce of strength her thigh muscles possessed. Her foot caught the back of his knee, the one at her side and he stumbled, throwing out an instinctive arm to stop himself impacting the back of the lift. Mayling chose the instant to launch her body back onto her feet. In the time it had taken her to do that though, the man had brought the weapon up into a firing position for the second time. Throwing the centre of her frame onto her left foot, she drove the right at the man's wrist. There was a satisfying smacking sound as pseudo leather met skin and the needle gun went flying from his grasp, hitting the wall of the lift with a dull report. Fiscarte recovered well though, bunched both his fists, he had no reservations about hitting a young woman, when she had some weaponry of her own. He rushed toward her one fist snaking out, aimed at Mayling's throat. In the brief but violent exchange, she had not had the opportunity to draw her hand weapon and she still did not then. The man's fist struck her a glancing blow on the side of her neck, but immediately she felt the sting of something sharp and glancing down at his hands saw was had done the slashing.

He was wearing a blade-ring and the tiny razor would have been coated with something that would soon render her insensible. Desperately she backed away from him and went for her Trebora Dicoidtree Electrique pistol. Almost at once the terrible knowledge that the drug, whatever it was, acted almost instantly and she felt herself slowing down as his fist crashed against her jaw.   Fiscarte   caught   the crumpling form of the girl's body Vinenovalidissimus was the fastest working toxin on the market, he was already holding onto a dead body.

Nigh rapped on the door of his Aunt's suite, several thoughts were crowding his mind at that moment but he least expected what happened next.

Nothing!

There was no answer. It had not occurred to Nigh that he might reach the room only to discover that the couple were not in it. Yet it had always been a real possibility. Now he was faced with a ship-wide search and all before the storm hit. Ironically he was running out of time! He should have arrived shortly after take-off, how stupid of him not to have thought of that before? Cursing he rapped one more time, but it was plain that the suite was unoccupied. Better to quarter the habitat ring as part of a team of two. He pulled out Paddie.

"Mayling, are you there? Mayling, please answer I've hit a major obstacle"? Then to the padfon itself, he asked, "We're still connected are we not, Paddie"?

"Negative"

"Please reconnect then, I asked you to keep connected"? Nigh felt his ire growing

"The connection was broken at the other end and I am sending, but there is no receipt. The padfon of your friend is no longer functional".

"A breakdown! Now of all the times for it to happen. Can you give me the location of the padfon the last time it was working"?

"Certainly the lift at the end of level 3, it was halfway between this level and 4 when the signal stopped abruptly".

"Surely not a power failure, the storm has yet to hit the ship"?

"No, the central processor suddenly failed".

"I don't suppose you have any idea why such a relatively new unit's CP would just pack up like that"?

"I have a theory".

"All right, let's hear it then"?

"A sudden and violent impact".

"She dropped it"?

"A more severe impact than that".

"Theorise, Paddie".

"The padfon was subjected to a sudden and violent impact".

"Right, which way to the lift, let's get moving"?

Fearful of what he might find, Nigh raced toward the location where the incident must have happened. He frantically thumbed for the lift and then waited anxiously for it to arrive. It seemed to move very slowly. Finally, the doors hissed to one side and Night gazed keenly around for any sort of clue as to what might have happened. He found a discharged needle on the lift floor, a few dints in the sheeting of its walls. Evidence of some sort of struggle and no sign of either a padfon or Mayling. If he could not act when the vessel got to Mars Decorum would no longer be on the Destino. If he could not find his companion and she was still aboard, then she would be the logical suspect and would end up in prison or executed. That was if she were still alive. He had to search for her and or his Aunt and her lover and locate them before whatever had happened – happened. He had never felt so helpless, so devoid of direction. The only place he could logically return to was the suite. At least he would get a chance to talk to his Aunt if nothing else transpired, for she had been in the suite when the storm had hit. Then he remembered that so had Decorum. Fool, fool - fool. He was making all the wrong judgement calls. If he had waited for the two of them to return, then he would surely have encountered them? He would have to worry about Mayling later, his priority was to the man who had disappeared and indirectly, Lynea. Now he was resolute he began to race back to the suite. He dashed past doors and finally was just turning the last corner by his estimate when....the corridor was plunged into darkness. The ship bucked and a strange sensation seemed to prickle his skin. He had wasted the time originally calculated to perform the rescue. As he tried to plunge further forward, he collided with someone in the darkness.

"Sorry," said the voice, who have I just banged into, crew or another passenger? Any idea of what is going on"?

"The ship has just flown into a geomagnetic storm", Nigh found himself saying into the darkness, "It will last a while but not indefinitely. Keep calm and everything should be fine".

"Oh, well I'm glad we bumped into one another then, my wife was very worried and I've come out here to see what I could find out. I never realised it would be pitch black. I recognise your English accent, I wish we had met under better circumstances, Sir".

English, sent out by his wife to find out what was happening. On the fifth level of the habitat-ring. Surely it could not be?

Nigh blurted, "My name is Nigh, Durango Nigh. Whom do I have the pleasure of addressing in the dark, Sir"

Nigh heard a sharp intake of breath and then nothing, as the man processed what he had been told.

Finally, the cultured English voice asked, "Durango Nigh? The Durango Nigh who went to Mars and tried to stop General 23 releasing the SX"?

"The very same", Nigh agreed, "Nephew of Lynea Morrelius. If I'm not mistaken I am speaking to Alexis Morrelius Decorum and you are travelling under the name of Pollopanie"?

"I was told you had some rather surprising powers, Sir. To be candid with you though I thought some of them exaggerated by the pride of a loving Aunt for her only nephew".

"Then you are Decorum"?

"I cannot see any sense in denying it as you seem to know the answer to that already".

Nigh said urgently, "We have to get to safety somehow. I believe you might be in danger, I have come to protect you"?

"From my Father and his unwholesome henchman, do you mean"?

"Exactly so", Nigh could not tell his Aunt's lover that she was an actual suspect in his future disappearance.

"Then we must get back to the cabin, to Lynea. Who knows what...".

"No, Decorum, you are going to have to trust me, but it is you who are in the most danger. I do not have time to explain just now, but I have to get you out of this corridor and go somewhere not near your suite".

"How can you expect me to leave your Aunt if you have reason to believe my Father is somewhere on this vessel? That is what you suspect isn't it"?

"Yes, but she is not Gravis' target. You are"!

"I don't see how even you can know that"?

"But I do! I'll explain when you're safe".

Nigh grabbed Decorum's clothing, felt fabric for the briefest of instances and then the material twisted out of his grasp. He heard footsteps retreat from him. How senseless Decorum was acting, they were in pitch darkness, he had no chance of finding the one room he sought. Yet if that was true, how could the similarly blind Nigh ensure his safety? There was only one way. Take him upwhen. To do that though he had to be holding him in a tightly grasping hold. Nigh blundered forward, hesitated, listened. Crept forward some more. He was so frustrated he could have wept. The futility went on for several minutes and then, the lights flickered back on. First at emergency power level, then full illumination. For an instant the two of them looked at one another, both with thoughts racing through their minds. Then Decorum suddenly turned and ran away from the location. A glance at the nearest door informed Nigh what he was about. Decorum was dashing back to the suite he knew he had left Lynea inside. There was no longer any need for Nigh to dash in pursuit. He, therefore, walked calmly, congratulating himself as he did so that he had foiled at least one crime – the disappearance of Decorum himself. After several moments he reached the open door of suite 595, it would be pleasant to see his Aunt for a brief while before returning to the 51st.

"She's not here"! Decorum's eyes were wide, his hair in disarray. He had just finished searching the rooms, which had not taken very long.

"She may have gone after you", Nigh tried to sound calm. "A search will doubtless discover her at some other location on the ship".

"You'll help me find her then"?

"Of course. You turn right out of here, I'll go left if she's not on this level we will meet at the lift and search each level until she turns up".

Decorum was too excited to reply verbally, rather he nodded furiously and left hastily without a backwards glance. Nigh followed at a more sedate pace, closing the door of 595 as he did so. By the time the two of them did rendezvous at the lift, however, he was beginning to feel less confident. Surely Lynea could not have stumbled so far without any light whatsoever. A certain nagging doubt was beginning to trouble him. What if.....

.... the person who had slain and disposed of Decorum the first time this thread of time had passed through the eye of duration had some sort of light source? Had found Decorum gone from the apartment, so had taken Lynea and....

Nigh was beginning to feel dread grasping at his guts. Could it be that in saving Decorum form the killer, he had directed him/her to his Aunt instead? Was the person responsible for Mayling's abduction, even now holding both women hostage somewhere on the ship. The public address system suddenly barked into life,

"Will Mrs Pollopanie please report to the steward's lounge, where her husband is waiting for her"?

Decorum had decided not to comb level 4 but instead sought the help of the crew. Maybe not such a bad idea? Nigh could not locate Mayling [or not] with the same time-saving device though, she was not even supposed to be on the ship! As it turned out, as Nigh grimly continued to search alone, the tactic Decorum had thought to employ was not bearing fruit, for the message was repeated a second and third time. Time was proceeding and all Nigh was learning was the fact that he knew even less regarding the circumstances of what was happening on the Destino. He could spend the rest of the voyage to Mars looking for people who could be moving - or no longer aboard, or he could go to the steward's lounge and simply wait with his Aunt's lover. He chose the less taxing of the two, physically at least.

"I thought you were here to protect us", Decorum greeted with an accusation.

"It was dark, remember, I was doing my best. I have lost a companion too", Nigh reasoned,

"Our best strategy now is to wait for rendezvous with the Ares and see who disembarks".

"And what if Lynea is missing? Then what? Where could she be"?

Nigh did not want to answer that frantic question, did not want to contemplate what his meddling in time had inadvertently resulted in. He was even beginning to see why Adalberto Almeida Sapientiae had urged him not to break the tempuslaws. The wait was not an easy one. Neither man felt like talking so they remained seated in maungey silence until the ship braked, clunked into a lock with the Ares and the public address told all passengers they should assemble at the airlock. It was the moment they had been desperately waiting for. Positioning themselves in a location that allowed them to watch everyone else presenting their etickets for inspection as they passed through the lock, they waited some more. At one point Decorum acted as though he recognised one man, but after a second glance decided it was not whom he thought it might have been. It was Gravis, but as the man was wearing a fleshmask, harmoan [special badly cut wig], coloured contacts and platform shoes, he fooled his son and everyone else as he passed him by quite closely. Fiscarte had already gone aboard the shuttle and similarly escaped Decorum's inspection. The queue finally exhausted and a member of the crew asked the two of them for their papers as they were waiting to disengage the lock.

"I cannot", Decorum announced, "My wife has yet to pass through this check".

The girl checked her pad, "But with the two of you, we will have the correct number", she objected, "You must have missed her, she will be waiting for you on the Ares".

"We've been here from the commencement of disembarkation and she has not gone onto the shuttle, check to see if you have Mrs Pollopanie"?

Looking puzzled and more than a little sceptical the girl nevertheless checked her pad manifest and her forehead consequently wrinkled in confusion, "That's very odd. You are right, Mrs Pollopanie has not passed through the check, but we are only two short of the correct total and there are you two ready to disembark"?!

Before Nigh could stop him, Decorum blurted, "I see why that is, Nigh here did not get on the Destino in Earth orbit, he got on later".

At such a bizarre revelation the girl made a quick hand signal to someone behind the two of them and Nigh turned to see a very attractive Latin woman approaching them, dressed in the uniform of an Italian lieutenant.

"Is there some difficulty here"? Plenusia Tazza Circumerario asked. Nigh thought even her contralto voice was enticing.

"My wife, Mrs Pollopanie, is missing", Decorum could not be silenced even with one of Nigh's best glares. The girl crew member added hastily,

"She has not gone aboard the shuttle to go down to Mars Tenent, but we are only two short in the overall count and when I pointed this out to Mr Pollopanie, he said this other gentiluomo had not gotten on the ship at Earth orbit"!

Nigh saw the good-looking donna's hand creep toward her sidearm as she asked in a gentle tone, "How then did you get on the vessel, Signore"?

Nigh was not about to let a woman dictate the course of the conversation though and he countered with an enquiry of his own.

"The explanation is simple is it not? I did not get on a ship that was travelling through space at tremendous velocity. What is obvious though is that a search needs to be made for the passenger your staff have misplaced – Mrs Pollopanie".

The crew member could not be contained though, she persisted, "If we find her we will have a person too many though"!

"A few moments ago", Decorum suddenly accused, "You did not even think *anyone* was missing, now your dubious records show you have too many passengers when my wife in unaccounted for. I suggest you check your manifest and put it right and I want to know when you are going to start looking for her"?

Both Nigh and Decorum stared at the lieutenant, which was not the worst thing one could do with one's vision. She seemed to conclude and called over two more of the crew,

"Start a ship-wide search for Mrs Pollopanie. Once we have located her we will recheck every passenger currently waiting to go down to the planet. I will let the Capitano know what is happening".

She turned to Nigh then,

"Can I see your papers, Signore"?

"I've had them inspected once already", Nigh lied easily, knowing the confusion would allow him to get away with that subterfuge, "Once Mrs Pollopanie is found I will present them when we are all checked again".

He was wondering if the search would reveal the body of his one-time Elucidator but suspected she, like his Aunt, had probably gone out through an airlock.

"Would you like to pass onto the shuttle then, Signori".

"No, *I* would not"! Decorum came to Nigh's rescue yet again. "I can search just as well as your crew".

"No, Signore you cannot", the lieutenant reasoned, "Certain areas are off-limits to you. Having said that if you wish to search the habitat ring and other areas that your wife might have visited, then I do not see why we cannot enlist your aid".

She turned to Nigh, "I did not get your name, Signore"?

"That is because I did not give it to you", Nigh grinned mischievously. "I will accompany my friend here, as I said before, you can task me once Mrs Pollopanie is found"!

His feeling of triumph soon transmuted into frustration and dread. Of either woman, there was no sign, not no sign of a body. Nigh did not wait around to see if the crew reported the use of an airlock before the storm. It made no difference. Whoever had killed Mayling had gotten rid of her into space and when he had done it was immaterial.

"I cannot help", he finally confessed to Decorum, "It looks like your father and his hired killer have slain your step-mother".

"But you were here to prevent that, how could you have botched the job so magnificently"?

"I came here to save you, which I have done, but the consequence is that while keeping your attacker at bay, he or they turned his or their attention to their secondary target. Don't worry I can still mend what has been done, I can arrive sooner and prevent what has occurred today".

"Oh, and what happens to me"?

"You will know no difference, but you will find Lynea and together the two of you will enjoy the rest of your lives on Mars".

"If my Father and his killer fail to harm either of us on this voyage, what is to stop them doing so once we reach the planet"?

"Me! I will stop them, no matter how many times I have to create tempusdoors, Decorum I will succeed".

It was as good a time as any to make good his escape and go down in history as the mysterious slayer of his aunt, but he would find a way to fix it, for now, it had become a personal quest for him. With the power of the andhera tantu and the techniques the yogi, Doshi had taught him, Nigh created another Phase-door through the ether and dimensions of four. He figuratively willed his being to step through it and emerge into the apartment in the year 5057 as the calendar of Earth reckoned the passage of the years. Of course, this time he was alone, Mayling was dead.

For the moment!

Nigh would rescue her, of that he was resolved so to do. He glanced around the apartment to make certain his tampering with the timeline had affected the future [his contemporary events then] in no deleterious way. For a while, it seemed that nothing was different in even the tiniest of details, but then he got a shock and found the first difference.

"Paddie, we might as well get it over with, can you connect me to Huahua so I can tell her of the failure of our first attempt"?

"Whom"?

"Huahua Morrelius, my distant cousin, the one who put thoughts of saving Decorum into my head in the first place. She gave us her number, just connect will you"?

"There is no such person in your contacts, Night"

"Don't be silly and do not add a 'T' to the end of my name, if that's a joke I'm not amused, you know I get it all the time and it annoys the Gehenna out of me".

"Mister Night, there is no contact in my memory banks of a person with the name you are giving me and you do have a 'T' on the end of your name".

Nigh thought about it. Of course, there would be no Huahua in the newly established timeline he then found himself part of. Lynea had never survived, never had children, as a result, Nigh was the last of the line and somewhere in the new records, the infernal 'T' had been added to Nigh's name. An error that he was now stuck with until he rectified it that was. A nagging doubt started in the back of his mind then, What if by tampering again he would solve some problems but create new ones? No matter! He had to try and save Lynea and Mayling, he was determined to go to the infernal space vessel again, at least once more at any rate.

"Forget I asked Paddie, I'm a tad confused. Do something else for me will you, Look of the SWW registry and find out if there is still a Mingfu Li living here and if one Aurora is still in Fuchow"? The padfon assured that there was. Nigh(t) was relieved, at least he would have someone to relay his first adventure to that evening. He found then that he had missed both the attractive landlady and his equally lovely admirer and he would feel much better once he had told them what had happened.

He was wrong!

When the door opened several hours later. Nigh(t) had relaxed in a nice hot bath and changed into housewear. With the entrance of Mingfu Li though every scrap of relaxed contentment vanished.

"You're back how did it go, where's my girlfriend. You promised you'd keep her safe"?

Nigh(t) looked at the youth and could not respond. Mingfu Li was a man!

It took him several seconds to reply and when he did it was to ask, "Have you ever had reorientation"?

Then it was Mingfu Li's turn to be puzzled, he asked,

"My sexual orientation do you mean because if you do, I don't like the idea of that sort of thing, I'm proud to be heterosexual and comfortable being a man. That's a strange question to ask me. Now, where is Mayling"?

"Dead", Nigh(t) saw no reason in prevarication, "I think she was killed by the very assassin who was going to kill Decorum before I prevented it".

Mingfu Li seated himself heavily on the couch and said nothing more. Nigh(t) felt obliged to add to his explanation,

"We split up to search for Decorum and I found him. Mayling must have intercepted the killer before the storm hit, but he or she must have gotten the better of her and she went out the airlock instead of Decorum. I could not save Lynea from the mysterious assailant either. I suspect it to be Fiscarte".

"So you took Mayling with you, despite my arguments, got her killed and your Aunt too. Great mission, Night".

"Not only that but Huahua has never even been born now", Nigh(t) was miserable.

"Huahua"?

"A descendant of Lynea who firstly got me interested in our family history".

"Never heard of her, you're sure you're not hallucinating, or maybe those black worms in your skull have turned you sort of demented"?

"You met Huahua when you were a girl", Nigh(t) persisted, realising only too late that it was a remark that was doing far from helping or clarifying the situation.

The male Mingfu Li

"How soon can you pack your meagre belongings and get out of my apartment"? Mingfu Li demanded angrily, "I'm sure Aurora will put you up".

So she existed still and was still willing to help. Nigh(t) saw no point in staying where he was not wanted, even for a short time. He asked Paddie for Aurora's address and got it and then returned angrily,

"I can be out of your hair in ten minutes Mingfu".

"Then do it"! The response came as the man slammed the bedroom door behind him.

Nine. Multiverse.

"May I come in", Nigh(t) asked the lovely creature before him.

She offered him an enthusiastic smile and held the door open so that he could pass through. Even before he was inside and looking around curiously, she asked,

"How did it go? Did you save your Aunt's lover? Who was it that had made him disappear? It wasn't other chronomen was it"?

"I failed, Aurora and in the process lost Mayling, she is almost certainly dead"?

"And the man that your Aunt was with...".

"Oh I managed to save him, but in the process whoever had gotten rid of him, took my Aunt instead".

"I'm sorry, Durango. What will you do now? Sorry sit, I'll go and make some tea, you can tell me exactly what happened then.

Once he was sipping the beverage Nigh(t) told the girl everything, even down to the change of his surname and the disappearance of Huahua whom she had, of course never, met. Her first response was,

Mingfu Li - a woman it's hard to imagine".

"I'm having a difficult time seeing her as a man, believe me. Anyway, he's thrown me out over Mayling".

"I wondered what was in the bundle. You'll have to stay here then, I'll make the bed up for you in the second bedroom, unless of course...".

Nigh(t) smiled tiredly, "Yes that would be most kind of you, I will pay my way, you do not need to worry".

"You know that sooner or later you will be pressurised by the government to take a wife, don't you? I will be devoted to you, I will work hard for you and do what I can to keep you happy and I will always love you".

"You barely know me, or that much about me Aurora. You're sweet and attractive and I can imagine that we could be happy together, but right now I have more pressing things on my mind than my happiness. Due to my incompetent stumblings, I have cost the lives of two people whom I cared about".

"You cared about Mayling? Did Mingfu Li know about it, he can be...".

"As a friend, Aurora, I cared about Mayling as my friend and when it came down to the important moment, I could not protect her".

"You cannot do everything, be all places at once. I think you are judging yourself too harshly".

"And I think I am not judging myself as harshly as Adalberto Almeida Sapientiae would".

"The question now is, what is your next move, Durango"?

"Good question and fortunately I have a plan. Firstly you will go and get bathed and ready to go out. Then I will take you out to dinner. Then we will come back here and get some sleep. In the morning I will take you back to the 33rd century and this time I will try and get things right".

Her eyes glittered with excitement, "We are going on a date"?

"A dinner-date yes. Dinner is just dinner, right"?

"It could be or...".

"Dinner is just dinner, right"?

She pouted her disappointment and nodded, "All right, it's just dinner. Tomorrow though, you're taking me with you"?

"You wanted to come the first time, now I'm giving you your opportunity. If you still want it that is".

She threw her arms around him and squealed, "Of course I want to time travel with you". Before he could stop her their lips were together at her instigation. It was far from an unpleasant surprise. She tried to mould her every contour into his and he playfully slapped her on her pert behind,

"Go and bathe and make sure the water is cool you're overheating you....".

"Saucy weasel", she laughed, "I'm a saucy weasel". She danced away so that he could not swat her a second time. When she was ready he had to admit that she looked stunning if sparsely dressed, but it seemed to be the fashion to wear as little as possible so who was he to criticise.

"Do you have a favourite place in Fuchow"? He wanted to know, "I will take you there".

It was called the Lü` gōngjī [Green Cockerel] and was on Aotou Fengling Road on the opposite side of the road to the Hakka Characteristic Side Dish Taocan Crock Shop, which had become a sky-scraping establishment of some thirty floors.

Both of them enjoyed an excellent Kung Pao Chicken and were sipping white wine waiting for their respective desserts when a figure from Night's past suddenly emerged out of the crowded interior and without asking for permission seated herself opposite him. He was so shocked and surprised, the arrival of the newcomer rendered him speechless".

"What is the matter, Darling? Don't say you have forgotten me. Though it has been 18 centuries for me, it hasn't for you has it"?

The devastatingly beautiful redhead android that was Ruari smiled and waited for one or the other of the Homini to respond. It was the Chinese girl who was first to find her tongue,

"Durango? Who is this person"?

"No person", the android replied in his place, "I am an android".

"What does one of the overseers want with us"? Aurora tried to bluff her way out of the situation, even though she guessed exactly whom Ruari had been sent by.

"General Acwellen demands your presence at Shattered Fang", Ruari said to Nigh(t), practically ignoring Aurora, "He thought that by sending someone who's body you had repeatedly used for your carnal desires and gratification, that you would not damage it".

Aurora gasped and then Ruari smiled cruelly and crudely observed, "Don't worry dear if he is currently cattle-prodding your oyster ditch with his love pistol, it's been 18 centuries since he squirted his saline baby gravy into my interior circuits".

"We are having dinner", Nigh(t) finally managed, "And there is no room for your crudity at it. Please desist at once".

Aurora sounded horrified as she asked aghast, "You lay with a machine, Nigh(t). You....you...."?

"And a very great deal of pleasure he had doing so as well. I hope you are keeping him satisfied in that department, little Chinese Homini".

"That's enough, Ruari", Nigh(t) snapped, "Leave the poor girl out of this. I fact leave. Go back to your master and tell him I do not seek a meeting, but thank you for asking".

"He is not requesting your presence before him, Nigh (she left the 't' off), it is a command".

"I think perhaps I don't want any sweet now. I think I would like to leave".

"Just one moment, Aurora and I will take you", Nigh(t) told her hastily, "Go please, Ruari you are spoiling our meal. Tell your master that I do not recognise his authority over me and respectfully decline his directive for a meeting".

"He has authority over all you Homini", Ruari returned glibly, "Therefore, as you are Homini, even if mutated in some way, his dominance over you is a given".

"No, Ruari. A23 has self-appointed governance over all the peoples of the 51st century. I am not from this time, I am beyond his authority, I have travelled ...".

As the very words left his mouth, Nigh(t) knew he had made a mistake by letting the android know that he had time travelled more than once.

"You can do it over and over? With control? Could you take My Lord Acwellen into the past"?

"So he could make his dominance over mankind span even more of history, forget it. The SX was bad enough once, he should never use it again, or he will have no subjects to rule over".

"He has done great good, Durango", Ruari reasoned then, "He sterilized the wound and saved the limb. Had he not done so the entire body would have become corrupt and died in its poison".

"I see 18 centuries have made of you - something of a philosopher", Night could not hide the scorn from his voice, "You speak in metaphor now, to hide the most heinous crime that was ever perpetrated against the human race".

"It is very doubtful that we will see eye to eye on the issue", Ruari reasoned, "So that area of our conversation should be closed now".

"As should any other", Nigh(t) added. "We are opposing forces who have divergent viewpoints, so for you to expect cooperation from me is also unrealistic, Android".

"Then I am authorised to use force to bring you before my supreme commander".

Should you try I will flee through time, just as I did with High and Mighty Machine number 23. Your task is thusly rendered redundant. You should return to him and tell him his authority is ineffectual against me".

"He hopes that I would be able to convince you to agree to a meeting, the force would only have been as a last resort".

"There is not last resort as I have already explained. Go home to Shattered Fang, Ruari".

"My Lord Acwellen does not suffer failure with magnanimity", the female android told him then, "He may decide to vent his ire on me".

"He has emotions? How can that be? He is a robot. An automaton, a mechanical contrivance - without emotions".

"Over 18 centuries he has managed to exceed his original programme matrix, Durango, he will be angry with me for arranging a simple meeting between the two of you".

"A simple meeting is optional, so I choose the negative option. As we have already determined I am the one human he cannot command. Therefore, he sent you on a fool's errand. I would not go back to him and tell him you had failed I would not go back to him at all".

"You think it possible that I could hide from him? Wherever I went he would detect me".

"Wherever yes, whenever not so".

Ruari blinked rapidly and enquired, "You would hide me in a different time"?

"If you wanted me too. To save you from the mechanical tyrant that A23 seems to have become. If disassembly is a real option and not just a device you were using to try and coerce my cooperation, then I would hide you somewhen".

"I must consider this as a real option", the android smiled, "Now I will leave the two of you to finish your meal in peace".

When she had gone, dessert promptly arrived, her presence delaying it. They ate in reflective silence for a while before Aurora noted,

"She was very beautiful, no human girl could hope to compete with that level of physical perfection".

"Perhaps you might be right, but she has some serious character flaws, not least of which is her choice of associates", Nigh(t) grinned. "One more drink before we go"? Aurora nodded eagerly. They tried to generate the same atmosphere as they had enjoyed before the android had intruded upon the event. It was not the same though, so they went back to Aurora's apartment. The girl showed him his room. Not quite as nice as the one he had occupied at Mingfu Li's bigger abode, but quite satisfactory.

"You do not have to sleep in here or try and move around in it you know"? Aurora tried once more, "The master bedroom is three times the size and we would be more than comfortable. Of course, If I repulse you then that's entirely different"?

"Stop being obtuse", Nigh(t) said a little briskly "I find you a very nice person and a very very pretty thing, but right now I want to focus my andhera tantu on other more pressing issues. If you wait till all this is over, then we will examine where we are Aurora".

"All right", she finally conceded defeat, the second female to do so that evening. "Good night then Durango".

"Goodnight", he did not move toward her, there would be no more caresses either snatched or instigated by either of them. He did not think sleep would come easily. Yet as his head touched the pillow he fell into an instantly dream-filled and troubled slumber.   Not surprisingly his dream was about his former lover Ruari, she was smiling and telling him that she had successfully converted to Homini. He asked what that meant, what had she done. She had revived the opposite of alterations a person went through to become a biotron. When each of her circuits was removed she had them replaced with stem cell culture-organs. Ruari had biologised herself in an attempt to become a woman. They could thusly be together she informed him then, for as long as they both lived. Something was wrong though, Nigh(t) could not conceive of a grown brain. After all, if the brain was replaced then the person was no longer the same identity. It was the mind that made the individual, not the body, in whatsoever shape or configuration. Then it was that he instinctively knew that Ruari was not a woman, never could be one, never could be anything other than a machine with biological organs. A train seemed to pull into the station backed by the oscillating sound of electronica. He felt a tremendous disappointment and awoke racked with the perspiration of Incubus. He glanced at the bedside-chrono 04:27. Too early to arise, too late to achieve deep restful sleep once more. He lay there simply thinking for an hour and then reluctantly arose. He realised that he had no better idea of a strategy than the first time he had jumped into the downwhen. History recorded events for certain. More so with the SWW than any other time that had gone before it. Even then though it did not concern itself with the minutia of everyday occurrences. Unfortunately, it was in the detail that the chronoman could succeed or fail. Nigh(t) still had no positive proof that Gravis or Fiscarte had been responsible for the disappearance and probable death of Mayling and Lynea. For all he knew in the second run of that fateful flight it was Decorum who had killed his mistress for some reason and been forced to add Mayling to his list when she happened upon the fatal act. On his second quest should Night concentrate upon finding the women, this time once again at the expense of Decorum? It was not so easy doing the right thing when one did not even know what the right thing to do was. Despite these shortcomings, Durango Nigh(t) was going to traverse the leylines of time by entering a tempusdoor once again. The trouble was he did not know which of a series of actions by him, would be the right ones to select?

*　*　*　*

"I will be your Tenent for the duration of the flight to Mars, Sir. The name is Plenusia Tazza Circumerario".

Matteus looked the tanned beauty up and down and thanked his lucky stars. His second in command could have been a right battleaxe. As it was she was very fetching indeed.

"Are all preparations other than my checks well on the way to being concluded, Tenent", he asked. He was impressed when she informed him,

"They are finished, Capitano, once you are satisfied all is in readiness for take-off, you can leave exactly at the appointed time".

"Good work. Can you direct me to the control room then, please?

"I am going there myself, Sir. If you care to follow me"?

Matteus did care to follow the rather tempting Tenent. She would probably already have someone taking care of her needs. He remembered his promise to Matteus but goodness it was not going to be easy if his second in command was typical of the temptations he was about to encounter. The duo entered the control room and an all-female crew looked up and were in turn introduced to their new commander. Matteus thought the Navigator, one Fiducia rather an appealing prospect as well. Very Italian, all flashing eyes and pouting lips, he could imagine her in a black sequinned low-cut frock, her hair tied back into a loose ponytail, long danglers in her ears. With only the greatest effort of will power, he pushed the fantasy to the back of his mind and tried to concentrate on what she was saying to him.

"....4.5 on the Coupland Scale, do you want to take any remedial action, Capitano"?

"A storm", he mused. His maiden flight postponed or cancelled, not likely, it would cast a long shadow over his service record, "We'll set off as scheduled, but make a detour if such proves necessary".

The Navigator nodded, but Circumerario was not satisfied with his decision and began to relate a nasty experience she had endured in the past as a direct result of a GS.

"You were most unfortunate, that is certain, Matteus acknowledged, "And we will react to circumstances as and if they arise, Tenent. Is everyone aboard yet"?

They were.

"Instruct the engine room we are going out and will need the appropriate power from the reactor", Matteus ordered. The Tenent was persisting with her objection regarding the wisdom of sticking to the schedule, however. Once he had heard enough Matteus declared,

"I appreciate your industry in that regard, Tenent and your objections are noted, but I am now engaging the main thrusters. No further comment from you is necessary, thank you".

It shut her up, but she continued to glower at him. Once the vessel was in coasting velocity, he declared,

"Fiducia you have the conn. Circumerario, you and I are going to the crew galley for a spot of working brekkers". He could not fail to notice the grin of satisfaction on Fiducia's features at the way she had been preferred over the Tenent to steer the powerful craft. The instant they were clear of the ears of her subordinates, Matteus asked,

"What in Gehenna is wrong with you Tenent? I gave you my decision once you had expressed your concerns and you wouldn't let it go. You were bordering on insubordination"?

"I told you why I was most concerned, Capitano. We are heading for an unpredictable and possibly hazardous phenomenon. I don't think, with respect, that you appreciate the level of disruption even a 4.5 can reap on this craft".

"Well, of course, I do", Matteus reasoned. "You, based on your past harrowing experience are overreacting. I have made the command decision to not delay the launch and should the GS prove a sticky situation then we can deal with it at the appropriate time".

"A GS is stickier than the stickiest thing you can think of Capitano".

"Just what are you implying by that remark, Tenent"?

"Only that the viscous and agglutinative nature of a GS is far more tenacious and viscid than you can realise, Sir, unless you have encountered one before. The theory does not do it justice".

"Are you trying to suggest I lack experience".

"General experience no, Sir. Involvement with a GS yes, as you have already told me you have never flown through or into one before. I'm thinking primarily of the safety of the passengers".

"Always a commendable consideration and one that does you credit", Matteus conceded, "Now, what would you like for your brekkers, I'm buying"?

*   *   *

Into a disused corridor, a couple of figures suddenly rippled the ether entering the leylines at the rate of a second per second utilizing an unseen doorway in the space-time continuum. The male was a rather average looking sort of individual in no way exceptional. Yet his appearance was deceptive because with the power of his brain alone he had just brought the pair of them back through centuries. The other person, an Oriental girl was far easier on the eye, but to date had done nothing of great merit in her life. She was eye candy without real substance, but certainly a visual treat. Nigh let Aurora loose from his embrace, she looked as if she had been enjoying the enforced intimacy.

"The first thing we have to do is find Mayling", Nigh repeated for perhaps the third time in total. Paddie, connect".

"Will it not be weird meeting your earlier self", Aurora was curious, "Which one will be you"?

"That's a question for philosophers or the superstitious", Nigh muttered as the padfon gave him directions to intercept the duo who would have just appeared seconds behind them. "Come on we have to stop the two of them splitting up, or the girl will be killed again".

"Not again though really", Aurora was suddenly introspective, "I mean it hasn't happened for the first time yet, so it can't be...".

Nigh grasped her wrist and jerked her toward the location given him by Paddie. The two of them broke into a trot and rounded two bends that both revealed the same corridor winding out of view each time. Then they found the couple they sought. The look on Mayling's pretty features was one of astonishment mixed with incredulity, but not so the earlier or later version of Nigh (dependant upon which view one was taking).

"Something went wrong", the Nigh who was with Mayling deduced at once. (Hitherto referred to as Nigh[m]).

"You are not to split up", Nigh who was in the company of Aurora (Nigh[a] from this moment onward) replied to himself, "If you do everything goes badly wrong".

"Then we shall stick together", Nigh[m] promised himself. "We have a little time, tell me briefly and factually what happened".

Nigh[a] did so and Mayling went pale at the news of her imminent death. Nigh[m] assured,

"You stay with me from now on, don't worry I'll keep you safe".

With that decision, Nigh had rethreaded the timeline. It caused Nigh[a] and Aurora to wink out of existence.

"Goodness, where have they gone"? Mayling gasped.

"Well I'm here and Aurora is back in the 51st", Nigh answered, as though it were the most natural thing in the world "You didn't want to be the girlfriend of Mayling Li did you"?

"I cannot think of a universe in which that would ever happen", the Elucidator responded. She and the former were rivals for Nigh's affections and barely tolerated one another.

"Right, we know now that my Aunt and her boyfriend, her actual step-son are not in their suite, so we can eliminate that possibility and look for them elsewhere. This means they will either be in the cafeteria or the interplanetary duty-free shops. Would you like to hazard a guess which"?

Mayling considered and returned, "A woman would want to go shopping, while a man would want to eat, so I guess it depends upon who has the stronger personality. Do we know that"?

"Not the sort of thing that usually gets historically recorded, so no, we do not know that", Nigh conceded. "So my earlier self has helped, but insufficiently it would seem".

"Don't be so hard on yourself, it was only your first attempt to save Decorum and in that task you were successful".

"At yours and my Aunt's expense by the sound of it. I cannot decide whether we should search for them, or Fiscarte and Decorum's father. What would you do if it was your call"?

"Stop those who want to do them harm and it solves the mystery of where Decorum went. He was murdered and tossed out the airlock by either the assassin the father or both".

It was not quite so black and white to Nigh, but he still found the notion more appealing than simply trying to protect a victim. To do that was surely only a temporary solution. They would follow the couple to Mars and catastrophe would only change location and date, but with the same result.

"Right then", he decided drawing his energy pistol, "Be ready to kick some ass Mayling".

"Why would I wish to treat a perissodactyl mammal of the genus Equus in such a way and what would it solve, Durango"?

"I'm sorry I used a 33rd-century analogy and Unwanted States vulgarity. I meant let's go and act forcefully or aggressively toward our enemies".

"All right, now you're yapping", Mayling tried to enter the moment, but the result was an amusing if abysmal failure. They went to the main thoroughfare of the habitat ring and began to look for Lynea, find her and it would lead them to those who wanted to harm her, that was the theory. Mayling had seen a holophote of Nigh's Aunt so she knew what she looked like, similarly, Decorum, what they did not bother with was images of the assassin and Gravis, for both would be expertly disguised. Suddenly a voice neither of them knew, or could be expected to, said in stentorian tones

"I am here to arrest you Durango Nigh, for breaching several regulations of the Chrononautical Code of conduct and breaking even more of its laws".

Nigh turned to see a tonsured tall man of some 200cms in height and with barely a gramme of fat, his frame being comprised totally of muscle.

"I'm sorry, Sir", Nigh tried, "But you seem to have me mistaken with someone else".

The Tempus Agent looked thoughtful for a second and then an image sprang to life in front of him, it was a perfect holophote of Nigh himself. It seemed some devices were built into the human body in the 77th century.

"Are you an android"? Mayling asked.

The agent shook his head, "I'm sorry how rude of me I am TA 5423Dorph and I am human. The abbreviation stands for Tempus Agent, my name is 5423Dorph".

Drawing his pistol in one swift movement Nigh shot him at close quarters and caught his falling body. The pistol was back in its holster before anyone had noticed anything amiss.

"What are you doing"? Mayling was surprised despite herself.

"When you have to shoot, you shoot, you don't talk", Nigh explained, dragging the inert form to some chairs on one said of a vast walkway.

"You've not killed him have you"?

"Of course not. I only kill when there is no alternative. He should be out for about an hour. That will give us time to get the mission completed and get back upwhen".

Mayling said no more, one thing about Nigh that she found appealing was his eternal optimism. They resumed their search for the elusive couple, but before they had managed to encounter them Mayling felt the hairs on the back of her neck rise when she ran her eyes over a man walking into a nearby store. She was experienced enough to trust her instincts and grasped Nigh's forearm.

"That man retreating from us, going into the fragrance boutique, I think he is wearing a realistic gel disguise".

"A silicone mask, how can you tell"?

"They are good, but not quite good enough to fool scrutiny to the trained eye. He is either Gravis or that assassin of his, you'll have to trust me on that".

"Very well, I do. If it is one of them we can be certain the other is not far away. I'll go after him, while you scan the place for a second gel, all right".

"What are you going to do"?

"Make certain he does nothing to Decorum".

There was only one way of assuring that permanently. But Mayling could see the need for it.

"At our present course, the GS is going to swirl around and catch us in the cross sweep". Fiducia told Matteus. "What do you want to do Capitano".

"How much of a course change do we need to make to avoid it altogether. Give me the answer in additional hours to Mars rather than kilometres".

The navigator did some calculations on her console before giving him options. "If we make the barest minimum change and still might catch the very tail of the GS it will delay us six hours, Sir. On the other hand, if we want to reduce our chances of disturbance to a greater safety margin then it will be twelve. If we wish to be certain that nothing and no one is harmed at all then we can either divert to Venus and go to Mars tomorrow or encircle the entire area resulting in eighteen hours of the moratorium".

"I recommend we divert to Venus, Sir", the cautious Tenent interjected before Matteus could even process the various options.

"Delay us a whole day on a half-day flight, that would not look rosy in the flight records would it, Circumerario"?

"Admittedly you would look very cautious by your decision Capitano, but everyone would arrive at Mars accounted for and well and the ship would suffer zero damage too".

"Had flight M3282-07-09 been an ordinary journey then the lieutenant would have been quite correct. As certain people knew though flight M3282-07-09 was anything but!

* * *

Nigh added hastily, "Try not to go too far away, I don't want to lose you again".

"I think I can handle the Father", the girl promised confidently.

Nigh followed the man with the strange inexpressive features, the closer he got to him the more he thought the back of his hair was just too perfect and it did not deem to move right. It was rather obviously a Harmoan. Many bald men wore wigs, but Harmoan's were the ones that stood out for their ill-fitting cheapness and poor colour matching. Named after the 2D comedy actor who had ludicrously tried to get the gullible to believe it was his hair. The masked face was furtively glancing about him, obviously searching for something himself and Nigh knew who that was. The store was crowded. The discounts were good. There was no help for it though. After all, the fight and resultant violent demise of one or other of them could well cause panic but Nigh would never see any of these people again.

Or would he?

"Fiscarte you son of a pig, turn and face me and take that ridiculous disguise from your naturally misshapen head", Nigh bellowed. Several people turned in surprise at the outburst as the killer, instead of doing as demanded turned to try and run away from his mysterious tormentor. He had his back to a glass and duristeel counter though, so had nowhere to flee to. Nigh performed a flying kick to the man's chest before he could decide what to do himself. The glass was unbreakable and the duristeel was not about to bend. So the softest matter that received the full impact of the blow gave way. Nigh heard the crack of several ribs even in mid-air and as he landed once more on his feet saw Fiscarte gasping in severe pain. He fumbled in the folds of his Edwardian frock coat and Nigh brought down the edge of his hand like the sharpened blade of an axe. The second crunch of bones caused the pistol to drop from nerveless fingers with a clatter of metal and nyloplanyon cushion-floor. Someone screamed,

"Leave him alone, what's he done to you".

He did not have time to go into a debate with someone whose business it was none of. So he pushed the sentence out of his mind in a split second, his arm shooting out like a lance. At the end of that arm, corded with muscle as it was, his hard fist punched the assassin with such power that it ruptured his heart.

"You've knocked him about enough now", the woman was pushing to the front of a crowd who had gathered to watch the fracas. "Leave him be".

Fiscarte's body was crumpling to the floor and Nigh had no further interest in his anyway. He knew the power of the Paanch Ungaliyaan maut ka Panch [five fingered death punch] had done its nefarious work. Only the father, Gravis, now threatened his Aunt and her lover. He shouldered past the interfering busybody and told her,

"Lady, I just don't have the time".

He had to find Mayling and make certain nothing happened to her, simultaneously hoping that by doing so it would lead him to Gravis as well. Glancing at his wrist-chrono that he had set to localised time he noted two details. The storm was twenty minutes away and at that time TA 5423Dorph would start to emerge from his enforced doze at the behest of the setting that Nigh's pistol had subjected his body to. Ironically no matter how he positioned himself in the past he never seemed to have enough time to complete the mission to his satisfaction. It would be of enormous help if he knew the sequence of exact events, but history never contained such mind-numbingly uninteresting minutia, uninteresting to everyone except he and Huahua that was. The other problem he had was that although he was able to gradually refine his technique of tuning into the correct period to *drop into*, it was still not possible for him to narrow it down to hours and minutes. He had been fortunate in the first two jumps, but get it wrong and he would arrive before take-off or after disembarkation when it would be too late to alter the natural sequence of events. Something he was currently aware of also was that the more jumps he did to the same point in time, in cosmic terms, the more damage he was doing to the fabric of the leylines in that period. An analogy that made it clear was that used by the Sapientiae,

"If time is like a bolt of cloth", he had said to his students and agents, "Then an incursion into it can be likened to a needle being pushed through a certain stretch of the material on it. Make several incursions into roughly the same point and what you would end up with is a hole. A void in the threads for that particular period would only make it more and more unpredictable as to what events would finally emerge from it. It is something that must be avoided at all costs".

Nigh was operating outside the constraints and regulations of the Ministro do Tempo Estudos e Tempo Viajando [Ministry of Time Studies and Time Travelling] though, unwittingly he could cause chaos unintentionally down the timeline if he made too many drops into the same few hours of times passage. He scanned the mall and could see neither Mayling nor anyone who looked strangely artificial. Once again despite his best intention, he had been separated from the Elucidator. There was only one thing for it. He had to find his Aunt and surely with twenty minutes running down on the clock, she and her lover would be in the suite on the fifth level. Nigh raced to the lifts. Before he reached them however something unscheduled happened which astonished him. Every system on the vessel failed and everyone aboard was plunged into absolute darkness!

'How can this be possible', Nigh wondered, *'The storm wasn't due for another third of an hour. The ship must have changed course! It did not change course though'!*

Historically the ship had flown directly into the very heart of the GS. This time-thread was not the one recorded in the history records, or the records were erroneous. Only then did Nigh, in a flash of insight propose a theory which was one that the chronomen of the 77th had been aware of for some years. If time was like a fabric, rather than a simple thread, then what his andhera tantu might have done inadvertently was landed in *roughly* the same spot both times. Roughly was not precisely and instead of landing in the same place he had landed upon an adjacent thread in the fabric. Even then it was close enough for him to have encountered the first expedition, but he would have to be careful in the future if he needed to return to the ship. If he jumped too many threads short of the fabrics thread, he might end up in one that was nothing like the one he desired. Thusly making a change in it would not affect the history of his Aunt at all, but a parallel Aunt on a different timeline to the one he occupied in the 51st. Little wonder that scientists had scrapped the idea of a universe hundreds of years ago, in favour of the multiverse. None of these philosophisings was helping the people he had come to rescue though. Due to meeting himself, he was not even certain he knew who *he* was and it seemed Mayling had been killed once, in one timeline, it was not something the ordinary mind could cope with for long and sever TA's had eventually gone demented with chrono-psychosis. Fortunately Nigh did not have an ordinary mind, so he hoped he was immune to such a threat. He stumbled around, found somewhere to seat himself and did so. There was no point in trying to reach the suite on level 5 in the pitch darkness and the lifts would be inoperative, which would mean using emergency ladders in total lack of light. Sensibly he decided to wait, there was no reasonable alternative. It seemed like a long time though. He could hear the occasional roar of anger, the odd scream. Once the tearing of fabric and a scream of horror quickly silenced. It sounded like one passenger had decided that rape would be easy in the pitched darkness. *That* had not been placed into history! The delay was interminable and Nigh could only hope that Gravis was just as immobilised as he without light or the use of any systems of any sort. Finally, the light came on and he hurried toward the closest lift. Three other passengers hurriedly joined him. Two were going to 7, the other to 4. The couple that was riding to a higher level than Nigh looked like they were together. One man, one woman. The woman looked flushed, her skin mottled and she and the man occasionally share a knowing grin following their eye contact, Nigh thought he knew how they had passed the time when the lights had been out! He got off at 5 and Mayling was in the corridor.

"Did you find Gravis"? Was his first question, but the Elucidator shook her head.

"I reached the suite that your aunt is in though. She's alone, Durango and worrying over Decorum.

"Gehenna's teeth"! Nigh cursed. "Gravis could have killed him".

"It's a possibility, Mayling did not sound fully convinced.

"What do you mean by that, Mayling"?

"What I say, there is another possibility, Durango".

"I know what you are going to say and I don't want to hear it", Nigh was obdurate. "How could she have offed her lover if she was with you while the storm had the ship systems disabled".

"She could not of course. She could have a body stored somewhere now that she cannot get rid of without alerting the ship systems. The only way to determine that is by going back to our own time and Fuchow. If history records that an airlock was opened after the storm...".

"Then Gravis could still be the killer of his son"!

"Or Lynea of her step-son".

"Are you determined to make a mystery of this? A mystery in which my Aunt is one of the suspects"?

"Vengeance or money, both are powerful motivations for homicide, Durango. Are we going to wait until the Destino docks with the Ares"?

"Gravis is still aboard and Lynea is still in danger".

"They are in danger from one another".

"I'm going to see my Aunt. Are you coming, or are you going to see if you can detect the elder Morrelius"?

"I'll stick with you, see what you make of Aunt Lynea".

"What do you mean by that"?

"You'll see in a few moments".

Annoyed, he turned away from her and went to suite 595, tapping politely on the door. Lynea answered and did not show any surprise at her nephew's appearance on board. Nigh simply reasoned that Mayling would have told her what was occurring.

"You are back in this century"? Was her initial reaction, "I do not need protection from Gravis, Durango I can take care of myself, see".

She held out n Hitachi 9mm needlegun.

"Even so Aunt, he is a man and you are girly, in the nicest possible way, you understand".

Lynea did not smile, nor seem especially pleased to see her nephew. Instead, she observed quite coolly,

"I thought there were penalties for unauthorised travel through time, Durango. Will you not get in trouble from that place in Portugal, in the future"?

"The Ministro do Tempo Estudos e Tempo Viajando in the 77th century. I can handle them, Aunt. My priority is to see that you arrive safely on Mars and with Decorum. He has gone missing I understand"? Nigh watched his Aunt very closely and she did not appear to be especially concerned, "He went for a beverage, he'll turn up sooner or later". Then Nigh knew! This Lynea, this version in this thread had no concern over the fate of either Morrelius. She might very well have killed the younger herself. Nigh glanced at Mayling, who simply nodded, she had come to the same conclusion earlier. There was thusly no point in staying aboard the vessel any longer. For whatever had happened to Decorum or was going to happen, was of no special concern to this Lynea Morrelius. They made their farewells and exited the suite.

"I cannot see the future being changed in any way this time", Nigh told his Elucidator, "After all what have we done, killed an assassin, that's all. He won't be missed". Nigh was still very naive when it came to the caltraps of time. Fiscarte had been killed ahead of his appointed time. Dead he could not continue his nefarious activities. Dead he could not be hired to assassinate the despotic leader of the Taiwan uprising - one Jiánhòng Chen. Such would change the face of China from that point onwards. Nigh still had a great deal to learn and soon he was about to do so!

*   *   *

The chronoman and girl released one another from the intimate embrace and glanced about them.

"This isn't Mingfu Li's apartment", Mayling noted.

What Nigh said next astonished her, however,

"No. You are right of course, but the strange thing is it is not Aurora's either. Or rather the room is the same dimensions but the entire décor and furniture were completely different".

They glanced about them. The walls were mid-green, not an especially attractive verdant. The floor and ceiling were brown. Not a rich nigger-brown though, but little more than a dark tan. The effect was insipid, to say the least. Gone too was the comfortable furniture, replaced with pale Camel-coloured Rattan from the Malay. It was the name for roughly 600 varieties of ancient world climbing palms belonging to subfamily Calamoideae. Some called it Manila or Malacca, named after the ports of shipment Manila and Malacca City, the trade name for Calamus Manan canes in Southeast Asia. Aurora has possessed traditional Chinese furniture. This was worrying. Suddenly a green door in a green wall opened and in stepped the owner of the apartment.

"Who are you"? Mayling asked.

"The girl asked, "Has her memory been affected"? She was talking to Nigh as though she knew him and it was not easy to reason that the young woman before them was Aurora.

"It's not that, it is the fact that we remember you with a different appearance", Nigh explained, "I doubt you have had augmentation since we departed have you".

"Augmentation"?

"Cosmetic surgery", Mayling added, "We all have it to help in the teen years don't we, Nigh wondered if you'd had an appearance chance, for some reason or other, although you didn't need one you was nice the way you were".

The girl that had been so familiar to them before frowned and observed, "I have no idea what you are both talking about. I know you though, Nigh and Mayling, you went to try and save your ancestor's lover".

"That's right", Nigh agreed uncertainly, "You just look differently that's all Aurora".

"At least you still look Chinese", Mayling smiled. The last observation drew an outburst of total rage from Aurora and she demanded coldly,

"How dare you say that to me, Mayling. You know very well that I am not a peasant. Take back the insult at once! At once do you hear me"?

Mayling paled and responded, "I apologise, I meant no slight. If you are not...what I called you, Aurora, what do you say your nationality is if you do not mind my asking"?

"I am Taiwanese of course", the girl returned, "From the city of Kaohsiung and I thought you knew that".

"A dramatic change it would seem", Mayling observed to Nigh. He asked Aurora,

"But we are in China are we not Aurora, so what brought you to the mainland"?

"This is Mainland Taiwan, Nigh. Has been for centuries since it was invaded by Jiánhòng Chen, centuries ago. Wait! Are you saying that you do not remember the *Subjugation*"?

"China was invaded by Taiwan, that's ridiculous they would not have the troops to be able to subjugate a country as vast as China", Mayling objected a trifle foolishly given that she and Nigh had just tampered with the timeline.

Nigh had been consulting Paddie meanwhile and he informed his Chinese friend, "I'm afraid it happened two years after my Aunt's flight, in the year 5059 to be precise. Guess who Jiánhòng Chen got to agree to supply troops for the invasion of what is now mainland Taiwan"?

Mayling finally leapt intuitively, "Gravis"!

Nigh shook his head, "23. This Jiánhòng Chen must have risen to power as a result of one person being missing from the timeline".

"The assassin"!

Nigh nodded.

Mayling noted sourly, "You killed the man who would have killed the man who killed my country".

"So what brought you to the mainland then Aurora"? Nigh tried to change the subject.

"I'm a manager of one of the many slave camps here, they produce coal, copper and other mined products".

"Slave camps"? Mayling was horrified. "Nigh, we have to mend this as soon as possible".

"Just a second", Nigh requested, "Firstly we need to see if Huahua is returned to us, if Mingfu Li is back as a female, even if Taiwanese and what happened to my Aunt in history. Then we can determine what our next course of action should be".

"I see only one choice", the Elucidator replied gravely. "That is to try and repair some of the damage our trips into the 33rd century seem to have created"!

Ten.   Male Order by Mail-Order

Nigh was wondering about his two friends Huahua and Mingfu Li. What if they had not followed the Japanese-Taiwanese line but were, Chinese slaves? Were they even still alive in this strangely twisted world that Nigh's tamperings had produced. How could he have envisaged such a bizarrely different world as a result of killing Fiscarte? He resolved that before journeying back to the same blessed ship yet another time, he would do his historical research. Who could have predicted how much a single family history could have distorted the future, with such a micro-change? Nigh had always expected there was a chance that his minor manipulation of events might result in a bantam-repercussion-transformation but instead he seemed to have achieved a grand-sequence-cataclysm!

"I'm going to look for Mingfu Li and Huahua", he decided verbally, "I know where they should be, but I am guessing the geography of the city is now changed, you would be very helpful to us Aurora, will you come with us"?

"While I cannot remember how concerned you were for the Chinese before, nor can I remember the women you speak of, I do remember what we meant to one another, so of course I will come", The Taiwanese replied with a half-smile. Mayling grinned at that, musing,

"You'll have to tell me more about that later. Can you forget for the moment that I'm Chinese"?

"Of course. I am not like some of my countrymen who think the Chinaman is some sort of inferior human".

"Chinaman you say, how did SX affect the population fo the two countries"?

"Oh, that might be different as well, sorry I keep forgetting how much you may have altered things. Well SX devastated China, those who remained were mainly men around 80%. Strangely in Taiwan, it was much different. 90% of those who survived were women, particularly as very few Taiwanese women were killed by the toxin. That's why I ordered you, Nigh".

"Ordered me to do what exactly"?

"Not ordered you to do anything made an order for you. You know on the SWW".

Mayling burst into laughter, "Durango was a mail-order groom"?!

"Well things had not yet progressed to that stage exactly, but yes we met on a dating site, as there are so many women to so few men, we try to look westerly for our partners now".

"Even if you have to share them", Mayling wondered if that had altered. Aurora looked annoyed but merely nodded.

"Shall we set off", Nigh encouraged. "Do you think much will be changed from our perspective, Aurora, in our original timeline there was no war, only the infamy perpetrated by the evil A23"?

"Then the city would look like it did before the flux-fusion bombings"?

"A coalition of modification is a strange way of describing destruction", Nigh noted.

Aurora shook her head, "That's exactly it, that is why flux-fusion bombs were used as opposed to more conventional explosives".

"Oh"? Mayling was intrigued, "How are they different"?

"Probably it would be better for you to see for yourself", Aurora decided and went to the door. They hurried onto the once familiar street and what greeted them was not something either Nigh or Mayling could have possibly imagined. The buildings were twisted and bent contorted into gnarled shapes, so so much so that they seemed to grow into a neighbouring structure. Gone were the straight lines and rectangular windows, there were no recognisable shapes at all. Fuchow looked as though it had been liquefied and then carelessly left to set with no pattern of shape and form.

"Gehenna's Teeth"! Nigh cursed forcibly, "What happened to the people who were inside these buildings that look as though they had been designed by a deranged bedlamite"?

Aurora looked chagrined, "Many were two badly deviated for their organs to continue to function, sadly they died in about a week. Some of the others were too contorted to be much use for labour, they were humanely disposed of".

"Humanely disposed of", Mayling flared, "Do you mean murdered"?

Aurora spread her hands, "Come on Xanthine, they were only Chinese".

"You were only Chinese when we left you to go back to the 33rd"! Mayling moved toward Aurora forcing Nigh to interpose the two of them with his own body.

"Might I remind you that to assault a Taiwanese person, as a Xanthine will incur the death penalty".

"Might I remind you that you would not be alive to see that piece of injustice fulfilled", the former Elucidator stormed.

"Stop it now"! Nigh cried. "We both know that Aurora is not responsible for what happened here. If you want to blame someone blame me, Mayling".

"She won't do that", Aurora smirked. "I've noted the way she looks at you, I know what's on her mind, or should that be much lower? Well, I ordered him, Xanthine, not you. Keep your lustful drives bottled up thank you so much".

"I may be a Xanthine, but you're a Saffronite".

"What's one of those"? Aurora demanded Nigh was puzzled also, never having heard the term before.

"It's a plebeian proletariat Taiwanese, a Saffronite".

"You just made that up, Xanthine".

"I know, Saffronite".

"Enough of this childish Xanthicology"! Nigh demanded, "Any more from the pair of you and you'll both go over my knee"!

"Ooh, me first", Mayling crooned and it caused Aurora to chuckle, despite herself.

"It was this way to Mingfu Li's, was it not", Nigh tried to stay on the quest.

"Xanthine cannot own accommodation, Durango", Aurora informed him then, "If you unknown friend exists it will be in one of the camps".

Nigh shuddered, he did not like the sound of that. He reasoned, "Well as the apartment was just a walk from here, can you take us to the closest camp then, please"?

They smelled it long before they reached it and it was not a pleasant combination of odours. Nigh could have made a mental list of the constituents of the stench but he was concentrating upon not dry hacking. He realised it had been quite some time since he and Mayling had eaten. For once hunger was a good thing, it meant they had nothing to bring up when the mouth got suddenly saline and the area at the back of the jaw began to ache. For her part, Aurora did not seem to find it as offensive and it was plain to the other two that familiarity had bred contempt in the Taiwanese version of their friend. They came to a metal gate in a huge mesh fencing and it was armed by two guards, when they saw it was Aurora approaching though they smiled and she explained to them,

"These two are with me. The woman is from the Island and has come for an unofficial inspection. The man is a real honest to goodness Lord. A peer from England who wants to see how we run our camps. The English might be using this place as a model for a setup they are contemplating in Hartlepool".

"Who do you intend to work in your camp, My Lord", The taller of the two Taiwanese asked him. A stout ugly man with a huge puckered scar running down the left side of his face from his jaw to his hairline. Cosmetic surgery did not seem to be so readily available in this version of reality, or this layer of the multiverse. Whichever way Nigh wished to regard where his tampering had taken him. Whatever he chose to call it, he did not feel it was an improvement on.....anything that he could bring to mind. It caused him to pause and wonder what England would look like in this drab version of the world he had once known.

"Who do you think"? He turned it on its head hoping to deflect and pass muster. The guard grinned. One of his front incisors had a huge ugly chip out of it too.

"Francosian, maybe some of the Belgiagermans from the police action in the North Sea recently"?

'Goodness to mercy', Nigh reflected bitterly then, 'Are we a race of beings damned to be eternally struggling with one another. Jupiter should come down and read the new regulations to us, force us to behave'. Not that he was superstitious, but if he had been he would have gone the way of the majority and felt that there were several gods and some of them were bad while the others were downright nasty.

"Those Belgiagermans, or Krautbelg as my unit called them, they put up quite a fight but they were no match for the Royal Navy. Your suggestion has merit, my friend, you enjoy the rest of your shift and keep up the good work".

"Oh I am doing", the talkative guard continued, his comrade had said nothing up to that point. "Why only an hour ago I had to heavily chastise one of the Xanthine filth for stealing some rice. He'll think twice before doing that again I can tell you, even when the bone sets".

Out of the corner of his eye, Nigh saw Mayling's expression and instantly sought to distract the sadist with another question,

"Tell me, my good man, do you know most of the prisoners by their given"?

"Every single one", the guard puffed out his chest with pride, "I don't need any padfon to tell me who is in my charge. Why do you ask, My Lord"?

"I have an interest in two prisoners, in particular, they are wanted by my government for crimes committed in English Columbia. Not that I have any extradition orders on my padfon on this occasion, but I can get some should such prove necessary".

"Who is it that you are looking for, My Lord"? The guard glanced at Aurora who nodded, saying without words that it was all right to give the information to Nigh if he had it.

"One of them is Mingfu Li and the other Huahua Morrelius".

A brief ray of satisfaction seemed to pass over the guards grizzled countenance at the mention of at least one of the names and he was quick to announce,

"Your government with have no further trouble from Mingfu Li in the near future, my Lord. Or indeed ever again".

"Because"?

"She was shot. About three weeks ago, if memory serves for failing to make her quota three days in succession".

"Quota"?

"In the Bauxite mine at Shandong Henan, we fly some of our slaves out there each day by jetflitter. One of them was your fugitive. The other one you mention, she is still with us, used as a farm slave up in the Yungui plateau peanut region, again flown there every day and brought back to this camp at night. Our citizens didn't want the slave camps all over Great Taiwan so they are all pretty much clustered in this zone, although you probably already knew that, My Lord. We Taiwanese like your country a great deal, we like how you have dealt with your enemies over the centuries.

Wincing at the misplaced admiration, Nigh turned to Aurora and asked,

"His Majesty's government would be most grateful if it became possible for me to interview Morrelius".

"I would have to confirm that with my superiors", Aurora admitted sadly, but then the garrulous guard shook his head informing,

"Duìzhăng [captain] Chow Kow has gone home, Lùjūn Zhōngwèi [lieutenant], when you enter the compound you will be the most senior officer in the place".

"Who is now"? Aurora seemed genuinely intrigued to discover.

"Shàowèi [2nd lieutenant] Wing Tan Kuo, Lùjūn Zhōngwèi".

"In that case, I believe I can take you straight to hut Shíwu᷉ [15], My Lord, if you care to open the gate now, Shēntĭ᷉ cháng máo [Lance corporal] I shall be certain to mention your efficiency to Duìzhăng Chow Kow when next I report to him".

The Shēntĭ᷉ cháng máo seemed delighted with that and hurried to do Aurora's bidding. Nigh and Mayling humbly followed her into their very first slave camp. The stink increased, the lights of the city, transformed as it may be, barely able to cut through a dark filmy murk that hung over the interior like a shroud of doom. Nigh heard Mayling cough and wondered if she were going to vomit. It was not unknown for hunger to cause that, but doubtless, the odour was more likely the cause of the girl's distress.

"When we get out of here we go and have something to eat". He promised her but the gagging girl did nothing other than hold up a hand as though to inform, *'after this, I do not think I will have much appetite'.* They passed through a maze of poorly constructed bamboo huts that were little more than sad shanties against the rain and would certainly not keep out the draughts of the evening. Fortunately, it being July, the cold was yet to be the slaves' enemy, but many would perish from hyperthermia when winter came, that was certain. Being something of a student of history Nigh reflected that the grim conditions of the Chinese under the Taiwanese were not disparate with the fate of slaves existing under the yolk of oppression in Roman times.

Lùjūn Zhōngwèi Aurora turned to them informing, "This is hut Shíwu᷉. Prepare yourselves for a grim scene or two".

"How could you let Huahua exist in a place like this, Aurora"? Mayling demanded.

"The Xanthine and I have never been anything other than captor and captive", Aurora responded not unreasonably. "She was the conquered and I belong to the superior race. I do not remember matters any other way".

She held open a poor excuse for a door and let them pass her into an inky den of iniquity. Both hesitated until Aurora threw a switch just inside the opening and harshly albescent LED illumination flooded the interior. Several rows of emaciated filthy individuals in rags that were rotting from their bony frames blinked at the trio of newcomers like startled owls.

"I am looking for Huahua Morrelius", Aurora instructed them and her tone had taken on a harsh quality which Nigh found he did not recognise. There was no response. Had Nigh's distant cousin expired that evening even as they had come to liberate her. Aurora cajoled,

"It is all right Morrelius. It is not about your quota, far from it. This English Lord from the Empire there has come to see you".

"I have come to liberate you", Nigh said loudly.

"I'm sorry but you will not be allowed to leave the camp with her", Aurora told him. Before he had the time to respond to that a timid voice asked,

"Durango? Is that you? Do you know who I am"?

The trio gazed at the filthy wretch who had hesitantly approached them. Covered in dirt, skinny beyond health and with the odd festering sore, it was what was left of Huahua.

"I know and I've come to get you out of this Gehenna damned misery".

"Durango, you cannot do that", Aurora persisted, "Without the appropriate expedition orders on your padfon you would be stopped at the gate, even if I allowed you that far".

"What do you mean by that far"? Mayling interjected. Nigh allowed her to, the two of them were of the one mind on the current issue.

"I am the Lùjūn Zhōngwèi of this facility, Durango but even I do not have the authority to release a Xanthine. I am sorry. You can visit her with clean clothes and food parcels, but you cannot take her out of here. Even if you overpower me and take me, hostage, you will not get past those two on the gate".

"Would they let us out to save your life", Mayling suddenly asked and her pistol was pressed against Aurora's neck in one lithely swift movement. Aurora gasped and asked,

"Are you going to let her threaten me, Durango. I who brought you over here to me my male-order mail order".

"Leave the Momo out of it for the second", Mayling grinned, introducing a new acronym to the Chinese vernacular, "If you don't do as your told Saffronite, I will kill you without a moment's hesitation and I won't regret it either".

Nigh was a little taken aback by Mayling's sudden enmity toward someone she had previously tolerated. That was when they were both Chinese though and they were both Chinese no longer.

Suddenly a voice new to all of them suggested,

"I would like to make a suggestion"?

It belonged to a small Chinese youth of some twenty years or so. Nigh asked him,

"Speak, I would do what I could for you all, but it seems I am most likely unable to help much".

"Give me that pistol at your side and the other one the girl has to one of my fellow prisoners and we will storm the gate. Some of us may go down in the fight, who knows maybe all of us, but it is better than rotting in this Gehenna dungeon".

"If you do get out where will you go", Aurora demanded, "There is nowhere to run in all of Greater Taiwan. Do you intend to go on a rampage of theft and violence until the combmen catch up with you and shoot you down"?

"Better that than what we have now", the youth returned not unreasonably. "We were planning to storm the gate once we had built up the courage anyway. Armed only with our fists and maybe some chopsticks we had stolen. With two energy weapons, it will not be a mass suicide, we will have a chance".

Nigh began to undo the flap on his pistol and wriggling Aurora squealed,

"What are you doing, stop, you'll all...".

Mayling fired her weapon and Aurora was instantly rendered unconscious. She lowered the girl's limp form to the dirty boards of the hut's floor and then passed her weapon to the youth,

"Good luck, You'll need it".

Nigh meantime had passed his own to a second youth who had approached. The first then grinned and then said,

"Thank you, give it a couple of minutes and then you should be able to simply walk out of here with Huahua. I hope it works out for you".

"And I, you", Mayling smiled, while Nigh nodded at the sentiment.

The poor wretched filled past them until only Nigh, Mayling, Aurora and Huahua remained.

"How did you know where to find me, Distant cousin Durango", Huahua asked.

"That is a very long and convoluted story", Nigh grinned. Before he could decide if it was the time and place to relate even a compressed version, the sound of shouting and the discharge of energy weapons cut through the air. For several long moments, there was the sound of pandemonium, but then it went quite suddenly - very quiet, very suddenly. The battle was over, but who was the victor.

"I think it time to see if we can get out of here", Nigh observed. As he did, he bent over and scooped up the stunned lieutenant. Though he was not especially muscular, the girl was diminutive and light and easily within his capabilities of carrying out of the camp. Mayling noted,

"She may fare better if we left her here? She could always claim we overpowered her, or the Chinese did and she would be blameless for what happened".

"On the other hand, if the Taiwanese authorities want to pursue us, we could hold them off if we have a hostage".

They followed him out into the warmth of the night. It was several seconds before they could see the scene at the gate. They were pleased to see that at least some of the slaves had made it out alive though, both the guards lay dead amongst those who had not found freedom. All four energy weapons were gone.

"The Saffronite are not going to take this lying down", Mayling noted, "I hope they do not seek reprisals by executing yet more Chinese"?

"It would not be sensible to reduce their workforce still further", Nigh argued. "Anyway, we cannot worry about that. We had to free Huahua".

"Where are we going, Cousin"? The girl in question desired to know.

"The one place where they will not think kidnappers would hold Aurora", Nigh grinned, "In her apartment. I hope she has some food in, I could eat an Iguana"! (the local saying to explain severe hunger).

* * *

"You look a great deal better already", Nigh lied to his distant descendant. In reality, she was still emaciated and though salve had been applied to her sores they would take a while to heal. Even Aurora look uncomfortable at the pathetic figure Huahua cut. The generously loaned clothes hung from her bony frame and the weight loss had shrunken her once fantastic bust. All of them had bathed and shared a welcome meal. Only the former lieutenant of the Fuchow Slave Camp seemed to be less than encouraged by the changes Nigh's arrival had made to their various conditions. Seeing this the chronoman squeezed her arm and cooed,

"Don't worry Aurora, I've sent a ransom demand to the government here. If no more Chinese are harmed you will be released in a couple of days unharmed".

"And if they ignore your threat, what happens to me then"?

"I would never harm you, Aurora, it is to shift suspicion from you that you were absconded with. There is no scenario where you will come to any harm from we three. Is there Mayling"?

Mayling grimaced.

"*Is there Mayling*"?

Finally, Mayling shrugged and grinned, "Of course not. We were on much better terms Aurora when you were Chinese too and Taiwan had never invaded China".

"I cannot imagine that", the Lùjūn Zhōngwèi returned frostily, "But in the spirit of the mission, whatever the mission is, I accept the word of a Xanthine for the first time in my life".

"Enough of the bigotry", Nigh was growing irritated by the use of the insulting titles, "No more Xanthine and no more Saffronite. Is that clear"?

"You know you were much more compliant when you were a Momo", Aurora joked. It was the first time she had attempted humour since their untimely arrival in the 51st and Nigh forced himself to laugh along with the others.

"So I'm guessing we go back to the Destino tomorrow, Nigh"? Mayling finally wondered, "What will become of Huahua here? Mingfu Li, will she remain dead? What about Aurora, can we change her back to her original nationality"?

"Ironically we must make certain Fiscarte is not killed. He must have been in some way responsible for stopping Jiánhòng Chen from coming to power and enlisting the aid of A23. I think if Fiscarte lives, then the subjugation of China never took place".

"You think", Aurora noted, "You do not sound 100% convinced. Are you sure you know what you are doing any more"?

Nigh was not.

"Of course! We just have to go back and put everything back the way it was before. Then we can see if we can still keep Lynea and Decorum together".

Aurora would not be fobbed off though, "Keep them together how, time travelling Momo, you do not know what the consequence of each action you take in the 33rd will do to us in the 51st. Maybe you should just leave things the way they are now and thusly avoid making it possibly even worst"?

"It could not be worse than this"! Huahua practically sobbed. "It is alright for you, Aurora, you experienced the changes on the right side of fortune. I did not"!

"We cannot let China remain in its current predicament", Mayling urged, "No matter what the alternative is".

"Go back and mess around with the time thread again and the consequence could be even worse", Aurora warned. Though she would urge further non-interference being in the more fortunate position. For once Nigh felt that he was struggling with personal conviction. What if it were possible to make the 51st even more unpleasant for many and he managed to blunder into that change? The door pinged then and the four of them glanced at one another in alarm. Could they have been pursued so swiftly? Nigh went to see who it was, he was unarmed, but trained in combat with only the hands and feet as weapons. When he saw the image in the inspection plate he groaned in annoyance. Swiping the speaker to the active position he demanded,

"Could you not have come at a more propitious time than this Ruari. Who sent you this time? Acwellen 23 or Jiánhòng Chen"?

"Not the android – Ruari", one of the women gasped, but Nigh could not decide which one for he was unlocking the door mechanism. The beautiful android glided through the aperture, which he locked and closed after firstly checking in both directions to make certain no one else was loitering without. As he turned the android put her arms around his neck and before he could react in any way, her soft lips were on his. It was pointless to struggle, she was several times stronger than he. It was pleasant enough anyway despite the circumstances and the audience.

"Excuse me"! Ruari objected, "Will you please leave my Momo alone, Mistress"?

Ruari grinned, "And what does that acronym stand for, Lùjūn Zhōngwèi Homini, or should I call you LZH now? I note that you are not bound, are you a willing captor in their illegal little enterprise"?

"I know what you want, Ruari", Nigh said to her, "But not how much you know. How resistant to change are android records"?

Without waiting for an invitation the android seated herself on the couch. Huahua promptly melted away, obviously exhausted she perhaps even went to bed. It was 11:37.

"My Lord General Acwellen knows that you are manipulating the leylines of the fourth dimension if that is what you are hinting at. In response, he has a very lucrative offer to make to you if you simply come with me. We cannot hold off the TA indefinitely".

"What do you know about the Tempus Agents"? Nigh was alarmed.

Ruari seemed to come to some sort of decision before she decided to tell him, "Put it this way, Durango, 5423Dorph now leads a team rather than trying to stop you alone. The team is four strong including him".

"And you've been keeping them off my back"?

Ruari nodded.

"Why, what's in it for you? Or should I say why is 23 suddenly looking after my interests such as they are"?

"He feels that with his aid you may consider a certain obligation to then use your strange abilities to help him with a little matter".

"I cannot even promise to consider it if you do not tell me what that might be"? Nigh was curious, even though he had no intention of ever forming any sort of alliance whatsoever with the Android General.

"He wants you to take him to the 77th", Ruari was tactless in her factuality.   Nigh guffawed in surprise,

"That metal-headed monstrousassorus thinks he can become an army of one and storm the Ministro do Tempo Estudos e Tempo Viajando? Either take Cientista de Extrema Aprendizagem Adalberto Almeida Sapientiae captive, or steal one of his Tempus devices! Even if he did so, he would not have the expertise to operate it".

"His Lordship is a very quick study, have no fear for him. The question is do you wish to continue enjoying his protection and once your quest is completed will reciprocate with the requested action"?

"Or"?

"Or he will withdraw it, the TA's will come for you and your little strangling band of concubines".

"The aloof disdain of the masters", Mayling noted, the first of the responses to the android to be from anyone other than the Taiwanese or Nigh himself. Ruari afforded her a withering glance, but Mayling merely glared at her in defiance.

"How is it that Your lord and master does not know that while I am tinkering in the past I do not make certain he is never constructed"?

"To date, you have created micro-changes in the 33rd", Ruari noted. "Yet they ripple down the leylines of time and the ripples become a tsunami in the 51st. It is felt by N359 and computed by Qiangdadeanao that you are not foolish enough to make such a fundamental change that would echo down the centuries indefinitely".

"Making A23 sort of like cancer, horrific but necessary to halt mankind from overpopulation to the point of implosion"?

"A somewhat colourful expressive, but essentially you see the world post-SX and it is better than pre-SX".

"Tell that to the Chinese", Mayling observed with sarcastic feelings.

"But surely the shortage of gametes was nowhere near as catastrophic as that which your future husband did to this country", the android observed with her usual sledge-hammer tact. All Mayling could mutter in return was,

"Durango has shown no interest in taking me as his wifone or any other status for that matter".

Reasoning that he could look at that situation when he had time to turn around, Nigh instead asked,

"If I agree to aid A23 once I have solved my family history problems, will he keep the TA's off my back"?

Mayling looked mortified by the contract, Ruari less so.

"Do you give your word as an Englishman"?

Nigh nodded without hesitation.

"Would you thumb a contract on my pad"?

Again the silent gesture of affirmation. Ruari held out a prepared agreement and Nigh thumbed it without even reading it. Then he asked,

"Will you go now please, Ruari. We Homini need our rest, it is going to be a very event-filled time, on the morrow"?

The instant the door had closed behind her retreating figure and all that remained of her presence in the apartment was her lingering fragrance, Mayling demanded,

"Are you crazy? If the General gets his metallic hands on a time machine mankind is doomed to eternal slavery"?

"I just gave my word to a machine", Nigh sneered. "That does not count as giving your word to anyone".

"You intend to renege on that contract", Aurora was shocked to incredulity.

"If I gave my word to that hypo-wave in the kitchen would you expect me to keep it"? Nigh chuckled.

"That is not quite the same thing", Mayling smiled a trifle sardonically. "The hypo-wave would not be upset when you broke it. Your word I mean. The hypo-wave does not have consciousness".

"Neither does A23", Nigh was suddenly serious, "The machine that is A23 has the programming that *simulates* thought and will, but it is ultimately artificial. A simulacrum of a mind and will, just like I agreed to a simulacrum of a contract with it. I do not even consider it breaking my word, therefore I am not doing any such thing in the normal understanding of such an act".

"It sounds a trifle underhand to me", Mayling grinned, "But you at least, seem to know what you are doing".

I just wish I did', thought Night then, *'I just wish I had a clue what the consequences of my next action will be'!*

* * * * *

All of them were tired when they arose the next day. It was good to see daylight. Especially for Nigh and Mayling who had not done so for many waking hours the period before. Even so, Nigh was on edge and spluttered over his beverage,

"What in the Nation of Tar is this"? He demanded when he tasted the rubescent fluid.

"Taiwanese Perryiaid", Aurora informed, unimpressed by his lack of appreciation for the brew, "It is a combination of Sherry and Port".

"And has inherited the worst aspics of both by the revolting taste", came the inappreciative response.

Mayling brought the subject back to the topic she most desired to discuss, "Have you decided who is going to accompany you to the 33rd this time, Durango"?

"I'm in danger if I am discovered", Aurora declared at once, "It should be me".

"Then you would stay Taiwanese", the Elucidator pointed out, "Perhaps permanently".

"That would be my wish", came the immediate reply, "I was born Taiwanese, why would I want to be demoted in the lottery that is the gene pool and birth".

"Well I want to stay", Huahua declared, "If what you told us is correct, then the changes you make would mean that I would never have been a slave".

"So it is just between the two of us that you decide", Mayling noted. "Do you leave Aurora as she is and accept her changed nationality, or do you take someone who can handle herself"? Nigh's head span. How to stop Fiscarte from killing Decorum [if indeed he did] without ruining China's future. Then there was Gravis running about on the ship and finally, Mingfu Li who seemed to suffer a worse fate each time he used the Tempus Doors.

"You want to stay Taiwanese"? He asked Aurora, "Chinese you were gehenned hot"?

"I want to go to the 33rd and avoid any unnatural transformations", the girl was firm.

"And I want to do the same, for the very same reason", Mayling observed, "I don't want to end up like Mingfu Li"!

"I see only one solution then", Nigh resolved. "The three of us hug and see if my powers of Andhera Tantu can take me and two passengers. If not we come back here and I go alone and all of you take your chances, agreed"?

Begrudgingly, the young women nodded their heads.

* * *

Ruari was smiling and telling him that she had successfully converted to Homini. He asked what that meant, what had she done. Why was this happening now of all times, it was not a convenient moment, not convenient at all. She had revived the opposite of alterations a person went through to become a biotron. When each of her circuits was removed she had them replaced with stem cell culture-organs. Ruari had biologised herself in an attempt to become a woman. Surely this was not real, this was a dream and dreams do not become reality except in tri-vidz or science fiction novels. They could thusly be together she insisted upon informing him then, for as long as they both lived. Something was wrong though, Night could not conceive of a grown brain. After all, if the brain was replaced then the person was no longer the same identity. It was the mind that made the individual, not the body, in whatsoever shape or configuration. Did that observations and set of parameters not make of Nigh, something other than Homo-sapien? Then it was that he instinctively knew that Ruari was not a woman, never could be one, never could be anything other than a machine with biological organs. She was not even there, not in a physical sense she was some sort of a train! Emotional instability pulled into the station backed by the oscillating sound of electronica. He felt a tremendous paranoia this was worse than the worst sweat racked incubus. The floor had suddenly disappeared from beneath their feet, just as had happened the first three times. This time though there was a vast difference. This time the mass was greater, the strain even more so. This time what he was trying to do was pushing him to his utter limits and beyond. Of course, for the first time, his outward was a trio. The aroma of fuchsia filled his nostrils and the gentle chimes of violaceous assailed him. He tasted the delicate music of Brahms as it swirled around in his mouth caressing his tongue. Vitality and zest filled his hearing and he felt excellence and sagacity touch his skin. Before him, a chattering whine of the temporizadoor opened in the throbbing of the firmament. The sensation was not so much disturbing as disorientating and strangely tremulous. His senses were capable of registering in areas hitherto closed off to them, he saw emotions, tasted hues, felt musicality and heard a luscious candy. There was a sense in his subconscious of an enormous digital clock with red LED numbers and a black face. Yet the clunky graphics they produced were in Roman numerals, not one to twelve though but in tiny characters, years. The M's and C's in rows as the clock became more and more stretched into a very long rectangle that would not have fit on most walls. He identified the correct year, the correct date, in a way he had no way of understanding he even found a locus in space. The point in time was in a vast swirling glutinous ocean, a sea of C's, a vast confusing lake of M's. Then the floor came up to meet them. The floor or the ground, he could not be certain which. The three of them, hugging tightly as they had been, were torn apart and fell in different directions. Nigh thought this might not be a very good landing nor a very good result as his fractured nerves cascaded into the inky bowels of unconsciousness.

Eleven. The Room that Had Everything

When consciousness finally returned to Nigh, he knew immediately that something was very wrong indeed. It was not the cool wet feeling that pervaded his back, caused by lying on dew-kissed grass that gave it away. It was not the curiously strange cawing of some unknown avian. It was the fact that he was under trees, the leaves of which were unknown to him and he was looking upward at a curiously lilac hued cupola filled with clouds. This was not the Destino. Nor was it the 33rd century. Thinking it was a good idea to have rearmed from a local Taiwanese bandit earlier nigh unclipped his holster as he carefully climbed to his feet. A distance away he could see the inert form of one of the girls and he began to take hesitant steps toward her. It was Mayling. Of Aurora, there was no sign. Nigh went over to the awkwardly positioned girl and carefully straightened her limbs, then he cradled her hand in one of his own, waited while her eyelids fluttered open. She smiled when her vision came into focus and asked,

"Are you going to kiss me Durango and turn me into a swan"?

"One of those mythical white birds that became extinct centuries ago, why would I do that"?

"You've never read any of 'The Grime Brothers Tales of Queers' as a child have you"?

"I read 'Hands Superstition Handerson' and 'One thousand and twenty-three Nights in the Nuclear East'. In those fanciful tales of fantasy, you would have to be a swan and my kiss would turn you back into a beautiful Chinese Princess".

"Gehenna! Struck-out again", she pouted, "No kiss then"?

"No kiss. Enough of this riotous banter anyway, look around you, I have messed up badly once again and this time it's a messomassinoromous".

He helped her to her feet and she glanced about her and then asked, "Durango, where are we? I'm guessing that this is not the good ship Destino. Call it a wild stab in the dark if you will".

"It's exactly what you'll get if you don't cease with the sarcasm", he grinned, "We are like two laboratory mice in a box with no holes".

"Access your ribbon things in your brain then and sense where and when we are"?

"My ribbon things"?

"Mirrors, ribbons, strands, it is all mysterious to me, just crack on before something happens and we are once more racing to keep up with events"?

"That point was valid and Nigh closed his eyes to concentrate. He regulated his breathing and heart rate and then went into a Yogi Doshi taught trance. Whilst in the semi-catatonic state he allowed his thoughts to flow into the andhera tantu and he  thought his way toward a hidden mental clock. He suddenly gasped and opened his eyes, swaying so badly that Mayling grabbed him lest he stumbled and fell to the ground.

"Is it a messomassinoromous then"? She asked half guessing the truth.

"You could put it that way. Or describe it conservatively as a messomassinoromous colossagargantuacatastrophy. Mayling this is the year 5929 and we have not moved from a geographical point of view. This land was once Fuchow"!

Mayling suddenly smiled incongruously in Nigh's opinion, and pointed down to his feet,

"Speaking of catastrophes, how auspicious is that"?

He glanced down and observed a white cat rubbing against his boho trousers, purring furiously and covering him with white hairs. He noted something his sharp eyes had discerned that had escaped Mayling's more cursory glance and groaned out loud at the implication,

"Oh no. I don't accept any set of changes that could have resulted in that"!

What is it"? Mayling glanced furtively about her, "What have you seen".

"The cat, of course, Look at the name tag, look at the cat's name"!

Mayling bent down and stared at the happy feline and gasped. Then she chuckled,

"It's Aurora, I always did think she was something of a pussy".

"It's not a scenario for levity   Mayling",   Nigh fumed, "How can our advancing into the future instead of the past produced anything like as bizarre a change in one of us as this"?

"I can answer that", a muffled voice was heard by both of them and Nigh pulled forth the forgotten padfon and demanded,

"Then please do so Paddie? This surely is not my fault this time. We have blundered forward nine centuries, it was not my doing I am happy to observe.

"Cause and effect cause and effect and sometimes it takes a while for the ripples to permeate the fabric of the leylines, Nigh", Paddie informed somewhat bored of the tome as though his prose were, in fact, prosaic when they were anything but.

"Enough of the riddles, just inform us what has happened in everyday speech if you please. Also how come you remember the unaltered timeline when it now is no more."?

"As to the latter question, that is simple it is because I am with you. Therefore the proximity to the loci keeps me immune from alteration".

"And the changes, how can changes occur when we have not been back to the ship this time"?

"Intent".

"Intent, that is your marvellously revealing explanation. Be more specific for goodness sake. What resolve and determined by whom"?

"Yours Nigh. You always intended to rescue Decorum from his fate on the Destino, is that not so"?

"Well, yes, but...".

"But you are now upwhen from the point at which you intended to do so and therefore ineffective in this particular timeline, hence the changes".

"You mean Decorum has to live, otherwise this place we are in now is the resultant new reality"? Mayling proposed

"And the prize goes to the hottie", Paddie observed in totally unpadfon-like tones. "To be specific it is the grandson of Decorum who is now not born and thusly missing from the timeline that results in the reality you now find yourselves in".

"So Decorum's Grandson does something or stops something that means China is transformed into....this"? Nigh waved his arms about him.

"Correct", Paddie confirmed, "The Grandson in question grew up to be General Alexius Morrelius Dilexitvehementer, none other than the leader of the Terran forces who stopped the Prædontt from invading Earth after destroying Mars and the forces of A23 on that world".

"A23 is destroyed"? Nigh sounded jubilant.

"Along with the planet Mars and all the peoples on it, yes".

"And what of Earth"? Mayling asked, "This looks like paradise, not a radioactive waste as one might have expected, what happened here, Paddie"?

"Without the leadership of General Dilexitvehementer, the poorly organised armies that each area could muster were soon defeated and what you see now is six centuries later".

"Well it looks peaceful", Mayling tried to look on a side that did not exist for them, the bright side for humanity, "It looks like one would imagine Eden to be if Eden had been in China".

"A23 destroyed", Nigh repeated to himself, tickling Aurora behind her ear. Her eyes close in pleasure and she leaned into his fingers.

"Unfortunately you cannot leave things like this, Durango", Mayling finally noted, "Can you"?

Nigh picked up Aurora, who snuggled into his arms and purred loudly, "We're armed and I have the Andhera Tantu if things get a bit hairy, what do you say we go and find some life around here, even if it is the Prædontt"?

"Curiosity killed the cat", Mayling smiled.

"I'll protect her", the chronoman grinned at the pun, "Come on you must be at least curious to see who the invaders are and what they look like. I also wonder why the Tempus Agents have not stopped the invasion before it happened"?

"Perhaps they did in another reality", the Elucidator offered, "Remember Roxbrough's theory of multiple layers of possibility in the leylines and the multiverse highway system"?

"The artist and science fiction writer", Nigh scoffed, "You're quoting that misguided fool as the source of your carefully considered hypothesis".

Mayling blew a raspberry at him then and flounced away, "Come on then, let's see if we can find life, or some bizarre version of it before you get turned into a newt or something else unwholesome".

"I *was* a newt once", Nigh jested. Causing the girl to turn and scrutinise him with a glowering glare.

"I got better"! Nigh joked and then hurried to follow her as she shrugged and stumbled away.

They found themselves traversing a vast plain of open grassland dotted with the occasional clump of bushes or trees. In certain areas, there was evidence of crop planting. The growths were strangely blue and alien to anything the duo had ever seen before. They assumed that the plants were those that had been cultivated by the Prædontt, their appearance so different they could not even guess what they were for, although it was most likely they were foodstuffs of some sort. The next feature of interest was a coppice of totally unfamiliar plants that Nigh could not even decide to categorise. They towered over their heads, yet did not possess bark and were a royal blue hue with leaves of what looked very like silver, the colour not the precious metal. They also had huge flowers sprouting from every branch. White petals with xanthic centres. The vegetation though so large was more like a huge frond than a tree. Some sort of fungus or parasitical infestation was present on many of them a type of alien white mildew. It did not seem to be killing any of the fronds though so perhaps the relationship was symbiotic.

"We know why the aliens came then", Nigh observed to himself as much as to the girl, "They were after real estate. Terra must have suited their needs much more than frigid Mars enabling them to destroy it with little compunction. It must have been a tremendous weapon to kill a planet, shame all the androids went with it".

"I thought that interstellar flight was exceptionally difficult". Mayling reasoned, "How far do you think they travelled just to subjugate one little world. Or are they also on Venus and the other human settlements"?

"I do not know that, but perhaps they have something even better than cold fusion. Let us call it frost fusion for want of a better nomen at this point. Hyperspace is not something they developed a paranoia about like humanity did. So then, with their admittedly vastly superior technology, they start branching out into space and we both know what happened to an inferior technological race when it is introduced to a superior one"!

"It gets its ass kicked".

"Not to mention every other part of its anatomy. Let's go further, I'd love to see one of them before we go back to the 51st"?

"Are we taking the moggy"?

"That's our friend Aurora you're talking about. Of course, we're taking her, she'll be restored on the way back, because I still intend to save Decorum from whatever fate it was that awaited him on the Destino".

Cresting the next rise, the city greeted their collectively excited scrutiny. Very tall and spired towers with high windows. Beneath the structures of concrete-type material figures moved but at the distance they then were, it was not possible to distinguish any features.

As they cautiously advanced to the outer limits of the city though, they could tell that the aliens were immensely tall. Possibly in the region of 275cms. The skin tone was also vastly different from any Caucasian or Chinese persons. The Prædontt were a bluey-lilac. Whatever was in their blood was not iron-based it seemed. Could they have the life fluid based on chemicals similar to copper sulphate which gave them haemocyanin?

They drew closer and with each trodden step made out more features on Terra's conquerors. In addition to their height and bizarre complexion, they had enormously fluted conical skulls and arms that were too big seemingly for their frames. Huge orb-like eyes of bright yellow and wide mouths that drooped in the centre, rather than being a straight line like those of human lips. Their chins were elongated and pointed to accommodate such an orifice. Their chests were multi-ribbed in a series of easily noticeable ridges, which hinted at hung lung capacity, obviously capable of extracting oxygen from Terra's atmosphere. The most noticeable feature of all they possessed, however, was the fours ears, serrated protrusions of tendril-like flaps that appeared twice, the second pair being high on the domed head, almost at the tonsured crown. They were still faintly mammalian if such could be applied to their classification, for they had large bushy eyebrows of dense black hair or fur. These above the dome-like eyes that were either side of a tall very thin nose.

"Humanoid", Nigh noted remembering the Zernoplat.

The closest of the Prædontt heard the expression, despite the distance, with its hyper-acute sense of hearing. It turned and gazed at the two approaching strangers and then did something neither one of them would have expected in an age. It waved at them, seemingly in a friendly way, certainly, there seemed no menace demonstrated by its detection of them.

Nigh took the initiative, "Hello, we are peaceful explorers, not from this place or even this time. Are we welcome? Where is this place, please? Can you understand me"?

"You are Solarian"? The voice lisped as though in such a gigantic mouth the tongue was half lost. It sounded like *tholarian* rather than named after the star of the solar system.

"No", Nigh decided to err on the side of caution. "We share many characteristics with the Solarian, but we are a side branch race we are Chronomen".

By then they were only four metres apart and the duo stopped walking.

"You are at the edge of Ooraşhaaasa", the Prædontt told them. Its entire mien and body language bespoke of peacefulness and a benign attitude. "My name is Băifotă, I am a biologist. Who do I have the pleasure of addressing"?

"Nigh, Mayling. We are explorers and cartographers".

"You have much in common with the Solarian".

"We are greatly advanced compared to them. Far more peaceful and intellectual".

Mayling remained silent.

"Mayling is what the Solarian call female, is that not so? While you are the alter-sex".

"We have two sexes yes, what about the Prædontt"?

"Four: meeso, deeso, uruşa and meedeeusa. It is not often that we propagate".

"I can imagine", Mayling could keep silent no longer.

"Have you and the female produced many ouălu to date"?

"Ouălu? Do you mean offspring"?

"The offspring come out of the shell once the meedeeusa has lain".

This was a bizarre opening conversation to have with a stranger but Nigh persisted with it. At least they were on civil terms,

"No we are not mates, we are colleagues. Can I comment on your mastery of the Solarian language it is masterful"?

"Yes, I am very clever. Is that not so"?

"You are an intellectual, that is the case", Nigh flattered, "I would love to talk with you on several matters as part of my study thesis. Would there be somewhere that we could go to facilitate my request, or do you have future pressing engagements, Băifotă"

"It is Odihnăzitor for we Prædontt, there is no work done during this planetary cycle. I can take you to my abode as honoured guests, will you come"?

Nigh bowed and returned, "We would be honoured". He then glared at Mayling who grudgingly curtseyed to a member of the race who had killed many many humans. Perhaps even all of them. That prompted her to ask as they began to stroll toward the tall narrow spires of the Prædontt City,

"Are all the Solarian vanquished, Băifotă, or do a few pockets survive"?

"Oh, many remain in this solar system", the Prædontt tried his best to get his short tongue around words that were difficult for it. The Solarian race remains on Callisto, Moon, Mercury and shares Venus with the Venuser. Just as we share Terra prime with them here. We have the Northern Hemisphere and they keep to the south, the landmasses of Solaria. Once the surrender was accepted all hostilities ended".

"What brought you to this system"? Mayling edged toward the less savoury aspects of recent history, wondering how the Prædontt justified what they had done.

"We ran out of space on our planet Proximaria Prime", Băifotă informed without any qualms at all. "So we began to study the cosmos with our deep range instrumentation and discovered the Solarian system firstly as it was so close to our own. We saw the effects of the illness that made native populations sparse and came to seek peaceful coexistence with them. Alas, they sent mechanisms against us, the androids, forcing us to use the Dezintemarmagrare. Thusly was the fourth world around Sol destroyed and the androids with it".

"Such devastation on a massive scale did not bother you"? Nigh frowned at the girl but she was resolute.

"We came in peace", Băifotă explained, "The first shot was fired by the natives of the system. The second by the Dezintemarmagrare, it was a war of ten minutes. Now we Prædontt are building a replacement world in the space that Mars once occupied, to secure the balance of the system. We will call it Aresolaria. The Dezintemarmagrare is something of a misnomer it reconstitutes without destroying, unfortunately not much can survive the recycling process, except inert matter. The Android and Solarian of Mars will be re-established into the new world, their base components will not be lost".

"Why did you not build Aresolaria in the Proxima system"? Mayling pushed.

"We did not have the matter, it is not possible to create something from nothing. It would have ruined the balance of our system also, even if we had found enough material. Aresolaria will restore balance to Solar System, not upset it. We must enter here, this is the way to my humble abode".

The next few moments Nigh and Mayling were stunned to silence by the emotions of awe and wonder. The entrance to the building could best be described as a vast chasm of light and sweeping lines, in a white material that unlike concrete had an illuminant glow of its own. What the light source was exactly was impossible to ascertain when every sweeping wall, every curve high ceiling was a supplier of lumens. Băifotă led them across a vast swathe of an empty floor, pure white and without a hint of dusk. It then beckoned them to take up places on a platform with only a handrail set into it on two sides. The back of the platform was flush to the back wall of the hall, the front remained open. Mayling gave a start of surprise when the platform began to rise and an opening in the high ceiling allowed it to pass through, closing beneath them as the *lift* continue upward. This happened several times until the platform stopped on one floor, divided into sections and segmented by a tall corridor. These were the living quarters of the Prædontt. Sure enough, Băifotă led them to one and the door opened without him uttering a word or pressing any contacts. Nigh looked for a motion detector, but found none, it forced his curiosity to frame the question,

"Where is the sensor, Băifotă"?

"My brain", came the reply, "This door is set to my brain waves so that only I can enter my rooms".

"So how will we get through the doorway"? Mayling was then curious.

"My mind has indicated friendliness toward you, the mechanism has detected this".

"Futuristic technology the like of which would only be in a science fiction yarn", she smiled,

Nigh replied in return, "We are in the future, Mayling, although I never witnessed anything like this in the 77th when we went to visit the Ministro do Tempo Estudos e Tempo Viajando. Here is an argument to present to Cientista de Extrema Aprendizagem Adalberto Almeida Sapientiae, justifying the use of the fourth dimension for the advancement of mankind".

"Tell that to the Martians", the Chinese girl returned with feeling, "Or to your cat there, or even Mingfu Li".

"The cat is of interest", Băifotă observed as it seated itself on an impossibly large sofa. "Is it for your evening meal"?

"No"! Nigh's response was unnaturally sharp. He apologised, "Sorry, I did not mean to snap at you, the cat was a friend of mine before events turned it from a chronowoman to a feline".

"An accident in the fourth dimension", the Prædontt gave the most bizarre grimace either of the humans had ever seen. "We do not tamper with it".

"That is wise of you", Mayling agreed with feeling and for the first time with the invader. "It has presented us with several *difficulties*"!

"But where are my manners, please be seated I can offer you refreshment and nutrients, will you partake please"?

"Will our anatomies be able to assimilate said"? Nigh asked. "We are identical to the Solarian in that respect".

"Easily", Băifotă assured, "Essentially you can eat and drink anything that I can".

There was the humming of some kind of mechanism and an opening appeared in the wall and from it a mobile cube of some 1000mm square seemed to glide across the floor. On its topmost face was an array of tiny metal dishes and three goblets. The metal looked to Nigh like rhodium so highly polished was it and so brilliant its lustre. Băifotă waved an arm magnanimously,

"Take one they are all the same".

As the girl took one brilliant goblet she sniffed at it and asked, "What do you call this, Băifotă and what is it made of".

"We call it Fluid", the dome-headed lilac figure told her matter-of-factly, "It eases thirst and it comes from the Văcprăoie".

"A plant"? Nigh asked as he gazed at the liquid which was a sort of blue of hue. Băifotă wheezed, the duo guessing correctly that it was the equivalence of Prædontt laughter.

"The Văcprăoie is a quadrupedal ruminant that shares many characteristics with the chevrotain of Southern hemisphere Terra Solarian Prime".

Nigh tasted the beverage and found it to be nothing like either milk or fruit juice. It was however delicious and very thirst-quenching. He turned his attention to the dishes and discovered to his relief that none of them seemed to display crustacea, molluscs or animal flesh of any kind. Instead was an array of slightly strange-looking fruit and nuts. He selected one that looked like it contained cashews and placed one in his mouth, as he chewed he noted to Băifotă,

"These taste exactly like cashew nuts, Mein Host".

"Das liegt daran, dass es Cashewnüsse sind, Nigh [That is because they are cashew nuts, Nigh]", Băifotă returned in adequate German.

"You speak German as well as the universal language of the humans", Nigh noted, "How so, Băifotă"?

"I speak twenty-three languages", came the reply, "As do most Prædontt, it helps with trade".

"Like cashew nuts".

"These are not Terran fruit though are they", Mayling asked, she was eating some orange berries that were as fat as strawberries but circular and seeded on the outside".

"They are văpşăportocal, they are in season at the moment and grown in the main landmass in the north".

"What do you call that country now"? Nigh asked. Băifotă looked confused.

"Northern Hemisphere of Terra Prime"?

"I see, you do not have separate nationalities amongst your kind"?

"Such would be inefficient and fractional".

"Tell me about it", Mayling observed with feeling.

"I would be pleased to ask you to stay here with me for a while"? Băifotă asked them then. "I would like to introduce you to my deeso, uruşa and meedeeusa and also to study you a little like a biologist. For example, I would like to see you both disrobed"?

Mayling gasped and blushed and Nigh was forced to return, "Only medical practitioners are allowed that privilege amongst the Chronos, Băifotă, we, Mayling and I, have not even seen one another dis-robed. In our culture, it would be a prelude to intimacy probably sex".

"And you would not engage in sex to aid my understanding of your peoples. I would do so with my three mates"?

"Such acts between our people are considered mainly private and personal, except for those who are engaged in pornography. I could find those for you on the SWW if you have access to it"? Nigh returned carefully.

"The Prædontt Webcast will have such images"?

"Undoubtedly. If I am any judge of the industry of which I speak some Solarian have already engaged in coitus with members of your race".

Mayling's mouth twisted in distaste, but she remained silent, as she knew it was doubtless the case. Many people of the 51st had no qualms in engaging in any mutual activity dependant upon it being pleasurable. So why would the 60th be any different?

"Then please be my guests for the evening and put me in touch with such broadcast, I will lead you to my terminal".

"We've not left a pan on the boil what do you think"? Nigh asked Mayling as he absently stroked Aurora.

"Well you are a chronoman, so the fourth dimension is quite elastic in your consideration", She noted, "The only trouble is it keeps snapping back on you and although I think I prefer Aurora that way, you still have your Aunt's lover to aid".

Băifotă had been listening intently to their conversation and pricked up all four ears at the mention of the fourth dimension. He interjected,

"Your cartography extends to the fourth dimension it seems to me. Tell me, have you reaped the desired effect whilst travelling through time"?

"No", Mayling beat Nigh to the punch, "In fact every time he tries the tempusdoors, it ends up making matters even more complicated".

"I can understand why", the Prædontt reasoned, "We found that the past has quite an obdurate structure and is best only observed rather than manipulated".

"I thought you did not involve yourself with fourth-dimensional travel", Nigh was suddenly very intrigued.

"We flirted with it briefly after creating the Urată-îndoită".

"Urată-îndoită", Nigh repeated, "Some sort of mechanism for time travelling perhaps"?

Băifotă nodded his enormous conical head, he must have possessed neck muscles of steel to be able to perform that motion without any sort of distress.

"In your language, you would refer to the device as a Duration-Vortex. It does exactly as that nomen suggests, creates a whirl or eddy through the ether and allows the user to traverse the inter-dimensional plexus of the generative element that is continuance".

"To move through time"?

"I believe I said that", Băifotă smiled its enormous smile.

"How accurately can this Urată-îndoită be focused, My Friend"? Nigh desired to know.

"I believe the Mark VI was accurate to within thirty seconds or so".

"I don't suppose we could either buy or borrow one"?

"Hahahaha, buy one, with what", Mayling guffawed.

Băifotă did not laugh though, instead, he returned shrewdly, "Mine could be bartered for".

"How large is it", Nigh was practically drooling by that point.

"It fits onto one's back and weighs approximately fifteen ivră. That would be six thousand eight-hundred and four of your grams".

"What would you require in exchange for it? You mentioned bartering. What are you after, Băifotă? Silver, Nyloplanyon, Durilight, Aluminium, Rhodium, Gems, Titanium....surely not Solarian money"?

"I told you I am a biologist, I would like to observe you and the other sex for my thesis on alien biology".

Mayling blanched and asked urgently, "Define observe for me, please? How intrusive are your observations going to be"?

"Aah the Solarian fear of probes, you Chronos share that myth. I said observe, Mayling, Not intrude or insert".

"And how long is this observation supposed to be for"? Nigh asked he wanted the Urată-îndoită more than anything else he could think of.

"How long does it usually take, on average and are you - average, Nigh"?

Nigh's brow furrowed in puzzlement as Mayling suddenly blurted angrily, "He wants you and I to dance the dragon's jig on the white sheet and he wants to watch us"!

"If I understand that euphemism correctly then yes, as a biologist I wish to observe a two-gender couple enacting coitus. It is not possible with my race you see".

"And it's not going to be possible with us neither", Mayling stormed. "What do you think we are, animals"?

"Yes", Băifotă replied without a hint of chagrinment in any respect, "As is the Prædontt".

"Think of something else you would like instead", Nigh tried.

"But I do not want to", Băifotă resolutely returned without hesitation.

Nigh turned to Mayling, "You've been after me for a while, haven't you"?

"Forget it", came the rapidly disgusted response, "I'm not your Methley".

"What if we were engaged to be married"?

"Jupiter, Vishnu and Wangmu Niangniang, you'd marry me to get your hands on a time machine, why, when you have one in your head.

"Speed and accuracy, efficiency, the ability to take someone with me without it turning them into a cat or a man or Taiwanese".

"Just direct him to some porn and then let's get out of here".

"If that had been acceptable to him he could have done it without any help from me. He wants to see mating, not sex. As in lovemaking not acting out something physical for the sake of the gratification of viewers.

"He's a pervert wanting to see us doing it".

"He's a biologist, to him we are not the same species. His is merely scientific interest".

"I find it curious that the two of you are referring to me in the masculine", the 'he' in question suddenly interrupted their argument with the observation, "I am not male, I am meeso".

Nigh was interrupted mid-thought and then asked,

"So does meeso have more male characteristics or more female ones"?

"We do not have either, we are quartersexual without all for sexes coming together we cannot produce the next generation. Tell me, Mayling would it help to dispel your reservations if I was not actually in the same room as the two of you when you perform your act of affection and intimacy"?

Mayling surprised Nigh at that instant by confessing, "Of course it would, but I do not wish to hear any details about how easily you could still see the two of us, either electronically or with mirrors or whatever. I will be honest with you, Băifotă, I have feelings for the man. I always wanted our union, if such there was going to be one, to be spontaneous and romantic. Not like two laboratory mice brought together to mate and procreate. On the other hand, if I cannot see you, he agrees to marry me when we get back to China (if we ever do) and we get one of those Urată-îndoită I am sorely tempted. The only trouble is now that we have discussed it so candidly, I find I am simply not in the mood".

The look on Băifotă face was not possible to understand as it was so alien, so he vocalised,

"I deduce you are referring to some sort of mental emotion, what sort is necessary for a female to mate"?

"A romantic one", Mayling declared a trifle hotly, "Do deeso, urușa and meedeeusa just do it at the drop of a hat"?

"What is a hat"? Came the honest response and why does one need to be dropped to make a female ready to copulate"?

"He, she or it is not helping here", Mayling turned to Nigh. The latter said to the alien biologist,

"Do you have any foodstuffs, herbs or medication which increase libido in any of your four sexes, Băifotă"?

"Yes, we have some powder which when ingested does that very thing, we call it Gălăgoraz Örinţă, which roughly translated means naughty and lustful. "I am not ingesting something which could harm me, possibly kill me", Mayling objected, not unreasonably. "If you let me take a tiny culture from you, I can test it before the evening meal and if it is not harmful my considerable laboratorial expertise will be able to assure you it is perfectly safe to use".

"A tiny culture"?

"All I need do is simply scrape the back of your hand, the exfoliation will not be noticeable to you".

Mayling smiled, "This is weird, naughty and I am out of my mind for agreeing to it, but all right. You can rub my hand and you can observe from a distance, preferably a great distance. I just don't want to see you and I'll try and put you to the back of my mind".

Nigh grinned as three other figures suddenly entered the room. Mayling gave an involuntary start of surprise and slight distaste. She had managed to ignore Băifotă's bizarre appearance, but the other members of the marriage were even more alien of appearance, were such possible. The deeso's skull was also pointed and fluted, but whereas Băifotă's grew tall from his grown, in the case of the secondary sex of the Prædontt, it grew backwards from the upper part of the back of the head. Like the meeso, the skin tone was a dark lilacy-blue. While Băifotă had large orb-like eyes though, the second sex had elongated and wide ones that were seated in very elongated sockets in the strange face. There were fours ear fronds but lower down due to the difference in head shape, the mouth was wide and the nose bulbous and large nostriled. Despite that, the overall impression the two humans got was one of femininity to Băifotă's masculine mien. The uruşa was something disparate entirely. The face of a ghost, reminiscent of *The Scream*. A fluted elongated face, huge elliptical eyes and tall narrow mouth. The nose was narrow and almost given no space in the quite disturbing features, made no less unpleasant by pure white hair and a great head-full of it. The feminist features were dark blue, the eyes a disconcerting red.

The last figure to enter was the meedeeusa and possibly most bizarre of the quartet. Its skull was shaped like that of a hammerhead shark, but the tiny eyes were in the usual place on a shrunken face that was mottled with a variety of shades of blue and amber. The nose was also very small and almost last in that huge head with very little actual middle features. Around a tiny mouth which must have made eating very time consuming was a vast bushy beard of navy-blue hair. Due to the facial hair, the meedeeusa gave off a very strong impression of maleness and so the couple were subsequently surprised to learn that it was the last of the four sexes who laid the egg - or Ouălu. Băifotă seemed proud to introduce his three mates, who were named; Nuovată, Puæm and Năcindubăit. The latter being the most vociferous of the trio.

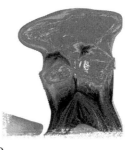

"I am honoured to meet you, Chrono's", *heshe* said in an equally tiny voice to match its tiny orifice. I look forward to seeing you produce your Ouălu".

"I don't", Nigh grinned, genuinely amused, "In our but binary sexual system, it is the female who produces the Ouălu and even then inside her body, so there will be no display for you I am afraid".

"Inside heshe's body, but then what when the shell starts to crack"? Năcindubăit was intrigued.

"There is no shell", Nigh remarked, "I'm surprised you have not noted this in the Solarian"?

"There is still much resentment over the destruction of Mars I'm afraid", Băifotă interjected then, "We have not been allowed to study any of them, that is why your arrival here is proving to be so propitious".

"Without a shell how do you protect your newborn, until it reaches maturity"? Năcindubăit asked Mayling.

"The offspring is delivered full term", the girl squirmed, "We are descended from mammalian ancestry. I suspect the evolutionary tree of the Prædontt is from a different classification of creatures".

"You are very astute", Năcindubăit complimented Mayling. Heshe seemed to have taken something of a shine to the Chinese girl, "In the ancient past when our primordial ancestors crawled from the soup that was our rich oceans we were amphibious. We only developed the waterproof shell after billions of revolution of our world around Proxima".

"Years", Mayling seemed to warm to the Prædontt too, "We call one cycle of orbit around the star Sol, a year".

"Aah, we call it a revolution, although it means slightly differently in Prædontt, but loses the nuances in translation".

"However you mean it and however disparate your heritage I am very pleased to meet you. We Chronos are peaceful travellers and have little to do with the warlike humans, you call Solarian".

"We are going for our community dip soon if you would care to join us"? Băifotă asked then. It seemed Mayling was not yet ready to share a pool with several naked aliens however and she too in a state of undress. She learned these details before politely declining. She asked the principal Prædontt if they could be shown the room they would be occupying that night instead. Both of them wondered what the furniture and fitments would be like. They did not fancy getting amorous on cold hard surfaces. To their astonishment, when Băifotă led them to it it was as Spartan as any room they had ever encountered. Gleaming illuminative walls like all others in the building, even though there was not only a window but also a huge rectangular light panel in the walls. On the white floor, created by the same material was a strangely shaped bed. Literally 'L' shaped, but at least it was upholstered with an alien mattress and covered with striped bedclothes.

"We will need to freshen up", Mayling pointed out, "Is the bathroom located adjacent to this room"?

"Everything that you need is here", came the confident reply, "Including a change of clothing should you desire such. You have only to desire and the facilities will provide".

"The servitor can detect our brainwaves"?! Nigh was astonished at such a level of technology, but there again the Prædontt had inter-stellar travel and had mastered hyperspace. The fact of the matter was though that the reality of it was even more fantastic than that.

"Not the servitor no", Băifotă afforded them both one of his incredibly wide grins, "The rooms facilities. I will leave you to discover those at your leisure for it would be unforgivable for me to delay the *bathing*"!

Before either of them could delay him any further with demands of a better explanation, he had exited swiftly.

"What do we do now then"? Mayling wanted to know.

"I guess we do as he seemed to think us capable and experiment".

"Go on then I wouldn't know how to start"?

Suddenly the wall to their left transmogrified before their very eyes and from it formed a sink. White porcelain with chromium-plated taps.

"How did that happen"? Mayling gasped, "Did you do that, Durango? How? What did you do? Did you use the fibriliance"?

"I just thought to myself we could do with somewhere to at least wash our hands. This building is way way beyond anything humanity could create, even in this century".

"Let me have a go then", she smiled and in the far corner of the formerly featureless room, frosted doors appeared. Mayling told him somewhat superfluously,

"You can get rid of your sink. Behind those partitions are a sink, shower and water closet. I've even imagined some large white bath-sheets and load of toiletries. Come on let's see if it's all as I imagined it"?

It was perfect, according to her, down to the tiniest detail and suddenly the joy left her face and was replaced by fear close to terror. Instinctively Nigh knew exactly what thought had just occurred to the girl.

"You're right", he told her taking hold of her slim arms, she was shaking with the trepidation of her reflections. "Mankind would not last one night with matter generators of this sophistication. It's like being Jupiter and all the other gods rolled into one. The Prædontt are far more in control of their baser instincts than we are going to be for millennia".

"If they ever had any base instincts to start with, maybe they were our exclusive property, although I read the Zernoplat were pretty unpleasant".

"Have you ever read the fanciful literature concerning the invasion hundreds of years before that, a race of some sort of insectivores that could hypnotise people or control their minds in some way".

"That would be nonsense, Durango, how could something so small be a threat to us? Enough chatter anyway, I'm going to take a long hot shower and while I do, you are going to imagine a frock for me to put on once I come out of the bathroom and before you ask, *I* will make my underwear".

She skipped away and Nigh was left with the reflection that if Gălăgoraz Örință was as good as the technology of the aliens, then he was going to be in for one Gehenna of a night.

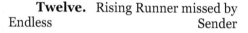

Twelve. Rising Runner missed by Endless   Sender

The evening meal was an extension of the snack they had enjoyed earlier. Prædontt did not seat themselves at a table but rather like the Roman tradition reclined on various couches while the servitor trundled from one to the other offering a varying array of fruit, nuts, tubers and berries. The fluids were both from animals and fermented berries or simply the juice of fruits.

"How do you find the growing of crops in, what to you, is alien soil"? Nigh was tempted to ask, "You seem to have a variety of foodstuffs that I have never tasted before".

Năcindubăit replied, "Terran earth is excellent for crops, filled with nutrients and creatures all working to keep it so fertile. It is 45% more productive then Proxima earth, little wonder some Solarian still refer to it by calling the planet after it".

Once the meedeeusa was present heshe was usually the one to talk to the Chronos. Băifotă was happy enough to fade into a less prominent position, it prompted Nigh to inquire,

"Your rulers. What system of apophthegm do the Prædontt follow and who applies them"?

"Our dynast is usually a committee of three", Năcindubăit replied, "The Triumvirate is voted for by the people once every revolution of Proxima Prime around Proxima, which is 421 revolutions in durations upon its axis. There is but one stipulation and that is that candidates who are proposed for consideration in the vote must be 60% meedeeusa, for it is they who lay the Ouălu".

"So you employ a type of cast system, where meedeeusa are considered of paramount importance in the governance of your society"?

"It is a trifle more complex than that, we have three casts if you choose to call them that, Nigh. As you rightly point out the meedeeusa are at the top of the system, but then there are two more depths rather than one. The second strata are the uruşa while the final cast is the deeso and meeso. This has developed over countless centuries when it was discovered that deeso and meeso leant themselves best to occupations of labour, while the uruşa seemed to have a natural bent toward the arts, literature and theatre. Finally, as you recognise, the meedeeusa is responsible for the continuance of the race and of course are born less often making them more greatly treasured as a result".

"Born, less often, so 25% of each sex are not born to a family unit"?

Năcindubăit shook its hisher weighty head, "Far from it, only 7% of hatchlings are meedeeusa".

"And the other ratio's"? Nigh was genuinely intrigued and could have stayed with the Prædontt months learning all he could about them, they were so...civilized.

"40% are deeso and the same percentage are meeso, the other 12% are uruşa".

Nigh's maths did not need to be brilliant to prompt him to point out, "That only comes to 99%? Am I to take it that 1% of Prædontt do not hatch"?

Năcindubăit's complexion seemed to go through several hue changes then, the equivalent of blushing and heshe muttered barely inaudibly, "No the fifth sex, the freaks are the other 1%".

"There is a fifth gender in the Prædontt genealogy, what do you call them, will I be given the chance to meet one"?

Năcindubăit responded with great care and it seemed chagrin as he informed, "It is not polite to talk of the *ciudaalincilægamogenetic* whilst eating, or most other times. I have probably given you too much information, Nigh".

"On the contrary, I find the existence of pentamerous sexual geology fascinating, you must tell me more about the mysterious ciudaalincilægamogenetic at some other time, Năcindubăit".

Once he had blurted out the inquiry Nigh knew he had committed a faux pas. It was Mayling of all of those present who came to the Prædontts rescue.

She suddenly ejaculated, "Băifotă, that powder you gave me I think.......".

Nigh glanced at her and her skin was aglow with perspiration, her neck was flushed and she suddenly gazed at him wide-eyed,

"......I think I would like a little lie-down, will you come with me please, Nigh"?

Out of devilment, the chronoman prevaricated, "I'm engaged in polite conversation without intriguing hosts, Mayling. I will join you anon".

The Elucidator had other ideas, however. Or rather one single impulse was promoting her desire, She jumped from her couch, not an easy thing to do in the long black frock Nigh had *created* for her and grasping hold of his boho shirt hauled him unceremoniously to his feet.

"You will join me now"! She declared most firmly, "I *need* you to come with me"!

"With wicked double entendre Nigh grinned and observed, "I'll do my best then babe, but it is not always so easy to get the timing exactly right but do not worry.......".

The last few words were strangled in his throat as the Elucidator dragged him from the room and the Prædontt hurried to what Nigh suspected would be a voyeur room of some sort.

* * *

Nigh lay in a film of his perspiration and gasped for breath. He tried to straighten the smile on his face, thinking he must resemble the Cheshire Cat, but he could not. The last forty minutes had been frantic, wanton lustful and very very pleasant indeed. Mayling had been like a tiger, a sexual-warrior and athlete and her appetite had known no bounds. She was beautiful and had the sort of figure that historically women had dreamed off never being able to possess and Nigh had possessed it for a while and very satisfying it was too. He arose and went to have a shower. He needed to rinse and cleanse away the rind and sweat of the acts they had committed and Mayling had certainly left no position out of her catalogue of lasciviousness. As he was towelling himself dry, now careless of his nudity the naked Chinese girl stirred and looked at him accusingly,

"You took advantage of that situation"!

"It's worn off then".

"Thankfully. I fear I was not myself, some of the things we did. Well, I'm......".

"We enjoyed one another and neither of us was being forced. Do not think of it as anything other than a rather mischievous interlude".

"But I was, I was *wanton*"!

"You let your guard down, for the sake of the success of our forthcoming mission. Don't worry I won't expect you to act in quite that way ever again. Now get showered and let's make our farewells because I want to put the timeline back how it should be".

Mayling picked Aurora up thoughtfully and cuddled her to one of her impressive breasts, "Won't this world disappear if we do that".

"I've ceased to think of time as a linear rope travelling through the ether of the cosmos", Nigh responded. "I think it is more like a fourth dimensional fabric and what we have been doing is skipping from one part of the weave to another. As long as we finally find ourselves on the weave where all else feels familiar and how we want it to be I do not think we have made any holes in the fabric. The Prædontt will still be here because they are here and the only thing that will change as a result of our travelling is when here is".

"That's so much double talk", Mayling complained, lowering Aurora to the floor, "But I'm ready for a nice shower and some more adventure, so I'll let you think you've convinced me".

As she passed him, he slapped her perfectly rounded yet pert buttocks and thusly had the last word on the subject. A word that was not a word. Time travel was helping Nigh to think in non-cogent parameters and instead consider simple leaps of intuition. The two of them left the room as they had found it. All the accessories had been reabsorbed back into the translucent walls. They were both dressed in one-piece black jumpsuits of a material that allowed the pores of the body to breathe yet was warm enough to keep out and drafts. The sneakers they wore were of the same wonder fabric. They went in search of the Prædontt, finding them unsurprisingly in the room designated as a lounge. Năcindubăit was very excited, "We could not have guessed, not have conjectured the different ways, the positions, just two sexes can get into"

Mayling blushed deeply, forcing Nigh to comment,

"I would imagine the more of a species there is the less room for manoeuvre. Now, we were promised a portable time machine"?

"Yes," Băifotă acknowledged, "One Urată-îndoită Mark IV if recollection serves me accurately, Allow me to show you out and back onto the plain where I can then give you a short course on how to operate the dials and switches. For your edification, I have created a device with the labelling etched in Solarian. I trusted it would be easier for you than having to remember Prædn, our language in other words".

"Most considerate", Nigh agreed diplomatically, there was no point in mentioning his eidetic memory and anyway Mayling might find herself in a situation where she might have to use the device. So Solarian or Standard or Chinese were all a better option than Prædn.

"I would like to bid each of you farewell in the traditional Chronosite fashion", Nigh lied, "By shaking each of you by the hand".

"It was then that for the first time the two of them learned of one proof of their host's amphibious ancestry. For when touching them it was like holding a frog or toad, obviously warm-blooded but ever so slightly damp. The Prædontt found the touch of the duo quite warm and would not have been able to hold on for long without being burned by mammalian internal heat.

Năcindubăit said to Mayling as heshe shook her hand, "Good luck with your egg, I hope you have what you desire as an offspring".

As Băifotă took them down to the vast entrance chamber of the building Nigh whispered, "I'm glad you did not mention your birth control, I do not know if Prædn mores allows for it and it's always better to leave on a positive note".

He was taken aback and the girl smiled asking, "I never saw you using anything".

"No"! Nigh gasped, "I meant the pill".

"I do not take the pill", Mayling chuckled, "Our marriage might be blessed with an early issue. You *have* remembered we are to marry".

"How could I forget", Nigh groaned.

"Is everything all right", Băifotă asked, seeing the expressions on their faces.

"Everything is just dandy", Nigh replied with a certain amount of observed sarcasm, "I just thought you would have the UI with you, can you produce it from the entrance chamber"?

"UI"?

"I abbreviated the Urată-îndoită Mark IV, it's a bit of a mouth full".

"The Prædontt do not do such things, we find it would lead to metal atrophy".

"You may be right at that", Mayling smiled.

"Well you are right, Nigh", Băifotă finally assured, "I can use any area in this entire complex to create what I desire, do not worry, you can trust the word of a Prædontt and the two of you certainly provided me with a vast amount of valuable data for my thesis. I do have one question though when you put that extendable rod of yours in Mayling's ......".

"Oh look we are on the ground", the girl cut him short. She had heard quite enough to know that any subsequent conversation would prove to be embarrassing in the extremis.

"I find I will miss you. I like you", Băifotă told them with his usual candour then, "Do you think when your mission is completed, that you might take the time to visit us once more"?

Nigh returned honestly, "I hope we are able, Băifotă. If we are, I for one would like to think that this is not my only visit to you and your heshes".

The Prædontt afforded them one of his hideous smiles of appreciation and then began to show Nigh how to operate the device that had just materialised out of the wall. It was not a difficult mechanism to operate, understanding it and using it wisely could take a lifetime or longer.

"It will be capable of operating to a much finer degree than your current unit", Băifotă assured him, "The one I deduce is somewhere inside your body or head. The miniaturisation is admirable in your case, but it might have sacrificed the accuracy to achieve it".

"That is it entirely", Nigh was grateful for the UIMF and did not wish to contradict his Prædontt friend in any way.

"I believe I can use this with confidence now", he assured the alien and the two of them once more bid the heshe farewell. They left the building and walked onto the plain at the outskirts of the beautiful city in introspective silence. Finally, curiosity got the better of the Elucidator and she asked,

"Are you trying to decide precisely which moment to sent us to, Durango"?

"It is a conundrum. I am wondering how best to unravel the threads I seem to have woven together in one way or another. Do I go back one step at a time, or jump right back to a time before any of the events, or jump back to shortly after the Destino launched? I presume you have an opinion".

"The girl flushed and then admitted, "If I were speaking from a personal point of view I would not alter my past, or I might fail to be your fiancé in the next created reality".

Nigh grinned, "We were good together were we not", at the expression of disapproval that remark created, he swiftly added, "And we make a good team too. In our endeavours. Perhaps we can stick together wherever we go and that will mean any changes we make as a duo will not alter either of us, how does that sound"?

To his unexpected delight, she hurried over to him, kissed him gently and confessed, "That sound like an admirable notion".

For the first time, he found himself thinking that being married to Mayling would not be such a terrible fate. He still wanted to help his Aunt though. Still wanted to see Aurora back as a human being. He wanted to cure Huahua of her injuries and bring Mingfu Li back to being the healthy landlady in China. For the first time, when he thought about everything he realised what a considerable task he faced.

'Not to worry', he thought to himself, "Now I have the UIMF it will be a piece of cake".

The trouble was Nigh had never been noted for his skills at baking! After a certain amount of pontification Nigh listened to Mayling s advice when she urged,

"Instead of diving headlong into what may turn out to be further contretemps why do we not go somewhere peaceful and quiet and simply take the time to reflect and formulate a well-considered plan? We have the provisions the Prædontt have placed in the UIMF so we don't need to interact with another living soul if we do not want to"?

"That's an astute observation, Mayling, Nigh acknowledged his new partner, now a companion as well as a collaborator. He was beginning to regard her on a new level. "But whatever period of human history we choose to journey too, there will always be the possibility of running into others, others bringing the possibility of adversity".

"The dial on the machine then, what is the highest set of parameters available to us"?

"Oh! I have not determined that, let me look before I give you an answer". He gasped after he had turned the UIMF on and looked at the number of zeros in the year section of the setting, "Jupiter, Vishnu and Oden, according to this readout, we can go back to the birth of our planet 45 million centuries into the past. The power source must be incredible, I hope it's completely stable.".

"So theoretically we can go the same distance in the opposite direction"?

"I should imagine so, I'll double-check but.....".

"Mayling noted the hesitation, "What is it, does it not go as far forward as the death of the sun"?

"Curiously no. It goes nowhere near as far, way much shorter".

"I believe the reason for that will be because the past happened, it is actual. The future is yet to happen and only extends as far as it does dependant upon what decision the occupants of the world make".

"Decisions, what does that mean to the future"? Nigh was impressed by the deductive powers his fiancé was suddenly displaying.

"We are on Earth and the unit will be taking us into the future of the Earth. Not the solar system or the galaxy or beyond that, but simply the future of this planet. Now, what if some despot shortly is currently bringing the world to the brink of a cataclysm similar to what the Prædontt did to Mars"?

Nigh smiled appreciatively, "Then the future would cease and until certain decisions *are* made, the future cannot extend. Going into that future is therefore dangerous".

"As is going to the past. So now you begin to see the caution of the Prædontt and the Ministro do Tempo Estudos e Tempo Viajando? Cientista de Extrema Aprendizagem Adalberto Almeida Sapientiae had a good reason for displaying to you and your companion, the caution that he advised".

"We'll be careful", Nigh promised.

Mayling chided, "You are a gambler, Durango. To achieve whatever ambition you possess at the time, you are willing to encounter any risk. Just remember the fate of more than you are now at stake? Mingfu Li, Aurora here, Huahua, Decorum and your Aunt. Why even the assassin, possibly the TA you fought as well. They have all become woven into your tapestry. The figurative drapery that adorns the wall of your Xanthicological habitation".

"Fiancé", Nigh objected in jest, "You cannot nag me until we are married, you know that right"?

"There is more at stake now that we are promised to one another", Mayling persisted in all earnestness,

"Not just my future but the future of our yet to be born offspring".

Nigh found himself mentally shying back from the latter notion, he was in his teens still, the thought of parenthood was not even on the edge of his mental horizon. He sensibly did not object vocally though, Mayling was Chinese and so, of course, would expect progeny. Instead, he told her,

"I've decided to take us upwhen, upwhen by a considerable distance and see how the Earth is getting on".

"He tapped the touch part of the Urată-îndoită Mark IV and let it race upward until at a whim he lifted his fingernail. The reading said 13248, or in their way of thinking the 133rd century. It was even beyond what the Tempus Agents had ever explored and it suited the duo's purpose at that point.

Nigh tapped the activation button - wonder of wonders! There was no disorientation, as was created by the Andhera Tantu, no confusion of the senses zero different tactile observations could be made at all for the transition was instantaneous and seamless. One minute they had been on the plain outside the fabulous city of Oorașhaaasa, the very next second they were in the 133rd.

"Oh dear", Mayling observed looking over Nigh's shoulder, "What a shame it was so beautiful".

Nigh spun on his hell and saw the ruin. As ruins went it was a magnificent one, on a scale with the Pantheon or Circus Maximus, but not in the same league as the Pyramids. The city was crumbling into strange mounds of some sort of heavy detritus. The tops of some of the spires open to the strangely pink-tinged sky. Truly it was a long time after the 60th and all things must eventually crumble to dust, but the city of Oorașhaaasa had seemed so permanent so timeless.

"Neglect, or attack", Mayling asked him, Which do you think"?

"How could I know enough at this point even to perpetuate a theory", Nigh objected.

"But there is one vital clue one piece of evidence"
The Elucidator was enjoying her superior powers of
deduction. "The sky, its hue, the dust in the air contains
huge amounts of ferrous oxide".

"You don't mean..."?

"Arresolaria. The Arresolarite has been in the air
over us, they could well be the ones who destroyed the city
of Ooraşhaaasa. Do you fancy going to see if we can find
out"?

"I thought we had come here to enjoy a period of
peaceful contemplation and relaxation", Nigh objected half-
heartedly.

"I am relaxed", Mayling told him, "And the city
looks peaceful now, I just wonder if there are any records in
its crumbling walls or even the odd Prædontt to interview.
You stay here if you want, I'm going to Ooraşhaaasa".

"Wait"! He cried after her then, "We're engaged,
remember, so we should now do things together".

The girl laughed and raced away. Forcing him to
trot after her, impeded as he was by the burden of the
UIMF. Her theory regarding the race she had referred to as
the Arresolarite proved to be gaining momentum for they
were soon kicking up plumes of rust with their passage. Had
Arresolaria began to decay? Was that the reason for the
attack? Had the Prædontt created an unstable planet with a
relatively short life cycle in cosmic terms? Or was it simply
revenge and the dust of Arresolaria clung to their vessels as
they set off to attack the cities of their ancient enemies? As
usual, the couple had no shortage of questions. Answers
were always that much more difficult to locate. As they
jogged their way to the ruins, suddenly Mayling stopped
dead in her tracks and Nigh collided with her unable to brig
himself up short in time,   "What
the...."!   "Jupiter, look"! His
fiancé gasped.   Nigh looked, in the distance and an
impossibly elongated figure was dashing toward the same
destination as themselves. The runner was taking huge
leaps into the air between covering the ground in vast
loping strides. She was wearing shorts and singlet, even
with her elongated limbs it was possible to determine that
she was human in general proportion and of course female.
On her long narrow feet were even some sort of running
shoe or plimsolls with chunky cushioned pads to reduce the

impact as she smote the ground that was trying ardently to slow her progress with both friction and gravity. Earth was not winning the strange contest however, the runner was making speedy progress, a pace that neither of the Chronos could hope to approach never mind equal.

"Come on", Mayling sounded like she was excited by the notion of a contest even if she could only hope to come second best to the rising runner. Before Nigh could either agree or urge caution, the Chinese girl was off in pursuit. He sweated and laboured beneath the weight of the Urată-îndoită Mark IV and could feel the front surface of the pack adhering to his back and jumpsuit with the tacky layer of perspiration he was bathed in. Nevertheless, he tried his utmost to match the pace of his fiancé and entered the open to the element entrance at the base of a once familiar chamber.

How different it was since before seventy-three centuries had passed. When Nigh considered the simple math of those passing aeons he realised it was lucky to be anything other than strange grey dust. Even the Prædontt could not create something eternal, something oblivious to the vast passage of the decades and centuries.

"Mayling"! He cried and heard her over to his left call out,

"She went up the stairs, the platform that took us up is no longer functional unsurprisingly, come on, she's practically flying"!

He wanted to cry out to allow her to fly away but was not going to be bested by his diminutive girlfriend. With a great sigh that inflated his lungs ready for the endeavour, he trundled after her, taking the stairs two at a time. He heard Mayling cry out from around the next corner, it was always the next corner,

"Up another floor".

The stairway was naturally winding negating much of the advantage his long legs could have afforded him and twice he jostled into the right-hand wall of the left-hand spiral. They had gone eight levels when he heard Mayling cry out,

"She's at the top, hurry she doesn't look too pleased to see anyone here".

Knowing it would soon see an end, Nigh pushed his lactic congested muscles to one last mighty effort. The stairs came to the eleventh floor and there was no twelfth. That level was open to the sky. When the strangely stretched figure of the runner saw Nigh her narrow eyes widened in astonishment, causing Mayling to smile and observe,

"She doesn't much like the look of you. I think she has oriental heritage judging by her eyes and complexion. She's acting like she's never seen a Caucasian before".

"Maybe she has never seen a human before. I'm thinking her body is so stretched because she was born in a world with lower gravity. You don't think that she's a descendant of the....".

"Arresolarite, those humans who went to the newly constructed replacement for Mars. In seven hundred and thirty decades it's reasonable to suppose that the humans would have grown gradually taller until they looked like her. I think it's time to introduce ourselves".

He took a pace forward and greeted, "Hello I am Nigh and this is Mayling, we are peaceful travellers. Can you tell us what happened here"? He indicated the building

"Chein numelu Ares estut"? The runner demanded.

"Of course", Nigh admitted, "Silly of me not to think the language would not change in seven thousand three-hundred and some odd years".

The girl cocked her fluted skull on one side and hearing Nigh speak suddenly reached into her shorts and pulled something out of a narrow pocket. Gingerly she stepped forward and held a small object out to Nigh.

He held out a palm, something not unlike a hearing aid was dropped into it. Straight away the tall runner indicated with gestures that he should place it into his ear. Nigh examined it and saw it would not get lodged, it was too large to reach near his eardrum, so he placed it in his ear as directed.

"What in Ares name are you"? The girl then asked.

Mayling was effectively excluded from the conversation for the time being.

"I am male, a man".

"I can see that you are male, but why are you so pale,? Are you also some sort of dwarf? No though, dwarves have the right shape head, it is just the spine that is truncated. You are not Arresolarite, are you"?

"This translation aid is a marvel", Nigh was momentarily sidetracked by the wonderful hearing and translating aid. "I am a Chronos. A human who can travel through time".

"An ancient? When the ancestors of we Arresolarite walked on the Planet of the Prædontt. Before they stole it from us".

"That is correct", Nigh admitted, "We are ancients, in my time not everyone had the complexion of my companion here, nor the eye shape".

"It is not a deformity then"? The girl was candid rather than insulting, "You do not have a skin condition, some sort of melanin deficiency"?

"No, the ancients were originally five hues of skin, yellow such as my companion and yourself, pink like me, brown, black and red".

"Black, hahahaha, don't be ridiculous no one could have black skin".

"Not even on Venus, Callisto or Moon"?

"Venuser have brown, but they are not Arresolarite, the Arresolarite on the other locations you mention are all like me".

So it seemed the Oriental races had succeeded in populating the solar system to the exclusion of all the other types. Of course, they would all grow taller as the gravity they all enjoyed was less than 1g.

"Are there any other Arresolarite on Terra any longer, or is this world now owned by the Prædontt", Nigh asked then.

"The Prædontt are somewhere but we do not know where", the girl intrigued, "They message us from the Endless Sender ".

With that, she stepped to one side and indicated possibly one of Earth's last Computer/SWW transmitter/receivers. It was still operational. Whichever generator deep in the bowels of the building was powering it, must possess a practically inexhaustible power supply, judging by the dust on every surface of the ruined buildings.

"I missed the message today but I will rise again on the morrow and race to this location".

"Was there a war here? Is that why you need to communicate through the erm, Endless Sender"?

"There was something". The Rising Runner agreed, "And the Prædontt had to flee. I am not sure why they went, but they did. Now I rise with the dawn, I run and I receive the messages from the Endless Sender. Today I missed the message though. It grows more indistinct every year".

Probably as the Prædontt journeyed further and further away, Nigh thought to himself, wondering what race was able to inspire such fear in them that they fled into space leaving prime real estate behind. Why did the other power not then settle on Earth too? Why had the Arresolarite grown so dependant upon the Prædontt that they still cared enough to receive their messages as well? Nigh had so many questions and precious few answers. He asked one thing he desired to know more urgently than anything else,

"Why do you rely on the Prædontt now they are gone, surely you can govern yourselves"?

"The Prædontt *knew*"! The girl intoned, almost as in a religious rite.

"Knew what exactly"?

"They knew what we needed to know and they told us and now they are gone. We have the Endless Sender though, so we will survive".

It struck Nigh then. Humanity had devolved. Atrophied into the girl he now spoke with, reliant upon their once conquerors. Now that the supervisors were suddenly gone, chased away by something even more powerful and malign, the supervised had no one to direct them. When the Endless Sender finally fell silent, what would become of what was left of humanity?

"This reminds me of Wells' Eloi", he remarked to Mayling who simply demanded to know the detail of their conversation and did not recognise the name of the ancestral writer of strange biographies. Nigh quickly explained what had transpired between him and the Runner, while the latter gazed soulfully at the mechanism which unyieldingly refused to cooperate with her.

"What will you do now then"? He finally asked the tall young woman, "You can stay with us for the night if you want, we can get a fire going and we have some provisions we could share with you"?

"Oh no that would not be how it is to be", the girl responded as if by rote. "I am the Rising Runner when dawn comes, I must rise and I must run and only then can I meet the Endless Sender".

It sounded more like a superstitious observance than logical behaviour, but Nigh knew better than to try to be logical with one who was superstitious, so he returned,

"I will give you your translator back then and we will delay you no further, Rising Runner. Good luck tomorrow".

"You can keep the Babel Fish if you wish, I have another spare".

"The translation earpiece, why do you call it that"?

"It is what it is called, it was thusly given such nomen centuries ago".

"Nigh nodded, there was no point in doing anything else. To the runner to call a translation device a fish seemed the most logical of things.

"Good luck then", he ended slightly lamely and the Rising Runner raced away she was never going to break her established pattern, she was always going over.

She turned and in an instant was gone.

"So now we have the city to ourselves do we"? Mayling asked, "What's the plan, Durango"?

"The plan is thought. Careful thought", he replied, "And once I have come to any sort of decision, with your help I might add, then you shall be the first to know".

"It would seem to me that the destruction of the androids was not good for the future of mankind", the Elucidator illustrated at once, "The Rising Runner came from a static society on the cusp of decay".

"Yet the Prædontt seemed so civilised and peaceful, surely ultimately what they did for the home-world, this planet, was benign rather than malign"?

"Perhaps they were too peaceful in the end", Mayling then observed, "Over the centuries it would appear that they forgot how to fight and whoever came after them was greeted with little or no resistance (The author explores this scenario in greater depth in:- From the Grave to the Cradle)".

"I think that astute observation. For now, though my chief concern is to gather enough detritus to make a fire for us. You go and look for somewhere where we might sleep once the light fails. I will give the evening over to contemplation and then come dawn we shall make some sort of plan".

Saying nothing by way of a reply, the girl nodded and went to do as directed. Nigh afforded himself a lascivious grin, anticipating the night spent with the Chinese beauty. After all, they were engaged to be wedlocked! That night they managed to find a room with a roof yet open enough to let the smoke of an open fire escape. It proved to be a wise manoeuvre, as there was a cloud burst while they were cooking their Prædontt provided provisions.

"No lightning, we are safe enough", the girl observed, though it was plain by her remark that she was no fan of electric storms.

"Good", Nigh looked out into the dark brown sky, "We will not have to take a Cloudburst Flight"!

When she did not smile, he was forced to add, "Cloudburst Flight. Like the famous Tangerine Dream piece".

"Tangerine Dream", the girl ran the nomen through her memory, "Do you mean the ancient minstrels who played archaic instruments with their actual fingers"?

"I do, possibly the very best exponents of their particular genre".

"I'm afraid though I have heard *of* them, I have not heard any of their stereo performances", she admitted to him, "I prefer the computemuzak of the 49th".

"Well, I am pleased to say I have not heard any of that. Nor would I want to how soulless - music computed. The whole point of expression in various notes and pitches is to show the quiddity of the composers. A machine is incapable of doing that".

"I listen to it when I am baking".

"Another mistake", Nigh debated, "To appreciate good music one has to listen to it. That means sitting down paying full attention to it and hearing every nuance, every key change, every single note the composer has committed to the medium. You cannot do that if you are distracted by another activity, no matter how mundane".

"Mundane? You have never tasted my cooking and baking. Your attitude to it will change once your palate has been delighted by some of my recipes. As you will discover once we are married".

"I am sure they will be as splendid as you are predicting", Nigh felt obliged to be diplomatic then. They ate their provision, then made love while the rain tumbled out of the sullen dark brown sky. Falling asleep in one another's arms on the cleanest bed they had managed to locate.

As dawn heralded its arrival with impossibly russet fingers of light in the eastern sky, the two of them awoke and Nigh eventually told Mayling his decision.

"There is only one sensible thing to do really and that is to go back further in time than we have done before and try and undo all the consequences we caused in each botched affair that followed it. Save Decorum's life, stun Fiscarte without killing him and warn Gravis to leave the couple alone".

"It's a tall order and you might remove the Prædontt from our timeline altogether"?

"Maybe they do not belong on our timeline at all, I think perhaps we have ended up on a different place in the weave than the one we started on. My hope is simply to undo all the complication and resolve our issue with my Aunt's lover all in one swiftly conducted mission. Can I rely on your assistance and support"?

"You know you can, I'm not even pleased that you asked".

Then let's clear up and get back to the 33rd, hopefully for the last time".

Ever the optimist was young Nigh. On that occasion, some of his optimism was not as displaced as usual. What the result of his further tampering would be, however, only *time* would tell!

Thirteen.   TMC.

"I have just noticed a strangely intriguing alteration to the readings on one of my instrument panels Capitano", Fiducia observed,

"Explain"? Matteus Crespo Gubernator requested tacitly.

"The payload of our vessel has just increased by 133 kilogrammes".

"You're saying we are now carrying 133 kilogrammes more than when we blasted off for Mars"?

"Precisely, Sir".

"What sort of anomaly could account for that? Surely not space-dust and we could not have been hit by a meteor our instruments would have detected the impact"?

"I have a theory, Capitano", Tenant Plenusia Tazza Circumerario offered.

"And what would that be, Circumerario"?

"The weight gain would be explained if one very heavy intruder was aboard, or more likely two less heavy".

"Would not our instruments have indicated the fact that we had been boarded"? Matteus could not hide the incredulous note of scorn that had entered his tone of voice.

"Normally, if the intruders possessed the same level of technology as ourselves".

"But"?

"If they were sufficiently more advanced to have some sort of steal technology then they could have achieved it without activating our instruments".

Matteus said to Fiducia, "Despatch an armed security detail to the area of the ship where the weight has suddenly increased".

"You think the intrusion is malign, Capitano"? The Tenant inquired.

"I think it can only be an invasion or a prelude to one. The newcomers did not announce their intention to come aboard", Matteus decided. "We need a show of force. Anything else would be a demonstration of weakness. Have the intruders caught and brought to my conference room Fiducia. Tell security if they resist, to use force, as deadly and extreme as is necessary if matters escalate. No one is going to invade my vessel and get away with it"!

"Permission to offer some advice, Sir"? Circumerario then requested.

Matteus was in one mind when it came to the possibility of invasion however, "Permission denied", he snapped.

"Firstly we locate Fiscarte and his employer, Gravis", Nigh said swiftly to his Elucidator and Fiancé. "I'll put the assassin out of action while you hold the father, then we'll have a little word with him".

Aurora was no longer with them, she had snapped out of existence when they had travelled through time and they had chosen to believe that it was a good thing. Somewhere - somewhen she was human once more... hopefully!

Before Mayling could as much as give a nod, he was striding off, despite the weight on his back. She could not doubt his enthusiasm, even if upon occasion it did turn out to be misplaced.

They covered considerable ground before a familiar if unwelcome figure suddenly appeared in the habitat ring's plaza.

"My fellow agents had to come back and rescue me before you murdered me, Durango Nigh", 5423Dorph told him. In his fist was a rather unpleasant looking flare-nosed energy weapon that was probably deadly. The agent had made a classic mistake, however. He had bothered to give the time-rogue an explanation for his appearance. Nigh himself would never have delayed in just such a dangerous way. He dove forward into a tremendous slide, his jumpsuit providing little friction on the polished metal decking of the vessel. His right foot caught 5423Dorph just beneath his left knee. There was the nasty grinding sound of cartilage damage and the Tempus Agent cried out in a combination of surprise and pain. At the same instant, Nigh snatched the weapon from distracted fingers and promptly smote the TA a rather enthusiastic blow to the temple. People began to stare as 5423Dorph crumpled on top of his attacker.

"Don't worry folks this criminal is now under my jurisdiction", Nigh calmed them with the authority in his lying voice. He pushed the inert form of 5423Dorph, who rolled onto the floor at his side. As Mayling helped him to his feet he grinned,

"That chap is starting to annoy me. Right, let's find the assassin".

"What are you going to do about him"?

"Someone, call a doctor", Nigh announced to the gathering crowd. "He's had one of his spasms".

The two of them melted away from the knot of onlookers and no one noticed them go.

Nigh handed the weapon to the Elucidator, "Can you figure out how to use this"?

Mayling grinned, "There isn't a weapon created that I cannot".

"Yes but that one has not been created, *yet*"!

The duo proceeded onto the next level of the habitat ring.

"Do you want me to take a turn with the time pack, it must be tiring you somewhat"? Mayling offered as the lift took them to the next floor.

"Have a girl carry something for me, I don't think so", Nigh laughed, "Don't worry about me, Babe, just keep your eyes peeled for that Fiscarte fellow. I've got a feeling we may have just changed our luck this time and the mission is going to be a resounding success".

Nigh's words proved remarkably auspicious because as the door of the lift opened, they almost collided with none other than Fiscarte and Gravis.

"Excuse me...". the assassin managed before the edge of Nigh's hand struck him on the side of the neck and he slumped half into the lift, half still in the corridor beyond. Gravis would have ejaculated a gasp of astonishment and trepidation were it not for the fact that his throat was on fire and he was struggling for breath. The perfectly straight fingers of the Elucidator had driven into his windpipe with alarming force and accuracy. Acting as one the Chronos dragged the pair into the first room on that level, which thankfully was unoccupied. Gravis was gasping and dry retching which allowed Mayling to handle him easily even though he was considerably heavier than her. Nigh had thrown the stunned assassin over a shoulder and carried him into the room fireman style before dumping him onto the first bed he reached. He gazed about him, found some wire that was attached to a lamp and soon was not and began to bind Fiscarte's wrists.

"Now listen to me, Alexius Morrelius Gravis", he began whilst still engaged in his task. "I am my Aunt's protector and that extends to the man she has chosen to be with, your son, Decorum. Harm either of them or have them harmed by this chimpanzee here and I will hunt you down and I will kill you. Nod if you understand me"?

Gravis, who's complexion was puce, did not even hesitate, he nodded miserably.

"Good. Stay here for the rest of the voyage and then disembark in your boarding disguises. Go back to China and never come to Mars again. Otherwise, you *know* what will happen"!

Gravis finally managed to gasp from his bruised larynx,

"Who are you"?

"Your nemesis", Nigh growled with all the theatrics he could muster. Nodding to Mayling the two of them left, closing the door behind them.

"Very good, now we can go back to the 51st and be reunited with the others *if* they are there"?

"We have not finished yet", Nigh surprised her. "If Lynea killed Decorum for his money we have not saved him. We need to know that such did not happen and the only way we can discover the truth is by meeting them once again".

"You are right of course. I do not see your Aunt is the killer though".

"Neither do I, but I do not want to have to come to this ship ever again. Come on".

Taking the lift to level five the duo raced down the corridor and pounded on suite 595".

"Stop what you are doing"! An unknown voice suddenly barked. "Throw your weapons to the floor, then lay down face first on it and do not move, or my men have orders to shoot with maximum prejudice".

Nigh demanded, "Who by Jupiter are you"?

"Ship's security, now do as you are told, take longer than three seconds and we will open fire"!

* * *

"I don't like this, they've been gone too long", Mingfu Li complained, "Something must have gone wrong"

She did not know the half of it and never would.

"It takes time to accomplish what Durango has set out to do", Huahua observed, "I'm certain they will be alright, both he and Mayling are more than capable of looking after themselves".

"I'm going to make some tea", Aurora decided, "Who would like a cup"?

Everyone decided that they would and Aurora went into the kitchen. Neither Mingfu Li or Huahua broke the silence, having nothing to contribute to the conversation. They both gasped when Aurora returned though, for she was not alone. A man dressed in unusual garb that was not recognisable as contemporary was holding the girl by the throat and some sort of pistol was pressed into her neck.

"Don't move", he hissed, "If you do, then your friend will not end up feeling too well. She might end up feeling dead".

"What do you want"? Mingfu Li asked, "Who are you and why are you treating us in this way"?

Huahua had a little more deductive power though and she guessed, "You are Fiscarte are you not"?

"It don't matter who I am. All you have to do is what I say and you get to live through all this. Try anything cute and...well, things won't turn out so well for all of you".

"Fiscarte", Mingfu Li repeated, "I know who you mean, Gravis' hoodlum, but how would he reach the 51st? He did not have the sort of technology to hand that the agents of the 77th had at their disposal. Not in the 33rd. No one had".

"That is true, but in their twisted way, the TA's have decided to recruit him to cause Nigh some difficulty. That is true is it not, assassin"?

The man grimaced, "The descendant, you're too smart for your good. Now shut your yap unless you want to wear your teeth on the outside of your pie-hole".

"Why would the TA's hire someone to break their time-laws", Mingfu Li asked Huahua. "We were told they were very particular about the manipulation of the timeline".

"Needs must when Pluto calls", the descendant of Lynea returned. "They want Nigh so badly and unbeknown to us have failed to detain him, so they've stooped to this thuggee to do their dirty work for them. That's right isn't it Soil-man"?

"I'm warning you one more word and I'll let you have it right between the eyes", the swarthy man with weasel-like features hissed. Huahua seemed unkowed though, she returned defiantly,

"You'll do no such thing. The TA's would never have permitted you to kill anyone. Not one of us anyways. Stop clamouring with that empty cage, Fiscarte. Just tell us what your deal is"?

"I'm telling you nothing", came the retort, but he had ceased to threaten or deny his identity.

"You are obviously to wait here with us and capture or kill Nigh when he gets back. Though I doubt the latter. You are to take him back with you to the Time Institute, yes that's it. Using one of us as pressure to force his cooperation".

"All right clever pants, you've finally guessed it. So will you kindly give my eardrums a rest now"?

"So you are Fiscarte", Mingfu Li was surprised,

"How did you get here then? Are you really at the behest of the agents from the Ministro do Tempo Estudos e Tempo Viajando"?

"I'm working for the Cientista de Extrema Aprendizagem Adalberto Almeida Sapientiae himself if you must know. Now, will you shut your rattle, the pair of you"?

"Let go of Aurora's neck, or I'll talk and talk until you find your brain melting and running out of your ears", Huahua threatened and to their collective surprise, Fiscarte pushed her toward the couch the two of them were already seated upon.

"Now shut it, or I'll break my promise to the professor and break something, maybe a bone in one of your sweet little bodies". Then a wicked notion crossed his mind. A dark expression of malice and lust lit up his feral features as he warned, "But that would get me into trouble probably, so strike that. No instead I'll take one of you lucky ladies into the bedroom and entertain myself with her body for a while".

That did result in nervous silence!

* * *

"How did you get aboard my vessel"? Matteus asked the male prisoner.

"By use of an UIMF", came the instant and seemingly candid response. Matteus hesitated and Fiducia came to his aid,

"What is a UIMF, explain it to the Capitano".

"The UIMF, to give it it's full nomenclature, the Urată-îndoită Mark IV is a transportation unit for travelling through not the usual three dimensions, but four. It allows the wearer to traverse the various threads of the leylines that exist like a matrix in the ether of the medium we all inhabit. I must point out that any attempt to tamper with the unit will result in an explosion so catastrophic that this vessel and thousands of kilometres of space surrounding it will be atomised to anti-matter. The unit is also duration sensitive, so if you delay us unnecessarily I cannot guarantee the safety of the vessel and her crew and passengers"!

Nigh had spoken with all the conviction he could muster, he and Mayling were currently incapacitated and he needed to be free very soon, or they would miss their window of opportunity. In his mind, he was hatching a scheme not only to convince the captain of the Destino to release the two of them but to help them to find his Aunt and her illicit lover.

Matteus was plainly out of his depth, he hesitantly requested rather than demanded,

"Could you put that explanation into less scientific terms and tell me what you are doing here"?

Nigh saw the rather striking Latino who her uniform indicated was second in command wince at the request and rightly deduced that of the two she was the vastly more experienced. He thusly turned to her and warned simply,

"Delay will result in peril for us all. Will you assist the two of us rather than hindering us, no one will come to harm if you do"?

"What do you want to do and how can we help, if it is non-aggressive", the Tenant returned, her rich contralto tones were as sensual as her appearance.

"I wish to find the two passengers who are travelling under the names of Mr and Mrs Pollopanie and simply assure myself they are safe. Then we will be gone from here"?

"What do you mean gone from here"? The captain interrupted, you haven't even told me how you got here in the first place. I want an explanation and I want it in everyday language, either Italian or Standard"?

"I'm sorry, Sir, but I gave it to you once and in language that was not particularly difficult to determine the intention to. In my sphere of normal existence, it is said that one does not need the greatest intellect to achieve the mandate of regulation, but rather to simply possess the loudest intonation".

"Capitano", the Tenant requested then, "With your permission I believe I can sort out this seemingly insoluble conundrum".

"I don't need your assistance, thank you Circumerario", the captain was belittled by the oblique suggestion that he was out of his depth, "I'll deal with the prisoners".

"Then do so, Sir", Nigh allowed the edge of nervousness to creep into his lies, "Because the chronometer is reducing our chances of survival at the rate of one second per second and you are letting them tick down. Failure will result in a detonating percussion of cataclysmically violent paroxysm that will annihilate not only we here - but future generations in the misty horizon of the quadrigeminal elemental ambit".

"Are you saying you have a bomb"? The captain demanded, suddenly querulous.

Nigh replied in as convoluted a fashion as he were able, "The only hazardous detonative on the control centre right now is the provocativeness of the luminary's injudiciousness".

The captain was confused, but he could see that the others of his crew manning the control room were beginning to look very nervous indeed at the garrulously oblique language of the stowaway. He, therefore, did what a good commander does when he knows he is out of his depth and that others in subsidiary positions could well deal with the problem better, he blustered,

"I cannot be bothered with this matter when I'm responsible for making sure this vessel does not fly into the GS. Tenant, you deal with the intruders"?

"Yes sir", the brunette beauty responded instantly. Nigh suddenly got a rather firm elbow in the ribs.

"What was that for"? He nearly yelped, for it hurt and it surprised him.

"Put her clothes back on"? Mayling hissed.

"What are you talking about"?

"You've undressed her three times"!

Amazingly the Italian brunette merely smiled indulgently, obviously used to the attention and rather enjoying the Chinese girl's show of jealousy.

She turned to the navigator and requested, "Put out a request for Mr and Mrs Pollopanie to come to the captain's conference room, Fiducia".

The captain affected not to notice what was being done or to take any interest in events, in the contest between them, Nigh had proved to be a comparatively mental giant.

"Come with me, please? The two of you can go, I will be all right". The latter instruction was to the security men who were still in the control room. Nigh followed a very nice piece of ass, to use ancient vernacular to the room in question. For his look of ill-disguised appreciation, he received another dig in the ribs.

"Don't worry", he sniggered, "A liaison would prove, difficult"!

"We will wait in here", the Italian either had not heard or found the remark unworthy of comment. She took a small implement from the lines of her uniform and sliced the nyloplanyon ties wraps from their wrists, the blade must have been edged by transparent carbon, for it to have cut the wraps so easily. From the desk, she then handed back what weapons Nigh and Mayling had taken from Fiscarte and Gravis.

"I thought you from the 77th", she admitted, "But those weapons are contemporary nothing more. Out of purely scientific interest, when are you from time traveller"? Her question was directed to Nigh alone, which annoyed the Chinese girl. She smiled at him too and further asked,

"Now you are once more armed and free, I am not likely to be attacked am I"?

"Not in any way", Nigh returned obviously. "Our mission is to save a life, we are peaceful".

"The husband or the wife, which is in danger and whom from"?

"Mr Pollopanie is in danger from an assassin called Fiscarte, who in turn is in the employ of one Alexis Morrelius Gravis. Neither of them has boarded in their real names and appearances, but you will find them on level five in suite 501. the killer is currently incapacitated. If you so desire you can hand them over to the authorities on Mars. Fiscarte will escape or be released subsequently though, but he will not have killed Mr Pollopanie. We are from the year 5057, I am a direct descendant of the couple I seek to protect".

"Then their injury would not have jeopardised your existence"?

"I'm a distant nephew, not distant son".

The lie was close enough to the truth to sound eminently convincing and the dusky Latino found it so. Before any more could be said the door opened and in stepped Lynea and Decorum. Nigh's Aunt's eyebrows shot up in surprise at seeing her nephew once again but the former quickly urged,

"Mrs Pollopanie, I'm here to stop Fiscarte and Gravis from doing you an injury. We have incapacitated them and put the Tenant here in the picture, you will both now be safe until you reach Mars and then you can disappear, whilst Fiscarte will be held in custody".

"Well thank you ....Sir, who-so-ever you are. I assume myself and Mr Pollopanie here have your blessing to continue our journey unmolested then"?

"All in a days work for the TA's of Ministro do Tempo Estudos e Tempo Viajando".

Nigh had told so many lies he was beginning to wonder if he would recognise the truth if it hit him right between the eyes. Suddenly Lynea grasped his hand and said earnestly,

"Thank you....erm, agent".

"Go with the guests and stay with them until they disembark onto the shuttle", Circumerario instructed the security member who had accompanied them into the conference room.

"Thank you, Tenant, we will leave the vessel now, good luck in the storm, but do not worry the ship will weather it".

"I have so many questions, but you would not answer even one if I asked you, would you"? The second-in-command of the ship asked.

"We're not allowed to give any such information out to straight-timers", Nigh's silver tongue was still fully operational, "On pain of death actually, so I hope you understand"?

"Of course. As I hope you understand in turn, when I ask you to get off this ship", the woman returned with a throaty chuckle.

"Right then", Nigh turned to Mayling, "Let's go back, I think we got it right this time"!

Getting it right was not necessarily going to result in a conclusion to the entire business though!

*   *   *

The transition into the apartment was seamless with the UIMF. The Prædontt certainly knew their technology. That reflection caused Nigh to momentarily wonder in what capacity the special race of aliens now existed on Earth in the future. Fiscarte was restored to the timeline and had assassinated he whose actions against the visitors had destroyed Mars. That meant that A23 very possibly still existed and that was not a comfortable thought for him. Adding to the confusion it might not even be the timeline he and Mayling now found themselves in. In a multiverse and an infinite number of possible combinations were possible.

"The place looks right", Mayling thought aloud as she was glancing furtively around. "I wonder how many of them made it this time".

"There is no reason to suppose that none of them didn't", Nigh argued, but he felt nervous. He had been confident before and it had always preceded yet further complications.

"Mingfu Li could be at work. How precisely did you set the UIMF"?

"Just with enough local time elapsed to make certain we never arrived back before we set off. Being as we didn't in our memory anyway".

"So Fiscarte killed Jiánhòng Chen and Aurora won't be a cat or a Taiwanese any more. Huahua will be alive and uninjured and Mingfu will once again be alive and female".

"For certain", Nigh felt anything other than certain, but he put a confident face on his prediction.

"So where are they then"? Mayling could be annoying, Nigh thought, when she really tried and she was certainly trying his patience at that point.

"You are currently in possession of the same information and sensory data as I, Mayling. So why do you expect me to instinctively know something that you don't"?

"Access your Andhera Tantu then", the girl demanded, "You still have the dark mirrors in your brain, do that yoga thing you do and find out where the girls are. In the meantime, I will access the SWW and find out how Decorum and Aunt Lynea lived out the rest of their lives".

"Yes! That is a good plan", Nigh felt slightly chagrined that he had not thought to try it without the girl having to suggest it, so he did as she instructed. He let his mind leave his skull (figuratively) and float about the room. All he saw was the room, admittedly with his eyes closed in concentration. So then he tried to manufacture a mental image of duration. It helped him to place a huge sand-glass in the middle of the lounge. An ancient timing device so large that instead of being an hourglass it was a day-glass. With the power of the fibriliance Nigh figuratively pushed the sand from the bottom of the glass back up into the top. He was imagining time flowing backwards and it suddenly yielded fruit. All three figures of his friends suddenly flickered into the representation of the lounge. They were not alone though! A man was in the room with them. A man who had his back to Nigh's imaginary viewpoint. Nigh imagined himself flowing clockwise to see the man's features, though why he expected to recognise him, he did not know. As the weaselly features swam into focus Nigh gasped and opened his eyes, the imaginary room promptly vanished and he said to Mayling, his voice dripping with dread,

"Fiscarte's got them! Fiscarte has the girls somewhere"!

Mayling looked startled, but then Nigh realised she had already had a rather grim expression on her fine features before she had heard the latest piece of news.

"Where do you think.......what? What have you learned from the records"?

"It's your Aunt, Nigh. I'm afraid her future from the Destino onward was not as fortunate as if we had not saved Decorum".

"Less fortunate than quietly disappearing into lonely obscurity"? Nigh noted with dread, "How less fortunate, Mayling"?

"Decorum. At first, it sounded like the two of them were happy enough, so I scrolled through the decades as you do and finally found the sensation six years later"!

"The sensation"?!

"Decorum's execution in Rothcaster, Saxonia in the Mare Cimmerium region".

"Executed! That only leaves a very decreasing list of possible crimes, for which, he will have been convicted! Tell me quickly it wasn't for murder? For the murder of his lover, my Aunt"?

Mayling hung her head and admitted, "He had become a Snufz addict and when Lynea would not release the last of their funds to fuel his addiction......".

"Quickly? Cleanly? Please tell me it was with a needle gun"?

Once again though the news could not have been much worse, "I'm afraid he was convicted of GBH, it seems your Aunt was so badly injured, she did not survive".

"The Azdogunoi (vulgar:- lit trans pond slime or pond scum) beat her to death", Nigh cursed.

Mayling nodded.

"We have to go back, but not to the ship this time to Mars. I'm going to kill him myself".

"What about the others? What has happened has happened, but the girls might be in peril now?! When do you think he took them"?

"You've just answered your question, Mayling", Nigh correctly deduced. "If the assassin can travel from the 33rd to the 51st it can only be with the sanction or even assistance of the 77th".

"But we cannot go up against them", Mayling whined, "Even we two would be no match for the TA's".

"True", Nigh admitted freely, we need allies and we know just exactly where to get them from don't we"?

"The 60th. We don't even know if the Prædon are still in this timeline. If they are why would they help us"?

"They are nervous about fourth-dimensional travel what better way to regulate it than by eliminating the Ministro do Tempo Estudos e Tempo Viajando? They would then be sole custodians of temporal doorways. As to the first part of your objection, my answer is, there is only one way to find out is there not"?

"I'm not certain why the Prædontt will feel obliged to help us", Mayling objected. Why do we not simply go back to the point where Fiscarte entered this apartment and kick his ass"?

"Two incursions into the same area of the thread", Nigh mused. "That sort of attempted manipulation has not turned out well for us in the past if you'll excuse the pun. Something tells me it might not be such a very good idea too".

"What tells you that"?

"If Fiscarte is working for the Ministro do Tempo Estudos e Tempo Viajando [Ministry of Time Studies and Time Travelling] then we can also assume that Cientista de Extrema Aprendizagem [Professor-Scientist] Adalberto Almeida Sapientiae hired him. If I were the Antigo Acadêmico I would have asked myself what Nigh (being me) would do when he discovered that the girls had been abducted. We know what he would thusly reason I think"?

"That you would attempt to do the very thing I've just suggested, so what"?

"So, what, if the Antigo Acadêmico set some sort of trap in the earlier apartment, knowing I would immediately blunder into it".

"More TA's"?

"Or an explosive device"!

"Would that not be breaking his own rules, the rules of the Ministro"?

"If the rules, as recorded in the computers are breached by Cientista de Extrema Aprendizagem Adalberto Almeida Sapientiae, then he can simply rewrite them can he not. He *is* the Ministro"!

"And you want to attack it"?!

"With help. I'm hoping the existence of the Ministro itself will be enough to convince the Prædontt that it should be removed, now that it is conducting a personal vendetta against me by allowing tempusa-kidnappia".

"Tempusa-kidnappia, did you just make that up"?

Nigh grinned", Of course. Are you ready to return to 5057 and see if the Prædon are still there"?

"Where else would I be but at your side, Fiancé"?

* * *

The huge fronds were present once again. The grass was a delicate shade of crimson that time and was dotted with silvery-white mushroom-like plants that grew in clumps hither and thither. Once again the fruits of the mottled blue super growths were white with yellow centres.

"They look like fried-egg trees", Mayling observed. The sky was not pink on that occasion though, rather a very deep and encouraging azure, possibly added to its lustre by the blueness of the tall waving fronds. Nigh had taken them to the same spot at ten minutes before they had appeared the first time they had journeyed to the 60th. This was not the same thread though, adjacent perhaps, but not the identical one. There would be slight variations, they even expected there to be differences. The sun was very warm, very bright and it filled even the more naturally cautious Mayling with optimism.

"Come on then, take my hand", Nigh urged, "I could do with a spot of tiffin".

"You seem confident that the Prædontt will still be part of Terra Prime's future"?

"Of course and look".

They had only progressed a few paces but the even higher and even more brilliant gleaming spires of the city were starting to crest the horizon.

"We never asked if they still call the place Fuchow".

Mayling responded grimly, "Nor did we ask where the original populace went"?

"Băifotă told us though, the southern hemisphere".

"And a good Prædontt always tells the truth", Mayling observed cynically.

As they drew closer to the city of white transparency and silver hues, a figure was approaching them, this was not Băifotă though, in fact, it was not even a meeso. Heshe had the elongated features of an uruşa. This one was far more attractive than Puæm. If any uruşa could be said to be attractive to the human eye.

"Greeting humans, what are you doing on this settlement"? The uruşa was direct.

"We are Chronos and we have come to ask for the aid of the Prædontt. The Ministro in the 77th is currently guilty of tempusa-kidnappia and we have come to find out what Băifotă thinks to their actions"?

"Băifotă my meeso? Even if heshe sympathised with your position of policing the Ministro, why would he be able to do anything about it"?

"Then we should talk to Năcindubăit perhaps? I am sorry but I do not know your name"?

"Năcindubăit is currently indisposed", the uruşa informed Nigh, "Heshe is about to lay an Ouălu. You do not know who I am because we have not met. Leastways not in my memory, but if you are Chronos perhaps in yours"?

"No this is our first encounter, I am Nigh and this is Mayling. We are a couple".

The duo received a shock when the uruşa informed in polite response, "I am Rheină JÝêvvïð".

"Two names? The Prædontt I have previously met all have but the one"?

"Rheină is my title, my nomen is JÝêvvïð (Pronounced gshevi)".

"A badge of office"?

"The closest you have to it in humankind is queen".

"Oh"! Nigh had cause to pause for once, some of his usual poise frozen by the height of Prædontt nobility he was conversing with.

"I am sorry, Majesty. No system of rule was established by your meeso when last we met".

"Think not of it", the queen was magnanimous in her forgiveness, "I am the first uruşa to be voted queen by our race anyways".

"Voted", Mayling finally broke her silence. "Queens do not inherit the title in Prædontt society"?

"That would be folly indeed surely", JÝêvvïð gave the deepest of smiles no human could ever hope to emulate, "To rely on judicious merit being passed down into one's Ouălu would be a genetic lottery".

"Of course it would, Majesty", Nigh toadied, there was never any harm in sucking up to a monarch. "I am sure your reign will be a peaceful and prosperous one with your wisdom guiding your people".

"The term is øampæni, not people", the queen explained, "I shudder to think what would happen if the Prædon became humanitized"!

"Do, perhaps, you mean humanized, Majesty"? Nigh ventured as politely as he could.

"One thing you must learn and learn very quickly, Nigh. Is that a queen always means exactly what heshe says heshe means. Why is a rumegătoarele [four legged creature that ruminated and was kept in herds by the Prædontt] like a fabricăpte [roughly translated:- diary, ledger or aged tome]"?

Nigh tried to guess, "Because what one yields the other sound like"?

"It's a whimsical brain-tormentor, Chronos, there is no right answer". The queen returned amused that Nigh had attempted to solve the riddle.

Mayling added, "A Carrollism then, or Jaberwockite". To both their surprise JÝêvvïδ seemed most impressed by the offering of the Chinese girl,

"Exactly, Chronos, I have read some of the great philosophies of Charles Lutwidge Dodgson. A great philosophical savant and Prædonical mentality, as too were Palin, Elton and Trubbshore".

"Then perhaps we have encountered the right monarch at our very first attempt, Majesty", Nigh returned wondering at a race so advanced technologically, yet impressed with bizarre whimsy and farce. "We will go to the city, you can meet Băifotă and Nuovată, who are my other three quarters. Do you know the latter as you seem to know my meeso and meedeeusa"? "We met in a previous trip on a different thread, Majesty", Nigh proposed, not knowing for certain quite if it were true or if all was beginning to be some strange flight of fancy to a demented mind. Constantly transforming the timeline was a messy and confusing affair and could easily lead to tempuras-psychosis. They followed the Rheină. Strangely shaped with a thin neck that did not look strong enough to support such a fluted skull. The shoulders were hugely muscled by way of compensation perhaps and the rest of the body alarmingly slim and fluted. It no longer concerned the couple though, they were growing accustomed to the unexpected. Into the base of a building, heshe led them. One very similar to what they had previously experienced. The same white walls with the strangely source-less illumination. The vastness of the domed cupola, the lack of ornamentation. They knew it could be imagined if required, but in their vast advancement, it seemed that the Prædontt had become aesthetic and Spartan in their tastes. JÝêvvïδ led them to the expected platform but the journey was far longer than previously. Of course, the Queen would inhabit the very upper-most of the luxury suites in the building.

It was exactly as they had expected. The uppermost apartments rose into impressively tall spires, the last few metres being completely transparent. This caused the apartment below to be suffused with natural light, thrown back in turn by the reflective surface of the white walls, made of some sort of semi-translucent concrete. Once in the habitation of the Queen, they met Băifotă and Nuovată again, but it this part of the fourth dimensional fabric it was for the first time, so they were not remembered as the Chrono's remembered them. Năcindubăit would not have met them either, were heshe present, but heshe was broody.

Once the five of them were seated and supplied by food and drink courtesy of the servitor, the monarch asked them,

"So you found who you were looking for at the first attempt, you said. Why were you looking for me then"?

"My friends have been tempusa-kidnappia by an assassin called Fiscarte, who is working for none other than the Ministro do Tempo Estudos e Tempo Viajando. We can also assume that Cientista de Extrema Aprendizagem Adalberto Almeida Sapientiae hired him to do so. These actions are in breach of their very own tempus-laws and if the Cientista de Extrema Aprendizagem Adalberto Almeida Sapientiae is willing to do that, then none are safe from his interfering reach".

"You, therefore, assumed I would want to know, assuming that I might be nervous that the Ministro might decide to act in such a way as to eradicate our øampæni from this and every other timeline, in which, we journeyed to the Solar System".

"I want my friends back", Nigh was candid, "I also assume you want your øampæni safe from tempusorial attack. I know you have sophisticated machines for defending the fourth dimension, as I use one myself. Do you want to even contemplate the implications of a protracted conflict with a determined organisation who decides to do that to you though"?

"Have you any reason to suppose that it will become their intention"?

"I have met Cientista. Sapientiae is starting with me because I simply want to rescue one of my family. That surely qualifies as a tempusorial micro-change of TSC. Your presence in the 60th will be a huge result in the $77^{th.}$ Making it look very different from what it would have done had you never come to Solarian Three. To put it another way a tempusorial macro-change or TMC. I thusly deduce that once Cientista Sapientiae has done with me he will turn his attention to larger issues. It is simply a matter of time. If he focuses his tempus phase-doors further back once ready, you could be attacked in an hour from now, twenty minutes, who knows. So I ask you to act with me and take the Ministro do Tempo Estudos e Tempo Viajando as soon as you can and put it under the control of yourself, Majesty".

"And incidentally free your friends during the raid no doubt"?

"For which I will be eternally grateful and agree to become an officer in your newly formed Tempus Comb-øampæni or TCO. I will report to you once I have settled my Family History problem and stay in your employ for as long as you desire me so to do. My presence in your newly formed TCO will be an example of how Prædon and Chronos can work together, how a man can befriend a Prædontt and successfully function at his side in the service of you, Rheină JÝêvvï∂ ".

To the combined astonishment of both Nigh and Mayling, the queen of the Prædon did not hesitate but treat the supposition with instantly decisive action.

"Băifotă, gather fifty of your meeso, have them armed and armoured and ready to go with the Chrono's as soon as you possibly can. You will be second in command only to Nigh here. How does that suit your purpose, Chrono Nigh"?

"It suits it admirably Majesty. When I return here it will be with my friends and with your meeso in command of the Ministro do Tempo Estudos e Tempo Viajando".

"And should you not return", the queen wanted to know.

"Then you will need to send far more than fifty meeso in your second wave, for I will be dead"!

Fourteen.   Robbed, Raped and Dead.

As Nigh was setting the mechanism on the back of one of his *troops*, he reasoned that ten rows of five meeso were an impressive sight indeed. It also freed him of his heavy backpack and he and Mayling would be the most mobile of those launching an attack on the Ministro do Tempo Estudos e Tempo Viajando. It was disappointing that they refused to carry anything other than level two needle-guns, essentially being a peaceful race, despite their conquest of Terra. On the other hand, Nigh only desired control, not some mass killing, so he reluctantly agreed that level two would be the best course. Using what he had learned during his military service in the Francosian-Saxonian war he split his force into three units. Ten Meeso would form a left rank and the same number the right, the rest would perform a frontal assault on the building. Nigh had dialled in the location, Portugal and the date, 76,540. The transfer was as instantaneous as usual, all he had to do was give the pre-arranged signal, a circular wave of his left arm and the plan went into action. He and Mayling were in the very vanguard of the central force, determinedly so. From the surrounding cover of the undergrowth, they raced, making no deliberate noise, though gasping from the exertion could be heard. The front doors were not guarded. No one ever expected the Ministro do Tempo Estudos e Tempo Viajando to be attacked. Not when TA's could then skip back to a period before the assault and reverse it with an attack of their own. Nigh   and   the   Prædon   had considered that possibility and that was why they would seize every single tempus phase-door generator in the entire facility. The coup, if successful would make only the Prædon masters of the fourth dimension, with the unique exception of Nigh of course. The door groaned in protest as nigh kicked it aside, two startled students of the Ministro were the first two to receive needles in their necks and they slumped to the floor almost in unison. Nigh was pleased that Mayling had fired her needle at the same instant as he. Then began a race through chambers and lecture halls. The aim to subjugate the students before any could use a mechanism and escape into either past or future. To negate this possibility, one of the meeso carried an instrument that measured fluctuations in the fabric of the ether. Its sensorial gauges were sensitive enough to not only indicate that such a journey had been undertaken but to where and when. During the scouring of the building, two meeso went through phase-doors in pursuit of said fugitives. The third according to Băifotă went to the 33rd.

"Don't pursue the assassin". Nigh requested, "He belongs in the timeline he has gone to. Merely find the Tempo Travessia Dispositivo he used and steel it stranding him exactly where he belongs".

Off went another Meeso Prædontt in pursuit. Finally after two of their own were stunned in subsequent battles, they reached the laboratory of the Ministro do Tempo Estudos e Tempo Viajando, which led to the oldest man any of them, save Nigh, had still supported, reclining in his protective webbing - laying behind his banks of instrumentation. Over his almost completely naked pate, he had once again swooped a few strands over his tonsured scalp. They still looked like snow-covered twigs and would still not have fooled anyone with anywhere near normal vision and deductive reasoning. From rheumy pale eyes that remained non the less vital, he regarded the tormentors and invaders of his Ministro. His skin had the quality of practically transparent parchment and even his wrinkles possessed wrinkles. When he spoke his accusative voice was like the dry whisper of the mistral passing chillingly through reeds,

"How *dare* you do this Night"?

"I was freed from the constraints of your temporal laws when you hired a common and brutish assassin to tempusa-kidnappia my friends, Sapientiae. Now produce my friends, or I'll turf you out of the webbing and then snap your scrawny neck with my bare hands".

Băifotă went a sudden darker shade of blue at the implied violence of Nigh's speech. He held his tongue though, the Prædon had wanted control of the Ministro for some time it seemed and were prepared to tolerate much to achieve that desire.

"You threaten *me*! Me, the Tempus-master of the centuries"?

"Yes", Nigh was brutally candid, "Your period of supervision over a dominion that does not belong to you is over Sapientiae, meet your replacement",

To everyone's surprise, Nigh waved at Băifotă.

"The Prædon are now custodians of time and I suspect they will do a far better job of it than your TA's. Now produce my friends and we will go, leaving you here in this obsolete building. Tied into the 77th indefinitely. You are shut down old man".

With a sigh of resigned defeat, Sapientiae told him, "You will find them in suite ĐÑØ568 completely unharmed. Will you at least leave me the master computer complex"?

"Sorry, no. With enough time and industry, you could use it to rebuild a series of replacement Tempo Travessia Dispositivo's, so even as we speak the stiks are being removed from it along with the motherboard and durasilicon chips. The door opened allowing the last of the resistance to suddenly storm into the laboratory attacking the meeso. The conflict was brief but especially violent. Nigh kicked the foot of one student who was launching himself at him. It threw him off balance and as he stumbled, Nigh brought his fist up with all his strength and heard the man's nose crush like a ripe tomato. By the time he looked up from defending himself, the attackers had all been dealt with but three meeso were injured and one was dead. The Prædontt was not the only casualty of the conflict, however. During the scuffle, someone had accidentally bowled the Cientista de Extrema Aprendizagem [Professor-Scientist] Adalberto Almeida Sapientiae out of his webbed crib. His frail body little more than skin stretched over bones had not been able to endure an impact with the tiled floor. There would be several obvious internal injuries, but as to whether an autopsy would be performed, was academic, for the fall had proved fatal to the first man who had created a Tempo Travessia Dispositivo! Nigh felt a reasonable sadness. Despite his strange moralising and his use of Fiscarte in an attempt to avoid the very sort of thing that had subsequently transpired, Adalberto Almeida Sapientiae had been a Cientista de Extrema Aprendizagem the first and last of his kind. Such gloomy reflections were evaporated in an instant however as one of the meeso brought Mingfu Li, Huahua and Aurora into the laboratory.

"Fu", Nigh heard himself cry and threw his arms around her, much to his fiancé's irritation. He tried to make it look less intimate by then embracing Huahua and Aurora in turn, but compared to how he had held his landlady, their embraces were sisterly. "You would not believe what we had to go through to get to this position in time and space", he finally told the Chinese girls.

Mingfu Li was gazing at Băifotă and the other meeso and she murmured, "I think I would".

"The big question is did you succeed in bringing Decorum and Lynea back together", Huahua wished to know.

A cloud passed over Nigh's face and he admitted, "We did but it did not turn out as well as we had hoped. Let us all leave here and return to Ooraşhaaasa".

"To where exactly"? The former landlady desired to know".

"Think of it as Fuchow in the 60th century", Nigh smiled, "China is gone but the land is beautiful and the Prædon have settled there".

"Your blue-friends"? Aurora requested confirmation, frowning at a meeso "I think I preferred her as a moggy", Mayling grinned.

* * *

"And you are now up to date, Majesty, on all the adventures we have experienced. You are the Rheină and Mistress of time. I left Băifotă in charge of mopping up, but I don't think he will encounter any further resistance now that the old man has sadly passed away. Of course, you can bring Băifotă back and have a replacement send to the 77th at your convenience. JÝêvvïδ considered this for a moment before agreeing, "Băifotă will make a very suitable Governor until we feel we can trust to leave the humans once more in command of the former Ministro. What about you, Knight of Nigh, what is your next move"?

"I think, sadly that I will have to replace Fiscarte as the assassin of Alexius Morrelius Decorum. Sadly my Aunt's fate could be worse than the one destiny gave her. It could be the one my meddling gave her. Decorum must not reach Mars, for if he does it will lead to the subsequent violent death of Lynea herself. Better a life of loneliness, at least it is a life".

"Once you restore the fabric of the fourth dimension to its natural weave, you will retire from tempura manipulata"?

"You have my word on that, Majesty", Nigh promised and at that very moment, he meant every word he said!

* * *

"I've changed my mind about going to the Destino yet again. That section of the weave must be threadbare by now, the number of times my great plates have hoofed through it".

"But you do not have large feet", Mingfu Li countered, "I've always thought your feet quite Chinese by their dainty size, for a man".

"Well saying my little plates, does not convey the same gravitas does it"? Nigh objected.

"What about Aunt Lynea then, surely you don't intend to leave her to such a miserable ending? Though she must have known the joy of childbirth before she died, otherwise I would not be here again, would I".

"She had a son, whom they called Alexius Morrelius of course and later became known as Alexius Morrelius Artium. He became a light painter using lasers and light-emitting diodes. When Decorum had killed Lynea, Artium fled west into Zephyria, in the Deutschesektor, to a town called Kreiggerät where he opened a studio and created his art pieces for the rest of his 117 years. He married whilst still relatively young and his wife provided the financial support all his life. Nothing sold until after his demise and then it did relatively well. The two of them had four children, the beginning of your direct line Huahua".

"So you go back to the ship and stop Decorum and none of that might ever have happened, you do not know when the baby that grew into the artist was conceived".

"True. I am going to time my arrival at the stage where Decorum 's snufz dependency is almost at its peak. That way when he turns up expired somewhere, Lynea will not be blamed. The death of a Snufzojunk, who will think it anything other than what it is - an accidental overdose"?

"Accidental as in *accidentally on purpose* by any chance", Mayling wanted to know. When are we going".

"*We* are not"! Nigh told her then, "I intend to risk none of you on this very last run. I go alone. Alone I can gain Decorum's trust more easily and there will be less chance of being spotted by the combmen. A good looking Chinese girl would be remembered in the sort of circles he would have kept at that point. I'll get some old work clothes from somewhere, forget to wash and I'll thusly blend right in. Once I'm close to Decorum I will give him some sort of cocktail of drugs which will react with the snufz and make sure he never makes that very last trip to see his by-then estranged wife".

"The last time you go back to the 33rd", Mayling noted hopefully. "For you have a wedding to arrange in the 51st".

"The only question is to how many girls"? Aurora simpered. "You'll only need one loving wife, Durango", Mayling tried. Nigh was a young man, however, with the average libido of a young man and the average appetites and he thought he was going to like life in the 51st century of China and the rule that any self-respecting male should take up to four women as his joint spouses! He ate, bathed, rested and then decided trying to sleep would be a waste of time. He could always take a nap on Mars.

The records were not as precise as he might have hoped, but he knew roughly where to start looking for his Aunt's murderous lover. It was in the IYWIWSI sector where the Tharsis plains were situated. Somewhere in the region of a town called Vrill. Decorum had originally worked there in the offices of If You Want It We Stock It. The offices serviced a Vrilludiium mine there, an element crucial in the manufacturing process of transparent steel. Decorum's services had been dispensed with by the period Nigh had timed his arrival. The reason being that his tardiness had broken all records when it came to poor time-keeping. The inherited wealth had run out six Emonths previously and it had forced the former wealthy figure to seek something as lowly as a plebeian occupation. Mayling made one last half-hearted attempt to include herself on the current expedition but was not greatly surprised at being rebuffed. The others were used to staying behind. Each made a personal farewell, promising much upon Nigh's triumphant (hopefully) return. Then he set the controls and flicked the toggle. He materialised in a provincial street and immediately detected the lessening of the gravity. He also shivered, having left a China where the air temperature was a balmy 27° C, to materialise into an equally balmy (by Mars standards) summer day on the red planet where the air was some 14° C. There was also a wind, a cloud of dust-filled wind. The wind was always dust-filled on Mars. The wind's chill factor was not helping, neither was the rust that was being blown into his face. Nigh flipped his goggles into place and glanced about him. The first thing he needed was an anorak to tug on over his boho linen shirt. Going into a store might also furnish him with helpful information. He had no intention of staying on Mars a moment longer than was necessary and there were two reasons for this. The first was the muscle wasting lack of gravity that would make his return to Earth so much more taxing. The second was the occupants of Shattered Fang. Should the latter learn of his presence on Mars.... He had to hope they would not, that was all. Nigh entered the airlock of Troubadours. An establishment 'dedicated to serving you with every fashion requirement', according to the mission statement. The place was filled with female androids who were there to help. Nigh felt a shiver run down his spine and not just from the relative coolness of the building's air conditioning. It was a while since he had been in such proximity to so many constructs. He was only too aware that every last one of them would be connected in some way to the central nexus that went by the nomen of General Acwellen or A23.

Glancing upward he followed the LED displays that indicated his course toward 'Gentlemen's Outfitting'. Behind the counter, one of the counters, at any rate, was the usual impossibly attractive android, that had probably originally served as a pleasure model.

"Yes, Sir, can I help you today"? The construct asked in a deep and husky contralto.

The designer had made her into a dusty blonde. Her hair was tied up in some sort of loose bun but a huge strand had drifted out of its restraints on the left side of her head, making a sort of side ponytail. She had unfashionably narrow lips, but she might well be an old model. The store uniform for staff was a black off the shoulder frock of black it seemed. Of course, the bosom was full and impossibly pert.

"I just want a serviceable anorak please Allia"? Nigh requested taking the opportunity to read the android's name badge and examine her breast at close quarters. The pseudo-skin was particularly impressive, being just the right shade of pinks and oranges and would doubtless feel exactly like the real thing. One fringe benefit of the birth of androids had been the almost synchronous death of human prostitution. What woman could hope to make a living selling the promises of her body, when the female form in perfection rivalled her at every turn?

"Certainly, please follow me, Sir"? Allia requested, and led him in the appropriate direction with a sashaying of her hips that Nigh would one time have tarried over. He quickly chose a navy-blue fur-edged hooded garment in XXL, suddenly wanting to get away from the blonde automaton as soon as he possibly could. Paying with cash caused a problem until he told the android he did not require change. Her response to this was,

"Perhaps I could compensate you in some other way, Sir, the fitting rooms are just over there, I'm sure that in ten minutes I could....".

"No, thank you", he responded firmly, disquieted by the lack of any sort of humanity in her admittedly lovely and beautifully crafted eyes, "My appetites run to the more almond shape recently and yours are those of a doll anyway".

Leaving her with a confused look upon her artificial features, he left the store, pulled out the anorak and threw it on, then stuffing the neoplas bag into a pocket headed for the nearest bar. The time was 09:19 the bar was open though. It was called rather insalubriously 'The Dirty Pog'. Once Nigh had passed through the doorway he knew instantly why the nomenclature. A brightly coloured creature by that name immediately came up to greet him, wagging its tail feathers in simple pleasure. Probably the creature did so to every poor drunken fool who wandered into the place at such an unhealthy hour to be imbibing alcohol. A pog was yet another of the geneticist Hoyle's bizarre creations. He had spliced the DNA of a terrier dog with that of a blue and yellow macaw. The resultant designer-pet had the body and head of a terrier and remained a quadruped. It was covered in azure and xanthic plumage however in place of fur and instead of a muzzle had a magnificent hooked and pointed beak. Nigh wondered idly as he patted its feathers if its diet was fruit and seeds, or meat, or perhaps both. He looked at the collar and saw that the creature was called Archiefeathers. Meant to be some whimsical version of Archiebald.

"Don't give the greedy getbag any treats"? A roughly harsh voice suddenly issued from behind the tall counter and Nigh looked over to see a tall, fat, unshaven man with very little hair on his head, polishing glasses by the simple expedient of breathing into them to cause sufficient moisture to accomplish the task. Shuddering at the lack of hygiene Nigh asked,

"Can I have an Orang-U-Can, please"?

"You want a glass with that, Mucker"?

"No, a straw, please"?

"Press your thumb to this then, Mucker"?

"I'll pay cash if that's all right".

"Cash?! It's a might inconvenient for a 25 sestertii tab. Where would I be if I had to journey to the bank in Chroze every week"?

"I was planning to give you a 5/- note. In exchange for some information, then you get to keep the whole deal"?

"Oh aye", the bartender looked interested at the mentioned sum. "What is it you want to know, Mucker".

"If you know one Alexius Morrelius Decorum and if so, where I can expect to find him at this hour".

The bartender's features took on an expression that bespoke a combination of avarice and intrigue. He asked,

"He owes you money or something? You're not a *dealer* are you"?

"A dealer"?

"Hey, Mucker, don't play the smarts with me, we both know what a dealer is and I run a respectable place here, I don't want the combies round here pulling my license".

"I am not a dealer, I'm a distant relative".

"You a relative of Decco, well I never! Well, a word to the wise, Mucker, he's one spaced out snufzojunk, so make sure he doesn't tap you for every Marshillin you have on you. He hangs around the dark district, down Undertaker Street. You armed"?

"I am, why do you ask"?

"'Cos nobody goes down Undertaker Street who ain't that why. You don't be looking after yourself and you gonna wake up dead in some gutter somewhere, robbed, raped and dead and maybe not even in that order"!

"It is jolly decent of you to forewarn me my good man, my heartfelt thanks. One more favour if you would be so kind, from here which way do I turn to locate the district you tell me of".

"Turn left out of here and follow your nose", the bartender supplied, "And good luck, Mucker, I can tell you right now that your smackhead of a relative ain't worth your trouble. You'd be well advised to forget all about him and get back in whatever transportation brought you here and get out of town. While you are still vital enough to be breathing, ifin you take my meaning"?

"I shall be careful", Nigh promised.

Huddled into the warmth of the anorak and finding it a little difficult to breathe in the thin atmosphere, he hurried off in the indicated direction. Stopping twice more to ask for further directions he found the street he was seeking and noted how ramshackle and rundown it seemed, even by Martian standards. One thing it did not lack for however was the presence of rather sinister-looking inhabitants. It was no more than a few seconds before he had drawn the attention of a knot of three. A triumvirate of malign intent if ever there was one.

"Stranger, what are you doing down here, this is my dominion"? The largest and therefore most menacing of them desired to know.

"I'm looking for someone", Nigh was pleased he had been asked, it might make his search all the more easy for that very reason.

"Someone in particular, or someone with a fair pair up top and a willing one in the middle", one of the Big One's lieutenants sneered. Nigh chose to ignore any other than the obvious leader. He sensed their intent but still hoped to bribe his way out of any sort of conflict if it were possible.

"I will pay for the information", he volunteered to the big man, situated with his cronies one upon each side of him.

"Oh I know you'll pay", the huge individual guffawed, "Any as is foolhardy enough to venture down here always does".

"Well, the man I'm looking for is....".

"The toll first", the leader demanded. "Then we'll see if we know your mate".

"Don't mess about Gharkey", the last of the trio hissed, "Just stick him and we'll take the lot".

The big man, who answered to the name Gharkey smiled menacingly and replied to his henchman with the rat-like features,

"Come on, Sunda is that any way to treat an honoured guest. Who wants the combmen crawling all over our patch when this gent here will like as not simply give us the money if we ask him nicely".

"Very well", Nigh replied reasonably, "What is the toll for telling me where I can find Decco"?

"I'm not talking about no toll for giving up a ...friend of ours", Gharkey grinned, "I'm talking about the ground toll, for walking down our street".

"The street is municipal property", Nigh heard himself argue, beginning to realise from that instant onward that confrontation looked inevitable. "But lead me to Decco and I will pay you two Marshillin".

"Two lousy Marshillin to give up our friend"? Gharkey spat onto the rust-covered tarmacadam, "I do not think you realise the sensitive nature of our imminent business arrangement, Mr Lah-de-darh. "Hand over your wallet now and I will see if it contains enough to merit my giving you the detail you wish to purchase"?

"I don't think that it is going to work that way", Nigh countered.

"You don't think"? Sunda repeated scornfully, "You don't think"?

Correct", Nigh returned, "I realise the concept of mental activity might be somewhat unfamiliar to you, but we higher vertebrates engage upon said activity all the time".

Gharkey burst into a bellow of mirth at the rejoinder and told his lieutenant,

"He just called you an idiot, Sunda".

"Well then I guess I'm going to have to make him bleed", came the response and Sunda pulled out the biggest flick-knife Nigh had ever seen.

"Please don't make this a physical confrontation", the ex secret-serviceman requested reasonably then, "I do not wish to, nor will take any pleasure in injuring you".

"Oh no"? Sunda danced forward, knife held out, ready to stab or slice, "But I'm going to enjoy cutting you a new one, town boy".

He launched himself toward Nigh, the knife aimed at the latter's midriff. Nigh danced to one side, grasped the wrist to the hand holding the weapon and twisted using the appropriate pressure against joints in a counterproductive motion. Sunda gave a yell of surprised agony and the blade fell from nerveless fingers. The hoodlums two confederates had not been simply observing idly however and both were reaching for needle-guns at the same instant. Nigh threw himself forward and downward into a controlled forward roll, snatching up the knife in his left hand whilst tugging his gun-free with his right. As he came out of the roll his left hand hurled the knife at the third hoodlum who screamed as it sunk into his shoulder causing him to drop his gun.

"Don't Gharkey"! Nigh warned as he skipped back onto his feet. "You'll be shot before you can get that weapon into a firing position. Trust me, I never miss"!

In that instant, Gharkey had the sense to hesitate to allow Nigh the instant he needed to advise him to drop his gun.

It fell into the red dust with a dull thump.

"You move faster than any man I've ever seen", Nigh's former tormentor suddenly admitted quite transparently, "I could use a man like you. What do you want with the useless piece of human refuse - Decco"?

"It's my turn to ask questions now and all I want to know is where to find him", Nigh responded brusquely. Talk quickly because my considerable patience is beginning to wear a bit thin"?

"You'll find him in the flop, two doors down over to your left - behind you. Not at this hour though. He comes back to doss down at around 22:00, right now he could be anywhere in the city, begging, borrowing or stealing, trying his best to cobble together enough lucre to pay for his next nostril-full. If it's information you're after from him, don't expect him to make a great deal of sense. His grey-walnut's been turned to mush for a while now. When he knows what's happening he cannot remember much and the rest of the time he's in a different head-space. Perhaps I could...."?

"When I come back this evening it might be better if I don't see you nor your boys. Otherwise, one side or the other are not going to end up overly healthy", Nigh warned and slowly backed out of the street so aptly named.

* * *

By the appointed hour it had grown bitterly cold as far as Nigh was concerned. In reality, it was 8°C, but the constantly buffeting wind made it feel considerably colder and the rusty dust got everywhere. Those who elected not to wear goggles looked as though they had applied red mascara to their eyelashes and red eyeliner to their eyes. Some of the less well off also possessed a permanently hacking cough and pneumoconiosis and even mycobacterium tuberculosis were on the increase in the Martian Ghettos. Most of these had sprung up when certain mines had proved to have only shallow deposits of whatever they were mining and had closed, suddenly putting entire town populations out of work at a stroke. In Vrill there had been two shafted veins. One was the rather obvious vrilludiium, which was still proving very rich in the mineral and very profitable became of its industrial applications. The second mine had been sunk seeking out veins of the even rarer prelliosite. Prelliosite was one of the chief components in the newly developed ultra-thin shielding for stellar vessels which had been given the name tsuyoigādo [Japanese for strong-guard]. A metal alloy that had been exclusively produced in Japan where the patent resided. With the crippling effects of SX, it was thought that the alloy would not be available again for some decades and thusly the demand for prelliosite collapsed and half of Vrill with it. None of this had much to do with Decorum though. His poverty had been created by drug dependency. He had been a snufz user for some time but felt compelled to start using de-lite when the standard strength no longer gave him the hits he craved. De-lite had been a military weapon in the Francosian-Saxonian war and never designed for commercial release, but as was usually the case in such scenarios, certain unscrupulous business interests got hold of the formula and it was now available on the black market under the trade name of *mindblast*. Jiánhòng Chen was associated with the illegal manufacture of mindblast from one of his pharmaceutical manufacturing depots on Taiwan. Operating under the newly formed umbrella corporation of Bakageta Kigyō Incorporated he had produced several hundred kilos of mindblast, sometimes referred to as *braintrip* or *khakkhead*. Whichever preparation, in whichever formulation mindblast was incredibly addictive and almost always proved ultimately fatal to the user. By the time a pusher had tempted Decorum with it though, most of his cognitive processes had already been heartily compromised, his mentality eaten away by deleterious chemical preparations. Thusly, finding him would not be difficult and in reality, it was incredibly easy. He was in the very flop that Gharkey had said he would be.

"Hello", Nigh looked at what was left of the wasted frame of his Aunt's former lover and could barely credit how he would have the vitality to beat her to death. Perhaps it would be during some drug-crazed episode of dementia, Nigh had heard people were immensely strong during certain unpleasant trips of that nature.

"What's up". Came the slurred response and it seemed that Decorum could no longer focus his eyes. It was obvious, he did not recognise the man who had saved his life in what would seem like a different lifetime ago.

"My name is Shrooze", Nigh lied. "I'm the co-founder of Shrooze, Vlyme and Shrooze Chemical Corporation, perhaps you've heard of us"?

"I can't say I have, Guv. You work with your chick then? Your contractee or missus"?

"The name? No, no relation, just a coincidence". It was a measure of how addled Decorum's mind had become that he did not question that incredible claim. Nigh went on,

"Anyway one of the reasons I mention it to you, Sir is that your name has been given to me as a gentleman of discerning taste when it comes to matters narcotic".

"I've done a fair nostril-full of khakk in my time that's true", Decorum slurred doing his best to sound self-effacing regarding the dubious accolade.

"Good good, then I suspect you might be the very man I am looking for", Nigh went on, "Because SVSCC is proud to announce the release of a very exciting new product called metaxenicerebral".

"Say what, Guv"?

SVSCC, Shrooze, Vlyme and Shrooze Chemical Corporation have just developed a brand new designer drug called metaxenicerebral".

"Is it the dogs"?

"Let me put it this way, one hit from this baby and you'll be smacked out of your tree and kaahkfaced for ...well, it will feel like forever"!

"And you could put me down for a few baggies, Guv, were it not for the fact that at this moment I have an impecunious cash-flow situation".

"You're indigent"?

"As the monkey with no ball sack"!

"Then today is truly your lucky day because I'm authorised by Vlyme and Shrooze [no relation] to personally hand out two-hit samples to future marketing opportunities".

"Well ifin I'm a market, Guv hit me with the freebie. I'm certainly one snufzojunk if that qualifies me"?

"It qualifies you admirably my good man", Nigh enthused holding out two syringes. His hand were protected by nyloplanyon transparent micro-mesh gloves just in case. For the syringe contained a lethal cocktail of snufz, mindblast, spinal soporific, H_3SO_7 and mortifervenenum.

The latter being a deadly toxic pesticide used to control the Martian Acrididae Caelifera, a type of locust local to the planet and ruiner of crops, if in great enough numbers. If ingested by humans it resulted in hot sweats, difficulty in breathing stomach and muscular cramps and finally, death. There was no antidote. By the time it had insinuated its chemical way into Decorum's already ruined nervous system, he would be uncaring anyway, such was the dosage of the other constituents of Nigh's carefully prepared formulation.

"Oh"! His target hesitated, "I don't like needles Guv".

"Not even if one small sting will take you on the ultimate cosmic ride you will ever experience".

"That good eh"?

"Let me put it this way, you will never, ever have another trip that you will say comes close to the one awaiting you right now in this little sticker".

Decorum held out a grubby paw and Nigh let the syringes tumble onto it. With that action, he had just become a cold-blooded murderer! He decided he needed a drink, maybe a sandwich and returned to the bar. He treated himself to a sweet sherry and a ploughman's lunch. Reasoning that by now Decorum would have managed to kill himself with the deadly cocktail. All he wanted was confirmation before he returned to the 51$^{st.}$

One of the things about the SWW was its incredible speed when it came to the supply of information. Ven the local combmen would be using the multi-stranded electronic information broadcast. All he had to do was get his pad and access the correct pages. Paddie had been left in the 51st, there was no sense in being caught talking to a device that had obvious future technology. So he had bought a throwaway Bero PP40TB once inside the outfitters and it was with this he kept checking the combmen podcasts. Three sweet sherries later he knew that Decorum had been found dead and Nigh's description had been supplied to the combmen by none other than Gharkey. The combmen would like to discuss why the man who had been looking for Decorum had sought him out to see if he could help them with their inquiries. Even then though, he doubted he would be a suspect. Decorum was already well known to the authorities as a snufzojunk, the very last thing the combmen would be suspecting was murder. Maybe they thought Nigh was a pusher. Whatever they wanted to talk to him about he was not going to wait to see what they wanted, it was time to return to Fuchow and the year 5057. There he could make his life with four very attractive young wives and begin to create a dynasty of his own. That was his intention, as it turned out however intentions and actuality often behaved in a very different way for the chronoman.

Fifteen. The Èshā.

 The apartment had a familiar atmosphere and look to it. Despite his tremendous optimism that had been something Nigh had worried over as the settings were dialled into the mechanism that had brought him back to the 51st century. With growing confidence he gazed about him, picking up the odd item and examining it carefully so that such inanimates would provide him with the clues he was searching for. The hairbrush that he knew was Mingfu Li's some long dark hair still between its rounded prongs. He deduced that Mingfu Li was thusly female and living in the apartment. Obviously at work at the hour he had chosen to return to 51st-century Fuchow. It was 09:18. Of course, Mayling would either be abroad or at her place. As would Aurora and hopefully not feline. Why was he worrying? This time his alteration to the fabric of the fourth dimension had ben a micro-change surely? He had removed a piece of human waste from the time fibre and made certain that his descendants would be restored. So his first visit in the time he was beginning to consider his homewhen would be to his distant cousin - Huahua Morrelius Felix. The later addendum to her name would be his idea, it meant fortunate, but the feline connotation also amused him considering what Aurora had been through in one incarnation. Now that he had a definite strategy he bathed quickly and changed into clothing that felt familiar and comfortable after the restrictive nature of the chronosuit which had been a trifle clinging and less comfortable as a result. It was July in Fuchow and the temperature was 23°C Fine until one started moving about, then the 50% humidity made matters a little sticky. As nigh left the building though it began to rain, not an actual downpour, but sufficient to wet him through. He let it.

There was no umbrella's in 51st century China the protective artefact had slowly disappeared into antiquity in the 22$^{nd.}$ Once his boho clothing was plastered to his skin Nigh soon grew slightly chilled. He ignored it for something else was beginning to trouble him. The streets of Fuchow had never been especially busy, but it seemed to Nigh that they were exceedingly quiet. SX had been 18 centuries antecedent, so why did the 51st feel so spares to him. He had been through the streets before and they had been quiet, but not so almost deserted as at that point. There was only one thing for it, he would have to ask a passer-by if there was a reason for it. He discounted the rain, after all, it was only water. He was just about to step off the moving walkway and intercept a young woman hurrying in the opposite direction when a motorcycle suddenly sped into a puddle in the gutter and a spray of cold water doused him. Nigh cursed volubly and the motorcyclist must have seen his reaction in one of the handlebar mirrors because the huge machine turned around sped behind him and then pulled up at his side.

"I am most terribly sorry", the rider began and then stopped speaking and gazed at Nigh in astonished recognition. At the same instant Nigh was equally mesmerised by the lithe beauty of the rider. She was tall for a Chinese girl, even seated it was possible to discern she must be almost 179cms. She even had a long face but with her narrow nose and perfectly bowed lips adding to her almond eyes and yellow complexion she was beautiful. The surgeons had done their usual fabulous job of creating a perfect pair of breasts for her [always a speciality with augmentation surgeons] and her long legs and long fingers added to what was overall a very enticing package indeed. Black faux leather riding gear of jacket and shorts with knee-high boots created something beyond enticing. It would have been so even if her zipped jacket had not been unzipped to her midriff to allow a shattering decollete to be on display.

"That's the first wheeled bike I've seen in a while, you don't like the flitter-bikes", Nigh finally managed to observe.

"It was my great-great-grandfathers, it's an original Honda Sekkusuapīru [sex appeal] 1200bhp".

"That's a lot of power to have between one's legs"! Nigh could not resist. To his delight, the girl smiled lasciviously and returned,

"Just how I like it Durango Nigh".

"How do you know my name"?

"You're all over the SWW Comband. General Xueling III has put out a plea for you to go to Combmen headquarters to assist the officers with their enquiries".

With a now-familiar sinking feeling in the pit of his stomach Nigh asked the handsome rider,   "Enquiries into what exactly, what am I supposed to have done. Or is this connected to A234 by any chance"?

"I don't think the androids have any interest in the case", came the puzzled response, "But how come you haven't heard anything about the murders when someone close to you was a victim last night"?

Murders! Victims!. Only then did Nigh realise why the streets were so sparsely populated,

"What do you mean by close to me"? He demanded the familiar dread of time manipulation consequence was beginning to grip his insides. "Who might that be, Young Lady"?

"The combmen have not released anything regarding identity, just that the victim last night was known to you and the General wants to interview you regarding the incident".

"As in interview the chief suspect no doubt"?

But the girl shook her head, "No. You were away while the other twelve were murdered. You were away were you not, on some foreign mission or other"?

Twelve more!

"There has been thirteen dead, the last one being one of my friends"?

"Look, why don't I take you to the combstation"? The girl offered, "I am Liao Lihong and it is a pleasure to meet you, I just wish it had been under more pleasant circumstances".

"Take me on the antique bike? On the none moving road, with no helmet or protective clothing"?

Liao Lihong smiled and promised,

"I will be very careful and the roads are practically empty. If I stick to 80   kph we should get there in one piece".

"I could stick to the moving walkways"?

"I will cut your journey time by a factor of around 1/50th "?

Nigh thought about it. It would allow him to put his arms around that divinely narrow waist. Smell the heat of the creature, push his nose into her hair. He was a dog.

"All right then, thank you, Xiaˇojiě Lihong".

"That's Liao, or you're not getting on", she grinned.

"All right Liao, it's Durango to you then".

He slipped a foot over the rear of the seat and positioned himself behind her. It was easily as sensual an experience as he had expected. She smelled of Lily of the Valley, her mesentery was tautly defined and her hair smelled of Apple Blossom. Five minutes later he was sorry to have to climb off and thankful his boho pants were not the clinging sort so that she would not notice his timber.

"Thanks for the lift", He said to her hesitantly and she smiled

"You are welcome Durango Nigh, do you want to swap enumbers"?

He did and they did. He loved 51st-century Androichina. His good mood evaporated the instant he set foot inside the combstation though. The instant he was seen by one of the officers he was hastily conducted to an interview room. He had barely settled down to wait when who should enter the room but General Xueling III herself. She too looked as lovely as ever, but Nigh was distracted by what Liao had told him and was all business.

"I've been in the past", he got straight to the point, "I only arrived back into this period last night, so I am completely in the dark regarding these murders. What can you tell me, please, General"?

"Before I tell you anything", came the serious reply, "You have a rather unpleasant duty to perform for me. I need you to identify a body, the body is the Strangler's thirteenth victim".

"The Strangler"!, Nigh repeated, "The killer is killing the poor victims with his or her bare hands, how incredibly horrible and primitive".

"There is no *her* involved, Nigh, we know for a fact that the murderer is male. Before he strangles his victims he rapes them. We have his DNA, we even know who he is".

Nigh began to feel a familiarly horrible dread begin to grip his vitals,

"By the way, you said that you seemed to suggest that I might even recognise the murderer, but I know very

few people here in Androichina and they are all female so....".

"Then let me give you the azdoguoi's name", the General cut him off before he could finish, "It is Numa Sabine Morrelius, to which we have now added the appellation Èshā".

"Morrelius"! Nigh gasped, "Èshā meaning strangler at a guess"?

The general nodded.

"You mean to tell me that this strangler is a descendant of...".

"Lynea Morrelius, your Aunt. I'm guessing you have not had time to look at the SWW since your return to us last night. Now I don't know what you did in the past Durango and frankly, I think it best if it stays that way, but Numa Sabine Morrelius Èshā is your cousin, many generations removed".

"My Aunt had children"?

"To her second husband, after she had divorced Alexius Morrelius Gravis. She met and married a man called Numa Hostillius back on Earth three months later, in England. They had five children, the one that concerns us was one Numa Hostillius Morrelius. It seemed they kept the name of Morrelius so that he could enjoy the reflected glory of the various corporations that Gravis was expanding at the time. Ironically Gravis gave the child, when grown, a job at his plant in the Pyrenees. To cut a long story short, Durango, Numa Sabine Morrelius Èshā is a descendant of the man, who was your Aunt's son. He also knows who *you* are and it seems by last nights action, he has bitter enmity toward you".

"Who, Xueling? Who did he violate and murder".

"That is why you are here, to tell us it is her for certain. Enough talking, come and identify her for us, even though we have DNA and know, it is an ancient tradition and you might wish to say goodbye anyway".

* * *

Èshā was satisfied that his hated ancestor would be suffering that morning when he woke from a deeply gratifying sleep. His latest murder would keep the demons at bay for a little while. Before even performing ablutions he reached for his snap-clasp box and opening it with the usual anticipatory click reached in with his finger and thumb grasping a pinch of snufz. The deep snort he took charged it up his nostril and began to be absorbed by the blood vessels of his nasal cavity. A sense of well being and accompanying sensation of floating coursed through his body.

It was not unexpected for Spurât to appear to him then, he always seemed to want to reduce the pleasure of the early high, known as *the hit*. On this occasion, Spurât was a harridan rather than either a gremlin or hideous creature of some kind.

"Well, was she good, did you enjoy deflowering her"? Spurât demanded.

"You're not real, leave me alone", Èshā dared, "If I did not snufz, you would be dead to me".

"But you are a Snufzojunk aren't you, Numa? A sad pathetic wasted individual who cannot function without the designer narcotic. I am not dead while ever you turn your already addled brain to mush. I am very much alive, she is the one who is dead. You koofed the sweet young thing, enjoyed her young flesh and then strangled the life out of her".

"**Why did I do that, I ask you**"? Èshā raged then, "Because all I wanted was her ass, her sweet young ass, but you wanted her quiddity, her essence. Always you drive me to extinguish their lives, always I hear your voice egging me on, '*Go on*', you mutter in my ear, '*Off the silly little păsăriă! So you've had your pleasure now it's my turn I want to eat her soul*'. *It disgusts me, I hear you slobbering and you tear the morsel from her still warm body and devour it while it is still barely diminished*".

"But you enjoy it too don't you, Numa? You like to rape them, you like to slake your lust while they scream in your ear and their eyes glitter with the terror of it. You rape their bodies and terrorise their minds, you sick koof".

"Why am I in such torment"? the demented young man sighed then. The hit had dissipated and his maudlin period was imminent, it always followed his moment of introspection. "What drives me to do such insanely cruel things to these poor young girls. Admitted I want to see them nude, admitted I want to even koof them, but why do I get so violent, so brutal, why am I the way I am"?

"Because of him"! Spurât gave Èshā the very same answer she/he always gave him. "You know who I mean the anathematized one. He who's meddling in matters that he should not have meddled in impreacated your destiny as surely as if he had lain execration of objurgation on your very being. He created you and now he will seek to destroy you. He is the enraged Jupiter, the demented god who is now horrified by his offspring, he will smite you and your bones and flesh will become as pathetic gory paste".

"But even if he does that it is now too late is it not"? Èshā suddenly giggled and the sound was as the gibbering cackle of a lunatic even in his ears. No surprise though, for that was what he was becoming. Or, had always been!

"Too late for her", Spurât enjoyed the moment. "Just as it is too late for all those who went before her. It will be too late for the next one also, for he cannot find you, no one can find you Èshā for you are guile personified, you can twist and turn like a twisting turnagement. You wriggle into places which until that moment are nonwiggle. You ooze into realms of antioozerama and you insinuate yourself into the personal space of those who are counterinsinuative".

"That's right I can do those things can I not", Èshā danced around the room his forehead glistening with the perspirations of the tormented. He snatched up a silicon mask from the room's dresser, waving it about like some sick war trophy. In his other hand, he snatched up the Harmoan [cheap wig, usually blonde, always rather badly fitting]. The rest of his *kit* was still on the dresser. Eye shadow and colour changing contacts, lip shaders, false ears of various shapes and sizes including the less popular Spocks. The suits were in the closet, some to pull him in, some to make him look heavier. The clothes were thusly of different sizes, dependant upon which weight he wanted to be before the attack. He could not stop what he was. He had a burning desire for young-pretty girls and he was not handsome nor blessed with social grace. Androids did not present him with any challenge. They had amused him for a while, but that had waned until it was something distasteful and left him feeling hollow and cheated. They were so quiescent even when supposedly awake. They let him *do things* even he did not want to do. It did not leave them in any sort of distress, but neither did it leave them in a state of appreciation nor pleasure. They were what they were, very lifelike and intelligent dolls. So he had turned to his first victim. Taken his time over observing her movements and then one night when his blood was like molten lava he had encountered her in a bar. His offer to buy her a drink had been accepted, as had his offer of a pinch [snufz]. When he had offered to see her home though, she had tried to fob him off. He had insisted upon just dropping her off at her door. Saving her flittaxi fare. Reluctantly she had agreed to that. She began to complain when he took the first *accidental*, wrong turn. When he pulled up and let his flitter settle to the deserted area's ground she had tried to scramble out, but the door locks were controlled by the driver. Her screams had been louder than the tearing of her flimsy frock, her body was as lush and ripe as he had imagined. Tearfully she had then agreed to, *'let you do what you want if you don't hurt me'*. She had even grudging blown him as the tears ran down her pretty made-up face. He did not last long. He had only been in her for maybe a couple of minutes when his lust exploded inside her. She turned her head away and endured his grunted shudders. When his hands slipped around her throat she did not even struggle. Only at the very end when her lungs were screaming for air did she spasm a little, but by then it was too late. He still remembered her fondly. Though not her name. She had been his first, twelve others had followed, but none of them had been as sweetly appreciated as her.

Except.....

Except for her last night.

Sure she was beautiful. All of them had been *fit* differently though. What set her apart was not *how* she was but *who* she was. She was *his* friend. She was the first who he had been affectionately acquainted with. She would not be the last. Spurât had been right about one thing, the best way to destroy him was a piece at a time!

* * *

Nigh had not expected her to look so.....so....peaceful. Peaceful and beautiful. Even in death Mayling in her second incarnation was a creature with a divine appearance. He had expected to be shocked, angry. What he had not envisaged was the tremendous sense of loss and the terrible feeling of dislocative pain. Only now that she was gone in a very certain way did he realise how he had felt about her. He had loved her after all. He would have married her. She would be his wifone, even if others followed, she would have had a very special place in his heart.

"I confirm that this is the body of the young woman known as Mayling Fuchow, previously known as Shen Huan the Elucidator. Èshā must be powerful or skilful in the art of combat to have overpowered her, she was very capable when it came to looking after herself".

"Observe the tiny puncture mark on the left side of her throat", the General urged, "You might have missed it due to the lividity of the bruising".

"She was shot with a needle"

"Level two. He is no warrior or brave assassin, he cowardly used drugs to subdue her while......Well, I think the web report covers the rest of it".

"Why do you not catch him and kill him"? Nigh asked coldly then.

"He has evaded us at every attempt so far", General Xueling admitted quite readily, "We follow his electronic footprint whenever he uses his saved funds, but he has quit his employ and he must be able to disguise himself because we cannot seem to catch him on any of our monitors. Not to mention that we are seriously underwomanned at the moment".

"So now he has raped and brutally murdered my fiancé you want my help do you"?

"Your fiancé"!? Xueling looked slightly disappointed. "Have you just the one at present"?

"This is not the time nor place, General", Nigh objected. "Come on I need to get out of here"?

When they had returned to Xueling's office he finally informed her, "All right General, swear me in, I'll hunt down Èshā for you"?

"Swear you in? You don't want to simply go back in time and.....".

"No, it doesn't always work out as one anticipates and anyway I don't want to do it easily for that monster. I want to find him and I want him to know what is going to happen before it does, not simply and mercifully wink out of existence. So I need to be a combman, otherwise, you will be able to arrest me, for his murder. If I kill him in the course of my duty though, well, you get the picture, you're a bright girl".

"And afterwards? Will you then go back in time and erase his very existence, so that the thirteen victims can never have died"?

"I will then have to try that yes. Unfortunately, if it is meant to be that a strangler terrorises Androichina I might have to go back quite a long way and do something unthinkable".

"How unthinkable what do you mean"?

"If I simply kill Èshā as a child, his sibling might then become the Èshā in his place. I have to make certain the entire line never was. I have to erase back to the point of creation. Xueling, my Aunt was originally to die at her drug-addled lover's hands, now, it would seem, she will have to die at her nephews"!

Sixteen. 未婚夫的

Aurora had been weeping uncontrollably for some considerable time when there was a knock at the door. Heedless of the redness of her eyes and the puffy nature of her features she went to the inspection plate and her heart lifted a little at the sight of her visitor. All would be so much better now Nigh was back. She released the lock and when he entered the apartment she gently took him in her arms and held him for several moments. Finally, she let him go and said simply,

"I'm sorry, Durango, what are you going to do? Have you seen Fu and Huahua yet"?

"I'm not sure I want to see my distant cousin. Life would be a lot simpler if the two of us had never met. There is another reason as well. If I want Mayling back then it may mean that Huahua never existed".

"I'll make some tea and you can bring me up to speed, I'm certain I don't know everything you've been through". She offered, he nodded. While she was doing that he pinged his former landlady and she told him over the padfon that she would join the two of them there. They waited for her to arrive before nigh quickly told them the latest version of their timeline.

"So you terminated Decorum only to realise that you had created a new family history that terminated in Mayling's murder. Do you intend to go further back and stop yourself from killing Decorum now? Put everything back the way it was in the very beginning"? Mingfu Li desired to know. Nigh shook his head,

"I don't want to change things back so that my Aunt is beaten to death. I have only one choice now as I see it and that is to go back before Lynea gets divorced and remarries and ask her to be sterilised".

"And if she disagrees with your solution, the one that will make Huahua disappear as though she never existed"? Aurora asked, "Will you go upwhen and try and stop the next generation being born"?

"I reason that Lynea is the ultimate source, she had more than one child. If I stop Èshā issuing from one of her five children who's to say a different branch of the family tree will not result in the strangler still becoming reality"?

"So Lynea has to be childless, there is no way to save Huahua". Mingfu Li noted heavily, "But what will you do if your Aunt will not agree to be made barren"?

"I think you know what I will be forced to do", Nigh returned heavily, "It is one life or thirteen"!

"When do you leave"? Aurora asked.

"Not for a while yet", he surprised the two of them, "First I have to find Èshā and bring him to swift and seriously fatal justice".

"But then the combmen will be after you, in addition to the androids", Mingfu Li noted sadly.

"Not this time", Nigh sounded smug. "This time I *am* the combman".

They stayed together for the rest of the day, shared a meal some sensible conversation and then retired. Nigh drifted off to sleep without any real trouble, he was very tired and having settled his intention in his head, there was nothing to worry over. Despite the protests of his two friend, on reflection his only true friends, he left them. He was on foot, had no idea where to start when the roar of the Honda announced the arrival of his newest acquaintance. She afforded him a charming smile and asked,

"Need another ride, Durango Nigh"?

"I might if I knew where I was going", he confessed openly before asking, "Don't you have work or something"?

"I do nearly all my work remotely", she told him. By padfon, hardly ever any need to report to a specific building or complex. A goodly number of Chinese did their occupations in just such a manner. With intense automation of production factories and produce itself all the jobs were in administrative professions anyway. The worlds modest population meant that the quota was easily fulfilled and starvation and disease were at a tiny percentage of the overall population.

"Maybe you can help me then if you have got a mind to"?

"What are you after, Bachelor"?

'*I know what you're after*', Nigh thought but asked instead, "If I wanted to lay low in this city, beneath the constant surveillance of the cams and vidz, where would I go"?

"You're hunting"! Liao Lihong guessed, "You're hunting the Èshā are you not"?

"I am. Do you want to help? You've got the mobility and I've got the weaponry. I'm also a newly sworn-in constable".

"You a Combie hahahaha. I would never have seen that coming".

"The Constabulary Of Military Beadledom is a noble calling", Nigh observed with mock solemnity, "Do you want to be my sidekick or not"?

"I was thinking of something more, romantic, but I can start as your sidekick if that's what you want. After a while, who knows how things might turn out for us"?

Nigh grinned, "Exactly. Neither of us at this point. So what's your answer, have you any ideas"?

"All I can tell you, Combie, is that I would not hide in the sort of places your colleagues will already have checked. Hotels, apartments, places where there are vidz and cams dotted all over the place".

"So, Rogue, where then"?

Liao Lihong burst into delighted laughter, "Did you just give me a love-name, Combie. Are we now officially *Combie and Rogue* crime busters"?

"You're the one wearing the faux-leather, you tell me"? Nigh liked her. She was shrewd with a good sense of humour and drop-dead gorgeous what was not to like?

"You have to consider the shanty tenements in Zhanggangzhen – Provincial Road leads right down to the waterfront and is crawling with Shui Fong 水房幫 (Lit. Water Room Gang), also known as the Wo On Lok or WOL. If I was foolhardy enough to go there it would be the perfect place to hide between crimes. Èshā may even be a WOL member, who knows"?

"Will you take me there on your antique machine"?

"You want to go riding into Zhanggangzhen?! We could get raped and then killed, or maybe even killed and then raped"?

"Have no worries, if things get hairy we will escape into either the past or the future, you have heard I can do that"?

She grinned, "So partner you want us to go on our first adventure together"?

"I want another ride with you", Nigh remarked lasciviously, only too aware of his double entendre.

"Will it be a good ride"? She took up the theme in an instant.

"You're the one with the clutch and gears"!

"All right, Combie, climb on and put your arms around me, I'll get you there"!

Laughing he did as requested. Once more it was a very pleasurable ride but he did notice as the bike sped along, that the surrounding began to grow increasingly shabby as it progressed. When they finally stopped Nigh glanced about him and realised the girl had been right. If Eshā wanted to keep away from the law, to hide in a dark and subfusc place, then Zhanggangzhen was the ideal location for the sick azdogunoi. Nigh was only just climbing from the pillion when the low life's of the slum began to ooze out of the run down domiciles, like some sort of vile effluvian sludge. The duo of invaders into this dark and forbidding realm glanced about them. Unsurprisingly the majority of those who were creeping toward them were female. They would not be classified in the same breath as Liao Lihong though. Perhaps some of them could have been presentable in another life, but poverty, filth and snufz abuse had done its work on their body chemistry and they were as dilapidated as the buildings they inhabited. One of the few male gutter-dwellers demanded harshly,

"Have you taken a wrong turning"?

"No", Nigh answered succinctly, "We meant to be here, we are looking for someone".

"So you're a Wūgòu [lit: contaminated, filthy, abomination, member of the law enforcement], combman"?

"Combman? Yes, I am. That does not automatically make me your enemy though".

"Can I humbly proffer you a small piece of advice, Officer", the youth grinned. His expression was one of showing teeth however, there was little good humour on display.

"Certainly", Nigh was not fooled for a second but he would let the youth enjoy his posturing for a while, he had a thick enough skin.

"Take your Yínluànǚ˘rén [woman perceived as sexually disreputable or promiscuous] and get back on her Yījīgtìdàipi˘n [substitute for a male member, an object designed to facilitate sexual stimulation] and go back to the nice clean world you came from".

Nigh smiled sardonically and observed, "You are beginning to intimate to me that we are less than welcome here. I could feel insulted by both your stance and the scatological language you are using toward me". A grimy girl suddenly took her place beside the youth and explained simply,

"We don't like Wūgòu around here. If we try and make you split are you going to bring down the heavy gloom on us officer"?

Nigh was momentarily floundering and Liao Lihong came to his rescue,

"No one wants to bring down the heavy gloom so mellifluent the vibe sister. All the officer wants is some information, if you have it that is"?

The youth responded to that,

"Information is product around here, Wūgòu and product are worth guap, after all, we all have to give to the man when we want our Bíyānz [snufz]".

"I am willing to enter into a quid pro quo negotiation for guap", Nigh agreed. The youth's attitude abruptly altered, he smiled and with a magnanimous wave of his arm invited,

"Then come to my office, officer and we shall officiate"? Grinning at the alliteration, Nigh gestured for Liao Lihong to precede him in the indicated direction. In her hugging faux leather riding pants her rear was well worth scrutiny. Nigh felt suitably appreciative as the two of them went into the filthiest dingiest apartment he had thus far encountered in all of China. He squinted until his eyes adjusted to the gloom, while the youth and the girl who had accompanied him into the hovel took the only two rickety chairs in the room and did not indicate where Nigh and his companion could comfortably position themselves. It left them with nothing to do other than stand. Judging by the lack of hygiene in the place, it was probably the wisest option anyway.

* * *

Mingfu Li rushed to the door in a state of annoyed agitation. Who found it necessary to repeatedly thumb the chime in such quick succession? She glanced at the inspection security plate and found she did not know the Chinese youth who was without. Angrily she snapped,

"All right already, take your finger off the buzzer, who are you and what is so blessed urgent"?

"You don't know me, so my name would not be of any use to you but I am a friend of your friend, Durango Nigh. It's all messed up and you have to come, we need your help".

Mingfu Li felt the floor of her guts suddenly disappear. "What do you mean it's all messed up, what is all messed up"?

"Look Lady he asked me to come here and he may not last much longer there was a lot of blood! Jupiter but there was so much blood! I'm not about to have a conversation through a locked door over a speaker. Do you want to open the door or....no forget it, I've got to get back".

He half-turned and Mingfu Li had to make a decision. She pressed the lock release, said urgently,

"I've opened the door if you.....".

She never got the rest of her sentence out. The door burst inward the edge of it catching her on the forehead. A lance of sharp brilliance coursed through her and she felt herself slipping into the black shroud of unconsciousness. When she came to an indeterminate period of darkness later he was on her and in her pumping away, grunting in satisfaction. Her clothes had been roughly torn from her, she could feel the pain of fresh bites in the flesh of her breasts and belly. She screamed and his fist contacted with the side of her head sending fresh waves of agony through her brain. Half dazed, she tried to push him out and off, but he had the maniacal strength of a psychopath. Through her absolute terror and revulsion, she heard him cry with triumphant ecstasy as he spurted his malign lust inside her. Then his fingers found her throat and began to squeeze. The digits were like bands of hot steel, she had not the strength nor the will to pry them free. Though her lungs screamed for air she was not sorry when the sombre folds of death drifted over her vision and she expired. Èshā climbed from between the body's rapidly cooling thighs thinking to himself that he had just enjoyed the best of his fourteen victims. It was such a shame that he could only assault and murder each girl once. He would like to have ridden that saucy mare many more than a single time. She had been even sweeter than the one before, the Elucidator, who had struggled so violently she had managed to hurt him. Not that it had saved her from her eventual fate. As he went into the bathroom to get himself cleaned up he was already thinking about the next one to entertain him in a carnal fashion. The last of those who his hated descendent had tarried with, the one called Aurora. Only when she was dead could he break his cycle and finally kill the man himself – Durango Nigh!

* * *

"So how much is the information you seek worth to you, Wūgòu", the youth asked. While Nigh hesitated to wonder whether to name a figure or simply ask how much he wanted the youth suddenly drew a needle-gun and shot his companion in the throat. Even as she tumbled from her chair to the filthy floor he snarled,

"Move a muscle out of place, Nigh and I'll shoot sugar-tits here next and these are level one darts. Escape into time and I shoot her, try for your weapon and I shoot her, try and access your back-pack and I shoot her. Now slowly and carefully nod your head to acknowledge your understanding of the situation"?

As Nigh, frozen into inactivity for Liao Lihong's sake nodded he also declared, "Èshā I presume ".

The Èshā grinned, "One step ahead of you all the way, cousin. Always one step ahead. Now, very slowly and carefully take that backpack off and drop your weapon onto the floor. Sugar-tits you do the same with your pistol. One false move by either of you and you get it, sweet-cheeks".

"What are your ultimate intentions, if I may ask"? Nigh wanted to know as he tossed his pistol into a subfusc corner of the hovel.

"Well they don't call me the Èshā for nothing", the insane tormentor of them both smiled and then licked his lips. "Sugar-tits here will be my sixteenth koof and I'm looking forward to sampling her goodies".

"I'd have to be dead first you sick koof", Liao Lihong snapped.

Èshā's grin grew broader still and he admitted, "I've not tried necrophilia yet but there's time and so many sweet young things to deflower and despoil. I think I'll take my time over you, Bitch"?

"You have fifteen victims"? Nigh tried to distract the heinous rapist's attention from Liao Lihong, "The combmen think it only thirteen, have they not discovered the last two yet"?

Èshā roared with laughter and was delighted to inform Nigh,

"The last two were two of the very sweetest, two of the best I've ever had. I believe you were acquainted, Bī-miàn duì [lit – vulgar ladies private area – face]. Their names were Mingfu Li and Aurora"!

Nigh would have risked his own life to hurl himself at the strangler at that moment, but he could not risk getting yet another person he cared about killed. Cared about?! That was disconcertingly quick, but true he realised, he did care about the rogue rider. Certainly enough to play for time and hope to avoid the fate the strangler had in store for her at the very least. The weapons were on the dirty floor, the backpack tossed out of reach, the two of them were now at the monsters mercy.

"You killed his friends you koofing monster", Liao Lihong suddenly spat at the strangler.

Èshā chuckled, "I Zuò'ài their cute little asses first though, they screamed with pleasure, just like you're going to do"!

"In your twistedly demented dreams ass-hole", the Rogue was getting more incensed by the second and Nigh was carefully watching for the tiniest of openings when he could..... Behind Èshā the ether suddenly looked....wrong. It shimmered and rippled rather like the air over a heated tarmacadam road in the height of summer. Nigh and the Rogue had the sense not to look beyond their tormentor, it looked like a beacon of hope to them and they had the sense not to douse it. When the first of the two figures emerged into the timeline, she grasped Èshā's chin with one hand that moved faster than any human possibly could and with the other drove the durasteel blade of the anlace in just beneath the base of his skull directly up into his brain. He looked startled for perhaps a second and then the film of death began to glaze his eyeballs. Ruari let his body topple sideways on top of the girl he had but too recently shot dead.

"When you want to shoot someone you shoot someone. You don't indulge yourself in a mind-numbingly tedious diatribe firstly", the android said.

Nigh was not often robbed of words, but at that juncture he was momentarily robbed of the power of speech, especially when the second figure materialised at the android's side, turning out to be a meeso.

"What by Minerva is happening"? Liao Lihong gasped, her eyes widening at the strange and to her alien visage of the Prædontt.

"Is that you Băifotă"? Nigh asked lamely given what had just happened before their astonished eyes.

The meeso shook his conical head and informed, "I am his grandson, my name is Dìjììdù pleased to make your acquaintance Durango Nigh and this must be your Rogue, otherwise known as Liao Lihong"?

To everyone's surprise, Liao Lihong replied with humour, "He's my Combie, I'm not his Rogue. Now does someone want to tell me what by Minerva is going on and who you two are? I'm guessing you're an android, no human woman ever was as beautiful"?

"I am Ruari, aid and lieutenant to Acwellen the Great", the beautiful redhead told Liao Lihong, "Dìjììdù and I are allies in the 101st century, we knew Durango would need a bit of assistance at this point in his timeline".

Nigh's head was spinning. The 101st century, he could not envisage how the androids and the Prædon would become allies and why the former would choose to come to his aid. Then Ruari explained,

"Acwellen sent me to this point in time and space, Durango. To save your life and the life of your partner here. He figures that means you owe him a debt of gratitude".

Nigh's heart sank, "What does he want, Ruari"?

"He wants nothing", the android told him, she explained, "Exactly nothing, no threat of destruction or some abortive attempt to storm Shattered Fang. He simply wants you to forget your feud, leave him alone and he will reciprocate. Now your life is your own and his existence is his. Do you agree to his terms, acknowledge your debt and wipe the slate clean at the same instant"?

Nigh sighed, "Very well. Tell him - thank you and I will not make any sort of aggressive move against the king of the androids either now or in any other period".

Ruari smiled, allowed Dìjīīdù to throw a metal toggle on her pack and promptly vanished.

"So, Dìjīīdù, how do you fit into all of this"?

"The Prædon owe a debt of gratitude to the Homini, my journey here was to assist Ruari if she needed it. As you can see however the aesthetic is perfectly capable of self-protection. Once I have reset my controls I am leaving too".

"You are wearing a plug so that the girl could understand all this"?

Dìjīīdù nodded, but Liao Lìhong complained, "I understand each word this blue chap speaks, but I'm still lost.

"I've enjoyed this briefest of incursions, but now I must go. As your records show, Nigh, you understand our reluctance to tamper with the fourth-dimensional weave. Otherwise, I might very well have come alone".

"I doubt Ruari would have allowed that for an instant", Nigh laughed, "Thank you for your attendance though Dìjīīdù as a protracted esprit and a profitable one".

Dìjīīdù ten put his arm behind him and threw a toggle on his backpack before vanishing. While the two of them picked up their weapons and Nigh put on his backpack, Liao Lìhong suddenly observed,

"You can explain everything to me later. Right now we have to get out of Zhanggangzhen – Provincial Road without the Shui Fong cutting our throats"!

"Good point actually", Nigh confessed, "Get your gun ready and let's get out of here. We're going to be blamed for the girl's death even if they discover Èshā was wearing some sort of identity changing devices. I don't think the Shui Fong will be open to reason".

They were not deaf either and were waiting for them. As they pushed their way past the rusty corrugated iron shutter that served as the hovel's door, two of them rushed forward in an attack armed with a lump of detritus, crude cudgels. Nigh shot both with his needlegun. Others crowded into the space left by them and both Nigh and Liao Lihong emptied their clips into the crowding bodies. When that failed to stop the huge gang Nigh took to using his Yogi Doshi techniques of self-defence kicking and punching whilst the girl at his side reloaded her needlegun with a second clip. The ferocity of the assault tapered off when the hoodlums of Zhanggangzhen began to realise that it would be incredibly difficult to overcome the two of them.

"Keep back and let us leave and no one else has to be stunned. I have to warn you that the next couple of clips I have in my pack are level two, so you would be launching yourselves into your death".

Someone shouted, "Use level two and we'll call the Wūgòu"!

"I *am* a combman, imbecile". Nigh called back and the throng of thugs began to melt away.

The Honda was untouched,

"This surprises me", Rogue observed, "How come they never stripped it down for parts"?

"Because they thought the whole thing would be theirs when they had dealt with us", Nigh reasoned. "I'm hungry do you want to go and get something to eat. After which I have to go back to the 33rd century for what I hope will be the very last time".

"I could eat", Rogue declared, "And while we do you can tell me exactly what this is all about and what is going on. I'll take you back to my place and cook for you, all right"?

Nigh nodded, he had been going to suggest a restaurant but suddenly wanted only the company of her, he had endured enough new faces for one day.

Two hours later Liao Lihong was in full possession of the facts of Nigh's family history and all its twists and turns through its various incarnations.

Laying down her chopsticks Liao Lihong declared, "It's a wonder all the changes you have witnessed are not starting to make you lose your sense of reality. Especially when reality keeps changing for you".

"Perhaps my Andhera Tantu has kept me grounded, who knows", Nigh smiled, suddenly quite fatigued by it all. "What's for dessert"?

Liao's features suddenly grew coy, "What would you like, you can have anything you want"?

Suddenly craving desire, passion, lust, call it anything he could think of, he wanted a display of affection. He rose from his seat rounded the table and placing his hand beneath her chin lifted her face to him so that he could kiss her passionately on the mouth.

* * *

Liao Lihong was not about to let Nigh go without a fight. Her honey-trap closed about him after the third time they enjoyed one another.

"I want to be your 老婆一个 [wifone]", she purred in his ear, "We are so good together, so good for one another, don't you want to have me whenever you want me"?

"There is something you should know", he confessed at once, "I was engaged to Mayling Fuchow, one of the victims of the strangler who I hope to resurrect. Her memories will be resurrected with her if my mission is successful, I promised her the position of wifone. I'm sorry, Liao Lihong I should have told you, but in the heat of the moment I was not thinking with my big head".

Liao shrugged. A very pleasant expression to watch she was naked, it made her breasts jiggle delightfully,

"How many 未婚夫的[fiancé's] did you have"?

"One, but two other girls were also hopeful of marriage to me, two more of the strangler's victims. Two more I hope to resurrect. They did not deserve the cruel fate that befell them because of him and because of their association with me".

How many of these girls had you slept with"?

"Just my fiancé, up until you".

Liao observed seriously, "So if you want me and the last few hours have indicated that you do, then I would have to settle for sharing you and for taking the title of 新娘 [witwof]"?

"I would be honoured to take you as my second wife", Nigh declared thinking to himself,

'If I can finally get the weave of my family history right I will be one lucky lucky dog. Even if Mingfu Li and Aurora don't want to be 伴侣[wifree] and 配偶[wifoure]'!

Technically the exact translation from the Chinese was not numbered however but described each union differently, they translated as; wife, bride, spouse and consort. Each title not quite as revered as the one that preceded it.

"I agree", the rogue rider declared, "Who knows the fiancé might break off the engagement when she sees me".

"You never know", Nigh admitted, but thought, *'I hope not though, Mayling is stunning too'!* "It's time I got bathed dressed and set off though, Liao. I don't want my friends in the deep freeze unit of the combstation for any longer, not that they will remember it, but I will".

"What about me"? Liao Lihong asked suddenly worried, "If you were not called to the combmen station I would not have driven past you and......".

"I have your address, I will look you up and I will honour our engagement, you have my word of honour as an Englishman. That is if things turn out quite as neatly as I hope they will. I must point out that such has not been the case thus far, but I am optimistic of success this time".

"Well if things do yield unexpected results, you know where to find me. Please find me, Durango"?

"I will, you can count on that".

Nigh did not feel the need to protract his leave-taking any longer and as soon as he was in his black jumpsuit, with the mechanism in its pack on his back, he was ready to make what he heartily hoped would be his last trip through time for some considerable spell. He threw the toggle on the preset UIMF and found himself on Mars in the 33rd century. Precisely, he was in the town of Karathanistra, which lay just south of Dead Man's Gap. He knew Lynea had been to the town, but as to whether she was still in the place, only time would tell him that. The truth, when he faced up to it was that he did not want to find her too quickly. He was not desirous of the outcome, he did not wish to become guilty of amitacide but could see no other way to put matters to rights. While ever she could have children she could start the line that would end up with the strangler. It included babies of either sex, for the gene that gave the desire to kill, was dormant until the 51st century. Once again he was immediately aware of the changes in atmospheric conditions and temperature. The thinness of the air, the lack of gravity, he felt the customary lightness of body and light in the head and forced himself to breathe deeply through the mask he had brought with him. The wind was seemingly increasing in intensity and swirling about huge clouds of rust. It was a northerly draught. Nigh pulled down his goggles and only then began to examine his surroundings. So close to Dead Man's Gap, Karathanistra reminded him of an ancient western town that he had seen depicted in tri-vidz showing the settlers of the Unwanted States. The buildings were made of ply and breeze, obviously heavier materials brought from Earth would have proved prohibitively exorbitant of price and Mars was young in the 33rd, not yet the industrial planet it would become later on. A sign squeaking as it swung to and fro in the gusting air proclaimed one building as the Vojaĝanto Resto [Traveller's Rest]. A boarding house of sorts, run by most likely those who immigrated from one of the areas that spoke romance languages and Latin, though it was not difficult to find words from German, English or Russian origin. Therefore any of European nationality may have thought to use Esperanto to name their establishment. Without hesitation, Nigh decided to get in out of the wind and cold. He pressed the air-lock chime and waited for the familiar click of the outer door releasing. It did so with admirable alacrity and he stepped into the lock. The whine of the vacuums could be heard as nearly all of the dust was sucked from his clothing and the air. Only once the machine read that the air was relatively dust-free did the inner lock then allow him to pass further into the Vojaĝanto Resto. Behind a faux-wooden topped counter, a hugely fat man slowly climbed to his feet and offered Nigh a yellow smile.

As Nigh approached the reception area though, a strange expression crossed the fat man's face. Nigh gauged it to be a combination of surprise and incredulity, it was not possible that the proprietor of that establishment recognised him. Although since Nigh had in the *past (or maybe even future)* achieved the impossible several times, it was of course impossibly possible. But the cynosure of the fat man's vision was not focused on Nigh himself, he discerned as he drew closer to him, but rather, over his shoulder. He turned instinctively reaching for his needlegun. A vice-like grip suddenly constricted his wrist, delaying the action and a husky voice told him,

"You won't need that against me, Pup".

Nigh looked into the grizzled countenance of the other entrant to the boarding house. The man had seen more than his fair share of action in the form of conflict. Down one side of his bristly face was a strangely lilac burn. No doubt the result of a close call with some sort of energy weapon. Why had the man not had it surgically restored? That was not the most noticeable of his injuries though. In place of his right eye was some sort of lens. Not fitted especially well. The skin around it puckered and red with further damage. Even as he looked at Nigh, the lens gave a soft whir as it focused on various parts of him and his clothing etcetera. Again a prosthetic vision organ would have looked far more conventional. Indeed some were said to be superior to those given by nature.

"You don't like how I look"? The veteran grinned, the result of that humour, a parody of good homie, a rictus that looked unsettling in the extreme.

"It is not my place to comment one way or the other, Sir", Nigh returned. Something about the man's mein instinctively informing him that he was due some respect, maybe even because of his injuries. The man pointed a metal replacement finger at the lens and informed, "I got this in the Synbarian Cluster in the 243rd. I might not be pretty but it has a macro facility and an f32 zoom to 500mm".

"It's a camera lens"?

The vet nodded, "A Hoya 3D with UV filter built-in. The Synbarian bought the patents in the 242nd and made a few improvements".

"You seem to have been involved in a few skirmishes in your time", Nigh grew intrigued by the vet.

Again that twisted grin, and the admission, "I've lived more adventure in my lifetime thusly far than the average man would experience in a score of them".

"So when you say the 243rd...do you mean, the...".

"243rd century"? A rasping sound like vines being dragged across old timber indicated that the vet was laughing, "That's exactly what I mean. Excuse the quality of my voice, Pup I had my vocal cords scorched in the trident Conflict on the Rim. I keep meaning to have a digital voice-box transplanted, but I've been kinda busy".

Nigh said reluctantly, absently admiring the burnished steel dome that was the Vet's replacement skull, a device that would doubtless involve far superior protection and certainly cut down on hairdresser bills,

"Then it is discourteous of me to delay you any further in my banal conversation, please go ahead of me, I am not even booked in yet"?

The man's laugh was like the cool breeze that blows through a graveyard in the early hours, "You don't recognise me do you"? "I'm afraid not, Sir. You have a certain familiarity about you, but......". He shrugged.

"Do you want your keycard, Colonel"? The fat man enquired. "I'm not sure", the veteran who now had rank mused, he turned back to Nigh and asked, "I have a bottle of Synbarian Vodka in my room, Fatso here will soon fetch me another glass, would you like to drink with me and discuss yours and my business here, Pup"?

Without waiting for Nigh's reply, nor asking him to book in himself, the fat proprietor found another glass and swiftly handed it to the veteran. Everything in his senses told Nigh to refuse politely, but he nodded and declared, "I would be honoured to have a drink with you, Colonel".

"Come then, I am in room 23 – naturally"?

Nigh followed the veteran officer up the stairs, the Vojaĝanto Resto possessed no lift. Despite the Colonel's age, Nigh struggled to keep up with him as he vaulted the steps three at a stride. The second floor was as insalubrious as the ground. Even painted in pale greys and faun insipid but designed to blend in with dust and lack of housekeeping standards. The trod down a bare floor of concrete that had at one time been given a coat of pale blue masonry paint but was worn away down the corridor's centre. Thousands of booted feet had eroded that building in the short time that it had hugged the surface of the red planet. At the door marked with the outline of a two, two screw holes declaring that the number had broken off leaving a lone three, the Colonel swiped the lock and it clunked undone. The old veteran waved an arm in a magnanimous gesture and urged,

"Guests first go in young Pup".

Nigh turned into the doorway and at that instant, something decidedly heavy delivered a rabbit punch to the back of his ear. Pin exploded before his vision bright stars of violet and xanthic and then he felt himself falling into blackness. When consciousness returned, it was accompanied by an intense headache that made Nigh gasp. Every time his heartbeat, he could feel it throb in his temple. He was seated on a hard-backed chair, his wrists and ankles secured by nyloplanyon tie-wraps, his side-arm gone.

"You are back", the Colonel noted aloud. "I tried to be as gentle as possible, but I didn't want you accessing your Andhera Tantu. Trying now would be unwise, I've injected you with neural blockers, the ability to sneak away into some part of the weave is no longer one of your options".

"Why are you doing this"? Nigh demanded, "I can guess you have investigated me, maybe even historically if you're from the 243rd so I have to ask who is paying you, how much and would double be enough to purchase my freedom"?

"I'm afraid none of that would be of any help to you, Pup-Nigh. I'm not working for anyone, if I introduce myself to you properly you will realise that this is the end of the line for you, My Friend. I am Colonel Durango Nigh and I was born in the 33rd century"!

Nigh was speechless. His assailant and nemesis was his future self. Or perhaps his alter-ego from another layer of the multiverse, it depended upon one's viewpoint and how one regarded the fourth dimension.

Finally Nigh reasoned quietly,

"It is not the end of the line for me, Colonel, because you exist. You, the man I will become"!

"I have learned", the Colonel began, "That the fourth dimension is not a rope, rather it is a tapestry and like that pictorial cloth has a vast design made up of many threads. The part of the tapestry I have been exploring is warlike and ...well, interesting for all its conflicts. I have also learned that my vitality increases the few alter-versions of myself exist. For that reason, I have taken to eliminating a few shadow-Nigh as I like to think of them. I am the body, they were merely adumbration of the original, which is me".

"You have killed other-us"?

"Pale imitations of myself", Nigh gave a gnarled and twisted grimace, "As are you, Young Pup. I'm sorry but your flirtations and preoccupation with the Chinese girls make of you a particularly easy version to dislike and therefore slaughter. I will do so soon and with the minimum of fuss and inconvenience to myself. Alas, there will be however a moment of extreme discomfort for you".

"You are loathsomely malevolent", Nigh observed, "I find it hard to believe I could ever be anything like you".

"You won't be", the Colonel assured simply, "Because once we have had our little drink, you will be dead".

"And you'll wink out of existence", Nigh tried. The Colonel declared at that,

"I have not yet and have no reason to suppose I will this time. For as I do not remember this deathly experience in my youth, then it is obvious that you are not an earlier version of me".

"So what do you remember? Did you ever come to Mars"?

The Colonel grimaced once again, "Such knowledge would be of no use to you for the few minutes you have left. I can, therefore, tell you that in *my* youth I was the ally of Acwellen, a service which ultimately led to the creation of the Arcticfusion Drive and the beginning of the explorations into the next system beyond the Cradle".

"The Cradle"?

"Oh yes, you call it the Solar System, as if it were the only one. It is merely one cradle of life amongst many".

"It sounds intriguing", Nigh tried, "I would join you, serve as your lieutenant".

The Colonel chuckled, "And we would never trust one another until one of us slay the other. My way is simpler for me and involves less risk. No, Pup, I'm afraid you must be annihilated, for my good. So let's have that drink and then get the show on my road and your cul-de-sac".

Wincing at the terrible pun, Nigh struggled against his bonds. All it served to do though was cause his head to pound with renewed ferocity. He asked,

"You don't have any analgesics do you, Colonel"?

"Your head hurts", came the other's reply as he was pouring out two glasses of clear spirit, "They would be a waste would they not, you will be dead before they even begin to affect your central nervous system".

The Colonel took a hearty swig of his drink and then, bizarrely held the other glass to Nigh's lips,

"Get a slug of this down you, it will help to kill the pain and then relive the pain of the kill".

"How did I become you"!? Nigh wanted to know, once he had taken a burning swallow of the moonshine. There was no label on the bottle it was quite obviously illegally stilled.

The Colonel looked thoughtful for a second and then shrugged,

"Don't know, just lucky I guess".

"And you remember Mingfu Li, Aurora and Mayling Fuchow and you are deliberately confining them to non-existence? Can you not remember how you felt about them"?

In that strangely and quite ludicrous instant Nigh realised that he had deep feelings of affection for all three of them. He added Liao Lihong to the mental list.

"It was a few good lays at the time, but let's face it Pup, they were Chinks, you strip 'em off, lay 'em down and once you've done the business you move on".

"What a sad and time-worn creature you've become, Colonel. Are you even a Colonel or is that title as phoney as all your other emotions"?

"That's right, Pup let all that venom flare-up, fill your being with animosity, it feels good don't it"?

"You do not even speak standard with the accuracy you used to employ", Nigh could feel hatred for his self-to-be welling up inside him.

"Cut these wraps, lose the weapons and we can end this man to man, primal, basic".

The Colonel chuckled, "It might be fun at that to twist that arrogant little head right off your shoulders".

Nigh felt a glimmer of hope, a tiny shaft of xanthic twinkling in the motes of the sable pit. "Come on then, hard man, show me what you've got".

The Colonel took another hearty swig of his drink and cut off the source of the ray of aspiration. He shook his heavily battle-scarred head and observed,   "I'm   not drunk enough to not realise that down that avenue lays an element of risk, no matter how slim a chance it is that you could beat me, it is none the less possible. No, I think I'll just use the blaster and avoid even the most minor of injuries to myself. Here, get the rest of this down you, it's the last drink you'll ever have".

Nigh let the Colonel lift the glass to his lips once more, he took the spirit into his mouth and then whilst the Colonel was still in spitting distance forced a jet of it into his eyes. As the surprised older version of himself roared in a combination of anger, pain and surprise, Nigh threw himself back against the chair which promptly toppled and crashed back onto the floor with Nigh still firmly attached to it. The Colonel was blundering around the room waving his left arm out in front of him, while his fingers of his right were trying to wipe the spirit from his precious lens and his other eye would doubtless be stinging mightily. Nigh desperately tried to calm himself sufficiently to enter a trance state, as taught him by the Yogi Doshi. He had been agitated and in a high state of upsetmentation for quite a while though - it was proving virtually impossible to achieve. Without it, he could not activate the andhera tantu with any degree of accuracy. The Colonel was suddenly lurching toward him and the neural blockers were still doing enough to deny him the ability to focus his thoughts appropriately. Colonel Nigh grabbed hold of Durango Nigh and with a swift, almost effortless haul brought the chair back up to the usual position. Then a mighty powerful fist crashed into Nigh's face and he tasted the iron of blood in his mouth.

"So we've played this little game for long enough", he snarled, drawing a flared nose blaster from a holster at his side. "Any last words before I blow that thread infested brain of yours half-way across the room, Young Pup"?

"Yes, actually", Nigh mumbled, he thought the Colonel had broken one of his incisors, "Koof you Mu˘quīnu˘xiào [vulg – a person who lies with and has carnal knowledge of his mother]"!

The pain had in some inexplicable way allowed him to focus his mind and granted him access to the fibriliance in his brain. He grasped the end of one fibre, mentally raced up it and .... Colonel Nigh roared in anger and frustration, the loathsome little squirt had eluded him and he could not follow. How could he possibly give chase to a person who did not even know *when* he was himself?

Seventeen.   Tribeuchre

The air was thin, there was less oxygen in it. The ground looked like it was hewn from Jet. The sky was filled with the giant swollen ball of brilliance that was the sun. It was an incredible 10 percent brighter than any star Nigh had ever seen in his past journeys. In his confusion under the effects of the drugs the Colonel had administered into his system, he had fled a ridiculous amount of centuries upwhen. It was the year 1,100,003,282 or the 11,000,033rd century. The temperature was 50°C and sweat began immediately to pour from every pore Nigh possessed. The resultant greenhouse effect that turned Earth into a planet very like Venus had been before it was terra-formed, without the acid though. Of course, Mercury and Venus were gone, incinerated and boiled away into space. This Earth's oceans had boiled, the ice caps permanently melted, and all water vapor in the atmosphere was gone. Under those conditions, life as Nigh had known it had fled or died, unable to survive anywhere on the surface, and the planet Earth was fully transformed into another hot, dry world of rock and the only lifeforms that could survive such incredible extremes. Deep down beneath the burnished sands, in pockets of life, where some moisture still existed, the ants and the scorpions warred for the tiny footholds of environment left for them to squabble over. A few arachnids still clung tenuously to existence and microbes, germs, termites and the most enduring of lifeforms, the virus was existing on borrowed time. Nigh lay gasping and perspiring, glancing about him in a combination of shock and awe. He was the last man to remain alive on the formerly third planet from the sun. Now it was the first and with it the eternal moon. Nigh wondered if there were any men still living under the satellites domes. Would they even be men though? Evolution can make powerful changes in 1.1 billion years. It might well be that homo sapien now enjoyed the heat on some of the moons of Jupiter and Saturn. It would doubtless still be cold on Pluto Eres and Persephone.

"I am the last of us", Nigh croaked to the scorpions and the ants, "There is no on even remotely related to me or my kind that will ever tread on this barren scorched ball of rock".

He was wrong!

Even as he was beginning to see if he could once again use the andhera tantu to escape what would otherwise be certain and untimely death. Two figures walked out of the shimmering heat and stopped before him. They wore suits of bright silver, masks over their faces, but even then it was

possible to see that one was a Prædon, whilst the much smaller and slight of the mismatched duo was a human female. A human female with olive skin tone and almond-shaped eyes. Nigh could tell the two of them were communicating to one another by some sort of mechanism in their masks. Then the Prædon bent over and effortlessly picked Nigh wilting sweat racked body up in his arms as though he were a feather-weight. Almost immediately the surrounding began to shimmer and oscillate and as nigh fainted, the Earth of the year 1,100,003,282 was before them. In front of them, in the future, for the planet would not have many

years left in the other direction. Nigh came too slowly, his body having been starved of oxygen and poached, bending over him was a very attractive girl who looked to be a mix of Oriental and Caucasian races.

"You had us worried, she even had a sweet voice, "You would not have survived much longer in that almost alien environment, it's a good job we found you".

"When, where am I? Who are you"? Nigh managed to croak.

The girl held a sippy cup to Nigh lips and he drank greedily.

"Steady"! She cautioned, "Just sip, don't take too much in".

The fluid was not as he had expected, water. Rather it was some sort of energy beverage. Seeing the fact register on his features, she informed him

"It is Orang-U-Can Re-Kuvva, it contains all the salts electrolytes your body requires at the moment and is pound for pound more nourishing and protein-packed than prime bovine".

"You are very kind, who are you"? He repeated.

"My name is Durania Durangia", the girl smiled, "Hello, Grandfather"!

Nigh had experienced too many adventures in time and space to be surprised any more. What did intrigue him though was who had sired this delightful creature and who had sired her mother/father before her?

"Are you my paternal or maternal granddaughter Durania Durangia"?

"My mother is called Durangia Nigh", the girl teased offering nothing further, "She was your daughter to one of your wives, do you want to guess which one"?

"I'm not even married yet", Nigh smiled raising himself onto an elbow and discovering the Re-Kuvva coursing through his veins was having the desired recuperative effect, "But it will be amusing for me to try. Was your grandmother Mayling Fuchow by any chance"?

The girl shook her head

Then I think my next guess would be Liao Lihong"?

"According to my records in the Cradleweave, you had only just met her at the point in your adventures when you encountered the Colonel".

"The Cradleweave"?

"Oh, that's right you still call it the SWW or Solar-wide-web".

"Do I ever get the better of the Colonel, that aspect of me was a thoroughly unpleasant fellow"?

"He is a time-fugitive in many aspects of the tempusweave. He will eventually be caught I believe, but not by the 101st, which is where we are at present".

Then the Prædontt was none other than...".?

"Dìjīìdù, yes. I was not born here, but I have joined the Prædon as an agent for them, but that is another story Grandpop, to be told at another time".

'Grandpop'! Nigh thought, *'Grandpop'!* He said nothing though merely hesitantly offered, "So your grandmother was Aurora"?

This caused the girl to frown, "You have one guess left and if you get it wrong I may have to slap you".

Nigh jumped from the gurney and objected, "Slap an old man, you wouldn't dare, your Grandmother was Mingfu Li. What happens now"?

"Once you are recovered you can leave. Go back and secure my Grandmother's existence, because if you do not, I will fade to nothingness myself. It is not as instantaneous as the ancient fictions would have had us believe, but make enough broken threads in the tempusweave and the pull will eventually make certain offspring and associates, relatives and friends dissolve and evaporate until they are nothingness".

"Well, we cannot have that Durania. I am not looking forward to the action I must take though. Do you think there is any chance at all I can convince my Aunt not to have any issue"?

"You would never truly know if you had convinced her. Until you got back to your somewhen of the 51st and by then her decision might have resulted in unforeseen consequences, as you have learned thus far".

"Only too well", Nigh agreed gloomily. "I could always then go back and.....".

"That section of the weave is becoming unstable, Grandpop. Think of it as threadbare. Do any more damage to it and it will develop a tempusian-hole. If that happens then the tempusweave will fray, ladder, start to unravel....".

"Stop. I get the picture. I have one more shot at this do I not"?

Durania Durangia nodded.

"I'll just have a quick word with Dìjiìdù than and then I will be on my way, and if I'm successful, it will be for the last time, the situation is beginning to cause me despair".

"Come with me, if you're feeling strong enough and I will take you to heshe".

Nigh paid his respects and made his gratitude apparent and then turned back to his granddaughter,

"I expect your Grandmother is still a very handsome woman", he smiled, "Do you get to see much of her"?

"I visit downwhen when I get the chance", the girl responded, "I'm sorry but regulations do not permit me from saying too much".

"Of course. I am pleased that such restrictions exist, I grow tired of discovering the dangers of trying to manipulate the timeline. So this is a goodbye for the moment then, the next time we meet I will probably be balancing you precariously on my knee".

Durania chuckled, "There's a thought. All right, Grandpop let me adjust your controls for you and you will find yourself back in the Vojaĝanto Resto, one hour after the Colonel has left. I think it is the last place he would think to look for you".

Before Nigh could comment in either agreement or otherwise the girl threw the toggle switch on the backpack and he found himself once more in the town of Karathanistra, which lay just south of Dead Man's Gap. In one room, another pack identical to the one he now wore would be residing and Nigh had to find it and return it to the Prædon. The Colonel would have no use for it already having one of his own. Nigh strode inside, past the startled proprietor and up to the room with half the number 23 missing from its door. Inside he found his original backpack and gun. Setting the backpack controls to the correct aligments, he threw the toggle and watched is disappear, the gun went back into his holster. Then he returned to the desk and with coin secured the room for himself for the night, asking the fat man if there was anywhere in town where he could get a good meal and if he had heard of either Lynea Morrelius or Mrs Pollopanie. Confirming Nigh's suspicions regarding his landlord, he knew nothing of the inhabitants of the town, other than the traders he dealt with. On the gastronomic front though he recommended Stufitintilurfull. A fast-food establishment that belonged to the Buckminsterfullerene Corporation who had made much of their fortune based on the type of fullerene with the formula C60. It was the cage-like fused-ring structure (truncated icosahedron) that resembled a football, made of twenty hexagons and twelve pentagons, with a carbon atom which has one π bond and two single bonds at each vertex of each polygon and a bond along each polygon edge. The Corporation used a laser to vaporize carbon in a supersonic helium beam. Its applications included the C60 forming complex bonds akin to the more common alkenes. Complexes were created with molybdenon, tungsten, platinum, **palladium**, iridium, titanium and most usefully durilite. The pentacarbonyl species produced by Photochemical Reactions also had a multitude of industrial capitalizations. $M(CO)6 + C60 \rightarrow M(\eta 2\text{-}C60)(CO)5 + CO$ (M = Mo, W). When the corporation decided to branch out into more domestic enterprises the chain of Stufitintilurfull was born, the brainchild of the then CEO Andrusius Demetrius Enuff, which was immediately noted, that when shortened read as A D Enuff. An alias. Although tri-vidz of Enuff showed a man leaning from portliness toward obesity, which in many parts of the solar system was then considered a heinous and immoral crime punishable by hefty fines and if that failed to rectify the offender the removal of extraneous parts until a target weight was achieved. Stufitintilurfull seemed to fly thusly in the face of conventionality, although the Buckminsterfullerene Corporation claimed the nomenclature was designed to indicate maximum value for expenditure rather than a desire to propagate over-indulgence. Nigh slipped his mask into place and stepped out into the frigid night. It was very dark. The moons of Mars were pitiful at providing illumination and towns like Karathanistra found street lighting financially non-viable. The place did not even have a council or any sort of ruling body, it was still in its infancy and very frontier. Thusly Stufitintilurfull was an incongruous beacon in the Spartan night of the town. A shining jewel promising luxury and civilisation. People did not merely go there to eat. Once inside they tended to stay all night, drinking, gambling and socialising. As long as they were occasionally buying something, no matter how inexpensive or meagre, the management did not ask them to leave. Stufitintilurfull was like a Community Hall. Nigh went threw the airlock, allowing the vacuums to remove dust from his boots and suit, before entering the dome-like structure of the inside of the building. The food outlets were situated closest to the entrance/exit, but that was only to be expected and suited Nigh's purpose anyway. He went to the high counter of the Lichburg Bar and climbed onto one of the high stools. Glancing at the display, he ordered a Bellivalu Lichburg meal, which for mere sestertii included in the one price a Lichburg in Lichbred with seeded crust lichtoes, lichttuce, lichion and mayo in addition to the burger. At the side of this mouth-watering repast was a portion of lichspud chips and a medium Orang-U-Can or NRG medium drink. All in all a fabulous bargain and gastronomic treat. Nigh concentrated upon his meal before raising his head to see what else was being offered by way of evening entertainment. There was plenty of possible sources of information and he would try several before admitting defeat. His granddaughter would not have sent him on a wild goose chase, he was sure of that. Where was the best place to start? Surely it would be at one of the card tables. If a man lost all his stake he would be willing to supply information in return for some sort of recompense for the evening's losses. Nigh slowly strolled in the appropriate direction and slowed at a Tribeuchre table. The game was considerably more complex than most, involving as it did a deck of some 75 cards subdivided into five suits of fifteen. These were swords, escutcheon, arrows, spears and trident. Each suit consisted of the numbers one to ten plus the picture cards which were novice, steward, soldier, knight and gladiator. To master the game one had to remember the placement order of the suits and the various rankings of the pictures. Nigh had played before with his father, but never when in possession of eidetic memory. He took his seat at one table which already had three men and two women around it. As there was a vacant chair no one objected. Tribeuchre was best played with six anyway.

"How much is the buy-in, please", he asked as a dark-haired man was expertly shuffling the deck.

"5 Marshillin repayable when leaving if one still has it", the dark-haired man told him. A considerable sum then, this game was not for little boys and girls. One of the women offered Nigh a pad to press his thumb to but he surprised them all by placing five Marshillin slips onto the green baize.

"How many chips would you like", the same woman, a well-preserved blonde asked, as an android approached the table. Nigh looked at the piles before each of the players and asked for a figure just over the player who was doing best. A thin man with sandy hair and crooked teeth. Strange, when such an infirmity was so easily rectified. Nigh could feel the dark man's eyes watching almost reverently as the chips were counted out, they gleamed like the smashed badger caught in the headlights of a flitter. He was so dark, that even though he had shaved that morning [defoliation was currently out of fashion] his chins lip and the sides of his face were almost a blue colour. The thin man with crooked teeth and contrastingly sandy hair noted,

"If you've finished shuffling those, it's my deal I believe".

No one had offered their names, so Nigh did not supply his. Perhaps it was some strange etiquette involved with the game of Tribeuchre? He still desired to identify his opponents though so he gave each of them a mental name, Dark and Thin were easy, so was the last of the men, a huge man who worked with his spade-like hands, became - Spade. The well preserved, but quite old, even by the standards of the century became Grandma, while the last player, a slim brunette of much fewer years was Babe. Babe had a very slim face and brown hair that would not have curled even if 220volts had been passed through her. Yet her elfin features were attractive in a vulnerable sort of way. She was the type of girl who would end up getting herself a *sugar daddy* and bleeding him for every sestertius. Nigh played a few giveaway hands, not trying to win, merely watching how the cards came and went back to the bottom of the deck. He was more interested in scrutinising his opposition than the cards they played. After a while, he was satisfied he had correctly read each of them. Dark smoked quicker when his hand was good. His dark head became subfusc at the centre of a cloud of blue smoke. Thin blinked twice when looking at his two *hole* cards. He did not blink if they were *superiors*. Those being either swords and arrows, which were worth more points than the other three suits. Although the gladiator of escutcheon could trump the number cards of swords and arrows, while the soldier knight and gladiator of spears and trident were also superiors. Each card carried a value the number-cards being obvious the pictures slightly more complicated. Each had a different value of growing value and the most valuable card of all was the gladiator of swords. Strangely the same card carried with it the superstition of being linked with violent death. Babe pushed a stray strand of hair out of her eyes if her *hand* was strong, while Grandma was forced to wipe a thin bead of perspiration from her top lip. Only

Spade was impossible to read, he was the quiet and sly card player and he was slowly winning the chips with no fuss and little comment. The hand was dealt out in the following order, the two hole cards and the first *showing* [face up] all being dealt in one deal. Bets were then placed according to who had the best showing card down to who had the worst. Yet this did not mean that the player doing so had the worst hand obviously and that was where the bluffing came into play. Finally, the fourth card was played and the second round of betting determined by the same valuation of the showing cards. In the final round the players could then either *stay* [keep what they had] or buy a single card which was dealt to them face down and they, in turn, surrendered one of their hole cards in exchange. The cost of doing so was the highest bid any player had thus made. Finally, all four cards that each player possessed were shown and the one with the highest-ranking took the pot. As with most games, it sounded simple, but there were games within games, bluffs, counter bluffs, the manoeuvre of bidding high to force others to follow if the wanted to exchange. One could also *quit* at any time, to save bidding on a bad low-value set. The experienced card player would sometimes quit with a good hand if he or she thought one of the other players had an even better one, thusly reducing the pot they won. Finally, a player could have the best showing cards and still lose if an opponent had high hole cards. Nigh settled into the game and watched Thin and Grandma slowly but steadily lose as the evening progressed. Dark and Babe were up and down and breaking generally even, while Nigh himself and Spade were ever so gradually winning. Then came the point where Dark had tremendous showing cards and was prepared to bet heavily that he would win the hand. Thin quit in the first round, Grandma and Babe after the second showing card was dealt, it left Spade, Nigh and Dark. Nigh calculated which cards were gone and determined that he had little chance of beating Dark, so he quit. He had also calculated that Spade had a good chance of having very good hole cards, possibly even the gladiator of swords. Dark had good showings and equally good hole while Spade had a fairly good showing and possibly superb hole. Neither of them bought a replacement and it was time to turn their hole cards over with a grin Dark revealed the soldier and knight of spears to add to his showing knight and gladiator of arrows and trident respectively. Spade even then could not be read, by Nigh, or, any of the other players, to add to his knight of the escutcheon and ten of swords the big man revealed the gladiator of spears and swords. He had two gladiator hole cards and beat Dark with the *quadproved* hand. Dark was done, his stash would not cover remaining in the game for very long and he did not have enough to bet and win back his money. He slowly climbed to his feet saying,

"Ladies and gentlemen thank you for a very pleasant evening, I will bid you all goodnight, but first I think I'll get me a stiff one at the bar".

"Wait", Nigh almost barked, scoping up his chips ready to change back to cash. "It would be my pleasure to buy you that drink, Sir, after all, some of what I have is your money anyway"?

Dark smiled without humour, but conceded, "Far be it from me to ever turn down a free drink, lead on".

Nigh bid the others good night and preceded dark to the bar. While they waited for two Sunset Yellows to arrive, Nigh learned that the dark man went by the name of Lyndon Mathers. It did not fit him, but then perhaps Nigh did not look like a Durango? The cocktails arrived [Lichpineapple, dark filtered rum and a shot of liquasnufz preparation] a very potent brew, even so, Mathers downed half of his in one angry swallow.

"Let me ask you something, Rango"? He demanded as he carefully placed the glass back onto the pseudo-glass surface of the bar.

Nigh had never had his first name shortened in such a way before, but he did not comment upon the sudden familiarity.

"Do you think Jared was cheating, dealing from the bottom or anything of that nature"?

Spade was known to Mathers it turned out then and his name was Jared.

"No, I don't", Nigh returned honestly, he is just a quietly confident and talented card player".

"Eyeing the pile of chips on the counter before Nigh, Mathers commented, "You're no novice yourself, Rango, you've won a handsome sum there, mostly from me once everything is totted up Seldine Seldinius looks to have broken about even while Gerania Galbanus and Alcasia

Cordulum have not lost that much considering they have spent a very pleasant evening here".

Nigh's hunch had proved fruitful, Mathers knew everyone in town. He would also know if someone did not belong in Karathanistra. Biting back the other enquiry he wanted to ask, whether babe was Galbanus or Cordulum he instead noted,

"I'll wager there is not a single person in this place that you do not know".

Mathers grinned, "I get around, Rango, after tonight not so much but I'll manage".

"What is I allowed you to pick up all those chips and cash them into your account for yourself "? Nigh enquired.

"What sort of opportunity"? Mathers dark eyes narrowed suspiciously.

"Nothing sinister really, although some would possibly read into it. I'm looking for someone. My Aunt and I have reason to believe she might be hiding here in Karathanistra. All I want you to do is either lead me to her or tell me where you think I can find her and the chips are yours".

"What's the woman's name, would it be Morrelius by any chance"? Mathers grinned.

Nigh smiled, stating, "You know exactly where she is. Will you lead me to her this evening and you can have those chips before we go there"?

With a nod, Mathers scooped up the plastic counters and signalled to one of the androids who were walking the floor. The chips were counted and added to Mathers' **thumb.** He quickly drained his drink informing,

"Morrelius is staying at the old Striantum drilling site. Dariopum Striantum vacated it a couple of years ago when the shaft stopped supplying argon. The fissure just played out, still, he'd made his load and off he went. Your Aunt is stopping at the bungalow there".

"Is it far from here"?

"Five kilometres, easy in a flitter. I wouldn't try and walk there".

"Do you have a flitter, Lyndon"?

"I run an old Sony HP125 short curtain when it's running that is, it's always breaking down. It's not that bad for a cheap two-seater".

Nigh finished his cocktail, "Is it running now"?

"You want to go out to the drilling site now, it's getting close to closing time, [23:00] and the town almost goes to sleep incompletenessss"?

Nigh nodded, "I want to be reunited with my Aunt. You can drop me off at the door and I'll enter alone if you don't want to appear rude. Have you met her by the way"?

"No", Mathers looked thoughtful, "I have not had the pleasure yet, she seems like a very nice person and physically she's a knockout if you don't mind me observing"?

Nigh smiled and nodded, "Not at all, you're right on both counts. Come on then, let's get out there and then you can get home to bed". As events were to unravel however, Lyndon Mathers would not be retiring to his bed that night!

Eighteen. Never Say Never.

The place was in darkness, not especially surprising given the hour when they finally arrived at the Striantum drilling site. They pulled up quietly outside the accompanying building. Mathers unbuckled his seat-belt but Nigh stopped him from climbing out the flitter with an arm across his chest.

"If you don't mind I'd rather go in alone", He requested. "Family reunion, perfect surprise, you know what I mean"? "Okay, I'll just wait to make sure you're staying and then I'll go back to town".

"You can get straight off if you are getting weary, my Aunt will insist that I stay with her", Nigh lied. Lifting the backpack containing the UIMF that he had thrown into the back seat.

"All my stuff is in here, when we collected it from my boarding house room I packed all my belongings into it. You can bet on the fact that I will not be going back into town this evening".

Nodding, Mathers put the seat-belt back on and as Nigh was climbing out of the vehicle retorted,

"Good luck then and goodnight".

Nigh strode confidently toward the building, but strangely the sound of the pile being reactivated in the vehicle was not heard over his shoulder. He seriously hoped the Sony had not broken down again and wondered how the notoriously unreliable firm was still in business. Pushing that out of his mind he began to recite the mantra of resolution under his breath. It was not going to be easy committing the heinous act he then contemplated, but he needed to do it to save the lives of fifteen others....unless. No, if he engaged in any sort of conversation with Lynea, his resolve would fail. If she refused to be sterilised to save her life, he would not be able to take it anyway. There was only one way he knew he could succeed. Slip into the building quietly, shoot her as she lay asleep and vanish into the upwhen. A level one dart was swift and efficient, she would never even wake. It was a demise that very many of the past and possibly even in the future would gladly settle for. No knowledge of impending doom, no suffering of any sort of discomfort or pain. Gently Nigh tried the airlock and was utterly astounded to discover that though sealed it was unlocked. He slipped inside and the soft whir of the extraction motors seemed unnaturally loud in the stillness of the night. A stillness still not interrupted by the soft susurration of the flitter gliding away from the bungalow and back into town. The noise stopped. Hopefully, it had not disturbed the lady lying in the double cot in the only bedroom the place possessed. Nigh opened the inner airlock which was only a mechanism for making it a sealed unit and it was no surprise that the lock was not thrown on that one. He drew his needle-gun and proceeded into the gloom. He did not waver from his purpose, to do so would be to fail and he could not afford failure. He did not glance about him, he dare not delay. He took no interest in the décor or items in the bungalow. He wanted to do what must be done and get out as swiftly as he could. Three doors were leading from the lock, from an entrance hall in which were hung some outdoor suits and a mask. Nigh tried the first door and found it led to the ablutive room. The next one led to a kitchen. Cursing his luck he strode through the last of them and into a long narrow lounge, at the end of which was another door. It could only be one room, there were no other alternatives left. He strode through the dimness, tiny night LED's around the perimeter of the room were on their very lowest setting, just bright enough to facilitate a trip to the ablutive room without the inconvenience of turning on the main lighting. It was all Nigh needed to cross the lounge and ease open the door beyond. In a double cot was a singly slim figure, beneath a duvet. Nigh strode toward the edge of the recliner, pointed his gun at the sleeping figure's neck and fired. Then he allowed himself to think. Sudden brilliant light flooded the room and Nigh spun on his heel to aim his gun at Mathers.

"Don't Durango, throw it over here before we end up with one of us shot and the other filled with guilt".

Naturally confused, Nigh nevertheless threw his gun to Mather's feet.

"Now look at who you just shot"?

Nigh half-turned and was surprised to see the figure in the bed rise from beneath the covers and pluck the lethal needle from her neck.

"Lynea!? How is it possible, I used a level two-needle, you should be.......".

"Dead", the woman seated in the cot finished for him. You would have shot your Aunty, shame on you".

Nigh stared at the figure who looked exactly as he had remembered her. How had she done it? Could anyone be immune to the toxins in a needle? How had she known someone was coming....unless.

"The Colonel! The Colonel told you I would come".

"You *are* the Colonel, Durango", Mathers answered.

"Will you please keep out of this, Mathers, it is, after all, a family affair. Why did you not drive back to town as requested"?

"Yes, you're right it's an affair of the family, Durango, but I am family you see".

Nigh turned back to his Aunt shocked to the soles of his boots, "Aunt Lynea, did you marry this ne'erdowell".

"I'm afraid Ænyl has not had vocal circuits built-in yet. I did not think it necessary to have a talking-sleeping simulacrum".

The sestertius dropped at last,

"This is an android created to resemble my Aunt in every detail. No wonder the needles did not affect her. Mathers, what have you done with my Aunt, where are you hiding her"?

"Why? Are you suddenly feeling protective toward the woman you just tried to murder? Or are you eager to get the job done"?

As Nigh tightened his muscles ready to do he knew not what, Mathers cautioned, "Don't try anything, Durango, whatever your plan, it cannot be as easy as my pulling the trigger on this needle-gun and *you* are no android. I have *no* desire to kill my nephew".

"You're married"?! Nigh gasped. Suddenly his shoulders sagged, "All right I admit defeat. You and my aunt have won. Now, will you tell me where she is"?

"So you can kill her"?

"So I can ask her to agree to irreversible sterilisation. Your offspring will be the beginning of a line that culminates in a homicidal rapist that assaults and slays fifteen young women, some of whom are dear to me and whom I would have my family history with".

Mathers nodded, "I know".

"The Colonel again. How much did he tell you"?

"Everything Durango, including things that are yet to happen, incidents of which, even you are ignorant".

"And as a result what is my Aunt's decision".

"Her decision", Mathers suddenly appeared to have a rather sardonic twist to his dark smile, "Was to become your Uncle. I don't expect you to recognise me, Durango, but I was Lynea Morrelius – L.M. I am now Lyndon Mathers, it saved having to alter my monogrammed luggage".

"Aunt Lynea, that is you"?!

"In the flesh, if you'll pardon the expression. You do not need to kill me now, Nephew, as you can see I could not be the mother to any offspring of any sort".

"You had SRS [sexual reorientation surgery], to live and know I would never be a threat to you"?

Mathers nodded, "And to save the life of the fifteen women in the future. My future that is your present and the Colonel's past. Try not to become him, Durango, though he saved my life I did not like him at all".

"I'm sorry Aun....Mathers. If it is any consolation I did not want to kill you. I simply had to".

"I understand even if I cannot find it within me to forgive the fact that you were prepared to carry it through, Durango. So do me a favour will you and this is the last thing I will ever ask of you"?

"Anything, you only have to name it"?

"Get the Hades off Mars and out of the 33rd century"!

*   *   *

The apartment looked exactly as Nigh had hoped it would. The instant he entered it he strode over to his landlady and took her in his arms, he kissed her at first gently and then passionately and she was soft and compliant in the embrace. When they finally parted she gasped,

"Do I gather you remember situations I do not"?

He nodded happily and told her, "I've met our granddaughter and she was lithe and beautiful and full of grace".

"Really", Mingfu Li smiled, "You presume a great deal, Sir".

To her surprised delight though, he took her hand and told her sincerely, "I love you, Fu".

"Hm, along with others no doubt".

"Well Androichina needs repopulating and I have certain responsibilities".

"To me and Mayling. I suspect Aurora too. So who is your fourth choice, or is that in my future".

"Everything is in the future now Fu, for I have done with the past and I have done with tempusdoors".

"What about General Acwellen, surely that is not resolved and will never be satisfactorily settled"?

Nigh grinned and told one of his future wives, "When it comes to the fourth dimension, My Love, one can never say never".

Printed in Great Britain
by Amazon